THE
PARADISE
BIT

Books by William K. Zinsser

William K. Zinsser

THE PARADISE BIT

a novel

LITTLE, BROWN AND COMPANY · BOSTON · TORONTO

Published simultaneously in Canada
by Little, Brown & Company (Canada) Limited

PRINTED IN THE UNITED STATES OF AMERICA

For

HUDSON G. STODDARD

The physical detail in this book is based on a trip through various islands of the South Seas. The plot and the characters, however, are imaginary. The time is summer of 1966.

I am grateful to Alan Williams for his generous encouragement.

W.K.Z.

THE
PARADISE
BIT

1

Every morning Denis Foote got up and rowed out to the reef and went skin-diving for shells. Then he sat in his boat and ate a banana or a breadfruit and thought how lucky he was to be in the South Seas and not in his native London, or any other place.

It was nice to think of all the places where he wasn't. Trenton often came to mind. And Seoul and Slough and Sidi-bel-Abbès. And Ulan Bator and the Rann of Cutch. Then he rowed back into the harbor of Falolo and walked to his office, ambling along the waterfront and stopping to talk with everybody. It was the perfect way to begin the day, eliminating any risk of getting to work too early.

Today the first person he saw was Millie Hawkes, proprietor of Millie Hawkes's Boarding House, the most famous and most minimal hotel in town. Millie, a round old widow whose success was blended — as was her bloodstream — of Polynesian laughter and white shrewdness, had just finished painting a sign to hang on her verandah:

BAR OPENS
8 A.M.
FOR YR. CONVENIENCE

"You don't need that sign, Millie," Denis called. "Everyone knows this is the one place in the islands where you can get a good belt of Scotch at any time of day or night."

"Why, Denis, what a sweet thing to say," Millie called back, smiling so widely that her gold front teeth glinted in the morning sun. "But I don't want to miss any strangers that might come in on an early boat. Business is slow."

"It won't be when your jukebox arrives," Denis said. At the word "jukebox" her eyes swept the harbor for incoming vessels. "How long is it now?" Denis asked.

"Three months, eleven days and two hours since I sent the money order. Just where *is* Memphis, Tennessee?"

Denis shrugged. He counted with gratitude, as Millie counted with dismay, every week that failed to bring the American machine. "Maybe they're out of red ones," he said. "You did insist on red?"

"Oh it's got to be red, Denis. With green bubbles going through orange tubes. Hoo-eeeee. You know the kind?"

"I know the kind," he said, waving goodbye and strolling on. Up ahead, behind a post that narrowly held the upstairs rooms of Fong's Laundry from falling into the street, he spotted "Doc" Bligh — hiding, and therefore hard at work. Doc Bligh owned a seedy hotel called the Bounty several miles outside town, and he intercepted boarders bound for other hotels by inventing dire tales of the conditions that they would find there. "You going to Millie *Hawkes's?*" he would say, seizing a newly debarked widow by her camera straps, his voice incredulous. "Don't you know the rooms are full of land crabs? Man from Texas had his leg bitten almost clean off just last week."

"Doing any business, Doc?" Denis called to the post, and the cadaverous old man scuttled out.

"Got two good ones yesterday," Bligh said, his rheumy eyes gleaming with remembered success. "Nice old couple from Brighton. Retired. Thomas Cook had 'em booked into one of those thatched bungalows at the El Tropiques, but I told 'em about the snakes."

"How come the scientists have never seen any snakes here and you see them every day?" Denis asked.

"Scientists don't use their imagination, Denis. Hey! Look

what's coming! Australian schoolteachers, if I'm not mistaken.
Gotta go, lad." He stole off like a pointer.

Denis felt a twinge of pity for the retired couple from
Brighton, robbed of their stay at an authentic South Sea
bungalow with a beautiful view across the lagoon to the
peaks of Tulala Ha'i. Soon enough he would see them
wandering forlornly through the streets.

But the next person he saw was "Literary Johnny," who
cadged drinks by pretending to remember every writer who
ever came to the South Seas — an idea that he had borrowed
from Gauguin's son in Tahiti, who would talk about his
father at the drop of a franc. Johnny was adept at guessing
the literary tastes of tourists and could tell a Robert Louis
Stevenson type from a Nordhoff & Hall type at twenty paces.
He gratified English spinsters with recollections of Rupert
Brooke.

"Sensitive chap, Brooke," he would say. "Stopped off here
in the fall of 1913 — that's when I got to know him. I
remember one day we had an apéritif together and he kept
gazing at the horizon — his mind seemed to be elsewhere,
don't you know? — and suddenly he got up and walked out
on that dock and wrote 'Clouds.' Yes, ma'am, he was a lovely
spirit."

Denis admired the skill, if not the integrity, with which
Literary Johnny fulfilled this basic need of South Sea
travelers, enabling them to retrace the path — or at least to
think they were retracing the path — of an author who had
long ago written a story that resulted in their being here
now.

"Did I hear you telling an American couple last week," he
said to Johnny, "that you remember Herman Melville?"

"Oh Denis, what do you take me for?" Johnny said. "I told
'em my father knew Melville — jumped ship with him in the
Marquesas and helped him write 'Typee.' I don't go back
personally beyond Stevenson, and that makes me about
seventy-five. How old do I look?"

"About fifty," Denis said, "which rather spoils the effect.
But you're aging fast under the weight of your beautiful

memories. Soon you'll look as old as your dear friend Somerset Maugham."

"Ahhh, good old Willie Maugham! I remember once in Pago-Pago it rained for three straight days, and we met this prostitute named Sadie Thompson, and Willie said to me . . ."

"Stop!" Denis said, shaking him by the shoulders. "It's me — Denis!"

"Oh, I'm terribly sorry, Denis. Forgot myself for a moment. Automatic reflex, you know."

"That's all right. How about a drink?"

"Any other time," Johnny said. "I thought I saw two Australian schoolteachers coming up from the dock a minute ago. Conrad types. I wondered where they went." He hurried off.

Denis went up on the verandah of the Kon-Tiki Bar and began to sort the garish shells that he had gathered on the reef. He identified them with the help of a small book that he always carried in his pocket and cleaned them with formaldehyde, pausing every once in a while to savor his favorite view: Falolo.

Falolo was the only town of any size in the island group of Tonji, which had been a British crown colony since 1879. Like all Polynesian towns of any size, it was built around a harbor, and its life centered so completely on the coming and going of boats that anyone who walked along the waterfront would soon know all the news and gossip of the islands, not only of Tonji but of Tahiti to the east and Samoa to the west and the countless other specks of land strewn so parsimoniously across two thousand miles of ocean. As a waterfront idler Denis felt that he knew more about the islands than the Governor himself, Sir Reginald Weems, awash though the Governor was in cables from Whitehall and other official reports.

Denis looked with amusement at Government House, perched on the hill in antiseptic symmetry, aloof and autocratic, symbol of an eighty-five-year effort to impose careful order on a careless society. How much better he liked the motley buildings that had grown up in a semicircle around the harbor. Flaking missionary churches of six denominations jostled gaudy saloons and dance halls. Modern banks and department stores, made of creamy cement, alternated with the shaky wooden offices of inter-island traders, which had outdoor staircases and laundry drying on the balcony. Copra warehouses sent their acrid smell into adjacent boarding-houses and into the long shed of corrugated tin that served as a movie theater on nights when the generator worked.

Beyond that, leaning quite badly since the last hurricane, was a tarpaper building occupied by Cheung Ho's Grill and by the London Missionary Society, which stored tracts and hymnals on the second floor and, as a result, sent its Protestant materials out to the heathen heavily scented in Confucianism. And beyond that, most incongruous of all, Denis could just see the shining white courthouse where the British tried to dispense impeccable justice, hampered by the Tonjians' habit of committing trivial crimes solely to win a comfortable week in prison. The Crown retaliated by setting them free after one or two nights, but they kept returning in the evening until finally a sign was posted that said: ANYONE NOT IN JAIL BY 9 P.M. WILL BE LOCKED OUT.

Denis finished cleaning his last shell, a brilliant cowrie, and ordered an ale from Fat Lou, the bartender, whose attention he was lucky to catch. Fat Lou lost a lot of business because his gaze could seldom be deflected from the harbor, nor could his conversation. A Dutchman confined to land because he was no longer agile enough to go to sea, Fat Lou sailed verbally on every craft that put in or out of Falolo, and Denis was glad enough to listen and to watch, for boats were perpetually arriving and leaving, threading their way through the narrow gap in the reef.

Some were outriggers and sloops and schooners, but most were the ungainly motor boats of inter-island trade, their engines noisy and fitful with age, nondescript vessels in every way except in the cargo that they carried, and this was of consuming interest. Everybody knew, for instance, that Tonji had just run out of beer. It was now Tuesday and the next shipment wasn't due until Friday on the "Elizabeth Rose" from Suva, or maybe Saturday if the seas were rough.

Occasionally a tourist liner would come for a visit, or a luxury yacht from Cannes owned by a millionaire or a movie star, and these were reminders that maritime life could be elegant. But nobody really envied the tourists when they were rowed back out to their bingo games, or the millionaire when he set forth again on the solitary search for whatever he was searching for. True romance lay in the nightly broadcasts of the next morning's small-boat departures, when the island radio crackled with euphonious names: the "Tolala" for Aitutaki, the "Moana Sue" for Mangareva, the "Te Mura" for Huahine, the "Vailima" for Nukulailai. Then the talk quickly turned to other voyages — to boats that had made it through the reef in a storm because of the skill of their Polynesian skippers, or to boats that were not so lucky, in which case the reef was always the villain. Every wreck was remembered — "she's lying off Raiatea now" — and every mystery. Boats were the source of life, as well as the agent of death, and there was no end of "yarning" about them.

Denis was happier than ever in his life. He had left London five years before to find his island, and when he found it he knew — as he still knew now at thirty-two — that he never wanted to leave. His friends had warned him when he went away that he would soon be back.

"It won't work, Denis," Freddie Beauchamp said. "It's an old dream, but it destroys everyone who follows it. Your brain'll go soft as a melon out there."

"You'll miss the theater," said Nigel Horne, who remembered how often Denis went down from Cambridge to catch the new plays and to attend literary salons.

"You're just trying to run away," said Peggie Beardsley, who wanted to keep him, like her collection of early glass paperweights, as an ornament to her Mayfair parties. "Don't you know you can't escape from the time and place that you were born into? I hate to say it, darling, but I actually think it's *weak*."

But he had gone anyway, and he didn't miss any of them.

He had his government job, a small and pleasant job that left him plenty of time for other small and pleasant pursuits. He had new friends and he had serenity, born of the belief that although the rest of the world was changing rapidly, Tonji never would. It was just small enough, just unknown enough, just remote enough to be left alone by the tourist hordes. Yet it was just big enough to be interesting. In its villages the fabric of Polynesian life was still pure, and in its white settlers and drifters it had an overlay of commerce and desire that made every day different and no day dull. This was the special harmony that Denis prized.

The Methodist church struck ten, beating the Baptist church by the usual forty-five seconds — an unintentional symbol, repeated hourly, of the tiny differences that divided the town's five Protestant sects and mystified their Tonjian converts, to whom the five brands of salvation looked as similar as five brands of toothpaste. Denis got up and strolled toward his office.

Along the way he passed the three Danes who were building a balsa raft to sail to Peru. Their voyage was to be the reverse of the one made by Thor Heyerdahl's "Kon-Tiki," which they scorned, and was meant to disprove his theory that the Polynesians came from South America. People on Tonji were obsessed by the riddle of the Polynesians' origin. Despite Heyerdahl's feat it was generally agreed that they came from the mainland of Asia and moved eastward across the Pacific. Denis had heard the great migrations discussed on into the night; he had heard songs and seen dances in the villages that reconstructed from race memory the long voyages made by entire tribes across the Pacific in giant double canoes. Now he braced himself for the volley of words that the Danes would blow at him as he went by.

"Soon we ready," shouted Karl Ullstrad, the expedition's leader, a white-bearded old man as tough as the bamboo reeds that he was plaiting for the cabin of his raft. "We show Heyerdahl, you wait and see! Goddam right!"

"Goddam right!" echoed Sven Olaf, throwing his only two English words into the cause.

Denis had been waiting and seeing, with admiration and wonder, for several months now as the three Vikings laboriously pieced together their crude boat. It was very small, and yet they intended to sail south to one of the least explored areas in the world. There they hoped to meet a westerly wind, which they thought a race of early Polynesian navigators used, and follow it five thousand miles to Peru.

Denis's wonder was directed not only at the lonely voyage that was about to begin, but at the fifty years of voyaging that had brought Karl Ullstrad to this point. He was one of those driven men who turned up in Tonji every so often, usually alone, having come by sailboat from Bristol or Marseilles or some other incredibly far-off port. They were exhilarating to Denis, these pioneers on a last frontier, using the barest materials, yet richer in resources than he would ever be.

"You'll show 'em, Karl," he called.

"Goddam right!" called Ole Johnson, waving his fist from the raft.

Denis walked across the street to his office. The thought of its smallness, of the four walls and ceiling that bounded it so tidily, demanding no hard decisions or bold acts, brought a wry smile to his intelligent face and nagged him with an uneasy feeling. He recognized it as a first vision of middle age, still on the horizon but running toward him at terrible speed. What would he have accomplished when the runner arrived?

Over the door of his office was a sign that said TONJI VISITORS' BUREAU. And beside it was a wicker rocking chair under whose cushion Denis generally kept the key. Now, however, the cushion supported the angular old body of Roy Quaritch, slumped in a midmorning doze. Except for his pink face and knees he was a figure of total whiteness. He was wearing white shoes, white knee stockings, white shorts and a white shirt, and his hair was snowy as silk. Denis's attempt to reach under him for the key startled him back to life.

"Sorry, Old Settler," Denis said gently. Quaritch was

founder and editor of the "Tonji Times," a daily newspaper known to local wags as "the two-minute silence," and for half a century his own column, "Old Settler Says," had hammered out a stern defense of the status quo. He often dropped in to talk with Denis, and Denis was always glad to see him, for he represented a continuity and point of view that reached back to the days of Victoria.

"Sorry to keep you waiting," Denis said as he unlocked the door. "I'm afraid I maintain rather casual hours."

"No inconvenience, Denis," Quaritch said. "One finds when one reaches one's seventies that one wants to rest one's legs now and then. Besides, it's no hardship to sit and look at the view that one loves best in all the world. Not that one knows many others. Would you believe it, Denis: except for my service in the First War I've never been away from Tonji. I was born here, and my father before me, and my children after me. But *their* children, I regret to say, will be born somewhere else."

"Have you heard from young Roy lately?" Denis asked.

"Yes, I got a letter on last week's plane. He made it quite clear he's going to settle in London for good. And Peter has gone into business in Sydney — even as a little boy he wanted to sail on every boat that ever left. And Beryl is a housewife in Minneapolis, and Heather's engaged to a doctor in Auckland, so there's nobody left in Tonji but the old folks. I must confess one finds oneself a bit wistful about the finality of one's line here in the islands."

"It's the call of the city," Denis said. "There's hardly a person over eighteen who can resist it."

"How can *you* resist it?" Quaritch asked.

"Oh that's easy, once you've lived there. In many ways I had the best of London — as you know, I was an editor in a publishing house — but I got tired of the noise. Cars and motorcycles and horns. And radio and television and newspapers and advertising and publicity — all screaming at us to buy things that don't need to be bought and do things that don't need to be done. The real miracle, Old Settler, is that people can keep their balance at all."

"*Do* they keep their balance?"

"Well, a great many don't. God knows I had to read a lot of manuscripts that seemed to have been written jointly by an author and his psychiatrist. Maybe that's why psychiatrists charge so much — they're trying to get their rightful share of the royalties."

"You mean these books are collaborations?"

"Not exactly. But five times a week the psychiatrist tells his novelist why he's so guilty and miserable and has transferred his guilt to his children and how everything is a sexual symbol anyway. You know: if a man won't drive his wife to the supermarket it's because he has a deep-seated phobia about the gearshift lever."

"Good heavens, Denis, whatever became of the kind of author one grew up on: Rider Haggard and G. A. Henty and that crowd? Wanted to spin a rousing tale and didn't give blazes for all that sex rot."

"They're gone, Old Settler. Today's writer turns deeper and deeper into himself until at last . . ."

"Capital writer, Haggard. D'you remember 'King Solomon's Mines'? There was a yarn!"

"And that, Old Settler, is why I came to Tonji. I wanted to live in a society that was serene and stable, and I wanted to come closer to nature. First I took a look at Tahiti, but it's got a jet airstrip now and tourists are pouring in faster than they can build exotic Polynesian-type hotels."

"I daresay Tahiti wasn't helped by those chaps who made 'Mutiny on the Bounty.' Rum lot, from all I hear. Especially that Brandeis fellow."

"Brandeis?"

"That's the chap. Marlon Brandeis."

"You're right, Old Settler. Let in a movie unit and you're asking for trouble."

"You picked the right spot when you came to Tonji, lad."

"It's ideal," Denis agreed. "I read, I write, I paint, I spend a lot of time in the villages, and I keep various journals. All I need is a wife."

"Pity my Beryl went off to the States. She'd have been a

girl of your stripe. How about the Governor's daughter — the older one? Maud. She looks a strapping lass, and I've heard she has an eye for you."

"Then it must be because I look like a horse," Denis said.

"That's all she can talk about. God knows *she* looks like a horse."

"Still and all, Denis, it would be good politics to give her a tumble. Stay in favor with Sir Reggie."

"I've heard that politics makes strange bedfellows, Old Settler, but Maud's a little *too* strange. If I lose favor with Sir Reggie it'll be over something bigger than Maud — not that there *is* anything much bigger than Maud. I've a feeling that Sir Reggie would like to shake the islands out of their sleep."

"Rubbish, Denis. He's half asleep himself — only wants to serve out his term playing snooker and dressing up in ceremonial regalia."

"You sell him short, Old Settler. He has an ambitious glint in his eye — the *only* glint in his eye, I might add."

"Odd you should say that — I took him for a harmless bloke."

"Don't you remember how quick he was to open a tourist bureau when he came here? How he called me for an interview and said he wanted an office that would a*ttract* travelers to Tonji, not just help them when they got here?"

"Strengthen the economy — that's always the official reason," Quaritch said.

"But he always has an *un*official reason."

"Make Tonji look bigger than it really is, you mean?"

"That's Sir Reggie. He has a highly developed sense of self-importance."

"Come to think of it, Denis, it's a bit thick having the cricket test matches played for the Weems Cup now instead of the Prince Albert Cup."

"A bit thick, to say the least. That's why I thought I'd better grab the job before he gave it to someone more aggressive." He glanced with satisfaction around the room: at the tapa-cloth hangings on the walls, at the native crafts attractively mounted and labeled, at the handsome booklets describing island life.

"I send these booklets to Sir Reggie," Denis went on, "along with weekly reports telling him how many people come in and how fascinated they are — which they often aren't — and so far it's a standoff. Though I did have to run that horrible Miss Hibiscus Festival last fall."

"Rotten show, that," Quaritch said.

"It was Sir Reggie's idea. But I've got to throw him a bone every once in a while."

"Lot of cheap claptrap, if you ask me," Quaritch said. "The natives hated it. Even Miss Hibiscus thought it was undignified."

"That's the danger, Old Settler," Denis said. "The worst thing that can happen to an out-of-the-way place is to be 'discovered.' It's the new game of the idle rich. The more out-of-the-way the place that they discover, the more points they get. Like collecting antiques: you start collecting old snuffboxes, and suddenly *everybody's* collecting old snuffboxes, so it's no fun any more and you've got to start collecting Benin bronzes or Thai sword handles."

"But surely a place like this, Denis, is so far off the usual path . . ."

"It doesn't take much, Old Settler. There are American magazines like 'Vogue' and 'Harper's Bazaar' that have chichi little sections, called 'Nomad's Notebook' or 'Lady on the Go,' written by girl reporters who stumble into places like this. Women of fashion are led to believe that they can't hold their heads up in Grosvenor Street or Sutton Place if they haven't seen the kris dance at Ubud or the twelfth-century mosaics at Cefalù."

"And do they actually go?" Quaritch asked.

"Oh yes. Every year there's a new 'in' place. It *has* to change that often, because by the end of the year so many people have descended on the in place that it's out."

"What sort of places are these, Denis?"

"Entrancing. Heavenly. Utterly unbelievable. You haven't lived till you've seen the sun rising over a goatherd on

Mykonos. One year it's Mykonos, where only seventeen people altogether lived the previous year, and suddenly simply everybody is there with his yacht and transistor radio, and the next year they all run off to Cozumel. But Mykonos is never quite the same again."

"You put the fear of God into me," Quaritch said. "I think I'll write a column suggesting we keep all foreigners out. Would that do the trick, Denis?"

"A bit stringent, perhaps, Old Settler. Why don't you start by keeping all girl reporters out?"

"Splendid idea, lad. Let's go have some tea to celebrate tomorrow's column."

Quaritch went out the door and Denis followed him. He was just closing it when a boy from the cable office came and gave him a yellow envelope. Denis looked at it with irritation, slid it under the door and started off with Quaritch. Then he came back and ripped the envelope open. The cable at last lay naked in his hand and the strange words swam before his eyes like oil on a sullen sea:

PACIFIC PALISADES CALIFORNIA

FOOTE VISITBURO TONJI

HAVE COLOSSAL OPPORTUNITY MILLION DOLLARS' WORTH PUBLICITY TONJI STOP LAUNCHING NATIONWIDE "WIN-AN-ISLAND" CONTEST IN PROMOTION TIE-IN WITH 2000 TRAVEL AGENTS AND TITAN PICTURES' UPCOMING FILM "DESERT ISLAND FOR TWO" STARRING MOONA MARONE AND TAB TORN STOP COUNTING ON YOU PERSUADE GOVERNMENT LEASE SMALL ISLAND TO LUCKY WINNER STOP AIRMAILING DETAILS BUT PLEASE CABLE ACCEPTANCE SOONEST STOP AM GIVING TONJI FIRST REPEAT FIRST CRACK AT SENSATIONAL OPPORTUNITY

REGARDS

MEL PARKER PARADISE UNLIMITED

COLOSSAL TITAN MOONA TAB TORN

Denis put the cable in his pocket and caught up with Quaritch at the Grand Polynesian Hotel.

"Whiskey," he said to the waiter.

"I thought we were going to have tea." Quaritch said.

"I had a sudden change of mind."

"Bad news?" Quaritch asked.

"Some Yank has gone round the bend," Denis said, handing the cable to Quaritch, who studied it slowly, his brow knitted in concentration.

"Absolutely potty," he said at last. "I can't make head or tail of what the chap is going on about. Sounds like a ruddy cryptogram. Is it some sort of code?" He studied it again as if it were some sort of code. "I say, Denis, does it mean anything to you?"

"Just enough to know I don't like it," Denis said. He tore a piece of paper out of his notebook and scribbled on it:

> PARKER PARADISE UNLIMITED
> PACIFIC PALISADES CALIFORNIA USA
> CAN'T MAKE FRIG-ALL OF YOUR CABLE STOP TONJI
> DEFINITELY UNSEEKING PLACE TOURIST SUN SOONEST
> LATEST EVER REPEAT EVER
>
> > > > FOOTE

He crossed out "frig-all," wrote "bang-all" in its place, and gave the paper to a bar boy. "Take this to the cable office and ask Mr. O'Hara to send it out immediately," he said.

"There," he said to Quaritch, taking a long and meditative drink. "That's the last we'll hear of Mr. Parker."

2

Denis had slowly learned in the South Seas to live each day as it came along. He forgot about yesterday and gave no thought to tomorrow. This simple principle, so manifest in the lives of everyone around him, had been amazingly hard to master. Not until he had lived in Tonji for nine or ten months did he completely cut his lifelong ties to the clock, the calendar and the engagement pad. He now saw that of all the gifts which the islands can bestow, this was the best.

He was appalled, reviewing his years in England, at how much emotional energy he had spent on fruitless glances backward and fretful looks ahead. He used to lie awake at night, replaying his day like a movie revival, wondering as the images flickered across the screen whether he had been right to do this or say that, or whether So-and-So knew he was only joking when he said such-and-such. Now he knew that So-and-So wasn't even listening.

Free now of every such chain to the lands of Was, Might-Have-Been and May Be, Denis didn't think any more about Mel Parker's cable after he answered it. Consequently, when the plane came with the mail a week later and he saw the words "Paradise Unlimited" again, he could hardly remember where he had seen them before.

What had come was a large and gaudy envelope distended with pulpy materials that turned out to be South Sea travel brochures. From their voluptuous photographs and florid syntax Denis recognized them as the work of someone who had never been near the islands — it was a style that he knew all too well. Among the brochures was a long letter from Mel Parker, which fluttered out onto the desk and lay there, its face up and shining — like a dog, Denis thought, asking to be patted and loved. His instinct was to kick the dog right out the door, but he reminded himself that his job was to read the mail and not just throw it away. Wearily, like a man who hates to swim but must show his hosts that he appreciates their swimming pool, he flattened Parker's letter out, gave it a last grim stare, and dove in.

The letterhead, printed in bright green ink, was a galaxy of names and numbers, most of them mysterious: PARADISE UNLIMITED. Mel Parker Associates. Melville S. Parker, Executive Director. 14012 Santa Aziza Blvd., Pacific Palisades, California 40967. Telephone 213-994-8787. Cable address LOTUS. Member AWTA. He moved his eyes hurriedly over the strange terrain to the letter itself.

DEAR MR. FOOTE:

Many thanks for your speedy reply. I don't wonder my cable left you a little in the dark, but I know you're going to cotton to this project when I spell it out.

As you undoubtedly know, AWTA (the Association of Western Travel Agents) came to me last winter with a problem. They wanted to publicize the South Pacific region and promote tourism out your way, so I formed Paradise Unlimited to do the job. Up to now I've been Director of World-Wide Publicity and Exploitation for Titan Pictures here in Hollywood, but I've always had a yen to visit "the South Sea Islands" and I'm no longer with Titan except as a consultant.

Some 2000 travel agents in up to 14 western states are affiliated with me, but so far we've let you folks down. Quite frankly, we just haven't come up with a promotion that dramatizes the islands. But now we've got a gimmick that will put Tonji on the tourist map forever.

Here's the pitch. Titan Pictures, which is an established giant in the motion picture industry, has just completed a $3,000,000 motion picture called "Desert Island for Two," starring Moona

Marone and Tab Torn, two of the hottest box-office properties of this or any other year. The plot twist is that they get shipwrecked on a small Pacific island together. What we propose to do is give away a little island to the person or couple that wins our nationwide contest.

All that the winner has to do is finish the title song of "Desert Island for Two." The music is all written — it's a honey of a tune, as you might expect from a cleffer like Julie Sping — and so are the lyrics by Sammy Forn, which tell about a fellow and his girl on a tropical island. But Titan has agreed to pretend that the lyricist is stuck for a final couplet, and that's where our contest enters the scene. The writer of the best final couplet wins the island. Titan will release the song at the same time as the movie and will put big dough into pushing it with the deejays, so publicitywise we stand to make real nickels.

All you've got to do is find us an island. We're willing to buy it or take a 25-year lease . . . anything as long as it's legal. You don't even have to think of a name for the island. We've got that already: Moona-Moona. Roll that one off your tongue and you'll agree that it really sings, not even counting its promotion values vis-à-vis Miss Marone.

It doesn't have to be a big island — just one of the offshore jobs with a few coconut trees that we can fix up. I'll be coming out to handle that part of it myself, so don't worry if it doesn't look like much. I'll be bringing along a top Hollywood photographer, Cy Rumble, who's handy with the props and the paintbrush, and we'll take some pictures that will look really authentic. Incidentally, Cy loves girls (understatement of the year), and I know you won't have any trouble rustling up a native looker to pose against the palm trees. (How about that nice bit of stuff that was Miss Hibiscus in that swell promotion of yours last fall?)

We'll build a Polynesian-type bungalow on the island, and our tie-in airline, Trans-Sky, will fly the winners out to live in it, and of course we'll have the world press alerted to that story, which is sure to be brimful of warm human values. And you won't have to shell out one Tonjian dime because I've got tie-ins with six household and appliance-type firms in the U.S. to furnish the cottage with all the necessities of life. They'll be taking a lot of TV spots and one firm is even scheduling a double-truck spread in "Life" or "Look." The bar is going to be stocked by Walter of Waikiki, who runs the restaurant in Hawaii.

Now that you know the details you'll have to admit it's a smash of a promotion and just what Tonji needs. All I need is the go-ahead from you and we'll be in business — the whole paradise bit. By the way, I assume you can get rooms for Cy Rumble and me at the best hotel and also for a "girl Friday" I hope to hire in the next week or two.

Warm regards
MEL PARKER

Bad, Denis thought. Very bad. But not hopeless. All land is held in trust for the Tonjian people and can't be bought or leased. The whole thing can be stopped with a cable saying that it's forbidden by law and that the Governor would never approve. In fact, the Governor needn't even know, Denis said to himself as he picked up a pencil and began to draft a cold reply. Then he noticed that Parker's letter had a P.S.

"By the way," it said, "I'm sure that Sir Reginald Weems will be very excited by this project. I'm writing him today to tell him what we are in a position to do for Tonji and feel confident he will want to move up soonest."

Denis crumpled the paper on which he had begun to draft his cable. Then he lifted the wastebasket up to his desk and swept all the brochures from Paradise Unlimited into it. This left only Parker's letter, no longer a lovable dog but a snarling mongrel, ready to chew Tonji into small pieces. The letter would not be so easily countered now. He would have to write an official reply and clear it with the Governor. And the Governor would have ideas of his own. Which was always the trouble with trying to clear anything with the Governor.

That afternoon Denis went around to the "Tonji Times." Quaritch was at his big teak desk writing a peevish column on the mismanagement of the pineapple crop.

"Sorry to barge in on you, Old Settler," Denis said, "but I thought you ought to see this letter. It's from the Yank who sent that weird cable last week."

"Oh dear," Quaritch said in a tired voice. Denis sat down and listened to the sound of tomorrow's edition taking shape in the cluttered room: to Mrs. Pedley harvesting social notes on the telephone, to old Mr. Glubb swearing at the linotype machine for its uneven behavior, to the singing of Nuraa, the Tonjian boy, as he heated the molten lead with a bellows. To these strains were soon added, as in a fugue, the contrapuntal voice of Quaritch as he plucked phrases from Parker's letter.

"You say Monica will be wearing an heirloom veil?" asked Mrs. Pedley.

"Screw the day I ever left the 'Liverpool Echo,'" said Mr. Glubb.

"Blo-ow! Blo-ow!" sang Turaa.

"What in the bloody hell is a deejay?" said Quaritch.

The fugue gathered momentum: "Alençon lace . . . goddam machine . . . blow, Mister Bellows . . . paradise bit? . . . Methodist cake bazaar . . . never left Liverpool . . . heat 'im up, heat 'im up . . . who's Julie Sping? . . . sister from Adelaide . . . bitch of a linotype . . . whoo-oo-ee, whoo-oo-ee . . . double-truck spread? . . ."

A telephone bell jangled into the fugue and cut it off. Quaritch picked up the receiver.

"Quaritch here," he said. "Mmmm. Oh it's you, Favisham. Quite. Jolly good. Ummmmmm. Eh? Rather! Splendid. Ergghh. Right you are. Quite. Hoomph . . ."

This would go on for quite a while, Denis knew. It always did when people talked to Favisham. He was one of those Englishmen who converse largely in sounds like "Ummmmm," delivered with such gravity that they seem to contain a deep thought. But as the other person has no idea what the thought might be, there is no choice but to meet one "Ummmmm" with another, to parry an "Ergghh" with a "Hoomph" or a "Quite" or an elaborate clearing of the throat.

Finally Quaritch was silent and Denis knew that Favisham was going to try to come to the point. Favisham was the Governor's aide-de-camp, a position that he took as seriously as if he were secretary to the Sacred College of Cardinals.

"Oh I see," Quaritch said at last. "You're looking for Denis Foote? He's not at the Visitors' Bureau? I see. No, he wouldn't be at the bar in the middle of the afternoon — Denis is a terribly hard worker, old fellow. Yes, he sometimes comes here. Actually, I expect to see him soon. Can I give him a message? The Governor will see him at five. Jolly good. Ummmmm. Ergghh. Cheerio."

He hung up. "I guess you heard," he said to Denis. "The Governor will see you at five. Did you ask to see him?"

"Certainly not."

"Then why does he say he 'will' see you at five?"

"That means 'be there at five.' It's a form of wording that Favisham and Sir Reggie use to make you think they're favoring you with a royal audience — which they think they are. Puts you on the defensive. What time is it now?"

"Four-fifteen."

"Crikey! I've got to clean up and get into my whites — if I've got any whites that are even reasonably white. Court dress, you know."

"Bit of a shave wouldn't hurt, either," Quaritch said. "I'd better drive you. You'll never make it on your bicycle."

"Thanks, Old Settler. Before we go, give me a quick brushup on land ownership in Tonji."

"Quaritch took down a book and thumbed through it hastily. "Yes, this is it," he said. "Section 37A of the Land Act. Listen:

" 'All lands which are in actual occupation by any tribe shall be set apart for said tribe and for no other use. Furthermore, all lands deemed to be needed by the Tonjian people in the foreseeable future shall be classified as 'native reserve' and shall not be leased or otherwise disposed of. All residual land shall be ceded to the government of Great Britain, not for the private advantage of Her Majesty or any individuals employed by Her Majesty's government, but to be held in trust for the Tonjian people and for the general good.'

"There it is, Denis: chapter and verse. All you've got to do is remember Section 37A. Come on — you haven't got much time. Miss Pedley, I'll be back at five."

Half a minute before five, Denis was dropped off under the porte cochère of Government House. He bounded out of the

car, paused briefly to check his fly, which he was surprised to
find shut, and strode in past the guard. He was as relieved to
be punctual as he was certain that Sir Reggie would keep him
waiting ten minutes. Sir Reggie kept everybody waiting ten
minutes. "Takes some of the pecker out of 'em," he told his
secretary, Miss Muggle.

At 5:10 Miss Muggle ushered Denis into the Governor's
spacious office. "Mr. Foote, sir," she said, and scuttled back
out.

"Orgghhh . . . omm-ummmmm . . . owshh," Sir Reginald said from his desk at the far end of the room. He did not
look up.

Denis walked in and stood in front of the desk. His eyes
ranged over the room and its objects, which during two years
had never moved by an inch. Queen Victoria and Queen
Elizabeth were still on the wall behind the Governor's desk in
huge tinted portraits. Between them, in smaller black and
white photographs, were Edward VII, George V and George
VI. (Denis suspected that the Governor had a mother fixa-
tion.) Edward VIII had been banished to a side wall, which
he shared with Chief Malalonga I and an aquatint of the
Cup Finals at Henley.

Another wall was hung with personal memorabilia. One
quick look told Denis that nothing had been added to this
bleak gallery or taken away. It was still dominated by an oil
painting of Weems Manor, a gray baronial pile in Devon.
Surrounding that were satellite pictures of Sir Reggie's class at
Harrow, his debating team at Oxford, his prize dogs, his prize
horses, his prize bulls, and a framed testimonial from the
natives of the Gilbert & Ellice Island group "for his unflagging
efforts to foster the game of cricket" during his years there as
a junior official in the colonial service. On Sir Reginald's desk
was a cricket ball dented in some tournament long since
forgotten except by him, and flanking it were photographs in
silver frames of his wife, Lady Weems, and their daughters
Winifred and Maud. Maud was nuzzling a horse, and in their
proximity — especially as Maud's hair tended to fall down her

back like a mane — it was easy to forget that they did not belong to the same species.

At length Sir Reginald looked up from his papers and feigned surprise at seeing Denis there. "Oh it's you, Foote," he said. "Didn't hear you come in. Ommmmm. Grffff." He gave a little smile but Denis took no comfort from it — he had always felt that in Sir Reginald's case it was not so much a smile as a dental problem. The Governor's face was circular and inclining toward fat, especially around the eyes, which darted out from little pouches that seemed to be building up with the purpose of enveloping them completely. His hair was sandy and thin, and he had a small moustache of the kind worn by druggists, which he kept tweaking as if to reassure himself that it had not flown away.

"Sit down, Foote," he said, waving Denis to a chair that was lower than his own. "Ummmmm. I daresay you heard from that Paradise chap in the States. Ehhh?"

"Yes, sir," Denis said.

"Good, good."

"Yes, sir."

"Ummmmm. Cheeky fellow."

"A bit on the pushy side, sir."

"Quite. Hmpfff. Still, I had to admire the chap's mettle. One finds that sort of thing wanting in the British character nowadays, don't you think, Foote?"

"Actually sir, I feel that restraint is a rather attractive quality."

"Gets you nowhere, Foote. Bunch of milksops, if you ask me, this new crowd."

"What new crowd is that, sir?"

"Your crowd, Foote. The new generation. Always so eager to conciliate — keep the peace and all that bosh."

"Still," Denis said, "I don't trust fellows of Parker's type."

"Parker? Who in blazes is that?"

"The American, sir. The one with the mettle."

"Oh yes. Ahhh. Spirited lad. Have you found an island for him?"

"Island! Surely you don't intend . . ."

"Surely I *do*," the Governor said, giving his moustache a hearty tug.

"It's just a cheap publicity stunt," Denis said. "Let people like that into Tonji and the place will be overrun with reporters and television crews."

"Then at least somebody will *hear* about Tonji," the Governor said. "Which, I might point out, is more than they do through *your* labors, Foote."

"I try to create an atmosphere, Sir Reginald, that will reflect your enlightened policies."

"Rubbish! Tourists are what we need! Can't you get that through your intellectual Cambridge head?"

"Why do we need them so desperately?" Denis asked.

"When you're at the top, Foote, you see the big picture — which is seldom visible to those lucky enough to be in the lower echelons."

"Lucky, sir?"

"It's devilish lonely at the top, Foote," the Governor said, stealing — Denis thought — a commiserating glance at Queen Victoria. "One is sentenced to solitary confinement, as it were, with one's decisions."

"Yes, I imagine that the burdens of power . . ."

"I don't suppose you've heard," the Governor went on, "that the copra crop is down eighteen per cent this year. Chaps like you don't want to muck around with anything as mundane as copra. Probably don't even know it's the backbone of the economy. Well, what's going to make up that eighteen per cent? Ehhh? Mmmmm?"

"It's been a good year for coffee," Denis said. "And taro and bananas. There's a new phosphate field over on Lufua. Tunafish is up. Yams. Pearl shell."

"That's not copra, old fellow," the Governor snapped. "Out here in the islands you've got to think copra. Eat, sleep, drink copra. You'd know that if you were at the top." He paused and conjured a look of martyrdom across his face. "And if copra is off, you've got to think tourists."

"In my opinion, sir, it's . . ."

"Look at Fiji! Copra and sugar were off — the economy

was an absolute dog's breakfast. Then they built hotels and jet aerodromes and got cracking on the tourist industry. Now the place is swarming with trippers and I hear the Governor is up for a K.C.B. on the spring Honours List."

"Tonji is a somewhat different case, sir," Denis said. "If I might point out, we have a fortunate balance here which . . ."

"Of course one doesn't want to end one's career on Tonji," the Governor went on. "Sometimes in the stillness of these island nights, Foote, one dreams of Hong Kong."

"I'd like to see you get Hong Kong, sir," Denis said.

"There's almost nothing left," the Governor went on, talking now to the ceiling. "When one entered the colonial service, one could aspire to — well, one didn't flatter oneself that one might become Viceroy of India, but one did think perhaps of Singapore or Malaya or Nigeria. Now one looks about and wonders if one is doomed to dribble away his days in . . . where? Aden? Mauritius? The Seychelles? Barbados?"

"Saint Helena?" Denis said.

The Governor glared at him. "Are you being facetious, Foote?"

"Certainly not, sir. I was merely sympathizing that the list has been reduced to such lonely outposts."

"Because if you meant anything by singling out Saint Helena . . ."

"Good heavens no, sir. I could as easily have said Honduras."

"But you didn't."

"Or Bermuda. Or . . . what else is there? Christmas Island?"

"No, that went with Singapore."

"Pemba?"

"No, that went with Zanzibar."

"Rotten luck," Denis said.

"I fancied Zanzibar when I was younger," the Governor said.

"Pretty little spot, I'm told," Denis said.

"Fmpfff. Born too late, Foote — that's one's trouble. Mind

you, though: I intend to make my name yet. The Colonial Office has not heard the last of Sir Reginald Weems. Now about that island. Which one can we lease to those American chaps?"

"Why, none at all, sir. We have no legal right."

"Anything can be made legal, boy. Don't you know that?"

"I know the Land Act, sir. Section 37A specifically forbids the sale or lease of land occupied by the Tonjian people."

"But there's a lot of land that they *don't* occupy — and never will, if you ask me."

"It's still theirs in trust," Denis said.

"Let's take a look," the Governor said. "We'll chase up something."

He walked over to a large map of the Tonji group that hung in a corner beyond Edward VIII. The cluster of twenty islands made a familiar shape to Denis, who sailed among them often. The Governor took a pointer and jabbed at the map.

"Now of course there's no question of using these," he said, indicating the two main islands.

"Of course," Denis said.

"Or these," he went on, pointing to six islands with native villages on them.

"Naturally," Denis said.

"It has to be completely uninhabited, you understand. Literally a 'desert island,' as the old cliché goes, eh, Foote? Hahaha. That's what those Hollywood chaps want. Americans go downright potty over that sort of thing."

"Yes, sir."

"Ummmmm. How about these three?"

"I'm afraid not, sir," Denis replied. "This one, Mapua, has a cove that the natives use for fishing — once a month at full moon. Turtles. This one, Felaa, has that team of botanists who come from Glasgow every summer. Very unusual ferns. And this one, Olo, has two cocoa plantations."

"Damn!" the Governor said. "How about this one — Kamolo? It looks just the right size."

"That's the one where Lady Weems likes to go for picnics

and swimming," Denis said. "You know — where she had the little beach hut built beside the lagoon?"

"Oh, quite, quite. Fffff. Can't use that one, can we, Foote? Haha. Even a Governor can't afford to get in bad with his wife."

"No, sir."

"You're not married, are you, Foote? Mmmmmm. Jolly times we've had over on that island. One needs a place where one can get away from the social pressures of Government House. And Maud is dead keen on it — feels she can let her hair down, don't you know?"

Denis gave an involuntary shudder. Maud's hair was a subject that he didn't like to think about.

The Governor resumed his study of the map. Eight islands remained. Denis eliminated four in one sweep — small coral atolls which, he pointed out, were under water at high tide. Three more went almost as quickly. Saluma had the famous "grove of the bats," where thousands of flying foxes hung downward all day and flew about in terrifying bands at night. Valonga had six immense blocks carved by earlier kings, and on Tuva the London Missionary Society was building a clinic to treat contagious diseases.

"That leaves this little one here," the Governor said, pointing to a speck of land several miles offshore from the main island. "Kula-ha'i. What do you know about that one, Foote?" he asked.

"I must say I don't know a thing, sir," Denis replied.

"Have a look at it tomorrow morning and report back to me." He strode over to his desk and looked at his engagement calendar. "I'll see you at three P.M.," he said. "That will be all."

"Thank you, sir," Denis said, turning to go.

"And Foote," the Governor called after him.

Denis stopped. "Yes, sir?" he said.

"If you value your connection with the Colonial Office here in Tonji — I trust you understand my meaning — you will bring back a favorable report about the feasibility of using this island."

"I understand, sir."

"Good. Ummmm. You may go."

"Well, Foote?" the Governor said the next afternoon at 3:10.

"Meager, sir."

"Any vegetation?"

"It's mostly sand and scrub and mangrove swamp, sir."

"What about palm trees?"

"One," Denis said. "Quite old."

"One palm tree!" the Governor said. "By Jove, that *is* meager. Was there any evidence of human habitation?"

"No, sir. The place was dead — hardly a jewel that we want the world press to come and see."

"I think we can count on Mr. Parker to tidy it up before the world press arrives. Wizard things those Hollywood fellows can do, I'm told. The main thing is that it's small and uninhabited — and available. I checked with Mulgrew of the Land Board this morning. He tells me there are no native claims of any kind on the island. So now that I have your report — such as it is — I shall direct Mulgrew to appropriate Kula-ha'i for the Crown, and then we will arrange to lease it to Parker's group."

"Is there a provision in the Land Act for such a transfer, sir?" Denis asked.

"Dammit, Foote, what d'you take me for? D'you think I'm a bloody pirate seizing land without proper authority?"

"Oh not that, sir. Certainly not."

"It's in Section 37A. Let's see — how is it worded?"

" 'For the general good,' sir? Is it that part?"

"That's it. Quite, quite. For the general good. One always wants to act for the general good when one is entrusted with solemn powers."

The Governor cleared his throat at elaborate length. He sidled over to the portrait of Elizabeth II and gazed at it for a moment, seeming to seek a nod of approval from the royal head. Evidently receiving one, he turned back to Denis.

"Then it's settled," he said. "I'll write Parker today giving him permission to proceed. You will also write him today describing the island in further detail and offering your fullest cooperation."

"Perhaps I'd better not describe it in *too* much detail, sir," Denis said.

"Suit yourself, old chap. Just don't make a balls-up of this one the way you did of the Miss Hibiscus Festival."

"No, sir," Denis said. "I'll remember it's for the general good."

"For what?" the Governor snapped. "What's that?"

"For the general good, sir."

"Oh yes. Splendid." He waved Denis out. "Send Miss Muggle in, will you, Foote?"

"Take a letter to that Parker fellow in California, Miss Muggle," the Governor said. "You have the address?"

"I have it, Your Excellency," Miss Muggle said.

"Ummmmm. No need to call me that, Miss Muggle. People might think it a trifle excessive."

"If it embarrasses you, sir . . ."

"That's it exactly," the Governor said. "One thinks of oneself as a modest man."

"Oh you are, sir, most definitely," Miss Muggle said, patting her gray hair into place and balancing her dictation book on a knee too bony to hold it level.

The Governor leaned back in his chair and clasped his hands around the great globe that was his stomach.

"Dear Parker," he began. "Her Majesty's Government have given prudent consideration to the scheme outlined in your letter of the twenty-seventh inst. It has been decided to grant your group permission to proceed and you may consider this letter official authorization to do so.

"New paragraph. Owing to constitutional restrictions on the use of Tonjian territory, only one island may be released, and I should inform you at the outset that it is not of first quality. Mr. Foote of our Visitors' Bureau, in fact, has serious doubts that it can be raised to the standard which you envision. He will communicate his findings to you by separate post. I might point out that Mr. Foote is of a skeptical mind and that you would be well advised to gauge his report accordingly.

"New paragraph. The island in question is named Kula-ha'i. It lies three-point-four miles northwest of Falolo, is less than a mile in circumference, is of negligible elevation and is, regrettably, undistinguished in appearance and vegetation. Your letter, however, leads me to infer that you have every confidence of being able to beautify it.

"New paragraph. Should you desire to implement your scheme with the aforementioned island, you may cable your acceptance to Mr. Foote. I know that he will want to begin making preparations to extend every courtesy to you and your party — whose acquaintance, needless to say, Lady Weems and I also anticipate making with the greatest of pleasure.

"I beg to remain, etcetera, Sir Reginald Weems, O.B.E. etcetera."

PACIFIC PALISADES CALIFORNIA

FOOTE VISITBURO TONJI

APPRECIATE CANDID LETTER RE KULA-HAI BUT ASSURE YOU HAVE KNOW-HOW UPFIX IT FABULOUS STOP ACCEPT OFFER ENTHUSIASTICALLY STOP LAUNCHING NATIONAL CONTEST CAMPAIGN TODAY STOP HOPE PROCEED TONJI WITH RUMBLE AND GIRL RESEARCHER SOONEST STOP CHEERS

PARKER

KULA-HAI UPFIX RUMBLE

3

Sally Merrill reports that she just got her M.A. in social anthropology from U.C.L.A. and is now hoping to do field work in "one of the new countries." We don't quite know what social anthropology is, Sally, but it sounds fascinating and we know you'll go far — literally!

THE "Pembleton Alumni Magazine" came in the morning mail just as Sally Merrill was leaving to apply for the job that she had seen advertised, and she turned instantly to her class notes to see what she was doing. Having satisfied herself of her own reality, she caught the bus to Pacific Palisades and settled down to read about the other people in her class.

This ritual, in the year since her graduation, had never failed to depress her. Pembleton was a Midwestern college of clerical origin, where the twin streams of academic excellence and charitable zeal still flowed from the principles of Amos Pembleton, who became its first president in 1857 upon his return from missionary work in Borneo. To any reader of the present alumni notes, in fact, it seemed that every graduating boy and girl came down from the commencement platform, changed out of cap and gown and into dungarees, and set out by nightfall to an underdeveloped land, first marrying — in many cases — a classmate of matching fervor. Sally felt that she was the only member of her class still within the continental limits. Oh, there was "Buffy" Tate in Arizona, but she was

living in a cliff with the Hopi Indians and "having a ball," so
she might as well be overseas.

The class notes began with a square blob of ink which Sally
knew would turn into a photograph if she looked at it long
enough. (The magazine was printed on a glossy paper that
had the texture of salami.) From the snapshot there slowly
emerged the faces of two adults and a baby, sitting in front of
an igloo.

Tom and Helena (Martin) Frobisher sent this picture of themselves and the "house" where they have spent the past year making
tape recordings of the little-known sun-worship chants of the
Agak Eskimoes. "We're just 20 miles below the Arctic Circle,"
Helena writes, "and loving it, especially since little Tommy came
along three months ago. No problem about air-conditioning here!
Any Pembleton guys and gals passing through are always welcome."

Well, she always was a drip anyway, Sally thought. I
wonder how many Pembletonians will be passing through.
Probably half a dozen in the next few months alone.

"Sel al'ochom!" writes Betty Begley, "which means 'Hi there!'
in Kurdish. I'm living in a mud-and-wattle village in north
Kurdistan, teaching phonetic English to an intriguingly primitive
tribe (and to the animals that also live in my 'classroom'). They're
delightful people and I hope to be here at least three years. The
name of the village is Wadi Ma'zoom, and any Pembletonians
passing this way are warmly invited to drop in."

Betty was lucky to be there, Sally thought, meeting problems and inventing solutions. She herself had spent a year in
graduate school learning solutions, and now she needed to find
some people who had the kind of problems that her solutions
would solve. She had told her father the title of her thesis
when she went home to Long Island for spring vacation, and
now she remembered that he gave a little moan. What was the
title again? "Tribalism: An Enquiry into Certain Socio-

Environmental Factors Inhibiting the Viability of Isolated Cultural Clusters in an Era of Emerging Nationalism."

"If you're an expert on isolated cultural clusters," he had said, "we've got plenty right here at home. Why don't you go work with the migrant laborers in Riverhead? They're isolated by all kinds of socio-environmental factors."

"Well, Daddy," she blurted, "it's just that working here in America . . ."

"I heard of a boy who's going to work in America this summer," Forbes Merrill went on. "You know our friends Lil and Harvey Potts in Westport? It's their boy Al. He wanted to do social work in the slums of Leeds, so they said 'Why don't you do social work in the slums of Bridgeport?' and he said O.K. A real pioneer. Every other teen-ager is spending the summer working in the slums of Rio or Berlin or Calcutta, where their parents have flown them at great expense. But not Al Potts! Years from now Al will be remembered as an American do-gooder who chose to do good in his own country. Why, I wouldn't be surprised if Congress decided to strike some kind of medal for Al. President Johnson will invite him to the White House and . . ."

"Oh, Daddy, you just don't get the point," Sally said, using a phrase more degenerative to the cells of a parent than any substance known to geriatrics. Forbes Merrill withdrew into gloomy contemplation of his forty-four-inch waist and reflected that he hadn't had a checkup in three months. Mrs. Merrill took up the fallen reins and turned the conversational horse around.

"It's the hope of the world," she said, "all these young people running off to foreign countries, even if they're not very good at what they do when they get there." It was the kind of sentence, it's second half seeming to cancel out its first half, which infuriated her stockbroker husband and which, he was only now beginning to realize, had just as much validity as his Dow Jones chart, though the laws that animated her vague beliefs remained a mystery to him.

Forbes Merrill was a believer in facts. He mobilized them as a general marshals his troops, and only when he was heavily armed did he give his clients the order to march into a rising market or to retreat from one that was shaky. So thoroughly did he study the metabolism of Wall Street that he was often able to tell his family, during their evening meal, that the three-for-one split of Universal Pulp & Gypsum had come as no surprise to him, for the company had recently struck a rich vein of bauxite in Costa Rica — a bit of intelligence which they greeted with a spontaneous burst of apathy.

Their indifference to the forward march of American technology and to his grasp of it, which enabled them to live well and attend the best schools, genuinely amazed him. He clung to the hope that while his wife wouldn't remember his nightly accounts in detail — even as he recited them, in fact, he would see stealing over her face a curious glaze, an abstraction from the present moment which meant that she was planning her week — she would remember them in principle. By now he was quite sure that Mrs. Merrill, if left to the chills of widowhood, would not sell her General Motors and buy "some fly-by-night uranium issue — the kind your brother always thinks is such hot stuff."

But they both also knew that she would first blow some of the estate money on a trip to Egypt, India and all the other places that Forbes refused to visit. His idea of travel was a trip to England on one of the "Queens." Alice Merrill was a romantic who spent much of her leisure time dogging the literary footprints of desert eccentrics like Doughty and Lawrence and Gertrude Bell, of explorers in Africa and voyagers to Cathay and diggers in the isles of Greece, envying them a life that brought the daily gift of the unexpected. She even subscribed to the "National Geographic," willing to swim its turbid rivers of prose for a color picture of dawn at Benares or sunset over Delphi that would set her still young heart racing.

In their daughter Sally, Forbes Merrill was pleased to see his own orderly genes triumphant. All through school and college she ingested vast amounts of information, from which she then drew sober conclusions. That her conclusions might be wrong never occurred to her — she had gone to too much trouble to conclude them. Her mother wished that Sally was

more impulsive, and she was glad that Sally's scholastic needs
had taken her farther and farther from the sheltering East
until she now stood at the very edge of the Pacific Ocean,
requiring only one more shove.

Sally herself was also impatient now — more impatient with
every mile as the bus carried her haltingly through Los
Angeles and the class notes continued to sound their holy call.
Len Putney was teaching metalwork to an "ethnic pocket" of
Peruvians high in the Andes. "Fuzzy" Morgan was walking
with the Indian saint Vinjar Bhave from Madras to Allahabad,
which she hoped to reach by Thanksgiving. Ted and Helen
(Parkinson) Ross were helping to run a clinic in Jogjakarta
for the World Health Organization. And all Pembletonians
passing through were warmly urged to drop in.

No item was as persuasive, however, as the one that
brought the column at last to an end:

Gil and Marian (Turner) Pratt are happily ensconced in Darien,
Conn., with little "Bo" and their terrier, Prince Radziwill. Gil is
with Mutual Underwriters Reinsurance, which he finds "tremendously satisfying," and Marian has her hands full running the
mothers' car-pool committee. "We'd adore to see any Pembletonians who might be passing this way," Marian writes.

"They're the only people who won't get dropped in on,"
Sally thought, slapping the magazine shut, deaf to the birdlike
cries for financial nourishment that continued to come out of
its interior, where the sluggish response to the $18,000,000
First Century Development Fund was tabulated on a huge
thermometer.

"Pa-ci-fic Pa-li-sades — end of the line," called the bus
driver, his voice tired and tinged with surprise that he had
again managed to cross the limitless city. Sally got out and
looked at the slip of paper on which she had scribbled her
destination: 14012 Santa Aziza Boulevard. From the size and
majesty of the address she guessed that the boulevard would
be only two or three blocks long. She sat down on a bench,
leaning back against an advertisement for a "fun funeral," and

took a last glance at the "help wanted" ad that had beckoned her, somewhat against her better judgment, to this far suburb. It was still not too late to call it off.

WANTED: BRAINY JILL-OF-ALL-TRADES FOR EXPENSES-PAID CULTURAL EXPEDITION TO EXOTIC POLYNESIAN ISLAND GROUP. APPLY 14012 SANTA AZIZA BLVD., PACIFIC PALISADES, TUES., WED., 11 TO 4. CREDENTIALS.

It was already Wed., and they had probably given the job to another girl — whoever "they" were. She hoped they were a museum or a foundation, but something told her they weren't. Still, an expenses-paid cultural expedition didn't come along every day. It would at least give her a start.

She didn't want to ask her father for more money, now that she had finished her education — especially money for travel. His xenophobia had taken a sharp turn with the seizure by Indonesia of a smelting plant in Sumatra owned by Consolidated Tin, a company he had been touting as a growth stock. And who didn't want to go to "exotic Polynesian island group"? One of her two favorite books in college was "Coming of Age in Samoa." She "identified" with Margaret Mead, as she often told her roommate, "Bibsy" Struthers. The other book was "Franny and Zooey." She identified with Franny. (Bibsy identified with Zooey, but then Bibsy always was a little hard to figure.)

Sally got up from her fun funeral bench, drew herself to her full height, a willowy 5 feet 9 inches, smoothed her black hair, which was drawn back in a manner generally called "severe," except that it was held in a bright red band, put fresh lipstick on her agreeably broad mouth, and walked to Santa Aziza Boulevard — a narrow lane that ran along the ocean and had twelve houses, beginning at 14000 and ending at 14012, her goal. It was a pink cottage perched close to the surf, and nothing about it spelled museum or foundation. It had a gate made of coconut husks, a path of crushed shells, and a sign whose capital "P" was a palm tree:

PARADISE UNLIMITED
Mel Parker Associates

A small sign said "Walk In," and she did. If the office wasn't paradise, the efforts to make it so were at least unlimited. Grass mats covered the floor; the curtains were blocked-printed in tapa cloth, and travel posters lined the walls in such profusion that the walls themselves were hardly visible. They exuded a scent so heady that the room seemed to shimmer and the mind to drowse. It was pure essence of adjectives.

Sun-kissed beaches, they said, and palm-fringed shores. And star-dusted nights and perfumed breezes and whispering tradewinds. They said moon-drenched lagoons and surf-swept coral reefs and honey-skinned girls. And throbbing drums. They said exotic, hypnotic, romantic, idyllic. They said bewitching, beguiling, alluring, inviting. And fabulous and mysterious, ever-to-be-remembered and never-to-be-forgotten.

To every inch of the room the adjectives sang their irresistible song, and so did the proper nouns that they modified: Tahiti and Papeete, Bora-Bora and Pago-Pago, Rarotonga and Raiatea, Moorea and Nukualofa and dozens more, names as round and soft as the Polynesian girls who formed the central motif of every poster, their heads as heavily wreathed in flowers as their bodies were thinly wreathed in grass, their smiles exerting the warmest welcome known to tourism.

Sally stood inhaling the sensuous office. It annoyed her. She had the scholar's disdain for excess, and into her photographic mind there now came, in a rapid series of prints, all the textbooks in which she had studied Polynesian culture as it really was. She saw the drab library bindings with their pedantic titles. She saw the unending pages of type, their sameness relieved only by footnotes clamoring to amplify a point that was already too ample. She saw the tenuous line-drawings of Polynesian handicrafts, the maps of their probable migrations, the tables of their annual rainfall. She saw the trailing appendices and bibliographies that directed her to still dryer books, which she earnestly sought out.

This arid vision, far from depressing Sally, thrilled her with the remembered pleasure of pure study. The very black-and-whiteness of her research was a warranty of its truth, just as the gaudy colors and verbiage of the surrounding posters made them false. Subconsciously she wrapped the parchments of Academia around herself like a towel, shielding her naked knowledge from the room's philistine spirits — a room which, she now saw, was occupied by a real secretary sitting behind a real desk reading an English paperback called "The Sussex Strangler."

"Aieo," said the secretary, massaging the word "Oh" into four syllables. "Have you come to see Mr. Parker in regard to our little notice?"

"I think so," Sally said. "Is he in — or one of his associates?"

"Associates? Aieo. I see what you're getting at. 'Mel Parker Associates' is Mr. Parker, actually. Quite a common device."

"Well, is he in?" Sally asked. "I mean, could I . . . ?"

"I'm afraid he's engaged at the moment," the secretary said. "In conference, actually."

At the word "conference" a door opened, emitting a whine of jazz and a crew-cut man in his early thirties, dressed in a hula shirt, blue slacks and sneakers. "Ursula," he said to the secretary, "I'm not any more in a goddam conference than the Birdman of Alcatraz."

"Than *who*, Mr. Parker? My word, what an extraordinary creature he sounds."

Mel Parker turned and looked at Sally for the first time. "Miss Whipple here, as you may have surmised, is an English secretary," he said. "English secretaries give tone to American industry and in compensation they get to arrest its flow. Nothing appalls them so much as immediate contact." He turned back to Miss Whipple. "So if anybody else comes, Ursula, go easy on the old engaged bit. Although," he added, turning back to Sally, "I've got a feeling that my search is over."

"I don't," Sally said. "In fact, I'll just leave quietly and that'll save everybody a lot of time."

"Don't go," Mel said. "Just because I'm not who you thought I was going to be . . ."

"I sort of thought . . ."

"That I represented the Ira J. Schmidlapp Fund, which disburses a modest annual sum left by Mr. Schmidlapp, who took such an interest in carved Maori spears, to send a deserving girl with a graduate degree in anthropology to Oceania to find more specimens for the little spear museum that he was just starting in the east wing of his country estate, Milworth."

"I've never heard of *that* one," Sally said.

"Oh hell, there is no Ira J. Schmidlapp. But if there were, you'd still learn more with me — and have more fun, too."

Sally looked past him through the open door of his office. One quick glance revealed a surfboard, a baseball glove, a replica of an "Oscar" statuette, an enormous picture of Groucho Marx, a phonograph playing progressive jazz, and an untidy pile of magazines that included "Variety," "Billboard," "Playboy," the "Racing Form," the "Hollywood Reporter" and "Mad."

The phone on Miss Whipple's desk rang. Mel picked it up and said, "I'm terribly sorry but Miss Whipple is in conference now, actually. Oh. Hiya, Sid. Yeah. No, that's O.K. Shoot. What's your problem?" He listened gravely. "Lemme get this straight. B.J. wants to go for a saturation booking in the nabes? And Fogelstein wants to day-and-date it hard-ticket? So what is it anyway, a sex-and-sand epic? An oater! Christ, Sid, you need big grosses fast to get back the negative cost. Did you talk to Metro? Sixty-two per cent and residuals! That's giving 'em an arm and a leg. Sid, if it was my dough I'd go for the blockbuster campaign. The whole schmier. Pitch the release to the Thursday P.M.'s, and two-to-one you'll also pick up a mention in Skolsky and the other weekend tabs. Yeah. Any time, Sid. Glad to. See you."

Sally picked up her handbag. "I really think I'd better go now," she said.

"Why do you really think that?" Mel asked.

"Because . . . look, you just had a talk on the phone that

I didn't understand a word of. Not that I was supposed to be
listening, but of course I was."

"Before the telephone call you were talking to kindly Dr.
Jekyll, boy humanist. The ringing of the phone turned him
into Mr. Hyde, the wicked press agent, who talks an entirely
different language."

"Is he an entirely different person?" Sally asked.

"No, he just talks that way. He can't help it."

"Then could he tell me — on second thought, I'd rather
hear it from Dr. Jekyll — just what I'm doing here?"

"He could. Are you free for lunch, Miss . . . ?"

"Merrill. Sally Merrill."

"Are you free for lunch, Miss Merrill?"

"Oh you don't have to take me to lunch, Mr. Parker. This is
a business appointment."

"To me, business and pleasure are the same thing."

"Like 'Parker' and 'Associates.' "

"Right. So are you free for lunch, Miss Sally?"

"I'm free for lunch, Mr. Parker — and Associates."

4

"LADIES and gentlemen," said the voice of the New Zealand airline pilot, "in just a minute you should be able to see the island of Niuafo'ou, better known as Tin Can Island."

Mel Parker stirred resentfully out of his sleep. How do these damn pilots, he thought, always know the exact moment when I've decided to take a nap? They probably send the stewardess back to check: "Watch that guy in seat 5B — if he dozes off I'll give him the old geography routine."

"You're probably wondering how Tin Can Island got its name," the pilot's voice floated to Mel, who wasn't. "There's a very colorful legend . . ."

Do airline pilots become history teachers when they retire, Mel asked himself. He recalled many flights in the United States when he had been awakened to look down at some dubious landmark like Bing Crosby's golf course. He felt that if he went up to the pilot's cabin he would find, instead of instruments and dials, the complete journals of Lewis & Clark, leatherbound sets of Francis Parkman, and a half dozen drawings by Remington.

"It seems that in 1921," the pilot continued, "a Mr. C. S. Ramsay went to Niuafo'ou as a trader, and he noticed that no ships could land there during the hurricane season, which lasted six months. Ship captains tried to send the mail ashore by rocket, but it often burned along the way, and one Sunday morning it landed on the thatched roof of the church and set it on fire. This put an end to the rocket deliveries — and to the church service."

A ripple of laughter and a "Can you imagine?" coursed through the plane.

"So Mr. Ramsay began to swim out to take and fetch the mail. He carried it in tin cans strapped to his side, while the islanders swam around him to beat the sharks away. Over the years he made the trip one hundred and eighteen times and the stamps became very valuable. When he was an old man Mr. Ramsay recalled that the captain of the 'Tofua' once said to him, 'Always swim out, Ramsay, whether we can launch a boat or not — otherwise people will think I'm a liar.' "

The voice stopped and the intercom clicked off.

"I'll be damned," Mel said to Sally, who was sitting next to him. "He *said* it was a colorful legend and it was. Never in my experience has such a thing happened." He rubbed his eyes. "Gotta have coffee," he muttered, pressing the stewardess's call button. "By the way, where's Cy?"

"He went up to sit next to the stewardess," Sally said, "so you may never get your coffee. Is he really a good photographer?"

"The best — when he's not thinking about girls."

"And when's that?"

Mel thought hard. "There's a period of about . . . I'd say about twenty-four minutes in every twenty-four hours when his mind can be deflected to his craft. Our job is to find those minutes and make the most of them."

"Are they consecutive?"

"Not necessarily. I've seen him drop everything right in the middle of a highly technical setup to chase some model."

"And is he often rewarded? He's not exactly irresistible." Sally could just see, up ahead, the top of Cy Rumble's bald head.

"Well, that just doesn't occur to photographers," Mel said. "They're a special breed. It's competitive work and full of indignities, but they survive because they've got gall."

"Aren't you afraid he'll pull off every grass skirt in Tonji?"

"He's capable of anything," Mel said. "Once we had him at Titan shooting a layout for 'Life,' and he used to drive around the studio trying to goose all the girls who were riding bicycles — a feat, I might add, that calls for the most precise timing. He said it was a popular sport with the G.I.'s in Italy. But the point is, he got the best pictures I ever saw. He knows what he wants, he works fast, and he gets it. He's an operator. And that's what I need out here. I can't afford to crap around."

"Would the ordinary photographer . . ." Sally groped for a word and didn't find one. "Crap around?"

"Oh, you know — I can't afford some fag from 'Mademoiselle' who made his name shooting the bazaars of Marrakech through a mauve filter and who'd wait five days to shoot Moona-Moona through a rainstorm at dusk."

Out of the front seat and up the aisle came the stewardess, a chesty girl confined within her airline uniform by the miracle of man-made fibers. And out of the adjoining seat, looking around in bewilderment, a boy who has lost his balloon, stood Cy Rumble. When his eye finally caught up with the balloon, bending over Mel Parker in all its roundness, he came charging in pursuit, but by then the stewardess had scurried off to get Mel's coffee.

"Of all people to push the call button!" he cried. "Just when I was beginning to make nickels . . . And stacked! Man, this New Zealand stuff is tremendous. Did you get a load of those booberinoes? I wouldn't mind putting my little old hand . . ."

"Sugar?" said the stewardess, coming back.

"Yes, honey?" said Cy, turning to her eagerly.

"I was asking the gentleman if he wanted sugar. Now unless there's some professional assistance . . ."

"No, no," Cy said with resignation, watching in wonder as she walked the length of the plane. "Cute little ass, too," he said to Mel.

"Professional assistance," Mel repeated, mocking her tone. "That's the corporate way of saying you're not allowed to lay the help."

"Red tape," Cy muttered. "Whole world is smothered in it. All my life I've wanted to get beyond the red tape belt, and if it's not in the South Seas it's not anywhere." He climbed into his seat, which was in front of Sally's, and turned around. "Hi, Sally," he said. "Howza kid?"

"Pretty good, Cy. Having troubles?"

"Troubles?" It had never occurred to him that she would hear his discussion of the stewardess. At such moments his mind blocked out everybody except the immediate players. "Oh," he said at last. "I'm sorry you heard all that. Kind of rough on the ears of a nice girl like you."

"I don't mind — within reason," Sally said. "But it isn't very gallant."

"I'm too old to be gallant," Cy said. "Forty last month and not getting any handsomer."

Sally looked at the forty-year-old face. It was one of those ageless New York faces that could be thirty-five or fifty, more gray than pink, more flabby than firm, bearing the imprint, especially beneath the eyes and in the thinly engraved lines that meandered across it to no particular destination, of countless cigarettes inhaled in haste, countless prune Danishes eaten but not digested, countless cups of coffee swilled down when they had just lost their warmth but not their taste of cardboard, countless subways caught at full sprint — mortifications of the flesh willingly borne by the city-dweller in his chase of the big break, the big deal, the big time.

By every rule of medicine, the men belonging to these faces ought to be almost dead. Yet Cy's face was typical, and in spite of its disrepair it was vastly alive. "He's right about not getting any handsomer," Sally mused, noting the shiny dome, the straggly black hair around it, the bent nose, the mouth that seemed to have a surplus of teeth when it smiled. But it almost always *did* smile, and so did the eyes — large brown eyes, warm and amused. The face made Sally homesick for New York.

"I think you're very handsome," she said. "You'll make out fine."

"Sally, you're an angel," Cy said. "For that I'm gonna fix you up with the handsomest young man in Tonji. A Polynesian prince with a big future in tunafish. Say Mel, you gonna make us go to work right away? Sally and I need a little vacation."

"Well, you're not going to get it," Mel said. "We've got to work damn fast. The contest begins this week in the States and nobody even knows what the island looks like."

"Do you?" Cy asked.

"I've got a feeling it looks lousy," Mel said, "and we've got to send back some pictures that make it look good. And we've got to build that native bungalow and get it furnished with all the tie-in products."

"Why don't you just furnish it with native materials?" Sally asked. "Wouldn't that be more authentic?"

"You miss the point of a tie-in campaign," Mel said.

"What *is* the point?"

"We get all these different companies to contribute something, so it doesn't cost us a cent. Like Trans-Sky is gonna fly the winning couple out. And in return they get a bundle of free publicity."

"Who else?" Cy asked.

"I've got Slumberama," Mel said. "That's the big outfit in L.A. that makes 'Sleepy Time' beds and patio furniture. You've probably seen their Napateria on Sunset Boulevard? No? I often go there for a snooze after a three-martini lunch. They're providing the twin beds and four reclining TV chairs. The sheets and blankets are coming from Snug-Fit."

"Isn't that a bra?" Cy asked.

"You're thinking of Form-Fit," said Mel.

"Good. I'll think of it some more."

"Snug-Fit is going to take a lot of radio spots," Mel went on. "Which reminds me, Sally — they want an authentic soundtrack, so when you go out into the villages with your tape recorder I want everything you can get: songs, dances, women talking, children crying. I need a platter . . ."

"A what?"

"A record that I can place with the deejays — the disk jockeys. Some Tonjian song with an unusual beat that would make a good new dance. The Moona-Moona. Get all America doing it."

"But they'll be singing in their own language," Sally said. "People in America won't be able to make any sense of the words."

"That's never stopped people in America before," Mel said. "When it comes to popular songs they flip over novelty. You could sing the Karachi telephone book and it would have a pretty good chance. Who knows what the Singing Nuns were singing?"

"I never dug those Singing Nuns," Cy said.

"They weren't your type. And don't worry, Sally, if the sound isn't perfect. I'll be sending the tape back to Buddy Eleganto, who's musical director at Titan and a genius in the echo chamber. He'll dub in some waves and add some whispering winds and it'll come out more realistic than the real thing."

"What else?" asked Cy. "I want to know what to shoot."

"Let's see. Cook-Eez is giving us the stove and sink and kitchen cabinets, and for the curtains I've got a tie-in with Folklore Fabrics. That's the outfit that makes ethnic weaves from forty-six countries out of Acrilan acrylic in a loft in Brooklyn."

"At this rate everyone in America will hear about Tonji," Cy said.

"That's what I want."

"Is it what *they* want?" Sally asked.

"Who?"

"The people in Tonji."

Mel didn't answer for a moment. "I don't know yet," he said. "The Governor wants it, and that's important. But the head of the Visitors' Bureau, a man named Foote, doesn't."

"How about the natives?" Sally asked. "Don't you think they're entitled to . . ."

"I don't have time to think that," Mel snapped. "Don't tell me you're going to wind up siding with the natives?"

"I warned you I might," Sally said. "Why did you hire me, then?"

"I thought you'd look good in a sarong. Nice legs — did anyone ever tell you that at Pembleton, or did you wear those damn knee socks for four years?"

Sally blushed. Nobody ever had told her that. Larry Poot told her she had "honest eyes," and Stan Flegler at grad school admired her "swanlike neck."

"Besides," Mel went on, "I needed someone bright — and that's you. And I wanted someone nice — and that's you. And I needed someone quickly — and that was you, a scholar impatient to take her learning into the so-called field."

"It was almost too quickly," Sally said. "If I'd had more time to decide, I never would have come."

"Having second thoughts?" Mel asked.

"Second, third and fourth."

"That's natural. There's no syllabus for this course. It's the first time you've set out on an academic path without knowing where it would end."

"It's not even an academic path," Sally said. She looked very young and vulnerable, Mel thought — a freshman going off to college. "What am I doing here anyway, on this crazy plane?"

It was a rhetorical question, not really posed to Mel. She knew what his answer would be: some lighthearted comment about life being the best teacher. And who was to say he wasn't right? Suddenly everything was tilted. She had always believed that orderly roads of research led to definite bodies of knowledge. Follow the road and the prize will be there waiting.

But what if the prize was not worth the trip? Or what if there were other roads — obscure and untidy trails that no scholar knew about, or would follow if he did, leading to other prizes more worth possessing? Could that possibly be? All that she was sure of, right now, was an upside-down feeling in her stomach, the feeling that she had had as a child going to a party or as an adolescent going to a dance, her unwanted companion on every occasion when she didn't know how it was going to turn out. Nothing was worse than not to know how it was going to turn out.

Sally fished out of her flight bag, which was so distended
with books that it hardly had room for her comb and lipstick,
a monograph on the hostility of remote tribes to meddling
outsiders. None of the case histories, she now recalled from
Professor Feldspar's course, ended well for the meddling
outsiders. She began to read and was halfway into a chapter
called "Fatal Miscalculation" when the intercom clicked on,
emitting a low gargle as it awaited its master's voice.

"Ladies and gentlemen," the voice said eventually, "we're
about to fly over Palmerston Island, one of the smallest in the
Pacific and — I think you'll agree — one of the prettiest."

Mel craned his head over to Sally's window and they both
looked down on a coral atoll that was no more than a mile in
circumference. It was an almost perfect circle of white sand,
pierced in one place by a narrow boat passage. Inside the
circle was a brilliant green lagoon. Outside, the ocean waves
broke blue and white against the reef.

"Oh, isn't it beautiful?" Sally cried.

"Mm! Really something! Man!" Mel said. His remarks
when impressed by a natural wonder were always fatuous
beyond his own belief.

"Just thrilling!" Sally said.

"I'll say," Mel agreed. What a stupid comment, he thought.
"It's something all right." Christ, he thought.

The intercom stayed on, gargling, while the passengers
continued to gawk at the white circle of land and to ponder
its strange isolation. Then the voice came back.

"There's a very colorful legend connected with Palmerston," it said.

"Another very colorful legend," Mel said. "I doubt it."

"Shhh," Sally said.

"It seems that the island was unoccupied until 1862, when
a Gloucestershire man named William Marsters settled there
with two native women — his wife and his wife's sister. A
third woman joined them later, and all three of them bore
children. The children intermarried and in time the population grew to one hundred."

Cy gave a loud and admiring whistle. "Hey Mel! Where can you get that kind of work nowadays?"

"Marsters insisted," the pilot went on, "that all the children be taught English. So if you visited Palmerston today you'd still hear them speaking mid-Victorian English with a Gloucestershire accent."

"I love stuff like that," Sally said.

"Two severe hurricanes in the nineteen-twenties and thirties washed away almost all the houses and coconut trees," the pilot continued, "and many families moved to other islands in the Cook group, but the population is still around one hundred. The original William Marsters died in 1899 and his son William ruled the island benevolently until he died in 1956 at the age of eighty-four."

"Eighty-four!" Cy said. "See? It's the secret of longevity."

"I'm sorry you heard that story," Mel said. "Now I'll never get you home."

"I can hear airline pilots of the future pointing out my island," Cy said. " 'See that atoll down there, folks? Populated entirely by one man. Yessir. Fella by the name of Rumble. Had ten wives and one hundred children. They say he ruled them benevolently and died in his sleep at the age of ninety-nine.' "

Palmerston disappeared behind them and all was ocean again. The intercom was still at full gargle. Presently the pilot's voice added a final word:

"In about an hour you'll begin to see the outer islands of the Tonji group, and not long after that we'll be coming down in the lagoon at Falolo, where this flight will terminate. Meanwhile your stewardess, Miss Overjoy, will be serving you cocktails and a light snack." Gargle, gargle. "Thank you." Click.

Tonji. Falolo, terminate. The words detonated inside Mel's head like a sparkler. He grabbed his flight bag and headed for the lavatory, pausing only long enough to say to Sally: "Please tell Miss Overjoy: dry martini, five to one, twist of lemon."

Five minutes later he emerged shorn of his business suit. In its place, garbing him loosely, was a pair of yellow slacks and a hula shirt that he had bought at the Fiji airport. The shirt was bright red and had a repeating motif, like wallpaper, of tawny girls bathing in a South Sea lagoon. They girdled him round and round, seeming to wriggle their generous bosoms as he moved. He was carrying his shoes and socks — his feet were now in sandals — and behind his ear was a hibiscus plucked from one of Miss Overjoy's snack trays.

"I'm ready!" he announced to Sally. "How do I look?"

"Terrible," she said. "But I've got to admit you look happy."

"The spell of the islands. It just reached up and grabbed me."

"Odd thing, that," the stewardess said, arriving with the martini. "A *lot* of men go potty at this stage of the trip. You should see the Tahiti flight. Absolutely fantastic!"

"You can't shame me, Miss Overjoy," Mel said. "I feel absolutely fantastic, and I'm not about to get back into that suit."

"Oh certainly not, sir. I was merely making a general observation."

"And an interesting one it was. Do you suppose, Miss Overjoy, that I could have another of these drinks in about ten minutes?"

"Righty-o," she said.

An hour later the Tonji islands came into view. The two biggest were green and tropical and had jagged mountains in the interior. The smaller ones were mainly coral atolls, their white beaches strung out like necklaces. Mel saw outriggers bobbing in the blue water and thatched villages beginning to appear among the palm trees, and their downward tug was as strong as if he were fastened to them by a rope.

He had flown over many parts of the world that excited him: the gigantic Alps, the matted jungle, the baking desert. But those were too overwhelming for him, a mere passenger suspended unnaturally in the air, to grasp, and certainly they didn't beckon him to come visiting. They aroused instincts so old, so primeval, that modern man seldom has any cause to

summon them. But the islands of Tonji sent up an invitation
that was warm and gay. "We're waiting for you," they called.
"We've always been waiting for you. Just for you. Hurry!"

Every person on the plane heard the call and recognized it
for what it was: a line between the irreversible past and the
pliable future. Some dream had drawn them all to this
remote cluster of islands, and nobody could say which of
them would make the dream come true and which would find
it a mirage. Their needs were too various, their ailments too
complex. But the mystery of the moment occurred to each
person as the flying boat began its descent and the lagoon of
Falolo rushed up to meet them.

Sally thought:

So this is how it is to leave the nest. The old havens far
behind. Thousands of miles. And thousands of years. All so
safe. The snug boarding school. Miss Primrose's. The pro-
tective New York dances. Junior Get-Togethers. The cozy
summer community. Egret Cove. Only "nice" people. Nice of
my parents to telephone the night before I left. How like
Daddy to ask, "Who is this Melville Parker? I couldn't find
him in Dun & Bradstreet." And you never will. And Mother:
"Couldn't I send you a sweater from the Bermuda Shop? It
might get cold out there, Sally dear. You never know." Sweet.
Like sewing name tags in my camp uniform. Camp What-
Was-Its-Name? Wamaquiggitt. "With a 'wa,' with a 'ma,'
with a 'q-u-i' . . ." The name tag in red block letters. SALLY
MERRILL. What became of her? Skinny little girl in black
pigtails who liked to ride a pony. Parents so well-meaning.
Did everything to prepare me for the world *they* live in. How
to tell them that that world will never do? Narrow old values.
Youth on the move. No more lazy summer vacations. Nigeria,
Malaysia, Bolivia, Mississippi. Peace Corps, Youth Corps,
Anti-Poverty Corps. American Field Service, Operation
Crossroads Africa, UNESCO. CORE, SANE, SNCC. Build,
heal, help. Redress the ancient wrongs, proclaim the ancient
rights. The serious generation. Are we too serious? Is that our
cross? Then what is our salvation? To do the job. To get on
with it. Do some good.

Cy thought:

So this is how it is to get away from it all. The weight of
detail lifting off my shoulders. Haven't felt so good since I
went overseas after a year at Camp Lee. A year of petty
authority. "Ten-HUTT! Colonel Prick will now pass among
you with a white glove to see if there is any dust on your
footlockers." Cruddy old bastard. Great to get overseas where
nobody cared as long as you won the war. Wasn't that what
it was all about anyway? You'd never know it. The Colonel
Pricks run the world. Wear you down with stupid rules. "We
like your pictures, Mr. Rumble, but we ran a layout on a
similar subject seventeen years ago and there's a company
policy . . ." "The best spread you've ever done, Cy, and if
the decision was up to me personally I'd buy it in a minute,
believe me, but the guys upstairs think we're getting a little
too arty and so . . ." Arty shmarty. They don't know what
they think, is the truth. Guys upstairs. I hate guys upstairs.
They knock the spark out, make hacks of us all. World's full
of hacks. I could have been better. I'll hack around out here
in the islands. Have a ball, do the job, and then back to
Hackville. After all . . . man, what crazy colors in that
lagoon. Never saw a green like that before. Maybe some
morning before Mel and Sally are up, I'll bring my camera
out and see if I can catch that. Do something good. Maybe.

Mel thought:

So this is how it is to follow the rainbow to its end. The
dream merchant comes to Dreamland. Can I spend my life
manufacturing dreams? Conning and conjuring, like some
teen-age magician in love with his own act? Or do I have to
grow up? But what could I do that would be more valuable?
I gratify the ancient urge to escape from a humdrum world,
and that urge is centered right here in the South Sea Islands.
You could see it at the New York World's Fair. All those
ladies who went to the Polynesian pavilion and got a paper
lei that they wore for the rest of the day. You'd see them
later, standing in line at the Festival of Gas or the Dynamic
Maturity Pavilion or some other bore-ass exhibit that they'd
been told to visit, and they were still wearing those cheap

orange *leis,* carrying the dream around their necks — gray-haired and frumpy ladies who had never gotten farther from home than their bridge club in Joplin. When they put on those *leis* they were shouting to the world: "This is the real me — the me that nobody knows." But nobody ever heard the shout. It came from too far inside. Buried too long. And nobody would believe it anyway. That frumpy old lady never was a girl with dreams. But she was. And part of her still is. I hope one of those frumpy old ladies wins Moona-Moona. At any rate, I'll bring thousands of 'em here vicariously and keep the dream alive. Is that hokum? Sure it's hokum, and I'm the hokum king and there's nothing that I can't do.

5

BLACK DAY FOR TONJI
"Yankee, Go Home"
By OLD SETTLER

To the casual observer it undoubtedly appeared that yesterday's flying boat brought only the usual mixed bag of tourists, beachcombers, "writers," painters and other types who make their way to our islands with regularity. Yet among the debarking passengers was a small group from Hollywood, U.S.A., who have in mind nothing less than the utter ruin of Tonji. It is not too much to say that it was a black day for this hitherto sunny paradise.

One can, of course, respect the sincerity of His Excellency the Governor in permitting this newest landing of Yanks in the South Pacific, but one cannot in all honesty applaud the wisdom of his move. On the contrary, Government House have once again proved themselves fatally blind to the long-range interests of the very people whom they are bound by an ancient and honourable trust to govern. Mark our words: Sir Reginald Weems will live to regret the day when Mr. Mel Parker and his colleagues set foot on . . .

MR. Mel Parker threw down the newspaper. "What a lot of crap," he said, aloud, though he was all alone. Solitude never stopped him from voicing opinions of this kind. The words just sprang out of his mouth, taking him slightly by surprise, but he was always glad to hear them, for then they had an existence, perhaps even a certain power, which they would never have had if locked forever in his cranium.

It was his first morning in Tonji and he was finishing his breakfast — a glutinous white porridge and a bottle of beer — in his room at Millie Hawkes's Boarding House. No rooms had been available at the Grand Polynesian or the El Tropiques, so Denis had booked Mel and his party into Millie Hawkes's. "It's central," he explained to Mel, who said "Jesus, what a dump!" when he saw the sloping old wooden house, so different from his preconceived vision of a luxury hotel. "Besides, Millie never runs out of whiskey," Denis added, "which you will find a most engaging faculty in a group of islands that frequently go dry."

The rest of Mel's "party," however, had not yet made it. Cy had spotted a Tonjian belle on the customs wharf and gone away with his arm around her bare waist, and Sally had been wheedled off to the Bounty by Doc Bligh, who told her that Millie Hawkes's was known throughout the islands for its ferocious rats. "Filthy big beggars, Miss, you wouldn't believe it. Teeth as long as my finger — and sharp! Many a time they've been known to chew right through Millie's metal roof."

Mel hoped that Sally was all right. He would go over later and try to bring her back. As for Cy, there was no use looking for him. He wouldn't be back for several days, and then he'd be too tired to work. Well, at least Mel himself could get started. He set up his typewriter on a shaky wicker table, lit a thin cigar, gazed for a few moments across the sparkling blue lagoon of Falolo, and began to type:

FOR IMMEDIATE RELEASE

ISLAND PARADISE TAKES SHAPE!

FALOLO, TONJI ISLANDS — Yesterday it was just another South Sea island, forgotten by time. The Polynesians called it "Kula-ha'i," which means "tiny jewel on the horizon," but nobody ever lived there.

Today the island has a new name, "Moona-Moona," and the name is being spoken from village to village here beneath the sky of the Southern Cross. The very palm trees seem to whisper that something magical is happening on the pretty little "desert isle" whose white beaches are washed by the blue Pacific and cooled by the ageless trade winds.

Smiling Polynesian men and women began this week to turn the unspoiled paradise into a tropical bower fit for a king and queen — the lucky Americans who will win Moona-Moona in a unique contest that already has millions of people from Maine to California gripped in frenzied competition. Using their ancient crafts to plait together a typical South Seas bungalow of palm fronds and bamboo, fringed with fragrant bougainvillea blooms and set among lush banana trees, the native workers — several of whom are handsome young sons of island chiefs — improvise songs as they go about their happy task, including one which tells about "the blond strangers who will come to live on Moona-Moona from the faraway land where the tall buildings grow."

When the bungalow is finished, later this week, it will be out-fitted with a complete selection of up-to-the-minute appliances and tasteful furnishings guaranteed to

"Mel! *Mel!*" It was Sally's voice, high and nervous. "Where are you?" She burst into his room and flopped into a chair. "Oh that horrible old man! I can't tell you what an awful place . . ." She was still panting. "Crumby little thatched cottage . . . land crabs as big as a cat, dragging themselves across the floor all night . . . I'll never forget that scritchy noise if I live to be a hundred."

Mel took her hand and gave it a squeeze.

"That's the first nice thing that's happened to me," she said.

"Me, too," he said. "I'll get you some tea and then I'll go over to Bligh's and get your stuff, and maybe kick him in his flabby old — well, I guess that wouldn't do any good. Mil-*lie!*" he called. Millie Hawkes came shuffling in. "Millie, Miss Merrill here has spent a night over at Doc Bligh's and . . ."

"Oh, honey, I'll get you some Scotch right away," Millie said.

"Maybe some tea," Sally said.

"Don't you worry any more. Millie's gonna take care of you from now on. That mean old son of a bitch! Someone ought to go over and kick him in the balls. Right, Mr. Parker? Ha-*haaa!*" Her laugh rang melodiously across the whole morning.

"That'd show him. Hoo-ooooo!" She ambled off toward the kitchen.

"I think we'll get along all right here at Millie's," Mel said. "That is, if we can stand the food. The room service is rather informal — Millie keeps wandering in and out — and there's a whole family of chickens and ducks under the floor, but in general . . ."

"How about rats?" Sally asked.

"No, I asked about that when I heard why you weren't coming here last night. Millie says there are no rats in these islands."

"Oh that horrible man," Sally said. "Are you really going to go and — I mean, punch him in the stomach or something? My white knight?"

"No, I'll just go and collect your bags. But first I've got to finish this release. The plane goes out this afternoon and it's the last airmail for two weeks."

Sally went over to read what Mel had written. "Oh, *bro*ther!" she said as her eyes moved down the page.

"Like it?" he asked.

"Cripes! I mean that is re*pul*sive."

"I'm glad you like it," he said. "It'll wow the natives."

"What natives?"

"The natives from Maine to California. They'll lap it up."

"But there isn't a word of truth in it."

"That's promotion, baby. That's how you get to be director of publicity and exploitation at Titan Pictures."

"I see why it's called exploitation," Sally said. "But what's the difference between that and publicity?"

"Well, let's see. Publicity is sending out press releases and pictures. And promotion is when you take the star of your new movie to lunch at Chasen's with a reporter. Everyone sees her having lunch, so that promotes the movie, and then everyone reads the interview, so that promotes it again. And then there's public relations. That's when you take some fink and manipulate him into what the public thinks is a great guy and the 'New York Times Magazine' does a high-class article on him, though of course he's still the same old fink. Or when

you take some big corporation that everybody hates, like the
bank or the telephone company, and you turn it into 'just
folks' — which, if it was, it wouldn't be any good as a corporation."

"And exploitation?"

"Is when you dramatize your product by some method so
unusual that the public can't help being tickled by it. Like if
you have a movie about, say, skin-diving. You know, the old
underwater stuff: boy and girl exploring sunken galleons.
Giant octopus, moray eel, monster of the deep. All that. Well,
the gimmick is, you hold the preem — the world premiere —
of the movie underwater. You charter a plane and you fly a
load of reporters and columnists to Nassau or Jamaica, and
you see that they get plenty to drink, and you rig up an
underwater tank and . . . Say! Of course! Christ, why didn't
I think of that before? Must be getting old. I wonder if it's
too late." He tapped his fingers in a rapid beat.

"Too late for what?" Sally asked.

"Shhh, will ya? I'm thinking. Let's see. I could send a cable
to Fogelstein . . . see if he'll go for the junket bit . . . hold
the preem here . . . gotta check the exhibitors . . . if we
can get Trans-Sky to pick up the tab for the plane ride . . .
but I'll have to clear it with Sir Reginald Whoozis . . .
maybe if I move fast . . ."

"What are you talking about?" Sally said.

Mel grabbed her impulsively. "Sally, baby," he said, "you
are witnessing the birth of the biggest tie-in campaign since
Noah's Ark."

"You really love this crazy business, don't you?" Sally said.
She looked at Mel, sitting down again now, his head tilted
back and resting in his interlocked hands, his bare feet
resting on his typewriter, a man wholly at ease with his
chosen world. His boyish face had what "Vogue" would call
"the American look" — it was amiable and amused and not
quite handsome, the face of a camp counselor or an Iowa
farmhand or a cowboy. It might become handsome in five
more years, at which point "Vogue" would call it "rough-

hewn and chiseled," or it might fall apart and revert to the pudding-like softness of babyhood.

Right now so few lines had been chiseled into Mel Parker's features that he could either be a man of great contentment or great sloth. To Sally he looked more like the latter: there was a current of laughter in his blue eyes that seemed to mock her seriousness, and this was a look that she never quite trusted. She associated these faces with friends of her parents who had "charm" but, as her father said, "never got to first base" or "went busted in business," men who got drunk at football games and reached their annual zenith at college reunion.

"Yes, I love this crazy business," Mel said. "I won't deny there's an element of the carnival barker and the rainmaker in what I do. That's part of the romance, and there's damn little of it in most businesses. But there's also an element of the faith healer. That's my fun. It was Mike Todd's fun — and Barnum's too, I suppose. We persuade people to find life gayer than they otherwise would."

"You must be a very unusual press agent," Sally said.

"I am one hell of a press agent. You know that old saw 'Politics is the art of the possible'? That's too depressing for me. The only art worth practicing is the art of the impossible."

"Yes, but who's going to print an impossible news release like this one? Everyone can see it's baloney."

"Everyone can't. The good newspapers in America won't touch it — you're right. But the other ninety per cent will be glad to see it, and half of 'em will print it. Do you know that hundreds of American newspapers print movie reviews that have been written and sent out by the company that made the movie? Or that their book reviewers simply lift the blurb that's on the book jacket: 'Mr. Birdland's long-awaited second novel is nothing less than a minor masterpiece. In his witty yet perceptive grasp of the human condition he more than fulfills his early promise.'"

"That's very discouraging," Sally said. "It upsets me when I find truth getting blurry."

"Welcome to the outside world," Mel said, "and to the age of the managed event. Times were never riper for the publicist — truth and fiction are hopelessly intermingled in America today."

"Well, if I have anything to do with it . . ."

"Truth will prevail!" Mel said in the tone of a Memorial Day orator.

"No fair teasing," Sally said. "After all, I did sign up with you and not with the Ira J. Schmidlapp Fund. Isn't that progress?"

"Tremendous progress — and I apologize. I'll try to respect your sacred codes."

Millie Hawkes came back. "I brought you some tea, Miss Merrill, honey, and a little snack to tide you over till lunch." She set down a plate on which a white viscous mass lay shapeless and inert, seeming to have never had any organic life.

"What's that?" Sally asked.

"It's anti-matter," Mel said.

"It's sago custard, honey," Millie said. "I don't suppose that old bastard gave you any breakfast, except maybe poached bat."

Sally's stomach did an involuntary turn of 360 degrees. "I didn't wait to see," she said. "Well, that's very sweet of you, Mrs. Hawkes. If you'd just leave the sago custard I'm sure that a little later . . ."

"There's nobody but calls me Millie. And Mister Hawkes has gone to his reward so many years now that I don't feel like Mrs. Hawkes, that's for sure. Eaten by a grouper, poor soul, while fishing off the reef. Went down just like Jonah, wristwatch and all."

"How awful!" Sally said, covering her mouth with her hand.

"The worst part was that the fella fishing with him — it was Charley Vavonga — but of course you wouldn't know him — big strong man, half Polynesian and half Australian — tried to kill the grouper with his spear, and more than likely he finished off poor Mr. Hawkes inside while he was at it. At any rate, they tried him for homicide, right here in the courthouse. I remember that the trial went on for weeks because it was so — well, you know, unusual. Judge Grimshaw said there was nothing like it in the history of the law that they could use as a guide."

"It's damn unusual, all right," Mel said. "How did it come out?"

"Oh, they let him go, and that was fine with me. Myself, I didn't hold it against Charley. If I was going to hold it against anyone it would be the grouper. Well, I gotta get to the market — you folks'll probably be ready for lunch around twelve." She wandered off.

Mel took the sago custard into the bathroom and threw it into the toilet, which flushed with a loud protesting noise.

"Does it always make that noise?" Sally asked.

"You should have heard it when my porridge went down," Mel said.

"So you haven't had any breakfast either?"

"Only beer and a cigar," Mel said. "Which I think — at this rate — is going to be my regular diet. Let's take a walk and try to buy some fruit. Just give me ten minutes to finish this release and I'll drop it off at the post office."

Sally sat back to drink her tea and to read the "Tonji Times."

"Nice little piece in there by 'Old Settler,' " Mel said. "Make you feel right at home." Then he hunched over the typewriter and attacked the keys at full speed, never pausing or crossing anything out. At one point he thought he heard a moan from behind the "Tonji Times."

Mel and Sally walked along the waterfront of Falolo, threading their way among the Tonjian women who had their wares spread on the sidewalk. Twisted strips of tobacco, pink betel nuts, bêche-de-mer and octopus and other exotic foods from the sea lay alongside straw hats and cricket balls and tinted postcards. Mel noticed a number of mango peels; he had seen an item in the paper complaining that a "leading citizen nearly had a serious fall" — a leading citizen whom he assumed to be "Old Settler."

Boats clogged every inch of waterfront space. Some had just come in; others were getting ready to leave, their ports of call written on a blackboard next to the gangplank. Lithe brown boys loaded and unloaded the countless items of island trade. Noisy pigs were hoisted over the side on ropes, flailing their legs in the alien air. Acrid copra was piled onto old schooners, its smell mixing with cocoa and fruit and spices and fish from other boats, just as the sounds of the harbor also joined together, the creak of winches and derricks mingling with the cries of street merchants and the cackling of crated chickens and the shouts of boys working on the dock.

"Talk about your swarthy Lascars and strapping Kanakas," Mel said.

"Who talks about those?" Sally asked.

"Somerset Maugham. It's every Maugham scene rolled into one. He must have sat right here, taking notes."

"He did, lad — I'm here to tell you," said a voice behind him. It was Literary Johnny, looking very professorial with a pipe and a book. "October of nineteen thirty and two, if I recall. He was working on 'Red' at the time — you remember that story, of course? — and he said to me, 'Johnny, if I could just spend a week sitting here in Falolo while you pointed out the different boats and told me the yarns connected with them, why I'd be the luckiest writer in the whole world.' Well, sir, I was glad to oblige, and many were the hours that Willie and I spent right up there at the Kon-Tiki Bar — you see, right where that man is having a long cold beer? He was so grateful he wanted to assign me all the dramatic royalties from 'Rain,' but I said 'No, Willie, I'm content to be a poor and simple man, wanting no more than an occasional cold beer or maybe a whiskey and water on a hot day like this.' "

"Did you *really* know him?" Sally asked. "I just loved 'Of Human Bondage.' "

"Gave 'im that idea myself," Johnny said. "There was a club-footed fella used to sail in and out of here on the Tolala, and one day I said to Willie, 'Buy me another Scotch, lad, 'cause I'm about to tell you a story that'll put you on easy street.' "

"I always thought that 'Of Human Bondage' was mostly autobiographical," Mel said.

"Check it with Denis Foote, if you don't believe me," Johnny said. "I see him up there on the porch of the Kon-Tiki Bar right now. And we might have a whiskey as long as we've got to go up there."

"All right, old scout, I'd love to buy you that whiskey," Mel said. "And I want to talk to Foote anyway."

They climbed up to the verandah of the Kon-Tiki. Denis was cleaning shells at his usual table and he waved the three new arrivals over.

"Good morning, Mr. Parker," he said, getting up and shaking hands. "I was going to come round a bit later to see if I could be of any help. Good morning, Miss Merrill. I'm sorry I saw so little of you yesterday — you vanished into thin air. I trust the accommodations were satisfactory."

So quiet and polite, Sally thought, looking into Denis's gray eyes and giving him the forthright American-girl handshake, the one that goes to prospective employers and parents of boy friends. So different from this nut I'm stuck with.

"Well," she said, "I'm afraid — though it was certainly not your fault — that I spent the night at Mr. Bligh's so-called hotel."

"Good God!" Denis said. "So he told you about the rats? There are no rats in Tonji, so it's safe to move back to Millie's. I'll go fetch your gear directly, and while I'm at it I'd like to give that old rogue a good kick in the teeth."

"Speaking of old rogues," Mel said, "we came up to get your opinion on a literary question."

"I imagined as much." He looked at Literary Johnny with resignation. "What is it this time?" he asked.

"Scotch and soda," said Literary Johnny. "The Yank has kindly offered to pay."

"The idea just popped into my head," Mel said. "How

about you, Mr. Foote? Beer? Good. That's two of us. How about you, Sally?"

"Do you think they'd have any Coca-Cola?"

"I do," Denis said. "Your national drink was brought to the South Seas during the war. In fact, American troops threw so many empty bottles into the lagoon at Bora-Bora that when the war was over, pearl fishermen found it more profitable to dive for Coke bottles than for pearl shell."

Mel gave the order. "Now, the question is," he went on, "whether the noted English novelist, storyteller and sometime playwright W. Somerset Maugham ever visited the Tonji islands."

"I see," Denis said. He feigned giving the matter serious thought. "Well, there's one school of thought," he went on, with an oblique glance at Literary Johnny, "which maintains that Maugham was here in — I think — October of 1932, gathering material for 'Red' and simultaneously stumbling on inspiration for 'Of Human Bondage.' This school of thought is worth at least one Scotch and soda on the open market, and I wouldn't impugn it for anything."

"Stout lad, Denis," Literary Johnny said.

"But would you agree with it?" Sally asked.

"There you back me into the tight corner of scholarship, Miss Merrill," Denis said, "and as one who did his reading in English at Cambridge I am compelled to say that I would not."

"Another truth merchant, Sally," Mel said, pointing to Denis with his beer glass. "It's getting dangerous, having two of you around."

Literary Johnny took a long swig of whiskey. "Denis, you undermine my source of income," he said.

"Oh, Johnny," Denis said, "you know how much I admire your work, however flimsily it may be based in fact. And I can see that Mr. Parker appreciates it. After all, his work and yours have a lot in common."

Literary Johnny turned eagerly to Mel. "You a writer, too?" he said.

"Mr. Parker and you," Denis went on, "are both masters of

what is known in America as the bamboozle." Silence fell like
a knife down the center of the table. Denis let it stay there a
moment, quivering in the wood. "Sometimes you win," he
continued, "and sometimes you lose, but the race is always
close."

Silence fell again. Mel knew what had been said, saw the
glove thrown at his sandaled feet. "The race is close," he said
to himself, "if you're up against a good racer." He looked
hard at Denis, searching, testing. The gray eyes that met his
were steady and quizzical. This was a good racer.

"Say," he said to Denis at last. "Are you, by any chance,
'Old Settler'?"

Denis gave a knowing smile. It was a smile that said "I'm
up against a good runner myself — one who does his home-
work early and puts two and two together for the rest of the
day."

"He doesn't *look* like 'Old Settler,'" Sally said, forcing a
social laugh to ease the sudden tension.

"No," Denis said. "I'm not Old Settler. I'm Young Settler. I
settled here because I love it, and I still want to be able to
love it when I'm Old and Gray Settler."

"What is it that you love so specially?" Sally asked.

"Just sit and look for a few minutes, Miss Merrill, at the
different people on this street — Victoria Street, as it is none
too appropriately called, considering its many saloons."

Sally concentrated for the first time on the human parade.
She thought she knew all about Polynesian types from reading so many books, but now she saw them in motion: proud
old Tonji chiefs, stopping each other to chat of tribal matters;
younger men, supple and handsome; women as graceful as
dancers, with thick black hair falling below their waists,
carrying their latest baby on their hip while their other
children ran ahead in aimless exuberance and their laughter
tinkled in the morning air.

By comparison the rest of the parade was dull. English
planters and colonial officials strolled along, sometimes with
their pale wives in flowered hats. There were Chinese merchants and Indian traders. There were half-castes represent-

ing strains as old as Europe's discovery of the South Seas. And among them all was a slender thread of white tourists who obviously had just come and would soon be gone again, leaving no mark on the island and taking nothing away except what they had recorded on Kodachrome and on the less reliable film of memory.

"There you see a society in remarkably good balance, Miss Merrill," Denis said.

"But don't the white people throw the balance off?" Sally asked.

"Not really," Denis said. "There aren't enough of them to do any great harm. Oh, the English colonials are a bit foolish in their way — and Sir Reginald is more than a bit foolish in *his* — but on the whole they've done a lot for Tonji, and besides, their day is coming to an end. The winds of independence may seem a long way off in Africa and Asia, but they'll blow across the islands soon enough."

"And how about the tourists?" Sally asked.

"Well, the government limits their stay to several weeks — too many other South Sea islands have been spoiled by beachcombers and bums and writers who went to pot — and that's enough time for most tourists. They're widows, or retired couples, or a pair of single girls, or freelance journalists with the thinnest credentials. Or they may be serious painters or photographers or oceanographers or — who knows? Anyway, they bring variety. We see them around, and they jog the rhythm of our lives, and then they're gone again. But the fabric of society remains intact — and here in Tonji that fabric happens to be very pure."

"Isn't it just as pure in all the other islands?" Sally asked. "I mean the substratum of indigenous culture?"

"Professor Feldspar, I believe!" Denis said. "If you took 'substratum' out of his vocabulary he wouldn't be able to write those damn books. Silly old clot."

"He was the most *won*derful lecturer. Honestly, all the kids were just crazy about his course."

"And 'indigene,' " Denis went on. "Someone told him that it wasn't nice to call people 'natives,' so now the official word is 'indigene,' which Webster defines as a native animal or plant. But to get back to your question, Miss Merrill: the fabric is *not* as pure on other islands. Take a place like Tahiti."

"Did you say Tahiti, lad?" Literary Johnny broke in, starting out of his whiskey as if shot with a syringe. "I remember once in 1935 Charley Nordhoff and Jim Hall were sitting with me — this will interest you, Mr. Parker — at a little bar overlooking the harbor of Papeete. I said 'Y'know, Charley, you fellers ought to find out what *hap*pened to Fletcher Christian and the rest of that crowd when they got to Pitcairn's Island. There's a yarn to be spun out of that, or I miss my bet.'"

"Boy!" Mel called to the waiter. "Another Scotch and soda for Mr. Johnny." He gave an admiring whistle. "This guy's got talent," he said to Sally.

"Maybe you could put him to work writing press releases," she said, giving him a disgusted look and turning back to Denis. "Go on," she said. "You know — about Tahiti."

"There's been so much intermarriage in Tahiti — mainly with the French, but also with the Chinese and other races — that the pure Tahitian is dying out almost as fast as the pure Hawaiian," Denis said. "The structure of the villages has disintegrated, and the town is geared to tourists who are flooding in on the new jet airstrip. In another ten years it'll look like Waikiki Beach — souvenir shops and hair-curlers and Muzak and the lot. America has evolved a new way of despoiling the underprivileged lands. It's corruption by cuteness — and more insidious than any armed assault. You can always beat the invaders back into the sea, but once you've put a stick of bubble gum into the collective mouth of a people you'll never pull it back out again."

"Crapola!" Mel said, his voice rising irritably over the verandah. "That kind of talk gives me a pain in the butt. In a minute you're gonna start talking about the 'noble savage' and 'nature's last aristocrats.'" He inflected the words with heavy sarcasm. "Well, you can't stop progress, buddy boy."

"You think it's progress to have these people in hair-curlers and T-shirts that say 'Hiya Pal'?" Denis snapped.

"They've got just as much right to be in hair-curlers as anyone else, and it's not up to you to save them."

"Or up to you to corrupt them," Denis shot back.

Silence fell again. Both men took long drinks of beer. Sally was the next to speak.

"Please, Mel," she said, applying a wifely pat to his wrist, the kind that is given so frequently — and with such infrequent success — to prevent a husband from rushing into a social disaster that he has totally failed to perceive. "I'm sure there's a lot to be said for both sides."

"You sound like a goddam labor mediator," Mel said, turning on her. "Well, I for one don't think there's a *thing* to be said for Mr. Foote's side. It's the classic position of an escapist running away from his own century. But I suppose you go for those effete types. They appeal to your feminine . . ."

Denis had gotten up and was coming around to Mel's side of the table. Sally pushed him back, knocking over a chair and a bottle of beer. "Please!" she shouted. People on the street stopped to look up at the tumult.

"Reminds me of a time, lads," Literary Johnny said, "when I was having a drink on this very porch with Jack London — he was a scrappy little bloke, too, always ready to swing a fist — and I said to him, 'Jack, boy, there's something in our natures that we can never quite tame. I think of it as the call of the wild.'"

Mel and Denis had turned to listen to him, and now they both burst out laughing.

"Johnny," Denis said, "you're worth every Scotch I've ever bought you."

"I'm sorry," Mel said to Denis, "I got carried away. Exaggeration is woven into my character — as you've already noticed. Nothing I say should be taken seriously."

"Forget it," Denis said. "Is there anything you need today in order to get cracking?"

"I've got to get out to that island as soon as possible," Mel said. "I want to start fixing it up and I'll need to take some pictures of native girls like leaning against the palm trees."

"Palm *tree*," Denis corrected.

"*Tree*, for Chrissake?" Mel asked. "One?"

"One," Denis said. "A relic old enough to be venerated."

"Will it last?" Mel asked, nervously.

"Well," Denis replied, "if you are a churchgoing man — and, as you see, we have a wide choice of main highways and side roads leading to the Christian God — you'd do well to pray for gentle winds."

"So . . . that means I'll need . . . let's see . . . is there a carpenter anywhere in Tonji?" Mel asked. "And some cardboard and plaster?"

"And I suppose you want a lot of green paint?" Denis asked facetiously.

"A *lot* of green paint," Mel said.

"Oh Crikey!" Denis said, almost to himself. "All right," he went on, rallying against the tide of his displeasure. "I've arranged to have a very good man work for you as construction boss. His name is Simeon Lafonga."

"A Jewish boy?" Mel asked. "Out here?"

"No, no. The missionaries give Biblical names to a lot of Tonjian boys and girls. Anyway, maybe when I turn you over to Simeon you'll let this servant depart in peace."

"Don't you want to come along to see the fun?" Mel asked.

"No, I don't want to spoil the joy of seeing the end product. Picturesque Moona-Moona! Eden of the South Pacific! Guaranteed genu-wine!"

"You'll love it," Mel said.

"So let's go find Simeon," Denis said. Mel paid for the drinks and they walked down onto the street. Literary Johnny said, "Many thanks, lads," and angled toward an oncoming widow in a Hawaiian aloha blouse.

"Then the only other thing you'll need right away," Denis said, "is a native girl of appropriate proportions."

"I've had a man working on that since the moment we arrived," Mel said. "In fact, I think he's about to report in."

Far down the street he saw, slowly approaching, the figure of Cy Rumble. Two Tonjian girls were with him, one on each side, and even from a distance Mel could tell that they were beauties. He could also see Cy's arms around both of their waists and his white hands pressed against their bare brown stomachs. All three were singing a Polynesian song, and their voices went ahead of them like heralds.

6

THE little boat spluttered out of the harbor of Falolo to where the waves broke on the enclosing reef. Simeon Lafonga, bent over the motor like an anesthetist listening for a skipped heartbeat, steered it through the narrow passage and out into the open sea. Then, glancing at his compass, he set a course for the northwest and leaned back to enjoy the ride, gripping the steering rod between his long brown toes.

Sally sat upright in the back of the boat and watched the island's receding shoreline. The whiteness of its beaches, the greenness of its palm trees, the blueness of the intervening water and of the overhanging sky stunned her with their purity of color, unsullied by urban grays and blacks and browns, untouched by soot or smoke, fog or smog. More and more villages came into view as the boat chugged slowly out, and each one, built so near the water that it almost tumbled in, seemed prettier and more perfectly adapted to its natural setting than the one before.

Mel had no time for such tranquil pleasures. He sat in the bottom of the boat scribbling in a notebook whose cover said "Things to Do." Occasionally he looked up to check some item in the mountain of equipment that lay alongside him. Cy's various cameras, meters, lights and cans of film were easy enough to identify, and so was Simeon's huge wooden box of carpenter's tools. Other bags, vaguely lumpy, gave no clue to what was inside.

"Hey, Simeon — what's in this one?" he called.

"Oranges, Boss Mel," Simeon said. "I made them for the big festival. Maybe you heard about it? Miss Hibiscus."

"Made 'em out of what?"

"Rubber. Look very good. I thought maybe you like me to bring them along."

"I like," Mel said. "Cy! What's in this burlap sack? Cy? . . . Oh damn!"

Cy was teaching a song to the two Tonjian girls in the front of the boat: "No, doll, it's not 'flying marine' — it's 'flying machine.' It goes like this." He sang the first phrase in a cracked voice. "Got it? Great! All together now!"

> *Come, Josephine,*
> *In my flying machine,*
> *Going UP she goes,*
> *UP she goes,*
> *Balance yourself like a bird on a beam . . .*

The three voices waltzed out across the calm Pacific, lilting and dipping and swooping, until the song ended in an avalanche of giggles.

"Terrific!" Cy said. "You kids are the most. Now you gotta teach me another one."

"How about 'Falalalonga Mura Lai'?" one of the girls said, still giggling. "Do you know that?"

"How the hell would I know that?" Cy said. "Let's hear how it goes."

"It's easy. I teach it to you quick-quick."

> *Falalalonga mura lai,*
> *Va'i, va'o,*
> *Sala puni tai.*

"Now you sing after me." She faced Cy and wagged her finger like a metronome as he roared out the unfathomable words.

"What does it mean?" Cy asked when he finally stopped for breath.

"It mean 'Every night I wait for you . . . underneath the mango tree . . . I do anything you want me to . . . why you never come around to me? . . . maybe tonight when the moon is full . . . shining on the big lagoon . . . we could' . . . how do you say?'"

"Make love," Cy put in.

"That's it," the girl said, giving him a big squeeze. "I like you, Cy. You always think about the love."

"It's mutual, doll," Cy said, breaking into song:

Love makes the world go round,
Love makes the world go ROU-OU-OU-OUND!

"Dammit, Cy," Mel called, "when are you gonna get serious? We got work to do."

"I'm *work*ing, Mel, willya? Getting my models in the right mood. You want Richard Avedon you should've brought Richard Avedon."

"Okay, okay. Say, what've you got in this sack?"

"Grass skirts," Cy said. "Nice and short. I thought the girls here would look really *zaftig* in them. You know?"

"I know. Good idea."

"Grass *skirts!*" Sally said, turning around to join the conversation. "How corny can you get? If you'd made even the most rudimentary study of Polynesian dress customs you'd know . . ."

"I've made a rudimentary study of these two dolls," Cy said, "and I know that when they put their sweet little tails into a grass skirt they're gonna look mighty pho-to-gen-ic. Right, girls?"

"Oooooooooo!" squealed one of the girls, giving a convulsive jerk. "Cy, you do that *too much!*" she said in mock sternness, slapping his hand.

"Well anyway," Sally went on, "you'd know that what they mostly wear is a sarong. Isn't that what I'm here for, Mel — to protect you from technical mistakes?"

"I'll put 'em in sarongs," Cy said, "when I shoot my sensitive photo-essay for 'Horizon' or 'Réalités,' and you can write the captions in rich scholarly detail. But if I know Mel he wants legs."

"Legs! Tails! You all talk like some kind of sex maniac," Sally said. "Don't you see that it's a *cliché*, that grass-skirt picture? And a false one? Why don't you be accurate for once? That's what people want."

"It's the last thing people want," Mel said. "There are certain false clichés that have become so popular that they've replaced the dull old truth. The western movie, for instance, is full of 'em. Give people the truth and they'll throw you out of the house."

"I'm afraid Mel's right, Sally," Cy said. "The only South Sea pictures that we can put over as authentic are the kind we're about to take. Say, where is that island anyway? Simeon!"

"Mister Cy, I been looking hard for that island," Simeon said. "Must be mighty small." The boat putted on laboriously. Mel looked glumly ahead toward the horizon. Sally turned around again, defeated, and trailed her toe in the water over the back of the boat. Three Tonjian boys, Simeon's helpers, threw fishing lines into the ocean. Cy started teaching the girls to sing "Yes, We Have No Bananas."

After a quarter of an hour Simeon said: "Hey! I think that's him." He pointed and Mel saw a flat sliver of land that hardly rose above the water. Coming nearer, Mel strained his eyes to find some distinguishing feature, some quirk of topography or vegetation that made this island different from all others. He saw none. The only thing that he could see, as the boat got closer, were hundreds of mangrove bushes, their ugly roots intertwined to form a continuous wall along the shore.

"Christ al-*mighty!*" he said. "Simeon! Sail around to the other side."

The boat veered to the right and began a slow circuit of the bleak little patch of land. Nothing on the east side improved Mel's spirits. The mangroves tapered off, but the ground was still marshy, and there wasn't a beach in sight. Finally, on the north, the ground became firmer and, to his relief, he saw a strip of beach. The strip was so small that it was almost an accident of geology. But it was a beach, and behind it Mel saw a solitary palm tree, tall and thin and shabby, an obvious victim of malnutrition. But it was a palm tree, and that was the main thing. He motioned to Simeon to head in toward the beach.

"So this is your pearl of the Pacific!" Sally said.

Cy gave a low whistle of disbelief. "Jesus, Mel," he said, "we've worked on some crappy sets in our time, but this takes the cake."

"There's nothing that *we* can't lick, Cy," Mel said, rubbing his hands together, his spirits brightening again.

"You're a pleasure to do business with, old buddy," Cy said. "A compulsive optimist."

Mel stood up in the boat. "Did you ever see 'Rose Marie'?" he said to Cy. Then he cupped his hands and sang to the sullen island: "When I'm calling you-oo-oo-oo, oo-oo-oo . . ." Back from the shore came a high antiphonal voice which Mel at first hoped was Jeanette MacDonald, but he soon realized it was a tropical bird. The bird had a nervous and erratic cry.

"What a spooky-sounding bird," Sally said, shuddering.

"Either that or Yma Sumac," Mel said.

"We call him bad-luck bird," Simeon said.

"By the way, Simeon," Mel said, "what do you know about this island?"

"My people never come to this island," Simeon replied. "I think maybe a bad tiki lived here long-long ago."

"What's that all about, Sally?" Mel asked.

"A tiki is a spirit — usually a little stone statue," Sally said, "that the Polynesians try to propitiate, just like any other race that has gods or demons. Maybe the natives have some sort of mystical feeling about this place."

"Well, whatever it is," Mel said, "there's no time to worry about it now. Come on."

They all jumped out, and Simeon pulled the boat up on the hot sand. Several dozen land crabs, their solitude abruptly broken, scuttled across the beach and disappeared into holes. An oppressive silence fell over the island, and only the occasional shriek of the bad-luck bird hailed them as they unloaded the boat. The rest of the animal kingdom seemed to have forsaken the island and gone to others that were more auspicious. Behind the beach was a small clearing of dry ground, but beyond that the island turned into a dense tropical growth, cutting out all sunlight.

Mel paced back and forth, appraising the terrain. "Let's see," he said at last, "we'll build the bungalow right here, just to the left of the palm tree. And we'll put the front door right about here" — he made a large X in the sand — "so that the folks can go right out onto the beach and take their morning dip."

He turned and looked back at the surly interior. "As for this stuff," he said, waving his arm, "it's got to go. Simeon. How long would it take to clean this jungle out?"

"Two-three weeks, Boss Mel. I bring my boys out here with big machete knife and we chop him down. Let's see what he looks like in there." Simeon beckoned the three boys and they began cutting their way through the matted greenery. Mel started in after them. "Want to come along?" he called back to Sally.

"No thanks," she said. "I'm staying here."

"Me too, Mel," Cy called. "I'm gonna start working with the girls." A long high giggle rose into the quiet air.

Mel turned and plunged into the jungle. His sneakers kept catching on tangled roots; vines reached down specifically, he felt, to press against his retina. Up ahead the dull thud of knives and the snapping of branches and the swish of leaves drew him on. Simeon had given him a machete, and now he also hacked away at the enveloping gloom. He regarded every inch as his enemy, a dragon to be slain with strong strokes and strong language.

"Bastard woods!" he said, slashing fiercely. "Son-of-a-bitching vines!" How would one go about "son-of-a-bitching," he wondered? The beautiful meaninglessness of army slang always delighted him.

"Save your strength, Boss Mel," Simeon called. "There's nobody got enough strength to cut the jungle and swear, too."

Mel caught up with Simeon and the boys. He was puffing

hard and was clammy with sweat. "I'd hate to see the temperature-humidity index for this spot," he said.

"He's mighty thick in here," Simeon said.

"He sure as hell is," Mel agreed. "Say, is there a bulldozer anywhere in Tonji?"

"I think I see him once," Simeon said. "The Governor used him to make a cricket field. You ask Mister Governor Weems. You know him, I bet?"

"No, but I'll ask him anyway."

"Very important fella, Mister Governor Weems. I see him wearing medals on his chest and a big hat with white feathers. Just like Queen Elizabeth."

They rested a few minutes and pushed on. Suddenly Simeon called, "Hey, come look!" Mel hurried ahead and found him standing in a cleared circle of land surrounded by bamboo trees. The ground was flat and sandy.

"Somebody here long-long ago," Simeon said. "I think they have meetings here. Maybe a ceremony."

"I'll bet you're right," Mel said. "Sure. It's like a little theater. They could fit a couple of hundred people there, sitting on the ground, and up at one end the chief or the medicine man or the dancers could get up on a kind of platform, and everybody would be able to see them, and it would be nice and quiet, and the acoustics would be . . ." He stopped short. Then in a loud voice he said "*Mama mia!* How about *that!* Hey, Sally! Hey, Cy!" He started running back over the path that he had just cleared.

"Wait!" Simeon shouted after him. But he was gone.

Emerging at the beach, Mel heard Sally say: "Can you hurry *up*, Cy! My arm is killing me."

She was on top of a stepladder holding a bunch of bananas so that they would appear to be dangling from a branch. Below, in grass skirts, the two Tonjian girls lolled on a small patch of grass, and one was reaching up languidly toward the suspended fruit.

"Now don't get my *hand* in the picture," Sally said.

"Don't you worry about old Cy, dear," Cy said, peering through his viewfinder. "Old Cy went to school in Hollywood, U.S.A., illusions our specialty." He fiddled with some knobs on his Leica, which was on a tripod fixed in the sand. "Almost ready now," he said. "Steady on the bananas, Sal. Melura, honey — raise your leg a little higher. No, the other one, doll. I want more of the . . . no, like *this*." He walked over and raised her leg to a more seductive angle, working slowly and giving the leg a few reassuring pats.

"Cy, will you for heaven's sake hurry *up!*" Sally said.

"Roger!" Cy said, going back to the camera. "Great," he said, squinting through it. "Ready, girls? Look happy now, kids. You live on this island, see, and you've got nothing to do all day but lie around and eat bananas and make the love. Right? Steady." Click. "Hold it." Click. "Keep smiling, girls." Click. "One more. Push your skirt up a little, honey — it's slipping down. Good." Click. "Swell. That's enough for the banana shot."

Sally gave a little moan of relief. Then, with a last spasm of energy, she raised her arm. "Here, Cy — you like bananas," she said, scaling them at him from the top of the ladder. They bounced off his chest with a metallic noise and he staggered backward.

"Hey, what's *in* those bananas?" Mel asked.

"Old bicycle parts," said Simeon, who had arrived soon after Mel. "I found them at the dump."

"Say, Cy, you'll never guess what we found in there," Mel said, pointing to the interior. "A perfect little . . ."

"Tell me later, willya, Mel," Cy said. "The light's just right now and I want to get some shots of the girls drinking coconuts and leaning against the palm tree and going for a swim."

"Where'd you get coconuts?"

"I bought 'em in town. And how'd you like that grass the girls were lying on?"

"Really lush," Mel said. "What is it?"

"It's that green paper that goes in the bottom of Easter baskets. And did you notice how I painted the trunk of the palm tree? It looked kind of motheaten, but now it's all fresh and shiny. Wait till you see how great it comes out." He changed the film in his camera, working rapidly and with relish. "Okay, girls," he said with chairman-of-the-board solemnity to his two models, who had both fallen into a voluptuous doze on the green paper grass. "You may wonder why I've called you together here today. My name is Richard Avedon and I've been commissioned by 'Bildgesprach,' the new Swiss magazine of experimental photo-imagery, to capture in a sixteen-page color portfolio the lagoons of these enchanted islands." The two girls blinked their eyes at him, cow-like, and didn't stir. "Which means: Get your cute little asses out there in the water, pronto." At this they got up and trotted off to the beach. "I'm just going to slip into my bathing trunks," Cy called after them, "and then I'll be right along."

The next hour was all Cy's. Standing waist-deep in the water, he shot the two girls splashing in the waves, always keeping the island's lone palm tree in the background. Then he shot them on the beach, drying their long black hair, and after that he shot them drinking coconuts and eating Simeon's rubber oranges and leaning against the palm tree, where the brown paint had now dried in the afternoon sun. Finally he called a halt.

"Okay, girls," he said. "That's all for today. Get your money from Mr. Parker on the way out."

They gave Cy a big kiss and went off squealing for another swim.

"It's not great, Mel," Cy said, "but at least it gives you a little cheesecake to send back to the States."

"There's nothing better for getting people interested in a contest," Mel said. "By the way, have you got any film left?"

"One black and white."

"Good. There's a picture I want of Simeon standing on the beach and looking at this picture of Moona Marone." He produced a glossy studio shot of Miss Marone on the set of "Desert Island for Two." "I'd rather have a chief but I forgot to bring one along. Simeon will have to do."

"The way *you* write captions," Cy said, "what difference does it make? By the way, what *is* the caption?"

"The caption goes like this," Mel said. He paused a moment to collect his thoughts and his adjectives. "Uh . . . 'What's in a name? Hereditary chief Simeon Lafonga of romantic Tonji isles expresses delight (no wonder!) at picture of gorgeous Moona Marone, star of Titan Pictures' forthcoming Technicolor epic filmed in living Pana . . .' "

"I know that part," Cy interrupted. "You don't have to give me the *whole* goddam caption."

"Sorry," Mel said. "It's hard to stop once I get started. Okay, here's the rest of it: 'Chief Lafonga stands on dazzling white beach of pretty Kula-ha'i island, whose name has been changed to Moona-Moona in recognition of Miss Marone's stellar performance as shipwrecked heiress in "Desert Island for Two," one of brightest romantic comedies of this or any other year. Moona-Moona will be given away to winner of nationwide contest now nearing climax in U.S. From his expression Chief Lafonga seems to be thinking: "And they say *we* have beautiful girls out here in the South Seas." ' "

Sally said, "That's the most hokey picture I ever heard of. You really are an optimist if you think any paper's going to print that."

"That's the one they *will* print," Mel said, "even if they don't print any of the others."

"You're kidding!" Sally said.

"No, seriously . . ."

"*Ser*iously!"

"Well, maybe that's not quite the right word," Mel said. "But that picture has a lot going for it. A super-star from the glamour capital of the world arrives, in a sense, on an untouched paradise in the romantic South Sea islands. The secret lies in juxtaposing opposite elements. Queen of urban sophistication meets the last of the noble savages. Readers see that in a newspaper and they're tickled by the contrast."

"Another example of the 'managed event'?" Sally asked. Mel nodded. "And how far do you think you can push a managed event?"

"Stick around for the main course, baby. I aim to find out."

Cy had put the black-and-white roll in his camera. Then he

took the picture of Moona Marone from Mel and gave it to Simeon, who examined the vacuous round face, the airline-stewardess smile that was obviously turned on by some inner button rather than by some inner joy, the soaring ziggurat of hair born of untold money spent on blonde rinses and dyes and untold hours spent in the adoring fingers of the studio coiffeur.

"What do you think of that, old chief?" Cy asked.

"Him very pretty," Simeon said. "Very pretty hat."

"That's her *hair*, for God's sake."

"That white stuff?"

"Yep," Cy said. "Now you just keep looking at that picture and thinking 'Him very pretty.' And would you mind moving over a bit? The other way. Thanks. I want to get that palm tree behind you. It looks good with the sun shining on the new paint."

7

LATE that afternoon when they got back to Falolo, Millie Hawkes was sitting in a rocker on her front porch. She was listening to Glenn Miller's "In the Mood" on an old wind-up Victrola. "Just got some new records in from Sydney," she explained.

"Hi, Millie," Mel said. He and Sally looked hot and ragged. "What's for dinner tonight?"

"Poached haddock and mashed parsnip," she said. "I hope you're staying. You must be tired."

"Er . . . well . . . Miss Merrill and I promised to meet some people for dinner over at the Grand Polynesian. You remember, Sally — we told Mr. Plunkett we'd be there at seven."

"Oh, that's right," Sally said, pushing a vision of poached haddock out of her mind and replacing it with Mr. Plunkett, a hearty hay-and-feed salesman from Billings.

"How about you, Mr. Rumble?" Millie persevered. "Maybe after dinner we could sit out here on the porch swing and listen to my new records. Have you ever heard 'Take the A Train'?"

"Thanks, Millie," Cy said, "but I've got a double date. It's not exactly a double date — there's two of them and one of me, but what've I got to lose?"

"Energy," Mel said. "Come on, Sal. Let's get cleaned up so we won't be late for the Plunketts."

"Your room's all ready for you, honey," Millie said, "and

Denis Foote brought your bags over from Doc Bligh's this afternoon. It's Room Eleven — right next to Mr. Parker's and with a connecting door. You know?"

"I know," Sally said. She went to Room 11 and flopped down on the iron bed, whose springs jangled beneath the weight of her fatigue, which she estimated at an extra fifty pounds. She had been in Tonji little more than twenty-four hours and already she was beat. The night had been ghastly and the day hadn't been much better. Not only was Kula-ha'i (she continued to think of it by its correct name) a steamy and enervating island. Her patience had also been strained by everything that Mel and Cy did there, and as for those two ninny girls! If only she could be . . . what was that word she saw in "Harper's Bazaar"? Larky. If only she could be larky and do things just for kicks, at least once in a while. She knew people who went to Bermuda for the weekend. That was larky.

She looked around the bare little room that was to be her home. Over in one corner were her bags — 44 lbs. of clothing and books, carefully chosen for the first venture into the field of a newly fledged M.A. Who did Millie say had brought the bags over? Mr. Foote. That was nice. She got up and began to unpack the suitcases. That would make her feel more settled: to see the drip-dry blouses and cotton skirts hanging in the closet, to see her few items of jewelry and perfume and cosmetics arrayed on the wobbly dresser, to see her paperbacks set out in alphabetical order, directly behind — as always — the small gold-framed photographs of her mother and father, taken when they were much younger, their faces only beginning to congeal into the older woman and man who were the parents she knew now.

She also took a moment to look at the picture of Professor Feldspar on the back of "Indigenes in Ferment," a disciple seeking some message from the eyes of the master, opaque though they were behind his metal-rimmed glasses. What would he have to say about the substratum that she was digging in today? The Hollywood substratum. Moona-Moona. She repeated the outlandish name, half aloud. Crazy.

But catchy. And almost beautiful, in some strange way. Is it possible, she wondered, that these purveyors of beautiful names and beautiful pictures and beautiful dreams are more on the track than the rest of us, scrabbling for facts and rooting every last detail to its original source? No, it's not possible. She banished the profane thought that had come knocking. Professor Feldspar, I will be true.

There was a rap on the connecting door. "Sally, dear," came Mel's voice, "don't forget we're having dinner with the Plunketts tonight."

"Tell me about them once more," she called back, briefly, tentatively, larky. "I don't remember our last meeting too well."

"Very big in corsets-and-girdles in Tulsa. Tall guy with red hair."

"Oh, of *course*," Sally said. "And she was head of the women's bowling league. A swell couple."

"I knew you wouldn't want to miss them."

"Peg and Walter, isn't it?" Sally asked.

"*Jane* and Walter, I think," Mel said.

"Well, I won't be long. Is there a bathtub or shower anywhere in this luxury hotel?"

"Just down the hall and past the kitchen. You turn on the hot water with a wrench that's hanging from the faucet."

"Okay. See you soon." She unpacked her one cake of soap, put it in the pink plastic soap dish that she had bought for her debut in anthropology, wrapped her bathrobe around her, and, feeling for the first time like Margaret Mead, at grips with indigenous plumbing, padded down the narrow hall. Two ducks scooted out of the bathroom as she arrived.

"You look beautiful, Sally," Mel said as she came out on the verandah fifteen minutes later and they started walking along the waterfront. "A nice dress and you smell good."

"Why, thank you, Mel. You look nice, too. Coat and tie. Did you go to all that trouble just for the Plunketts?"

"No, just for you." They strolled along contentedly, the abrasions of the day wearing off. An almost full moon had come up and the air was scented with flowers. After a while they came to the Grand Polynesian Hotel. Though hardly grand and only barely Polynesian, being one of those white-washed stone structures that the British throw up in all their colonial outposts to house their own sort, it was at least a bona fide hotel. Palm trees dotted its impeccable lawn, flowers bordered its gravel driveway, and under the porte cochère a Tonjian boy in a white uniform opened and closed the doors of taxis that came and went.

As Mel and Sally walked toward the door, a pale and thin man of about forty darted out and jumped into a cab. Looking around as the cab pulled away, he saw Mel and said "Oh, hi!" And then he was gone.

"Who was that?" Sally asked as they walked through the lobby and into an adjoining bar.

"It looked like a ghost," Mel said. "So pale and going so fast. But I've seen that face somewhere. Let's see. Uh. I'll think of it in a minute. It's . . . I know. It's Brian Bellows, the Southern playwright. You remember he had a critical success on Broadway two seasons ago? It was called 'Somber Bliss!' "

"I remember. It was about a homosexual who found . . . what *did* he find?"

"He found acceptance by a hostile society when he ran for dogcatcher and won, or some involuted thing like that. Well anyway, the screen rights were bought by Hess & Rossiter, the independent producers, and they brought Bellows out to Hollywood to write the screenplay. What they didn't tell the poor schlepper was that they had bought the property for Debbie Reynolds, or some other actress, and were changing the homosexual into a nymphomaniac. Better box-office."

Mel had ordered rum punches and now the bar boy brought them, tall and full of exotic fruit and radiating sweet fumes. "Gosh, that's good," Sally said. "I'm beginning to feel human again."

"Anyway," Mel went on, "that's where I met Bellows — at some Hollywood party. Hess & Rossiter are real sadists and they drove poor Bellows almost up the wall. Hess used to say

'We'll read the reviews over your grave, Brian,' and then they'd both laugh like hell. Finally Bellows's analyst ordered him to take a long cruise to get away from it all, and I guess the cruise ship has put in here."

"It's the perfect place to get away from it all," Sally said. Rum had slowed her motor to the same speed as the fan on the ceiling overhead, whose giant blades turned just fast enough to keep the air in circulation, and when Mel led her for dinner to the hotel's outdoor terrace, which jutted into the lagoon and was lit only by candles on the various tables, she felt a removal from worry so complete that she thought it must be deeply sinful. Across the lagoon she could see the contorted peaks of Tulala Ha'i outlined against the enormous moon, and where the moon fell across the water she occasionally saw the moving shape of an outrigger canoe and of Tonjian men fishing on the reef. They sang as they fished, their voices sending in to the diners on the terrace a series of Polynesian tunes, distinctive in their lazy rhythm and pure major melodies.

Mel and Sally were having lobster and white wine and chatting of unimportant things. "Isn't it a relief not to know what's going on in the rest of the world?" Sally said.

"Sure is," Mel agreed. "And there's no way of finding out till the next mail."

"I know I should care," Sally said, "but somehow — at least tonight — I just don't."

"Me too."

"No worries at all?" Sally asked. She ran her little finger around in her wine in idle circles, absentmindedly chasing a small piece of cork. She had taken her shoes off and was vaguely thinking of asking Mel to dance with her.

"Only one," Mel said. "It's the same thing we were just talking about: how to keep in touch with the old mainland. Like I had a great idea today, but I don't know if they'll go for it. It's too hard to explain in a cable — I've got to dis*cuss* it with 'em. And there are no overseas telephones." He looked out at a fisherman casting his net in the path of the moon on the water. "Pretty," he said. "Oh well. There's nothing I can do about it, so why fret? Hey Sal, how about a dance?"

"I'd love it, Mel." They moved indolently around the terrace, their steps at half speed to the tempo of the guitar-and-drum trio. Around them, other couples — mostly British and American tourists — did a desultory fox-trot, their faces abstracted and serene. "It's not just me," Sally thought, watching them. "The mood of the islands is on us all. It really works — you *can* get away from everything." They danced and drank wine and danced some more. Nobody wanted to stop.

Around eleven, back at the table, Mel was jogged by the sound of another chair being drawn up next to him and Sally. It was Brian Bellows, just back from wherever he had gone, and in a highly agitated state. He lit a cigarette, burning the shaky and nicotine-stained finger that held it, and inhaled so deeply that he seemed to drain its entire tobacco content into his lungs. Then he squashed the cigarette out in the dessert dish where the last chunks of Mel's papaya lay soaking.

"You're the only person who will under*stand* this," he said to Mel in a high voice, the words spewing out like machine-gun bullets.

"Mister Bellows, Miss Merrill," Mel said, breaking in for a formal introduction.

"How d'you do," Bellows said, with a minimum loss of time, and went on. "You know that Spanish epic that Hess & Rossiter made before they bought 'Somber Bliss!'? Called 'Sons of the Cid.' Remember? Well, they opened in sixteen cities across the country and it bombed. I mean, it absolutely ex*pired*. Hee-eeeee." He gave a long demented giggle.

"Fine, fine," Mel said, cranking his mind unwillingly back toward California. "For your sake I'm glad."

"Glad!" Bellows piped. "The only time to be *glad* is when those two monsters drop absolutely *dead!* Do you know they've decided to make 'Somber Bliss!' into a *mus*ical? My delicate little *flow*er that was runner-up for an Antoinette Perry Award on *Broad*way! The drama of which the 'New York Times' said: 'Make a note this morning that a *lumi*nous new talent has come out of the South to shine the searching torch of *truth* into the dark places of the human heart. Make no mis*take* about it: this is pure theatre.'"

"Oh, you've got to expect changes when you sell your work to the movies," Mel said in what he intended as a comforting tone. "They think they understand the mass market."

"Under*stand!* Those two *rep*-tiles! Hess used to say 'Don't bug *us,* little boy Brian. We're *quality* producers and you're just a schlemiel from *Cul*peper who happened to hit it rich.' Can you imagine the absolute *nerve?* Those apes who wouldn't know *quality* if it hit them in the *face!*"

"They can be pretty unpleasant," Mel agreed, still trying to soothe the quavering playwright, his mind drawn almost completely back from the lagoon now and winging rapidly toward the pretentious Sunset Boulevard office of Hess & Rossiter.

"So you *see,*" Bellows went on, his voice rising in a parabola, "why it's so absolutely de*li*cious that 'Sons of the Cid' did the worst opening-day business of any picture that *any*body practically *any*where can ever re*mem*ber."

"Yeah, that's great news," Mel said. "By the way, when *was* that? What day did it open?"

"Today," Bellows said.

"To*day?*"

"Yes. Absolutely today."

"You mean . . . today?" He leaned over and shook Bellows by the shoulder. He was sure now that the playwright was in a psychopathic state where reality was only an occasional visitor. "How do you *know?*"

"On the *ra*dio, of course," Bellows said.

"But there's no radio here except a local station."

"The short*wave,* silly," Bellows said.

"Who? Where?" Mel said, every nerve tensed again.

"I'm a ham radio operator — though I don't suppose you had any way of *know*ing that," Bellows said, "and whenever I go any place I ask if there's another ham around. You might call it the freemasonry of the airwaves."

"I might," Mel said. "So who did you find here?"

"A French planter named LeClercq who lives up in the hills. That's where I've been tonight."

"And you made contact with someone in Hollywood?"

"Yes, though I must say it was the *sheer*est good fortune," Bellows replied. "The Frenchman was trying to raise someone in the Aleutians, of all places, and instead someone in Los Angeles came back to him, and the guy in Los Angeles put a phone-patch through to a friend of mine in Beverly Hills."

"A phone-patch? What's that?"

"The ham at the other end throws a switch and patches his transmitter and receiver into the telephone circuit, and you can talk to whoever he calls up, and vice-versa."

"Really?" Mel said. "You can do that? Well, come on, Brian, old boy, let's get going."

"Where? What on earth do you mean?"

"Up to see the Frenchman, of course," Mel said, getting up and signaling the waiter for the check.

"Oh, *Mel!*" Sally said. "Not now! *Please!*" She took his hand and tried to pull him back down.

"The girl is right," Bellows said. "It's very late and the Frenchman lives absolutely *miles* up in the hills."

"Would he mind?" Mel asked.

"He seemed *aff*able enough, though I did have the feeling that he was a bit miffed when I came crashing in. He seemed desperate to talk to somebody in Kiska — heaven knows why — when all of a sudden I heard Sheldon Sheldrake calling him from somewhere out in the Valley near Universal. He . . ."

"Wait a minute. Sheldon Sheldrake the director?"

"Right."

"*He's* a ham radio operator?"

"All his life."

"I know Shel! Crazy! Call the Frenchman and see if we can come on up."

"I really don't think it would be too polite, considering that the hour is . . ."

"Come *on,*" Mel broke in. "Shel will probably have some

late dirt on 'Sons of the Cid' and Hess & Rossiter. He hates those two creeps almost as much as you do."

Bellows's furtive eyes brightened. "Oh all right," he said. "If you absolutely insist."

"I absolutely do," Mel said. He paid the check and started to pull Sally's chair out. "Hey, Sal — what's the matter?"

"Don't you *know?*" she said.

"It's gonna be a ball," he said. "Nice scenic drive after dinner. Very romantic."

"Some idea you've got of 'very romantic,'" she said. Her eyes misted over and she blew her nose. "You just can't get away from it, can you? Not even for one night? And you never will."

"It's a lucky break, Sally honey, and I just can't let it slip by. Won't you come along? Please."

"No, I'd like to be dropped off at Millie's. I've had it. But it was a lovely evening."

"You insist?"

"I absolutely insist."

"Of course you understand, M'sieur Parker," the French-man said, "in California it is about four hours in the morning — how do you say?"

"Four o'clock."

"Yes, four o'clock. *Alors*, I do not think your friend will be awake. He will *dormir*, yes?"

"Not Shel, he's an insomniac," Mel said.

"*Qu'est-ce-que . . . ?*"

"Sorry. I mean he doesn't *dormir* very good."

"Ahhhh."

"Nobody in Hollywood *dormirs* very good," Mel said.

"Ohhh. *Les pauvres!*"

"They're absolute *beasts*," Bellows said. "They don't de-*serve* to sleep!"

"So if you'd give him a call, M'sieur LeClercq, or listen for him," Mel went on, "I'd be most grateful." He pointed to the mysterious mass of radio equipment spread out in front of the Frenchman, awaiting his touch. From the innards of its speaker came an unpleasant crackle of voices, far-off and indistinct.

"Even if he is awake," the Frenchman said, "your *ami* may not be in his shack." He put on a pair of headphones and slowly tuned the receiver. He listened intently, but for several minutes it was apparent that he was hearing nothing. Suddenly he smiled with satisfaction and said "Ahhh! *Bon! Bon!*"

"What is it? Have you got him?" Mel bent over the Frenchman eagerly.

"A doctor in Kyoto, *très gentil*. It is several months since we talk." He began to call him excitedly.

"Oh no!"

"Shh, I have him," the Frenchman said, pressing the earphones tighter.

"You're too far west!" Mel shouted. But the Frenchman was snug within his earphones, caught up in the gossip of Kyoto. Mel wigwagged to him occasionally without success, and it was fifteen minutes before M. LeClercq re-emerged from the Orient.

"The doctor, he is very *intéressant*," he reported, bright-eyed with new medical facts. "He was telling me a *petit conte* about an operation he did — you know, *avec* the knife? — on a man who could not make the babies."

Mel, whose stomach had constricted during the interminable visit to Japan, felt a further tightening elsewhere. "Never mind that," he snapped. "Go to the East! *Le East! Comprenez?*"

"You must have the patience, M'sieur." The Frenchman tinkered with the dials again. Soon his face illuminated with pleasure.

"Have you got him?" Mel asked.

"Oui, oui," the Frenchman said. "It is Valparaíso."

"Oh for God's sweet sake!" Mel shouted, slamming his fist onto the table. But M. LeClercq was already exchanging call letters with the Chilean and stumbling through a difficult contact. Mel tried not to listen.

"No," the Frenchman was saying. "No hablo español. *Vous parlez français?* . . . *anglais?* . . . *deutsch?* . . . *Italiano?*

. . . *Je regrette. Dommage* . . . *Alors,* seventy-threes, old man. *Bonne nuit.*" He signed off. "Myself, I do not speak the Spanish, *malheureusement,*" he explained.

"Yeah, yeah," Mel said. "Now will you *please* try to get someone in the America?"

"*Bien sûr,*" the Frenchman said. "I will try." After a few minutes of listening he looked up inquiringly. "Where is *Le Buffalo?*"

"*Too* far east," Mel said.

"They are having breakfast in *Le Buffalo.*"

"Great," Mel muttered.

The Frenchman listened again. "I have a lady in the Santa Fe," he said.

"You're getting closer," Mel said. "Here, lemme put those things on, willya?" He grabbed the earphones away from his host, clamped them on his head, and sat down at the receiver. He tuned and listened, straining his ears to catch some meaning in the voices that occasionally rose above the general crackle and hiss, voices which babbled in odd ham-radio language and which, judging by the proper names that periodically filtered through — Nairobi, Tegucigalpa, Montevideo, Dakar — came from half a world away at least. One name that he did not hear, however, was California, and he began to resign himself to failure.

Then suddenly he let out a whoop. "Hey, it's Shel!" He got up and grabbed the Frenchman. "I heard him! He's talking to someone! I heard old Shel plain as day!" He grabbed the microphone. "*Shel,* baby! Hiya! It's me — Mel Parker. Can you hear me?"

M. LeClercq snatched the microphone away and ripped the headphones off his head. "M'sieur Parker, we do not do it that way!" he said, very angry. "Do you wish that I should lose my license?"

"But it's Shel!" Mel pointed at the receiver. "I'd know that voice if I . . ."

"There are certain procedures . . ."

"Okay, okay."

". . . it is not like the telephone."

"Just don't *lose* him, for Chrissake."

"You must have the patience." He sat down slowly at the receiver, put the earphones on and stared into space.

"Well?" Mel said, very patiently.

"He is finishing," M. LeClercq said. He was quiet again.

"With someone in Brisbane."

"Just don't . . ."

The Frenchman raised his hand and started calling the California station with great urgency. He paused and listened, and then began to call again, and then listened again, and then a smile came over his face.

"Yes?" Mel said.

"Yes," the Frenchman said. He got up from his chair, handed the microphone to Mel and walked away, as if to disavow all responsibility for the fracturing of regulations that would follow.

"*Shel*, baby, how the hell are ya?" Mel blurted into the microphone. . . . "Who do you *think* it is, for God's sake! *Mel Parker!* . . . Where am I? Tonji. . . . That's right. 'T' as in 'Technicolor.' Brian's with me . . . Say, any notices yet on 'Sons of the Cid'? . . . Crowther said *what?* . . . 'A modern masterpiece'? . . ."

"Ourgghhhh!" Brian Bellows gave a hysterical scream and bolted out into the night.

"Say, Shel," Mel continued, "do you think you could get Fogelstein on the phone for me? You know, one of those phone-patches? So what if it *is* almost 5 o'clock in the morning? *You're* up, aren't you? . . . Sure, he's a big man in the industry, but he's not *that* big. . . . Would I *ask* you if it wasn't important? . . . Of *course* it's an unlisted number. You think Fogelstein wants every starlet in town calling him up at 5 o'clock in the morning? Me he'll be *glad* to hear from, I promise . . . How're you gonna find his number? *Here's* his goddam number: GRanite 5-5729 . . . Thanks, old buddy . . . Yeah, I'm still here . . . *Nat*urally his phone is ringing eighteen times. He's got eighteen phones in his house and doesn't know which one to pick up . . . Good! . . . Yeah, I'm ready. Why wouldn't I be ready? . . . HARRY!

How *are* ya, guy? . . . *No* I couldn't pick a better time to call. I'm not just down at Hollywood and Vine in a phone booth, you know . . . Is it *my* fault you put away too many Scotches over at Marilyn's? You ought to take two of those benzedrine pills before you hit the sack. Dr. Vilbiss has 'em, down at the studio. All you want . . . Say, Harry, you got a minute? . . . Have you made any final plans for the world première of 'Desert Island for Two'?"

8

THE next day was Sunday, and Mel and Sally sat on the porch of Millie Hawkes's, trying without luck to digest a breakfast that Millie identified, upon their request, which they instantly regretted, as fried mullet and corned silverside. Bells rang from the big pink Catholic church and from the five wooden belfries of Protestantism, and Tonjian families streamed along Victoria Street to answer their call, the children neatly dressed and carrying hymnbooks. Upon the scraggly group that occupied Millie's porch, however, the bells exerted no pull. The various guests remained slumped in the broken wicker chairs and on the tattered canvas of the porch swing, men and women of disparate origins, their only bond the drowsiness of Sunday and the growling of their stomachs.

A sallow Indian trader, his efforts completed earlier in the week to peddle silk to the local stores, sat with his samples on his lap, staring at the harbor for the boat that was to take him on the next step of his lonely journey. He never spoke or took his mournful eyes off the horizon. A Chinese banker from Hong Kong, trying to establish a branch in Tonji, swapped monetary tales with an importer from Norway looking for new sources of tapioca. A Tasmanian woman scribbled postcards, going from one picturesque view to another with no break in the rhythm of her pen stroke. Two American girls, whose sinewy legs more than supported their claim of having made a forty-two-mile bicycle tour of the island after getting off a tramp steamer, sprawled in denim shorts that were brief enough for their comfort and too brief for everybody else's.

Mel, the only porch-sitter who was inherently sociable, asked the two girls what they did when they were not on vacation.

"We're embalmers," answered the taller one, who said her name was Liz. "Aren't we, Diz?"

Diz nodded.

"*Both* of you?" asked Mel, who had never heard of even one lady embalmer and now glimpsed a horrid new vision of his body's ultimate fate.

"That's right," said Liz. "Isn't it, Diz?"

"Yes," Diz grunted.

"Well," Mel said, compelled by the code of a sociable man to keep aloft any ball that he has thrown into the air, "that's certainly . . ." He couldn't think what it certainly was. "Well, that's certainly . . . uh . . . out of the usual line."

"You don't get much conversation," Liz said. "Do you, Diz?"

"No," Diz said.

"The customers don't talk back," Liz said. "Isn't that right, Diz?"

"That's right," Diz said, studying a bruise on her upper thigh, which in its stringiness reminded Mel of the drawings that hang in an osteopath's office.

Millie Hawkes ambled out and sank into an aging rocker. "Thought I'd get a little fresh air," she said, genially. "That kitchen gets mighty hot when you're stuck in there fixing lunch." She smacked her lips. "Kidney dumpling and crumbed sardine."

"Blwugg froomggh," Sally said, rushing over to the porch railing. The Indian and the Chinese banker and the Norwegian made piteous noises.

"Sounds good," Liz said. "Doesn't it, Diz?"

"Yum yum," said Diz.

Sally came back and sat down, the crisis narrowly averted. Mel fanned her with a copy of the "Pacific Islands Monthly." The Chinese banker asked if he could have it next, and after fanning himself briskly he handed it on to the Norwegian. The Indian mopped his brow with one of his silk samples. Silence settled over the little band.

"Sunday in Falolo," Millie said, dreamily. "My favorite day." The church bells stopped, their flocks safely gathered in, and from the open windows of the nearby Seventh-day Adventist chapel came the piping strains of "Jesus Loves Me, This I Know." Mel hummed along quietly. No other sounds dented the morning air. The harbor and its machinery lay idle; time hung suspended, and for ten or fifteen minutes the only sign of life was Doc Bligh, scuttling from post to post like the badman coming to town in a western movie.

A motorcycle courier in a white government uniform broke the mood, pulling up in front of Millie Hawkes's with an imperious roar. He dismounted and climbed the stairs, stepping over a dog that was asleep, and announced that he had three letters to deliver.

"Who for?" Millie asked, her nose aquiver at the royal blessing.

"For Mr. Parker Esquire and Mr. Rumble Esquire and Miss Merrill," the courier said.

"I'm Mr. Parker Esquire," Mel said, "and this is Miss Merrill. I'll take Mr. Rumble Esquire's for him. He's not back yet from a cultural expedition."

The courier left and Mel opened his envelope. It contained a stiff white card with a gold crown embossed at the top. Beneath that was a formal invitation:

His Excellency the Governor
and
Lady Weems
Request the Pleasure of the Company of
Melville Parker, Esq.
at Dinner
On Monday, July Eleventh
At Eight O'Clock

Government House   R.S.V.P. to
Black Tie   the Aide-de-Camp

Millie had come around to read the invitation over Mel's shoulder. "Dinner at His Nibs's," she explained to the others, who looked up incuriously. The Tasmanian woman kept writing postcards and the Indian continued gazing out to sea.

"It's for tomorrow night," Sally said, studying her own invitation. "And it says 'black tie.' Oh Mel, I don't have a thing to wear."

"Pompous old ass!" Millie snorted. "He once had a party in the middle of summer in *tails*."

"*Here?* In *summer?*" Mel asked. "Well, *I* certainly don't have any formal clothes."

"You've got to *do* something, Mel," Sally said. "I'm dying to go. Oh, won't it be just beautiful?"

"I don't know if it'll be just beautiful, but I'm as anxious to go as you are. I've got business to do with the old boy."

"And while you're at it," Millie said, "do something for me. Give him a kick in the . . ."

"What I'm gonna do for *you*," Mel said, "is drum up a little action around this burg. Better get ready."

"Hoo boy!" Millie said, clapping her hands. "Maybe I should put up a little sign that says 'Home Cooking.'"

The dog on the steps gave a long howl.

"Is there any place where I could *rent* a dress suit?" Mel asked.

"No," Millie said with finality. "The only formal clothes in all of Tonji belong to the British colonials. They bring 'em when they come and take 'em when they go. For all I know, they're *born* in 'em, back in England."

"I do believe that is a medical fact," Mel said.

"I remember one old British gentleman," Millie said, "who sent his shirts to Paris to be cleaned and boiled. Said it was the only way to get 'em done proper. The shirts went back and forth for years on the ships of the 'Messageries Maritimes.' One day he died, but his shirts kept arriving for three months more."

Mel was hardly surprised. One of man's strongest urges, he realized, was to plant his dearest customs on foreign soil, however inhospitable that soil might be. Only yesterday he had peeked into the British courthouse and seen English barristers sweating under the thick periwigs and long robes that connote justice in their own clammy islands and therefore must be worn in the steamiest outposts of empire. And as for Millie Hawkes's cuisine, that was the supreme symbol of a nation foisting on the outside world an art that was intolerable even at home. Let the British build roads and schools and civil-service systems, Mel thought; let them establish Anglo-Saxon law and justice; let them even bring cricket and bowls to the deprived masses. But spare their God-given taste buds. He thought of all the hotels in cities surrounded by paradisiacal fruits and fish and vegetables — Colombo and Singapore and Mombasa and Kingston and dozens more — where the kitchen presumably had three faucets, one for cold water and one for hot water and one for white sauce. He saw, as in a dream, rivers of white sauce gushing forth from London and Southampton and Plymouth to cover the earth and drench its natural delicacies, and in the same flash of revelation he saw the real reason why the empire had been lost. That and orange marmalade — eternal, unescapable. So now he was to be balked from meeting the Governor because he didn't have a goddam tuxedo, out here in the sweltering tropics, thirteen thousand miles from Mayfair.

He got up and went to the wall telephone in Millie Hawkes's front parlor. Through the screen door Sally could hear him cranking the petulant machine, which, like its parent phones in England, jingled when he merely lifted the receiver and continued to ring at spasmodic intervals, signifying nothing except poor technology. After a while the call was put through and Mel asked for the Aide-de-Camp. Total silence followed and then Mel began to talk. So resonant was the phone, so rich in metallic echoes, that Sally could only hear fragments of what he was saying. But she knew from his ingratiating tone and elaborate courtesy that he had chosen his best instrument, had decided that if custom could raise stupid barriers, charm could knock them down.

". . . feel tremendously honored," Mel was saying. "Such an unexpected surprise . . . really so considerate of His Ex-

cellency . . . shouldn't have gone to the trouble . . . looking forward to it with the greatest of pleasure . . . heard so
much about British hospitality out here . . . yes, you've put
your finger on it exactly . . . no more than we're looking
forward to meeting *him* . . . and of course Lady Weems,
too . . ."

On and on the voice purred. He could keep that up all day,
Sally thought. Ten thousand words when he starts on a
charm job. Like a hypnotist. Old Aide-de-Camp must be
beginning to nod.

". . . would have been so disappointed to come all this
way and not meet some of your gracious blm-mmble-mbb-
blgug-woorm . . ."

Gracious what?, Sally wondered as the telephone swallowed up the noun.

". . . always had such admiration . . . warm memories of
my last visit to London . . . lucky enough to catch a glimpse
of the Queen . . . oh, you're absolutely right . . . yes . . .
well, eight o'clock tomorrow then . . . only one small thing
. . . limited baggage allowance . . . quite impossible to
bring evening clothes . . . wouldn't dream of risking any
offense to His Excellency . . . so perhaps it might be better
to decline . . . rather than embarrass . . ."

Mel stopped, and in the sudden shutting-off of his cascade
a silence filled the porch that was almost as loud. For at least
a minute nothing broke the silence. Sally awaited the verdict
in gloom. He's pushed it too far, she thought. Or else he's put
the Aide-de-Camp to sleep.

Then, just as suddenly, Mel's voice resumed. "You're *sure*
now? . . . it *did* happen on one other occasion, you say?
. . . and Sir Reginald was not too put out? . . . good of him
to understand . . . the penalty of traveling by plane . . .
this modern age, everyone going so fast . . . couldn't agree
with you more . . . a *defi*nite loss of values . . . well then
. . . if you'll convey to the Governor our most mmble-mm-
grr-boof . . ."

He came back out on the porch. "Okay, Sal, it's all set," he
said. "I'll wear my white linen suit and you wear your best

dress and the Governor will understand. The Aide-de-Camp
says he's a very informal and tolerant fellow."

"*That* old bastard?" Millie exclaimed.

"That's what the Aide-de-Camp said."

Lights twinkled from every window of Government House,
promising joy and laughter within, when the taxi carrying
Mel and Sally drove through the white gates at 7:59 the
following night and sped up the curling driveway. Both of
them had a well-scrubbed American look, achieved at the
expense of a full day's search for a tailor who could press
Mel's trousers and iron Sally's black dress and for such items
as shoe polish, fingernail polish and a tie somber enough to
be worn at a funeral, and they now faced the evening confident that they were as respectable as possible within the
harsh limits of possibility. Cy had not come back from a trip
to take pictures in a native village, but before setting out he
solemnly promised to turn up at Government House soon
after eight in his darkest suit.

Mel told Sally that he had never seen a girl so fresh and
beautiful — an authentic Cinderella, palace-bound.

"I *feel* like Cinderella," she said, her blue eyes sparkling.
"Do you really think this dress is all right?"

"Sure do, honey," he said. "You'll forget all about its not
being a floor-length gown."

Their taxi pulled up to the porte cochère, but two other
cars had arrived just ahead of them, and a guard in stiff white
attire was helping the occupants out.

"Mel, *look!*" Sally gasped. "*Medals!*"

"And a *sword!*" Mel said.

What they both hoped was a mirage, some optical quirk
causing an unnatural glitter, turned out to be a man in full
military uniform, a sword gleaming at his side and so many
decorations fixed to his tunic that Mel seemed to hear the
sound of bugles and to see, charging across his chest, whole
brigades of sepoys and Fuzzy-Wuzzies and Gurkhas. Emerging after him was a lady in a lavender dress so long that only
the tips of her evening slippers peeped out, and a shiny

lavaliere swung in the empty space long since relinquished by her bosom.

"Oh dear," Sally said. "Well, maybe the next couple won't be so . . ."

The next couple consisted of a lady whose gown fell behind her in a brief train and whose hair glinted with what appeared to be a small tiara, along with a man encased so rigidly in his tuxedo that he walked like a mechanical toy, only his feet seeming to move. Then they too were gone, gobbled up by the huge white mansion.

Mel and Sally's taxi moved up and the guard opened its door. Sally stepped out into the headlights of another car just arriving, a car in which she dimly saw swirls of taffeta and a diamond stickpin. Conscious of her long white legs, cruelly trapped in the beam of light like a rabbit on the highway, she felt that she had somehow put on a miniskirt by mistake, and her hands reached down in an awkward reflex to see if her dress was still there and to smooth it over her knees. Mel followed, brushing imaginary dust off his lapels, and escorted her up the stairs, at the top of which he saw a tall young man in a coat looped with gold braid. His face was so thin, despite a bushy moustache, that it could only accommodate his molars and bicuspids, leaving the canines and incisors to an extraterritorial life out in front.

"Is it Mr. Parker?" he said. "And Miss Merrill?" His eyes made a quick, disdainful tour of their clothing.

"No," Mel said, "I'm Mr. Switzer and this is Miss O'Gorman. We were just driving around the island and saw the lights on."

The thin face faded from the color of cream to the color of milk. "Look here," he said. "I'm afraid that won't do at all. *Most* irregular. I shall have to ask you to . . ."

"Oh hell, I'm Mr. Parker," Mel said. "Just a little joke, old boy."

"Well, it's not in the least funny."

"And this is the one-and-only Miss Merrill. To whom do we have the pleasure of . . ."

"The Aide-de-Camp. Favisham's the name, in point of fact."

"Pleased to meet you," Mel said, reaching out to shake the hand which he assumed, incorrectly, Favisham would extend. "Sorry about the joke," he added, withdrawing his hand and scratching his ear.

"D'you mind having a look at this before we go in?" Favisham said, thrusting at Mel and Sally a seating chart written in cursive letters. "It's quite clear, I think. You, Mr. Parker, are to take Lady Weems into the dining room. And you, Miss Merrill, will be taken in by Mr. Foote, whom I believe you know."

"Yes, slightly."

"Jolly good. Shall we go and meet the others, then?"

He led them into a spacious room where "the others" were standing in a shapeless group, sipping drinks. Favisham took Mel and Sally around and made brief introductions. The man with the sword was Brigadier Chitty, late of India's northwest frontier, now retired. And Mrs. Chitty. The man in the rigid tuxedo was Mr. Agnew, colonial secretary for Tonji, and the lady in the tiara was Mrs. Agnew. Then came Mr. Satterthwaite, minister of finance, and Mrs. Satterthwaite, and Justice Grimshaw and Mrs. Grimshaw, each dressed with utmost formality, and the Misses Maud and Winifred Weems, lank maidens of twenty-six and nineteen.

"How d' you do?" they all said, their eyes departing for an instant, so brief that anyone would have missed it except Mel and Sally, to note the apparel of the two Americans.

Favisham steered them on. "And here is a compatriot of yours: Major Funk, who is president of a meat company, and Mrs. Funk. His Excellency always tries to gather the important visitors to Tonji for these little informal evenings." They proceeded to a man with a round bald head and steel-rimmed glasses. "Professor Kalbfleisch, from Munich," Favisham explained, "who is here making certain anthropological studies." Both the Funks and Professor Kalbfleisch had thought to bring evening clothes on their travels, Mel noticed with resentment as Favisham pushed him and Sally back into the center and abandoned them.

"How are you enjoying our little island?" Mrs. Satterthwaite asked.

"Oh we're just *loving* it," Sally said, reverting to the bubbly verbiage of the Eastern sub-deb whom she thought she had long outgrown. "I mean it's just — everything's so *won*derful. And the town is as cute as can be."

"I do think it's the last of the colonies where the natives still behave properly," Mrs. Agnew said. "Don't you, Pamela?"

"I do, Ann," Mrs. Satterthwaite said. "They know their place."

"And so they should!" boomed Brigadier Chitty. "I've no patience with all this flapdoodle about Brown Brother."

"What flapdoodle is that?" asked the voice of a new arrival, a voice relishing its own question. It was Denis Foote, looking almost as misplaced, Sally thought, as she herself did. Technically Denis had satisfied the rules: all the correct clothes hung on his limber frame. But unlike the other men, whose clothes appeared to have been poured over them in liquid plastic, which then solidified and became their outer skin, Denis and his suit did not give the impression of knowing each other. Sally was greatly cheered by this feat of Denis's, preserving his identity within the carapace of the establishment. She gave him a warm smile.

Brigadier Chitty, who had shot off his statement about Brown Brother with complete assurance that it would meet no answering fire, looked stunned and then bewildered, unable to grasp how he had been pinked.

"What, what?" he said.

"You were saying, Brigadier," Denis went on, with the gentle politeness of a young man reminding an old man of the point where his previous sentence trailed into vapor, "that you have no patience with all this flapdoodle."

"Indeed not! No patience at all!" the Brigadier said, slapping his sword such a thwack that it rattled in its scabbard. "Self-government for Brown Brother — that's all one hears. Why, he's no more ready to govern his own affairs than those monkeys up in the rain forest!" He jerked his thumb toward the western end of the island. "Look at Kenya! Look at Malaya! Look all over the Empire!"

"The former Empire," Denis said. "The sun occasionally sets on us now, and we'd better recognize that Brown Brother — as you call him — is our equal in the councils of the world."

The Brigadier's face seemed to inflate, like a purple balloon, and he gripped his sword. Mel pictured him running that sword, years ago, through Afridi scouts who stole down from the Khyber Pass to spy on the British position, and just as easily he pictured him running it through Denis now. "It's you young Communists who have stirred up all this trouble," the Brigadier spluttered.

"Well, what *I* think is a blessing," Mrs. Chitty broke in, "is that we still have such a nice golf club. I do think it's so important in a colony to have a nice golf club, don't you, Mr. Barker?"

Mel, who hadn't realized that he was being addressed, now saw the watery blue eyes of Mrs. Chitty peering into his face in search of an affirmative answer. That there might be any connection between the health of a colony and the health of its golf club had never occurred to him, nor did it even occur to him now, despite the steady narrowing of the gap between Mrs. Chitty's eyes and his own.

"Oh yes . . . *so* important," he said at last. "Nice club . . . can't overestimate that," he added, and the inquiring old face receded.

"This will interest you," said Major Funk, edging into the conversation with the one phrase which, in Mel's experience, guaranteed as stupefying the words that would come next. "I was playing the fifth hole today — it so happens that golf is a little hobby of mine — and I got a good drive of approximately two hundred and four, maybe two hundred and five yards. Well, as you recall that leaves a dogleg over a little creek, and I didn't know if my seven-iron . . ."

"Did Favisham say you were a major?" Brigadier Chitty

interrupted. "What outfit, old chap? Weren't at the Somme, by any chance? *There's* a place the Hun won't forget."

"Oh shucks," Major Funk said with a self-deprecating laugh, which turned into a coughing fit as the profusion of Brigadier Chitty's medals began to dawn on him. "Heck," he went on, mopping his mouth with a handkerchief that had *FRED* stitched on it in italic letters, "I'm just a major in the Quartermaster reserve. Got my rank in the First War, and when I was mustered out the boys down at the plant took to calling me 'Major.' I sort of enjoyed it, to be honest with you, and I've been Major Funk ever since. Silly of me, I suppose."

"Yes, quite," Brigadier Chitty said. "Pity you missed the Somme."

Maud Weems drifted into the group. "Oh Mr. Barber," she said to Mel, "I'm dying to know all about this scheme of yours. I hear that . . ." She stopped as abruptly as if a cone of chloroform had been clamped over her nose, and so did everyone else. In the ensuing silence all heads turned toward the door, where Sir Reginald Weems and Lady Weems were making a measured entrance. Their faces glowed with the pleasure that their arrival was conferring upon the group, and they moved along the receiving line, which the guests hurriedly formed, like two figures on a Swiss clock, not walking so much as being propelled by some mechanism under their feet.

Sir Reginald wore a tapa-cloth cummerbund around his portly waist and a mirthless smile beneath his pencil moustache. Lady Weems, a thin woman several inches taller, had a carrot-colored evening gown that fell around her, obedient to no discernible pattern, in loose vertical folds of silk. Her equine smile had already preceded her in the person of her daughter Maud, to whom that dominant gene had been passed intact, but what the smile thereby lost in originality it regained in persistence, remaining fixed at maximum wattage throughout her tour of the guests.

At the sight of Mel's white linen suit the Governor and Lady Weems were unable to suppress a fleeting look of repugnance, and Mel offered a quick apology as they shook his hand and said "So glad." But what they mumbled in reply to his apology — assuming that it was a reply and not merely part of their dental condition — he had no idea, and therefore no way of knowing whether he and Sally were in bad grace or adequate grace. He ruled out good grace entirely.

The conversation that had died with the hosts' arrival now flickered back to life, tiny sparks of chitchat seeking the oxygen that would fan them into a larger blaze. But the temperature was perceptibly colder, and where a certain emotional warmth had prevailed, primness and protocol now laid their gray suede gloves. In fact, had it not been for the abnormal hush, nobody might have heard the commotion outside. Almost as one head, however, the guests turned to see what could be causing a conjunction of noises so strange, so un-British. Male shouts mingled with billows of female laughter and with the sound of scuffling bodies.

Presently the forces pushing the invaders forward overcame the force trying to hold them back, and into the room at full momentum lurched Cy Rumble and his two native girls, followed by one Tonjian man with a guitar and another with a drum. The girls, under Cy's chaperonage, were drunk to the maximum and dressed to the minimum. They wore only two strips of greenery, narrowly covering the natural wonders beneath, and the honey color of their young stomachs went forth as palpably as a heat wave, so real to the English men and women that they could feel it rub against their pallid faces and imprisoning clothes.

Cries and gasps pierced the room. Mrs. Chitty said, "I think I'm going to faint," but as Brigadier Chitty didn't hear her, having inserted a monocle to focus on the navels that providence had thrust into his vision, she changed her mind.

Mel said, "Oh my God! That blows it! There goes the whole ball of wax."

Sir Reginald stalked over to Cy. His face, already the shape of a tomato, now took on its color, and his mouth worked feverishly to find the words that were locked somewhere inside it. "What is the meaning of this?" he said, the mouth and the words at last synchronized. "Well? Well?"

"I come bearing gifts, Your Excellency," Cy said with an artless smile. "Seymour Rumble, sir, of Mosholu Parkway, New York City."

"Gifts? Gifts? Do you mock the hospitality of Her Majesty the Queen, Rumble?"

"On the contrary, sir, I bring an offering. You have heard of the famous American drink, the dry martini?" He waited for the happy murmur of assent which he knew would come and didn't. "I have poured its ingredients — gin and vermouth — into this pitcher."

"Sir Reginald," Lady Weems said, pushing through the crowd, "I insist that you stop this vulgar demonstration."

"What I am about to demonstrate, ma'am," Cy said, "will be a boon to the economy of Tonji, touristwise."

"Tourist what?" asked Lady Weems.

"Wise. Touristwise."

"Perhaps, my dear," the Governor said, "we should give Mr. Rumble another minute to clarify his scheme." He drew his gums back in what was apparently a comforting smile.

"Now the problem that has always bugged us in America," Cy continued, "is how to chill the martini without bruising the gin by stirring it or shaking it up and down. I am happy to report that in your beautiful islands I have found the perfect solution."

A proud little hum went around the room.

"First I pour the martini into these two shakers. Like this. Then I put the lid on tight. So." He walked over to the two native girls. "Now at the back of these, uh, skirts I have devised a loop that will hold a martini shaker." He turned the two girls around and hung a shaker on each of them. "Then, simply chill the martini, Tonji style."

He snapped his fingers. The man with the guitar began to play a Polynesian tune, setting a tempo so fast that his fingers were a blur. The hands of the drummer flew, slapping the taut skins. The room throbbed with rhythm and the two girls began to undulate from the waist down. Mel had seen hula dances before, but never anything like this, nor could he still believe what he was seeing. It flouted every law of anatomy. How could the pelvis be going forward and back in such rapid thrusts and still be going around in complete revolutions? And so fast? And for so long?

Cy stood in a trance. Even more than the way of an eagle in the air or a snake upon the rock, it was too wonderful to comprehend, and he was so far gone in wonder that he couldn't repossess his senses. On and on the dance went, more erotic with every minute, the girls now seeming to be in the final throes of some primeval sex rite.

A woman screamed. Cy's face was a mask, sealed off from other mortals.

Mel acted fast. He stepped in front of the two girls, clapped his hands, and yelled at them to stop. Seeing him, they did — the rotating engines ground to a halt — and so did the guitarist and drummer. Cy emerged from hypnosis, blinking to see where he was.

"Thanks, girls, that was very nice," he said. He lifted the martini shakers off the belts and carried them to the Governor. "And that," he declared, "is a chilled dry martini, Tonji style."

"Most edifying," the Governor said. "And now if you will be so good as to remove these persons . . ."

"Aren't you even gonna *taste* it?" Cy asked.

"I'm sure it's an amusing little concoction. I'm quite willing to take your word on that. Quite willing."

Cy gazed into Sir Reginald's eyes to see if he really meant it. He really meant it. "Anybody else?" he asked. But nobody stirred. It became obvious even to Cy, never a student of etiquette, that the Governor's refusal was binding on them all. "Nobody?" he pleaded.

"I'd like to try one," said Denis Foote, stepping forward. "Very good of you to go to all this trouble, Mr. Rumble. The reputation of your dry martini has gone round the world and I . . ."

"That's quite enough, Foote," the Governor said. "Spare us

the remainder of your academic drivel." Denis took the
poured drink and withdrew. "And now," the Governor continued, "as I'm certain there will be nobody else . . ."

"*I'd* like one," came a high voice. "Do just let me step
through, will you?" It was Maud Weems, striding out as from
a forest, her horsy smile a beacon to light the trail.

"Dear God!" the Governor said. "Maud, are you out of your
mind? I forbid you!"

"Now, Daddy," Maud said, making it clear from her inflec-
tion that there was more to come. But the next sentence
waited while a long whinny flew out of her and curled
around the chandelier. "I'm quite of age," she went on.
"Besides, Mr. Foote has had a sip with no ill effects. Am I
right, Mr. Foote? Where are you?"

A surprised slurp came out of the interior of the crowd.
"Yes, right here," Denis's voice called. "Cheerio, Lady Maud.
Quite all right, thank you."

"Well then," Maud said, turning to Cy. He gave her a glass
and poured a martini. Major Funk then decided to have one,
and Cy turned away long enough to provide it. Turning
around again, he was puzzled to see that Maud's glass was
empty.

"Didn't I . . . ?" he began.

"Oooh," Maud said. "It has a lovely aftertaste."

"*After*taste? What about the during taste?"

"Oh, I thought it was supposed to be — you know — 'bot-
toms up.'"

"You're supposed to *sip* it. Like wine."

"Righto," Maud said. "Do just pour me another one then."

Cy obliged and then turned to pour one for Professor
Kalbfleisch and for Mel, who told him to "get rid of those
bimboes before they screw us up for good." Even as he
spoke, however, it became obvious that it was not the two
bimboes who would falter next.

"Oh Mr. *Rum*ble," came Maud's voice, high and with a
queer straining noise.

Cy turned just in time to see Maud keel over onto a sofa,

where she lay motionless, eyes closed, the vital spark apparently snuffed out. Her mouth was open and she looked like a beached whale.

"Rumble!" the Jovian voice of Sir Reginald Weems thundered. "What have you done to my daughter?"

9

DINNER began late and without two of its expected
guests, through whose calligraphic names on the seating chart Favisham drew a thin line. One was Maud, whom
four of the men carried off in pallbearer style. The impression that they gave of being cemetery-bound was reinforced
by Lady Weems, who followed with a strenuous display of
grief. The other guest who didn't stay for dinner was Cy. His
departure, like Maud's, was swift and involuntary. "Remove
yourself this instant," the Governor bellowed, "and take your
bloody troupe!" Cy complied, pausing only long enough to
turn at the door and say, "Goodnight all."

Presently Lady Weems came back. Word was passed that
Maud had regained consciousness and that Dr. Thurlow was
on his way to Government House. Then, in response to a
signal that was transmitted, as far as Mel could see, in
absolute secrecy, all the guests were suddenly grouped outside the dining-room door. A man's arm was offered to each
of the ladies, with the exception of Lady Weems, who said in
a shrill tone, "Oh Mr. *Walker!* If it's not too much inconvenience." Mel bounded to her side, gave her what he belatedly
saw was the wrong arm, and they strode into a room whose
long table glittered in the light of many candles.

Sally was escorted in by Denis. "I'm glad you're with me,"
she said, noticing the three different wine glasses and the
graduated rows of knives, forks and spoons, each ordained
for a particular kind of food. But which kind of silver was for

which kind of food? "You can be my Emily Post," she told Denis. "You must be up here often."

"No, it's my first time, too. I guess I was invited because your project falls in my bailiwick. Anyway, we're off to a merry start."

"I don't think you'll want us in your bailiwick. We're accident-prone."

"Oh, I'm delighted to have *you* in my bailiwick, if not necessarily Mr. Parker and the project," Denis said. "You can sit down now," he whispered, pushing her in and seating himself at her right. The Governor was on Sally's left, at the head of the table, and across from her were Mrs. Agnew, Professor Kalbfleisch, Mrs. Chitty and Major Funk. Lady Weems was at the other end, with Mel at her right.

"Well, Miss Merrill," the Governor said, harpooning a piece of shrimp with the smallest of his forks, "the dinner commences at last. Ehh? Hmmmm? *Le jeu est fait* and so forth. Hahaha."

Sally gave her social laugh. She knew, as every woman knows, that in the trackless wastes of small talk a laugh which seems to acquiesce in what has just been said is the best answer. It throws the ball back to the man, who can't understand how he got it again so soon. The Governor pondered Sally's non-reply and realized that it was his turn.

"That's it precisely," he said. "Quite. Hahaha. Doesn't one?"

"Oh . . . that is . . . yes, very much so," Sally said, pleased to have come up with an answer for "Doesn't one?" It was still, however, her turn. "How pretty the table looks," she continued, skating out with confidence onto a familiar surface.

"Bit of a balls-up there at the beginning," the Governor said. "Oh well, that's all by the bye now. Nothing that a good English dinner won't make us forget. Ehh? Fffff." He impaled another shrimp.

"What brings you to Tonji, Miss Merritt?" Mrs. Agnew asked.

"Well, it's hard to explain," Sally said. "I suppose it begins with my having a degree in anthropology . . ."

"Woods are full of you anthropology chaps," the Governor broke in. "Dr. Kalbfish over there is in the same line of goods. Right, Professor?"

"Yah," Kalbfleisch said in the guttural voice of a Warner Brothers U-boat captain. "*Natürlich.*"

"You and the professor will have to get together," Denis said to Sally, pumping the conversation ahead. "It must be exciting to meet another scholar from the same discipline."

"Speak the same language, is that it, Foote?" said the Governor. "That what you're trying to say?"

"Well, sir . . ."

"Good, good."

"Mr. Foote is right," Sally said. "If I were to talk with Dr. Kalbfleisch we would have a, you know, scholarly frame of reference and . . . I mean, our methods might differ but our objective would be the same."

"And what is that, my dear?" asked Mrs. Chitty.

"To find scientific truth," Sally said. "We are bound by our academic vows — isn't that so, Professor?"

"*Ganz recht,*" Kalbfleisch said, nodding his hairless head.

"Well, you two are in for some good talks," the Governor said. "Never went in for that sort of thing myself. Mmmm."

"Are you out here on a special study, Professor?" Denis asked. "A grant of some sort?"

"Ahhhhhh," Kalbfleisch replied, signifying yes. "Ze people who are zponsoring me . . ."

"You've got a Guggenheim, I'll bet," Sally broke in.

"Zey share my deep curiozity about . . ."

"Rockefeller Fund? Ford Foundation?" Sally asked.

"No-no-no-no-no-no," Kalbfleisch said. "It is ze . . ." He foraged about in his pocket and found an advertisement from a paper. Bringing it close to his steel-rimmed glasses, he studied the type at the bottom. "It is Priapic Press, 432 Bleecker Street, New York Zity. Very zerious people. You know zem?"

Sally shook her head.

"Here," he said, handing her the paper, which was grimy in

its folds. "You read it for ze whole group. My English is *schrecklich.*"

" 'Sex Rites of a Primitive Culture,' " Sally began in a thin voice. " 'Untold centuries ago there seemingly flourished in the Tonji islands of the uninhibited South Seas a Polynesian tribe dedicated to weird erotic practices and an extreme form of phallus worship, characterized by . . .' I think perhaps somebody else should read this."

"Nonsense, my dear," the Governor said. "Science knows no such thing as a blush. Ehh, Foote? Hmmm?"

"If this *is* science," Denis said.

"Ztupid!" Kalbfleisch hissed. He motioned Sally to read on.

" 'To this oft-disputed forgotten paradise Dr. Hans Kalbfleisch, eminent Munich University savant and author of numerous learned articles on sexology, now brings his archeologist's tool . . .' "

Major Funk gave a long and dirty laugh. "Oh, that's rich," he said. Denis took the paper out of Sally's hands. "I'll read the rest," he said. "That is, if it *has* to be gone on with." He looked at the Governor.

"A few more sentences, Foote, to give us the general drift."

"All right, sir. That last part, Professor, could use a bit of rewriting. Next time you're in touch with Priapic Press I suggest . . ."

"Go *on,* Foote, damn it all," the Governor said.

" '. . . and his unquenchable curiosity about erotic customs which a less sensitive observer would regard as unnatural, or at the very least bizarre. It goes without saying that there is no intent in this volume to be sensational or prurient, nor to titillate the senses of the lascivious reader. No! It is to the mature seeker of recondite pleasures in the art of love that Dr. Kalbfleisch addresses this his latest and best work. Profusely illustrated. Check X for plain wrapper.' "

Denis handed the paper back to Kalbfleisch. "Is the book already written, then?"

"Moztly," Kalbfleisch said. "I have zummed up what previous zcholars have zurmised about zis lost civilization — which, I must zay, is very zpicy. Zese chapters are in galley proofs. Now must ze important last chapters be gewritten. First-hand rezearch! I muzt find evidence before I can conzider my task done."

"See here, old boy," the Governor said, "you're not going to muck about in the villages scaring up a bunch of naked chaps dancing around a maypole, or some rot like that. Wouldn't be good for the colony, you know. Not good at all. Not one bit. No indeed. Mmmmmm." He tugged at a section of moustache.

"No worse for the colony than Mr. Parker's project," Denis said, "if you ask me."

"Nobody did, Foote," the Governor said. "It's quite a different kettle of fish. Quite different altogether. The publication of Dr. Kalbfuss's book will bring us a stream of undesirable types. Misfits and that other lot."

"What other lot is that, sir?"

"Perverteds," the Governor said. "And . . . you know the sort."

"Writer-photographer teams from 'Paris-Match,' " Denis added, "and documentary film-makers and . . ."

"Chaps from the telly."

"That's right, chaps from television — I mean the telly," Denis went on, "all selling sex behind the respectable mask of anthropology. Why, I wouldn't be surprised if some little store in San Francisco put out a line of 'Lost Paradise' gifts. Dirty ceramics."

"Quite, quite," the Governor agreed. "Keep the blighters out, I say."

"But wait till you see the crowd that Parker brings in. They'll ruin you just as fast as Dr. Kalbfleisch's sex fiends."

"I think I'm competent to decide that, Foote. Or have you forgotten the little chat we had several weeks ago? Ehhh? Hmmm? Forgotten it already, have you, Foote?"

"No, sir. Indeed not."

"Indeed not what?"

"Indeed not forgotten it, sir — the little chat we had."

"Because if you are under the apprehension that I intend to relinquish . . ."

"Good heavens no, sir."

". . . I have absolutely no intention of retiring from . . ."

"Certainly not, Sir Reginald."

The Governor tweezed a few strands of moustache between his forefinger and thumb. Then he dove with hearty appetite into a long fish that lay across the plate and over its edges, the soup course having come and gone.

At the other end Mel was engaged in one of the trickiest holding operations of his career. Lady Weems's thoughts kept stealing upstairs to "poor Maud," who, she reminded Mel, "was very nearly done to death by that vulgar associate of yours." Alternately the hostess reflex, as if triggered by wires running up her chair, led her to make polite conversation with Mel about his country. She warmly praised "your wonderful Senator McCarthy" for throwing out the Bolsheviks "back when General Adenauer was President," and she chided the Americans for electing a man — President Jolson — who thought that "the black masses" were ready to hold jobs like everybody else.

Mel, feeling like a baseball catcher who has been stripped of his right to call the pitches, lunged gamely for everything that was thrown. In they came in all speeds and sizes — the wide breaking curve, the tantalizing knuckler, the beanball and the fast one down the middle. He gathered them into his glove and trotted back to the mound with comforting words.

When the talk veered to "poor Maud" he pointed out that Mr. Rumble was merely trying to provide a treat and "undoubtedly didn't know that in rare cases gin and vermouth provoke a toxic reaction." When the talk veered to America he deflected it back to Tonji, hinting of all his plans to give Sir Reginald's "not unimportant colony" (he loved a good slippery double negative in such cases) "its proper glow in the sun of empire." Thus he came to the end of the meat course punchy with fatigue but relieved to find that he and the project were still alive.

Suddenly, on his right, Mrs. Grimshaw plucked at his sleeve and handed him a bottle of port, which, he realized, had made its way down the table instead of being poured by the waiters. He filled his remaining wine glass and handed the port to Lady Weems, who filled her glass and sent the bottle on via Mr. Agnew. As the bottle proceeded, Mel turned back to Lady Weems, but her thoughts appeared to be elsewhere. In fact, he noticed that the conversation along the whole table was dying down, leaving only an isolated pocket here and there, until even these ebbed out and in the echoing void, as Lady Weems took her glass and began to rise, the lone voice of Dr. Kalbfleisch finished a sentence still in progress:

"Und zo we believe that he had a phallus eighteen feet long."

"My *word!*" said Mrs. Chitty.

Lady Weems, now fully standing, lifted her glass with dignity and said "To the Queen." Everyone rose and successive murmurs of "To the Queen" were heard. The toast completed, everyone sat down again and relapsed into silence. As a group they had the stunned look of tornado victims in a photograph.

Sir Reginald moved heroically into the disaster area. "The Professor was telling us, my dear," he called, "about a stone god — a *stat*ue, you understand — that some anthropology chaps think is here is the islands." He retracted his gums to give her a soothing smile.

"I quite understand," Lady Weems said. "Now Mr. Satterthwaite will tell us about his trip to Darwin and Perth to study a new Australian program of bond debentures that might help the economy of Tonji. Don't leave anything out, Clive — the little that you told me was thrilling."

Mr. Satterthwaite saw his duty and floated whole series of long-term bonds across the Pacific, nursing them to maturity only when dessert was safely over. The guests, if not rapt, were at least grateful, and each one hung from his features the mask of fascinated attention that is always ready, just behind the cheekbones, for such an occasion. As the last morsel of cake sank below the horizon, slipping past Mrs. Agnew's tonsils and allowing her to lay down her fork, Lady Weems rose as on a spring and said to Mrs. Funk and Mrs.

Grimshaw, her two nearest feminine neighbors, "Shall we go round the corner?" The other five ladies also heard the question, and all eight rose and paddled out like a column of ducks.

Mel welcomed their going because the talk would now turn to island matters and he would be able to broach his own ideas to the Governor. What better time, when Sir Reginald was suffused with food and wine and the company of his fellow men? The Governor was obviously in his optimum mood — the tugs that he gave his moustache were happy tugs, confident in the manner of a ballplayer swinging three bats.

Mr. Agnew acknowledged the mood with a contented harrumph and launched the topic of conversation. "Here's one for your collection," he said, proceeding to tell a dirty joke. Mel had never heard a joke less worth telling, but Sir Reginald chuckled and said, "Very good." Then he turned to Judge Grimshaw, who told a joke of equal quality, after which Sir Reginald's glance elicited dirty jokes from Brigadier Chitty, Mr. Satterthwaite and the Aide-de-Camp, all of whom had taken the precaution of finding one in advance.

Denis's turn found him at his usual loss to remember a joke from one minute to another. He flailed about in aimless despair and at last recounted a quip that he had seen in the "Listener," one of many magazines that came to him from London. Nobody understood the quip or even knew when it was over. "I can't stick that kind of humor, Foote," the Governor said. He skipped past Dr. Kalbfleisch, evidently feeling that he had said enough, and brought his eyes to rest on Major Funk. "Well, Major?" he asked jovially. "How about you? Hmmm? Don't let America down. Hahaha."

Major Funk, being a golfer, as partial to the nineteenth hole as to the preceding eighteen, seemed to hear from afar the clanking of metal lockers and the relating of a hundred dirty jokes by men in towels and brown paper slippers, and his only difficulty was to pluck one from such an ample hoard. He managed, however, and the Governor repaid him with a bawdy laugh. Then he stared expectantly at Mel.

Mel's problem was different from Denis's. He could remember jokes well enough — in his business they were required currency, valuable as gold. But the jokes were hatched in an environment so small and subsisted there on foods so special — on the plankton of showbiz gossip and the algae of psychoanalysis and the darting minnows of Yiddish slang — that they couldn't survive in the outside world. Mel thought of one joke after another, rejecting a dozen in quick succession, until finally his silence became too heavy to bear and he said to the Governor, "I can't think of any."

Sir Reginald's features blackened. "Dammit, Parker," he said. "I'd heard you were a clever fellow. Hmpff. Must have had it wrong. Fffff." He looked around the table to see if the men had finished their brandy and cigars. "I believe there are some games of chance laid on in the other room," he said to Mel and Denis, getting up. "Chitty! How about you and me standing Trevor and Clive to a game of snooker?"

The four men ambled off to the billiard room. The others drifted back into the living room, where the ladies, having been round the corner, were engaged in various games. Mrs. Satterthwaite and Mrs. Agnew were playing lawn bowls on a long green carpet. Cramped by their long years and long dresses, they nevertheless kept stooping to roll the heavy black balls toward the white one at the other end, and Mel sidled genially over to Mrs. Grimshaw to ask her to explain the rules. Mrs. Grimshaw began by pointing out that Mrs. Satterthwaite's ball kept veering off to the left. "Poor Pamela hasn't a clue about biases," she said.

"Oh *there* you are, America!" trilled Lady Weems, striding across the room and taking Mel by the wrist. "We've been waiting for you. We're all going to play the cork game!" Cries of approval greeted her idea, and Mrs. Agnew asked what the cork game was. "*You* remember, Elspeth," Lady Weems said. "The game that H.E. invented."

"Who's H.E.?" Sally whispered to Denis.

"His Excellency," he whispered back. "Sir Reginald."

Lady Weems was still trying to kindle Mrs. Agnew's memory: "We were in the B.S.I.P., and we had gotten tired of the game where we passed the ping-pong balls from nose to nose, and one night H.E. said why don't we . . ."

"What's B.S.I.P.?" Sally whispered.

"British Solomon Island Protectorate," Denis said. "Their last post. They've nothing to do after dinner but invent these silly games."

To a large round table at one end of the room were now brought several large bath towels. These were laid on top of each other in the middle of the table to form a thick padded surface. Somebody else brought the lid of an enormous silver soup tureen, and Winifred Weems brought a dozen corks and fastened a long piece of string to each one. The corks were then placed on the matted towel so that their strings reached out like spokes of a wheel to the edge of the table.

"Now each of you take a string," Lady Weems said, steering twelve of her guests into position, including Mel and Sally. She gave the great silver lid to Denis and told him to grasp it firmly by the handle.

"Now can you all see this pack of cards?" she asked. "Good. The Aide-de-Camp is going to turn the cards over, one by one, and every time a jack comes up, you are to pull your string. And meanwhile *you*, Mr. Foote, will slam the lid down onto the towel and try to trap the little corks before they get away. Hahaha. Everybody got it now? Marvelous! Ready, Mr. Foote?"

Denis nodded grimly. He was standing over the table with the lid clutched in his hand, ready to pounce.

"All right then," Lady Weems said. "*Go!*"

Flip, flip, flip, flip went the cards. Ooooooh went the players when the jack came up. BOOOOM! went the lid as Denis crashed it down onto the towels, shaking the entire table.

"Who got caught?" asked Lady Weems, lifting the lid to find three little corks nestled there, the other nine having flown away. "Jolly *good*, Mr. Foote," she said, marking the three victims on a scoring pad. The corks were replaced on the towel. "All set? Here we go again!"

Flip, flip, flip, flip. Oooooooh. BOOOOM! "Too fast for you, Pamela? Haha. You too, Miss Merriam? Shame! All set?"

Flip, flip, flip, flip. Oooooooh. BOOOOM! "Splendid, Mr. Foote! *Four* that time. Isn't this smashing fun?"

Flip, flip, flip, flip. Oooooooh. BOOOOM! "How's America doing? Oh I *am* sorry, Mr. Parker. Why don't you replace Mr. Foote for a while? Don't be silly — of *course* you won't bring it down on somebody's hand. Perfect! Watch out now, everyone — Mr. Parker is a wild American Indian. Hahahaha."

Flip, flip, flip, flip. Oooooooh. BOOOOM! "They *all* got away? Good heavens, Mr. Parker, you've got to be faster than *that!* Here we go!"

On and on the game went — and on and on. None of the English men or women seemed to flag, except for Denis, or to tire of its stunning monotony. Mel's arm ached and his mind swam. He was a prisoner in some weird tribal circle. He would look at the faces in the circle, seeking some break in the catatonic pattern, some sign that the ceremony was over. But the faces were a blur of happy smiles and never changed. Then he would look at the clock, and it didn't change either. Time had stopped. He was doomed like Sisyphus to push a rock into eternity — a silver rock with an ornamental handle.

BOOOOM! BOOOOM! BOOOOM! Again and again and again he slammed the lid down, but never hard enough to catch the corks, most of which bobbed merrily away. For he knew that if, at any moment in the long and lugubrious history of the cork game, some unforeseen circumstance should move Sir Reginald Weems's hand onto the towel, there to have its metacarpal bones splintered by the man with the lid, that moment would be now and that man would be him. Out of the corner of his eye he saw Sir Reginald, back from his game of billiards, hovering and kibitzing, meting out a "Damn good" here and a "Rotten luck" there. At one point, when the Governor stood near by, Mel asked if he might have a word with him to discuss his project. "Of course, old boy — any time," the Governor said and moved away.

Flip, flip, flip, flip. Oooooooh. BOOOOM! BOOOOM!

BOOOOM! BOOOOM! The booms reverberated in his head. His mind spun. Around him in the tribal circle his captors grinned.

Then suddenly it was midnight and he was in a line at the door saying goodnight to the Governor and Lady Weems. Out the guests all filed, shaking the hands of their hosts, mumbling their thanks for a lovely evening, being directed out by the Aide-de-Camp as precisely as he had directed them in so many hours — or was it days? — ago.

Mel stared into the pouchy eyes of Sir Reginald and from his deepest reserves of charm and expediency summoned a sincere final speech. The Governor listened with appreciation.

"I thought you might be amused," he said, "by one of our typical British evenings."

10

THE next morning, his brain a Fourth of July display containing all the colors of all the wines that he had drunk at Government House, framed in the white of Maud's face as she was carried from the room, Mel received the cable that he had been awaiting since his talk with Fogelstein on the shortwave radio:

FULL GO-AHEAD TONJI PRESS JUNKET AND WORLD-PREEM MID-AUGUST COINCIDING ARRIVAL CONTEST WINNERS STOP ASSUME COOPERATION ISLAND BIGGIES STOP BLUESTONE MOVING SOONEST STUDIOWISE REGARDS
FOGELSTEIN
WORLDPREEM BLUESTONE

"What's the date today?" he asked Sally as they sat on Millie Hawkes's verandah drinking coffee so thick with caffeine as to be almost hallucinatory.

"July twelfth — I think," she said, trying to talk above the noise of the cork game, which continued to resound in her head. She glanced at the cable. "What's the Bluestone part?" she asked.

"Harvey Bluestone," Mel said. "One of the p.a.'s — press agents — at Titan Pictures. Nervous little guy, but good at this kind of thing. He once took a dozen Eskimos across America by train to promote a crappy picture called 'Ugzak of the Frozen North,' or some damn thing. They stopped every day for personal appearances in towns like Greensboro. The railroad company finally threw them off the train in Pocatello Falls because they smelled too bad. Anyway, Harvey will go to work on the junket now and bring the columnists out next month."

"And who are the biggies?"

"Ordinarily they're the heads of the different movie companies. You'll see in 'Variety' that some guy 'jetted to the Coast to huddle with biggies.' But there's only one biggie here, and that's Sir Reginald, and Cy may have blown the whole ball game last night."

"Your cork game needs work, too," Sally said. "And so does Maud. Cy could have killed her with those martinis."

"It'll take more than that," Mel said. "My hunch is that we're okay with Sir Reggie — he's more interested in tourists than he is in Maud. It's just a question of getting permission from him, but I don't know if I can face those piggy little eyes so soon again."

"Your own don't look too good this morning. See him now and you'll be about even."

Mel went to his room, put pen to paper — the pen a quivering reed, the paper a trembling leaf — and began to write.

Your Excellency:

I realize that no apology of mine could possibly make up for the most unfortunate mishap which befell Lady Maud during last night's otherwise delightful festivities. I can only assure you that it was an evening which Miss Merrill and I will never forget. There remains only the question of describing to you the plan by which I hope to make your lovely islands more widely known to tourists in my own country, and perhaps if I could impose on a few moments of your valuable time in the next day or two . . .

Walking into town to post the letter, he stopped to watch the three Danes working on their balsa raft. "Hey!" he called to Karl Ullstrad, who was stitching a piece of canvas which he evidently thought would catch enough wind to blow them across half of the Pacific. "When are you guys leaving for Peru?"

The old man counted on his fingers. "About five weeks," he said.

"About the middle of August?"

"Middle of August. Full moon. Goddam right."

"Hmm," Mel said, mostly to himself. "I'll get back to you," he called to the old Dane.

In town he bought a can of Nescafé, a bottle of aspirin, and a notebook for keeping a journal. Not to maintain a daily account of what he was doing, along with letters and clippings and other relevant scraps, was to invite certain failure. The difference between a good press agent and a fair one, he knew from experience, was to keep watch over every detail and to remember that no detail was too small to be handled properly when its proper time came along.

The notebook began to fill up rapidly. Fogelstein's cable was pasted on Page 1, as if to invoke a blessing on the enterprise, and other entries followed from day to day.

JULY 14 — Summoned to interview with Sir Reggie. Inquired after Maud. Sir R. assured me she was "quite out of the woods — in point of fact, she's dead keen to get another of those drinks from that photographer chap." I said Cy was in the villages taking pictures for several weeks. He said Maud would find him wherever he is — which is more than I'll be able to do. Told Sir R. about the press junket and world premiere and how reporters would come and send stories back to the U.S., etc. He said that was just the kind of thing he'd been "trying to get that blithering ass Foote to do for several years" and that he would go along with any scheme. Said he'd even mention it in his speech on Cession Day — whatever the hell that is — and tell any interested "natives" to get in touch with me. Cased the town on the way back to Millie's. Deadsville for the junketing scribes. Pep it up. Discothèque? Rock 'n' roll?

JULY 15 — Learned that the biweekly plane arrives August 17. Also cruise ship "Tonalela." Danes sailing at approxi-

mately the same time. A package there. Sent cable to Fogelstein:

COMPLETE BIGGIE OKAY STOP SUGGEST JUNKET ARRIVE
AUGUST 15 VIA TRANS-SKY TIE-IN STOP GET SEATS FOR
WINNING COUPLE ON COMMERCIAL PLANE DUE AUGUST
17 STOP WORLDPREEM FOLLOWS ON MOONA-MOONA
ISLAND STOP BEAUCOUP PACKAGES STOP IMPORTANT
BRING MOONA MARONE ALONG STOP REGARDS PARKER

JULY 16 — Plane in today with letter from Harvey Bluestone (pasted below):

DEAR MEL:
First of all, the "Win-an-Island" contest is off to a smash start.
Good coverage in the dailies, entry blanks in the supermarkets,
Life, Look, Post, etc. Every day I go over to that crazy office of
yours to check the mail — when that Ursula broad will condescend
to let me look — and the replies are pouring in. Seems that everyone wants to win an island. Anyway, we should be able to pick
a winner by August 1. I assume you'd prefer a lovable middle-
aged couple from the Midwest for the warm-human-values angle.
I'm eager to get pictures from Cy to plant in the dailies — hope
he's not too busy at his other occupation.
Meanwhile I'll make tentative plans for the junket pending
your final O.K. Moona Marone is definitely set to come along —
says she'll participate in any "reasonably dignified" project that
will further her "career." Which, incidentally, will need a lot of
furthering — I saw a rough cut of "Desert Island for Two" last
night and it's Dog City. Not that it matters for your purposes. As
for what is "reasonably dignified" for Moona Marone, you can
permit yourself your usual wide latitude. She was caught in a
reasonably undignified fracas the other night at Chasen's between two shack-up rivals, but we managed to hush it presswise.
As for the journalists to be brought along, I think I dig what
you want. You and I have been through plenty of these wars, old
buddy. Remember "Secret of the Aztecs" — the trouble we had
getting out of that goddam pyramid in Guatemala? Question:
could you stand having Bobbie Baxter? Her "Bobbie Sez" column
is very hot right now — syndicated in 142 papers. She just got

back from leading an all-girl safari and her stories went over as big as Xerox. Terrible "dark continent" stuff: "There I was all alone, without a friend in the veldt, and there was this crazy cheetah-type bounding toward me, and it wasn't Baby Jane Holzer either." I'm willing to take the risk, but how are you fixed for Miltowns?

Best,
HARV

JULY 17 — Cy came in with a lot of photographs that he's been taking on Moona-Moona. Every day he and Simeon go out there with the two bimboes and some native carpenters and they've got the bungalow half built — the front half, enough to photograph, thatched roof and all. Even the palm tree looks as if it's going to live, though Cy says, "It's not any tropical paradise yet, you can bet your ass." Which I am not about to bet. But the pictures look romantic as hell. I'm captioning them and getting them off to Harvey on tomorrow's plane. With those two honeys leaning against the bungalow we'll make half the newspapers in the good old sex-crazed U.S.A.

JULY 19 — National holiday. Cession Day. Evidently the grandfather of the present chief, Malalonga I, got tired of all the tribal strife that made it impossible to govern the islands, so he asked the British to take over, which they willingly did, and Tonji was ceded to Queen Victoria in 1879. The present chief, Malalonga III, is a more progressive type. From what I hear, he'd like to throw the rascals out. I see his point — it was a damn strange holiday, everybody celebrating the loss of his liberty. A reverse Fourth of July. But they all seemed to enjoy it, even the speeches. Sir Reggie looked like some character in "Pinafore" in his ceremonial costume and white plumed hat, and his speech was full of oratorical crud, but he did make a point of announcing my "scheme" and urging the people to cooperate.

I wonder how Sally's getting on. She went out into the "field" three days ago with a tape recorder and a lot of notebooks. Eager to go it alone and get started in the Margaret Mead business. Should I worry about her? Go looking for her? The truth is, I guess, I miss her.

JULY 20 — Article in the "Tonji Times" about the Cession Day ceremonies and Sir Reggie's speech:

Nature lent her favour yesterday to the traditional rites of Cession Day. Blue skies and soft breezes greeted the joyful crowds who flocked to Albert Parade to celebrate the unique partnership that has joined the people of Tonji and the people of Great Britain for almost a century of friendship and growth.

Bands played a medley of songs including "Rule, Britannia!" and Tonji's hymn to the lagoon god, and, as in the past, the afternoon was climaxed by the presentation of the royal Tonjian mace to Sir Reginald Weems by Chief Malalonga III, symbolic of the act by which his grandfather ceded the islands in 1879 to Her Majesty's special representative, Sir John Fuddington-Smythe. Sir Reginald received the mace with his customary graciousness and in his formal address took cognizance of the "warm fraternal bonds which, for generation upon generation, have joined our two peoples in mutual affection and respect."

Only in one regard did His Excellency depart from the usual amenities of a Cession Day speech, and that was his announcement of "a most propitious scheme which has been laid on for the middle of August by our American cousins and which the Government believe will greatly strengthen the economy and renown of the Tonji Islands." Pointing out that production of copra is down by 18 per cent and that the outlook for sago and vanilla "does not warrant optimism," Sir Reginald asserted that the best hope of fiscal soundness "ultimately lies in the development of a thriving tourist industry."

To promote this industry, he said that the Government have consented to allow the world premiere of a new American film, "Desert Island for Two," to be held here next month, in connection with a raffle being conducted in the United States, and that a group of American journalists would fly to Tonji especially to write stories and "take films for the telly." He elaborated on the many opportunities open to the Tonjian people to take part in the week-long festivities and pageants, urging those interested to

call upon Mr. Melville Parker at 135 Victoria Street, which, he
added with a characteristic chuckle, "is better known, I believe,
as Mrs. Hawkes's establishment."

The speech was followed by light snacks and other refreshments, and the impressive ceremony formally concluded with the
singing of "God Save the Queen" by the girls of Kitchener Elementary School.

JULY 21 — Sir Reggie's speech seems to have irritated a few
people, especially "Old Settler" (see column pasted below).
Who is Old Settler? Not too old to punch out some lively
copy. He'll ruin me yet. How can I get to him? Take him to
lunch and get him oiled? If this were Hollywood . . . But
it's not, that's for damn sure.

BETRAYING A TRUST
By Old Settler

If irony is your dish, you had a full meal of it in the Cession
Day speech of Sir Reginald Weems. Here was a sacred event held
to commemorate, to solemnize once again, the proud moment
when the people of Tonji entrusted their dreams and their desti-
nies to Great Britain for safekeeping. Theirs was the faith of an
innocent child; ours was the pledge and the promise.

For more than eight decades we have kept that pledge with
honour. No tawdry commercial tricks have been played upon the
guileless children of nature who make Tonji one of the last places
on earth untarnished by the greed of Western man. Yet Sir
Reginald chose the hallowed occasion of Cession Day to an-
nounce that a thundering herd of Hollywood journalists, undoubtedly in their usual state of intoxication, will descend on our
placid islands to take part in a week-long orgy of publicity stunts
designed to lure American tourists to Tonji. One does not need to
be a mind-reader to know what sort of claptrap they will write
for their newspapers and what kind of vulgar pictures they will
take to satisfy the erotic needs of the American magazine reader.

As for the "honour" of being selected for the world premiere of
a film called "Desert Island for Two," it is difficult to conceive of
a more dubious privilege. One has seen enough Hollywood films
purportedly set in the Polynesian Islands to know that they are
sheerest balderdash, their sole intent being to display a bevy of

blonde girls clad in grass skirts of the minimum length allowed under the obscenity laws of the United States.

Is this the sort of publicity that one wants for Tonji? Is this the image that we would present to the outside world? I say "NO!" There come periodic times in the life of every colony when the rulers must re-examine their moral obligations to the ruled. One of those times most assuredly is now. Old Settler says to Mr. Parker: pack your valise and go back to Hollywood where you belong!

JULY 22 — Despite Old Settler's column, the natives aren't exactly unwilling to get a piece of the action. All day yesterday and today they've been trickling in to see what's in it for them. Luckily, the ones who are crying the blues about business being slow are the saloon-keepers along the waterfront. They want advice on how to get fixed up "like we see in the Hollywood movies and the Life magazine." Millie Hawkes wants to have the swingingest place in town, needless to say, and if her jukebox arrives she ought to get her wish. I only hope some new records come with it. I'm getting damn tired of hearing "I'll Never Smile Again" on that beat-up old phonograph. There's a little cottage out in her back yard that we could use for a discothèque. But the other dives need live entertainment — native stuff, real drums, grass skirts, the old "pelvic thrust," as the highbrow dance critics call it in the U.S., except that I never saw any till I came out here. Maybe I went to the wrong ballets — I don't remember any pelvic thrust in "Swan Lake" and "Les Sylphides," where the Willies keep coming in from the wings in long underwear.

The trouble is, all the best dives are right next to the churches, and I've had a few calls already from ministers and missionaries threatening me with fire and brimstone. Like the most hip place on the whole street, "Jerry's Authentic South Sea Emporium," is alongside the First Baptist Church, and both Jerry and the Rev. Elmer Bloodgood were in today with salvation on their minds. Jerry wants to save his business and the Rev. Bloodgood wants to save souls, mostly mine. He gave me pause, I must admit. The way he described Hell was the scariest thing I've heard since I listened to "Inner Sanctum" as a kid. He was preaching so loud about sin that Millie came in and chased him out with a broom. She said, "Reverend, if you keep talking that kind of crap you're gonna end up spoiling religion."

JULY 23 — Same as yesterday: one hotelkeeper, two owners of dives (Dirty Eddie's and Club Gauguin), five bimboes wanting to be "Miss Tonji" or "Miss Hibiscus" or "Miss Breadfruit" or Miss Anything that I might dream up (they all had excellent credentials, too — about 38-24-37), and one minister, Methodist. A testy column by Old Settler noting the "veritable parade of undesirable types who have been seen entering Mr. Parker's so-called office since His Excellency's most regrettable announcement on Cession Day." How does he know? Is he keeping watch out there? Or does he have someone feeding him these items?

JULY 24 — Letters in the newspaper by both ministers complaining about being called "undesirable types." I rather like the Rev. Bloodgood's phrasing.

TO THE EDITOR:
SIR: For a man of the cloth to be described in the public press as an "undesirable type" is surely inconsistent with the standards of honourable journalism, not to mention the laws of libel. Has your newspaper so mislaid its senses as to forget that in the eyes of God there is, of course, no such thing as an undesirable type? Oh sinful man! Wilt thou cast the first stone?
There are, however, undesirable values, and if my esteemed Methodist brother, Rev. Boggs, and I have erred by visiting Mr. Parker in an attempt to forestall the undesirable values which he intends to impose on Tonji, then we plead guilty! Yes! We are guilty of trying to preserve a wholesome abode for Christ's flock. We are guilty of believing that pagan revels and heathen entertainments should not be helped to gain an even stronger foothold among these children of nature, but, rather, should be eradicated with all the wrath of a righteous Jehovah. Is this heresy? Editor, heal thyself!

> Very truly yours,
> REV. ELMER BLOODGOOD,
> First Baptist Church

So I've got the church against me as well as the press. And
Denis. And what about Chief Malalonga? If there's one thing
I don't need it's a native uprising. Oh hell, I've seen too many
movies. Natives don't uprise except in B movies where some
Susan Hayward type is on safari and she hears drums throbbing in the night. Which reminds me: where's Sally? She'd
know the mood of the people. She wanted a week to live
among them and size them up for me. And get some tape
recordings — which I ought to be sending off for the deejays.
The week is up. Shouldn't she be back?

11

"I HEARD drums throbbing in the night," Sally said to Denis, explaining how it had all begun. "I sat up in bed and listened, and it sounded as if the men of the village were gathering down by the lagoon. The drums got louder and more — you know — insistent, and then the men began to sing. It was an eerie melody, more mournful than the usual Polynesian tune, and it built to a long high climax, faster and faster, until it ended with a tremendous shout. Funny, it had the quality of — well, sort of a war cry."

"Could you catch any of the words?" Denis asked.

"I heard 'tiki,' and I heard 'Hito,' who I think is the fishing god — at least it is in Tahiti . . ."

"Here, too," Denis said.

"And then I heard, over and over again, 'Kula-ha'i,' which of course is the name of Mel's island — only he's changing it to Moona-Moona, as I guess you know, because of Moona Marone."

"Where does someone get a name like Moona Marone?"

"From the executive vice president in charge of names at Titan Pictures. I asked Mel. He said she was born Gertrude Fossenkemper in Tulsa, Oklahoma."

"Go on about the song."

"Well, the name turned into a chant, strung out very long, like this: 'Kula-ha'i-i-i-i.'" She cupped her hands and wailed. "I couldn't get back to sleep for a long time, thinking about it — honestly, it was so *strange* — and in the morning at breakfast I asked what it was. That's when things began to pop. The men looked very dark and started to jabber and they pointed to me — I guess I wasn't supposed to hear it, but the wind was just right and it was such a soft evening — and then several men got up and came over toward me, looking very angry, and several others tried to hold them back, and the angry ones were getting nearer and nearer, and the meanest-looking of them all was about to grab me, and then . . ."

"Then?"

"You came along. I was never so glad to see anybody in my whole life. It was just like a fairy tale: rescued by the prince. You quieted the wicked ogres, threw my bicycle into your jeep, and drove me off to your castle."

They were sitting in Denis's thatched bungalow, looking across the white beach and the bright blue Pacific beyond. The room was full of books and magazines, and Denis had put an Ella Fitzgerald record on the phonograph. "I like your castle," she said. "It's like a dream, too — still part of the fairy tale."

"I'm glad you do. It's my only home — I've cut all my ties to wet old England."

"Denis?" she asked. It was the first time she had called him that.

"Hm?"

"How did you happen to be right there? I mean, in that particular village at that particular time?"

"You don't think I'd let you go out all alone among the savages, do you? I know you're a graduate in anthropology, but you've never met the subject except in a book — unless you count Dr. Kalbfleisch at the Governor's dinner last week."

"I don't," Sally said. "I hope he never finds his old eighteen-foot phallus. But Denis," Sally went on, and then paused.

"Yes, Sally?"

"I've been out in the villages a week. And yet the one day when I was in trouble was the day you came to find me."

"The first day," Denis said, "you bicycled to that village

about ten miles down the coast. Lolua. They greeted you warmly and you stayed there three days and took a lot of notes. No trouble. Then you crossed the island to that pretty little village at the end of a cove. Rongatela. Made some tape recordings of their songs. Then you went up into the hills and . . ."

"Were you watching my every move?" Sally asked. "That makes me feel like an awful fool."

"No, of course not. Once a day I'd drive out in your direction and ask one of my friends in the villages how you were getting along, and they said fine, and maybe they'd tell me a little bit about what you were doing, and then I'd come back to town. Maybe I should have gone and asked *you*, but I wanted to respect your first plunge at independent research. Were you lonely?"

"I think I expected to be," Sally said, "but I wasn't. I've never met people with such natural hospitality."

"It's in the Polynesian character," Denis said. "Any stranger who wants to stop is their honored guest. And by the way, if any of them ever come to New York — is that where you live?"

"Not far away — a little town called Locust Valley."

"Well, if any of them ever come to Locust Valley, they'll expect the same of you. Full honors."

"I'll remember. Did they . . . what did they say about me?"

"They liked you. They hoped you'd come back and see them again. And they said you were very serious. One old chief said you looked as if you wanted to change the whole world, though he didn't see what was the matter with it now."

"He *didn't?* Why, the schools need improving, there's sickness, there's poverty, there's dirt, there's . . ."

"Easy, easy," Denis said, gently. "There's laughter, too. Did you ever hear so much laughter? Do they laugh like that in Locust Valley?"

"They certainly don't," Sally said. "I'll try to remember that, but it'll be hard. I'm starting from a totally opposite position. It's the curse of modern American youth — if I'm still youth. Half of America is now under twenty-one, and I may be over the hill."

"You're youth," Denis said, "and you're beauty. But what's this curse you're talking about?"

"We're activists."

"Ac-ti-vists?"

"Yes. America's full of that kind of jargon nowadays. Like, nothing just works any more — it's got to be viable. Nobody's poor — they're disadvantaged. Nobody's dumb — they're underachievers. Nobody's . . ."

"Stop!" Denis said. "Is this the mother tongue that we sent forth from England a mere three centuries ago?"

"You'd never know it," Sally said. "Anyway, we activists feel driven to take action against all the social ills that earlier generations have created by *in*action."

"That's odd. I get the impression from your magazines that modern American youth doesn't do anything but dance the frug, sleep together, get pregnant, ride motorcycles, play the guitar, quit college and take LSD."

"It's because our magazines need to invent a new crisis every week, so they take any alarming tendency and blow it into a trend. You can picture the headlines: 'God Is Dead on Campus,' 'Our Unwed High School Mothers,' 'Marijuana in Elementary School,' 'Kindergarten Dropouts,' 'Adultery in the Suburbs,' 'You and the Pill,' 'Why Your Doctor Is No Longer Respected,' 'Hospitals in Chaos' . . . That takes care of education, sex, dope, teen-agers and medicine. Then there's one long article on the searching reappraisal of the Catholic Church from within, one on the growing alienation of Protestants from their faith, and one on the seeds of discontent in presentday Judaism, and then . . ."

"The whole cycle starts again?"

"Right. Almost the identical articles. Anything that's going right in America you never read about."

"You mean 'Good news is no news'?"

"That's what I mean — and a lot more briefly. I'm sorry I got so wound up. But honestly, I don't know anybody who's just sitting around a swimming pool this summer, the way they used to. I hardly even know anybody who's in the United States. My friends are scattered from the Peace Corps in Zambia to the tenements of Caracas. We're on the move and we're active. My being here in Tonji wouldn't strike most Americans as unusual — except Daddy, of course. He thinks I'm insane. And I don't mean I don't appreciate *your* keeping an eye on me. That was sweet of you."

"Even Margaret Mead probably needed some watching over in the first week or two," Denis said. "But don't hug your activism so tightly that you rob us of the pleasure of protecting you. That's where I'm an activist."

"I won't. I still believe in fairy tales."

"But tell me: is there some law that says you activists have to function outside the United States?"

"No," Sally said, "and that really bugs Daddy, too. If we *do* work in the United States we tend to work in the Deep South (the civil-rights beat) or in states like West Virginia (the poverty beat). They're the glamour areas, though heaven knows the *work* isn't glamorous. Otherwise we go abroad. It feeds our sense of mission to help another underdeveloped country instead of our own underdeveloped country, though there's as much poverty work to be done in *New* London as in London."

"And how about the poor rich of Locust Valley?" Denis said.

"They'll have to help themselves," Sally said. "In many ways they're in worse shape than the man who lives in a hut in Swaziland, but at least they've got enough money to pay for their psychiatrist and their divorces and their tranquilizers and all the other instant remedies for their long-range troubles, which never turn out to be remedies at all."

"Then your parents," Denis asked, "are they? . . . I mean . . ."

"No, they're happily married, and Daddy loves his work — he's an investment counselor — and they both really believe that their way of life is still, you know . . ."

"Viable," Denis said. Sally laughed.

Denis got up and opened the screen door and picked two

bananas from a bunch that was hanging just outside. "Second breakfast," he said, handing one to Sally. "So you're rebelling against all that?"

"Oh, I'm no screaming liberal," Sally said. "I suppose it's even possible that I'll marry the boy next door, who's a junior vice president in some business, and we'll buy a house with a swimming pool and belong to a country club and bring up our children just the way we were brought up."

"But the boy next door won't be next door," Denis said. "He'll be in Zambia."

"And he won't be in business," Sally said. "The boys in my generation look down on business. Talent scouts from all the corporations are beating the bushes to find their future junior vice presidents."

"And you wouldn't marry him anyway," Denis said. "Or is there such a boy?"

"No," Sally said. "There isn't. And I don't *think* I'd marry him, though I suppose you never can tell what you'll do when he comes along, this Ivy League knight with his tweed jacket and lovable old pipe. But I *know* I wouldn't send my children to exclusive schools — the kind that only take boys and girls from 'nice' families — or make them go to those terrible dances that were such agony for me. Or any of that stuff. So I guess I'm at least a partial rebel."

"You're a very honest rebel," Denis said, "which not many rebels are. I mean, you're fair to your past. You appreciate what it did for you — good education and everything — and you're not trying to pull down the whole temple. You just want to build a better one."

"And maybe I won't," Sally said. "But anyway that's why I don't think it's so bad, all this running off to work in foreign countries. Because when we *do* come home to America we'll be broader than any other generation, and then maybe we *will* teach in the schools of Harlem and work in the slums of New London. Though I must say that what I'm doing here in Tonji — so far — is not my idea of . . ."

"Why do you say 'so far'?" Denis asked.

"Because when this crazy job is over I'd like to stay and do some social work that *is* important."

"Which might be," Denis said, "to undo the work that Mel is about to do — with your help." The smile went out of his eyes. Goodness, how serious he looks, Sally thought. Then the smile came slowly back. "I should qualify that," he said. "You are a mere lieutenant in Mel Parker's flying circus. He's the brains and you're the research. You're only playing Dr. Watson to his Sherlock Holmes."

"Dr. Watson never quite knew what was going on, did he?" Sally asked.

"Not that I can remember," Denis said.

"Then I'm Dr. Watson."

"Or are you his Galatea? Or his Trilby? The innocent pawn being bent to the will of a cunning master?"

"No, I'm Dr. Watson," Sally said. "Dumb old Watson. I guess you think I'm pretty stupid to get caught up in this thing."

"I'm sure you had a good reason," Denis said, "though I'd like to hear *how* you got caught up in it. Hey! How about a swim? You can tell me while we're cooling off in the lagoon. And I'll take you skin-diving — you won't believe the colors of the fish. Got a bathing suit?"

"Yes, but . . . aren't you going to your office today? We've wasted most of the morning already."

"No, it's a holiday."

"Again? What holiday is it?"

"The first day that you came to my house," Denis said. "Besides, I've got so many helpers now that I can relax. My job is to nurture the delicate flower of tourism, and it's been taken over by Sir Reggie and Mel Parker and God knows how many people in Hollywood, so who needs me?" He paused as if to listen to his own question. "I'll tell you who needs me," he went on, finally. "The people of Tonji. As their director of tourism I have a sacred duty to keep hordes of tourists from landing on these shores."

Sally looked to see if he was joking. He wasn't. "What have you got in mind?"

"Today, nothing," Denis said. "It's a holiday, remember? Put on your bathing suit and let's go. The guest room is through that door. Your towel is in the bathroom on the right and there's a pair of sneakers in the closet so you won't step on any live coral."

"You almost sound as if you've been expecting me," Sally said.

"I think maybe I have," Denis said.

It was midafternoon when they got back to the house. They had taken a long swim in the lagoon. And they had rowed out to the reef and put on snorkels and looked at fish so dazzling in color, so infinite in the variety of their stripes, that Sally thought she must be looking through some child's kaleidoscope instead of ordinary glass. As Denis had predicted, she literally couldn't believe it.

Then they had sat in the boat, eating the lunch and drinking the rum punches that Denis had packed and telling each other of the events that had brought them to Tonji. Sally described the four years spent at Pembleton in solemn pursuit of truth and hearing the evangelical call of social reform — years which now seemed to her, afloat in the middle of the blue Pacific, gray and remote, almost irrelevant. Then she told Denis about her interview with Mel Parker at the office of Paradise Unlimited. That visit, at the time, had seemed wholly unreal, a freakish turning off from her proper road. Yet here she really was, and the paradise really was unlimited.

Denis recalled his years at Cambridge and in London, years which pointed to a satisfying life in the best cultural circles of his country. But he had also turned off the main road — not, however, by chance, Sally saw, as she had, but by decision. He had run away to paradise by cool resolve; she had stumbled into it by accident; and Mel created paradise wherever he and his typewriter happened to be — and he was here now, fabricating a desert island to fit the popular dream. Instant South Seas. They had come by three different approaches — the escaper, the reformer and the conjuror — but they had all landed in the same net, their lives tangled together, and they would not all get out as easily.

Denis explained that he had left London because he couldn't stand the clamorous voices of advertising and publicity, pressing their artificial claims at every turn. And Mel, a living synonym for publicity, had sneered at Denis for being an escapist. Could Mel have been right about that? Certainly it *was* easier to run away from something than to run towards something. She hoped that she at least was running, however skittishly, towards a valid goal.

The question nagged her as she took a shower and changed back into her clothes. Denis's guest room, like the rest of his house, with its books and pictures, its tranquillity, its idyllic views past bougainvillea blossoms and banana trees and rustling palms to the Pacific, was an adman's vision of total retreat from the modern world and its pressures. Even the ocean was tamed before it reached the shore, breaking its power on the reef, so that it lapped up onto the sand, barely audible, instead of crashing in huge breakers that hinted of hurricanes and high seas.

"Denis, did it bother you," she asked, coming back into the living room, "what Mel said last week about being an escapist — you know, running away?"

He watched her cross the room. "Crikey, you look great," he said. "Positively Polynesian — I mean the bare feet and the tan and the long wet black hair. All you need is a flower in it. And the beautiful legs. You ought to spend more days in the lagoon and less time on research."

"But Mel is paying me for research," Sally said, "and I'm going to report in to the boss before this day is over. Otherwise I'll go soft in the head. I'm so muddled already that I hardly know what's real and what isn't — or what's important."

"Don't go to Mel looking for any answers on reality," Denis said. "And don't expect any quick verdict here in the islands on what's important. It can be deceptive."

"I guess it can. My sense of time is all fuzzy."

"It'll straighten out in a month or two," Denis said. "First there's the exhilaration of actually *being* in the South Seas. It's like a drunken jag. Then there's the indolence. That's the hardest phase because it has an element of boredom: you don't think you can stand how little seems to be going on. A lot of people never get over it and they go back home. But if you *do* get over it, you want to stay forever."

"Like you," Sally said.

"Like me. I guess you think *I'm* going soft in the head, or that I will. My friends in England thought I would, and you and Mel have every reason to feel that I'm a deserter from twentieth-century battles that I don't have the stomach to fight."

"Oh, I never said . . ."

"But we all have our own battlefields," Denis went on, "and *I* don't think I've run away from the field of honor. On the contrary, the shooting is just about to begin."

"And what if you lose?" Sally asked.

"I'll antagonize the Government . . . get known as a sorehead . . . probably get kicked out."

"They could do that? Make you leave?"

"Sir Reggie would find a way. He doesn't like opposition."

"And you'd risk that?" Sally asked. "You'd be willing to give up this house and everything, just to defend the status quo? You must be a raging conservative."

"Oh but I'm not," Denis said. "I'm far more liberal than Sir Reggie and all the other pompous asses who are running this place — you met some of the choice ones at dinner last week. I'm all for the end of the Empire. I'm all for the Tonjians having self-government, if they want it — and they soon will. But when that time comes I want them to have islands that are worth self-governing. I want to cede back to them essentially the same Tonji that they ceded to us, not a honky-tonk resort full of neon lights and motels and bowling alleys. If that makes me a conservative it's because I want to conserve the best of what's already here."

"Not make it better?" Sally asked. "Is it perfect now?"

"Of course it's not perfect," Denis snapped, "but it's better than it will be when it's been officially improved. Beware the Greeks bearing improvements — and you Americans are the modern Greeks, planting your little colonies of superior knowledge on foreign soil."

"Denis, that's un*fair!*"

"It's unfair to you personally, and I apologize to you personally, because your motives are pure. You really do think you can make Tonji a better place, and if you stay here you will. But in general I'll stick with what I said. Wherever Americans go they feel a compulsion to change what they find. They can't wait to speed up the rhythm of life and introduce the latest technology, though in America itself this has hardly beautified the landscape or led to spiritual health."

"That's certainly true," Sally admitted. "But you're awfully bitter about it."

"Not bitter, really," Denis said. "It's just that sometimes the best way to help a country is to keep things from getting any worse. Does that still make me a conservative?"

"Maybe. Or maybe an idealist."

"A negative idealist," Denis said. "But remember, I've lived with these people for five years. I know them very well, including Chief Malalonga, and my commitment is to them. I haven't run away from England just to be committed to nothing. And I haven't run away just to go soft in the head. I'm working on all sorts of projects that may have some value when I get them written up. Those journals over there, for instance . . ."

"I was going to ask you about them," Sally said.

"They're records of the early Polynesian migrations, and I think I'm on to some new clues about their routes and their language."

"And how about those ornithology books?"

"Another of my serious hobbies," Denis said. "I'm trying to see if the flight patterns of certain birds can . . . But that's not the point. The point is, I've got a five-year equity here — five years in which I've been getting ready, without realizing

it, for the Battle of Kula-ha'i. Or Moona-Moona, if you
prefer."

"I don't prefer."

"Good."

"And am I going to be caught in the middle?" Sally asked,
her voice suddenly apprehensive. "I like you, Denis. This has
been one of the nicest days I've ever spent. But I'm also fond
of Mel, and he *did* bring me out here, and I'm learning a lot
that I never learned at college. He's a nut, but I don't think
there's anything devious about him."

"I don't either," Denis said. "And I like him, too — it's hard
not to like him. That's what makes him so dangerous. He has
this boundless assurance that he can make anything happen — or appear to happen — and he can charm everybody
else into helping him perform the trick."

"What do you mean, 'appear to happen'?"

"Mel's a dealer in images. That crazy island, Moona-
Moona, won't really look like a tropical paradise — it's a
scrubby little piece of land. But he's got a lot of paint and a
good photographer, and the pictures that he sends back will
seem authentic. Then he'll invent a lot of activities for the
visiting reporters that have never happened here before and
never will again, and they'll write picturesque stories about
the South Seas 'as it really is.'"

"It's what he calls the managed event," Sally said.

"It's a non-event. It has no life of its own. It only becomes
real later, when pictures of it are seen in newspapers or
newsreels by people who weren't there. But by then the
damage has been done and the image has gone out."

"Is there any defense against it?"

"We'll see," Denis said.

"Are you going to tell me what it is?" Sally asked.

"Sally . . ." Denis began. "This has also been one of the
nicest days *I've* ever spent. Let's not spoil it now. And let's
have another one soon. Will you come again?"

"Yes. Next time you can tell me about the flight patterns of
the birds."

"There may be a moment when you'll have to decide which

side you're on. But now you're on Mel's side and you've been away too long. I saw him in town yesterday and he looked gloomy — not the same bright-eyed boy we used to know. So get your stuff: I'm going to drive you back."

"I hate to leave," Sally said, taking a last look across the beach, now turned pink in the descending sun.

"I hate to have you leave," Denis said. "It just won't be viable around here without you."

12

Come on and dance the Moona-Moona!
Didn't you hear those trade winds blow?
Didn't you hear the palm trees croon a
Rhythm that says "Go, go, man, go!"

When you begin the Moona-Moona,
Brother, you'll never want to stop,
Gotta be crazy as a loon, a
Stick-in-the-mud if you don't hop!

Trade winds blow!
Ev'rybody know
Moona-Moona means "Go, go, go!"

"I'M just spitballing, of course — just trying it on for size," Mel said. He stopped putting words to the tune that Sally's tape recorder was playing on Millie Hawkes's porch and listened to the rest of the melody, borne on the wings of a Tonjian guitar. Then the song ended and out of the machine came the disconnected voices and sounds of village life.

"You said you wanted women talking and children crying and all that," Sally explained.

"I do," Mel said. "It's a nice tape." He listened to it contentedly. "And it was *really* nice seeing you come back last night. I missed you." The tape tinkled with laughter and with the splashing of women in a lagoon. "Are there any more songs?" Mel asked.

"That's the best one," Sally said.

"It's a honey," Mel said. He flicked the tape recorder off. "What's it about really?"

"It's the Tonjians' turtle-calling song. Every month at the third quarter of the moon they go to a certain cove and sing that song, and after a while the turtles begin to arrive and the men catch them, and I guess it's turtle soup for the next week."

"No kidding? You saw that happen?"

Sally nodded.

"Crazy!" Mel said. "Well, I don't blame those turtles. That tune is catchy as hell."

"Do you honestly think you can make it into a dance record?" Sally asked.

"It's a natural. Sally baby, you've earned your salary already." Suddenly he started to laugh.

"What's so funny?"

"They'll have to put a label on the record that says: 'Warning! Do not play in the presence of turtles!' Disk jockeys will have to tell people to turn their radios down or close the windows. Otherwise turtles will be coming up out of the woods in Darien and Princeton and all those places that are zoned for four acres and have a cute little brook running through the property. Turtles will come right up on the patio and ask for a dry martini. They'll crawl out of glass tanks in every pet shop in America. It'll drive 'em buggo. Man, what a promotion!"

"You can't just enjoy it as an amazing fact?"

Mel wasn't listening. "I can see the story now in the 'New York Times': 'RESTLESS TURTLES VEX SUBURBS. Puzzled residents of fashionable Fairfield County expressed surprise yesterday over a virtual plague of turtles assertedly leaving their natural habitats and attempting to enter the houses which comprise this normally quiet, well-to-do community.'"

"Why 'yesterday'?" Sally asked.

"A canon of journalism," Mel replied. "Even if the turtles

have been bothering them for weeks, the residents expressed surprise yesterday."

"And why 'virtual'?"

"Because it isn't a plague until some herpetologist comes and officially declares: 'This is a plague.' And the turtles are 'assertedly' leaving their natural habitats because the reporter hasn't actually *seen* them climbing out of the goddam brook, though he can see them all over their *un*natural habitats like the barbecue terrace and the outdoor breakfast nook. They're the hedging words of a timid profession, scattered in every article like hurdles in a track meet. A reader can't even round the first turn until he has cleared one 'allegedly,' one 'observers generally felt,' and one 'it was learned from usually reliable sources.' "

"So how will you cash in on the turtles that are allegedly vexing the suburbs?" Sally asked.

"Well, I'll let the newspapers keep the story alive for two weeks. There'll be follow-up articles from various sections of the country — they all will have noticed the same virtual plague of turtles yesterday — and the 'Times' science editor will write a Sunday piece speculating on changes in the American ecology 'about which we know all too little,' and then the letters will come in. Some will blame it on the atomic tests, and some will be sure it's sunspots, and some will say it's pesticides and others will claim it's detergent wastes, and somebody will say it's a famous forty-seven-year cycle and he clearly remembers it happening when he was a boy in Scranton, and someone will blame it on the Cubans, and someone else will say it's part of Bobby Kennedy's take-over plan, and some Englishman will write that it reminds him of a similar balls-up in the Orkneys after the inordinately wet spring of 1938. And then I, Mel Parker, will telephone the 'Times' and say that I know precisely what's behind it, and they'll send a reporter around and the next day on Page One you'll see RIDDLE OF TURTLES LINKED TO DANCE FAD, and the subhead will say 'Pop Hit, Moona-Moona, Held to Derive from Islanders' Fishing Chant.' And that, old friend, is promotion."

"Well, I don't think the song is going to have an effect on turtles anywhere except in Polynesia," Sally said. "So there."

"Probably not. But it's fun to think about. Keeps me on my toes. Because for every twenty ideas that won't work, there's one that will. It's just a question of knowing the mentality of American journalists."

"You don't seem to hold them in very high esteem."

"They have certain automatic reflexes, like the 'allegedly' reflex. Or like the automatic questions that reporters ask at press conferences or TV reporters ask at the scene of an accident: 'Just what did you think, Mrs. Gusenberger, when you saw the moving van run over little Marvin?' Take the group that's coming out here in August — I know exactly what kind of story each one will be looking for. I could write their stories myself. In fact, if they're too drunk I will."

"Do you know who's coming yet?" Sally asked.

"Yes, I got a cable from Harvey Bluestone while you were gone. It's a small junket — about twenty — but very influential. Harv and I want to keep it manageable but still reach a big circulation. Like there's Arnold Arkin, the syndicated gossip columnist. If you've ever studied his column, 'Arnie's Alley,' you know . . ."

"I haven't. Pembleton doesn't offer that course."

"You know that Arnie doesn't want gossip in the Winchell sense. He wants anecdotes — vignettes with a little joke at the end, though it's no cinch to find the joke when Arnie gets through with it. So I've been collecting local anecdotes. I've been getting 'em from Millie and Literary Johnny and Fat Lou and . . . oh yes, from Eddie Terhune, who runs Dirty Eddie's, which, by the way, we're changing to Dirty Eddie's à Go-Go. I've cabled Harvey to order a red neon sign that says 'Dirty Eddie's à Go-Go' and bring it out on the plane, and for entertainment I've found these bimboes with the biggest . . ."

"Don't tell me — I want to be surprised," Sally said.

"I was sure as hell surprised," Mel said. "They had the biggest . . ."

"All *right!*"

"Well anyway, Eddie's got anecdotes by the bushel, and altogether I'll have fifty or sixty good ones by the time Arnie arrives. He's got a daily column to fill and I'll feed him about ten a day. Like vitamins."

"How can you be sure that all the anecdotes will be — you know — *ap*plicable?" Sally asked.

"I'll *make* 'em applicable, for Chrissake," Mel said. "I'll apply six or seven to Moona Marone, so her name will keep getting a mention, and I'll hang a couple on Sir Reggie and a few on Chief What's-His-Name and some on Millie, and maybe one on you or Denis."

"Keep me out of this," Sally said. "And Denis, too."

"Okay, okay. But that's how I'm getting ready for Arnie. Then there's Mickey Dolan, the 'Tribune' columnist. You know his style — the soft-hearted tough guy. Or is it the tough-hearted soft guy? I'm arranging some sentimental slop just for him: maidens dancing in the village at sunset."

"But they *never* dance at sunset," Sally protested.

"So does he know Tonji from Flatbush? What's for *him* to be accurate all of a sudden? He'll think it's a scoop because none of the other journalists are there — because I'll arrange for Harvey to take them somewhere else — and Mickey Dolan will feel all good about digging out the hard news while his colleagues are schlepping around the pool . . ."

"Pool? What pool?"

"We're putting one in, over at the El Tropiques."

"With the whole Pacific out there, you're putting in a *pool?*"

"It goes with the tourist image, baby," Mel said. "If the whole place was underwater you'd still have to put in a pool. Why, this could be the biggest tourist paradise in the entire South Seas — even bigger than Waikiki if I play it right." His arm described an enormous arc. "Four or five luxury hotels along that beach . . . a golf course running through the banana plantation up in those hills . . . a casino here in the main street, maybe with a little marina out behind . . . chic stores from Paris and New York . . . the complete package. But every hotel has got to have a pool. That's the key image for the guy reading a travel brochure. He sees himself lolling beside a pool under the whispering palms."

"Yes, but with the whole Pacific . . ."

"So what about all those resort islands in the Caribbean that are grabbing the tourist trade, though nobody ever heard of them till they were 'developed' five years ago? Antigua, Dominica, Grenada, Aruba — dozens of 'em. Aruba shmaruba. They've got the whole Caribbean to swim in, but when the luxury hotels go up they all have a pool."

"Can you build one at the El Tropiques so quickly?" Sally asked.

"Easy," Mel said. "I cabled a company in Houston that caters to the leisure boom — it's called Big-As-All-Outdoors — and offered them the usual plugs, and they're flying a pool out here on August 8 in their own plane. They said they had to go to Moorea anyway to deliver a private airstrip — they make one of Durahemp that can be rolled up at night — to a petroleum king who has a weekend cottage there. It's a prefab pool. All we've got to do is dig a hole, put the pool in it, connect a few pipes, and before you can say 'Jackie Robinson batted .342 in 1947' you'll see Arnie Arkin out there in the pool in his batik surfing shorts, relaxing on a foam cushion and writing his column with a waterproof pen."

"Which you brought along for him."

"Harvey's bringing it. And the foam cushion."

"Honestly, Mel," Sally said, "when I listen to you I think I'm losing my *mind*."

"So to get back to Mickey Dolan . . . he'll think of his rivals schlepping around the pool while he's got an exclusive on the maidens dancing at sunset, and he'll take out his portable typewriter, the one with all the stickers on it from Vietnam and Santo Domingo, and the prose will flow like Mazola."

"What'll it say?" Sally asked.

"It'll say . . . let's see . . ." Mel closed his eyes for a moment and summoned Dolan's muse. Then he began: " 'Suddenly it was there. And you could hardly believe it. You were just an ordinary Joe from Flatbush and you were too old to believe in miracles. You'd seen the posters and the brochures and the travelogues and you knew it wasn't that way. Not really. You'd been around and you knew the ropes. All of them. You weren't going to be suckered by some two-bit dream . . .' "

"Who's 'you'?" Sally asked.

"Him," Mel said. "Mickey Dolan."

"Then why doesn't he say 'I'?"

"He's a 'you' writer. Please don't interrupt — the column is building. 'And then suddenly it was there.' "

"You said that already."

"I know — that's part of the building. 'You were coming around an ordinary bend in an ordinary path to an ordinary village called Bonga-Ronga. Just an unknown stop on the road to nowhere, and you knew that's all it was. You'd slogged along too many roads not to know that they all came to the same end. You weren't born yesterday. And then suddenly it was there. Like maybe you were on pot and you didn't know if it was real. You wanted it to be real and yet you remembered what Tim, who used to sling beer at Moriarty's in Greenpoint, once told you about . . .' "

"Hey, Mel! Can I come up?" a voice called from the sidewalk. It was Literary Johnny. Mel waved him up.

"Mornin', miss," Johnny said to Sally as he climbed the decaying wooden steps. "Funny, it gave me a turn seeing you on that old wicker settee with your long black hair hanging down. Put me in mind of a day I was strolling along here with Joseph Conrad and we looked up on one of these porches and saw a head of hair like that. A stunning beauty she was, or my name's not John Buchan."

"Is it?" Mel asked.

"Named for the writer, lad. There's been ink in my veins since I was a tot. Well, you can imagine that neither of us could get the girl out of our minds, and we just walked along, keeping our thoughts to ourselves. Finally it was I who broke the silence. 'Conrad,' I said, 'a man could give it all up for a piece of stuff like that, don't you think? Never go back home — become sort of an outcast of the islands.' Well sir, he gave me a look that I'll never forget. Seemed to be staring into my very soul, Conrad did — eyes like shining agates, the man had. 'Outcast of the islands,' he repeated to himself. 'By God, Johnny, I'm damned if you don't have something there.' He brooded for the rest of the day, and that night he locked himself in his room over at Almayer's Boarding House — that's gone now, swept away in the hurricane of '32 — and began to write."

"Millie!" Mel called. "A Scotch and soda for Johnny."

"Imagine! Joseph Conrad!" Sally said dreamily. "I just adored 'Lord Jim.'"

"Couldn't stick that one myself, miss," Johnny said. "Symbolism is not my cup of tea."

"Neither is tea," Mel said.

"He should never have left the islands, Conrad," Johnny said. "Told him so myself. 'You've got the islands in the very marrow of your bones,' I told him. 'If you go back to Europe you'll turn all hifalutin'.' But he went — sometimes you just can't tell a writer what's best for him. Now Robert Louis Stevenson, he was different. I remember he said to me once, 'Laddie, your advice has always been good. I wonder if you'd give me your opinion . . .'"

"Johnny, lad," Mel broke in, "I wonder if you'd tell me what you wanted to talk about."

"Ahh, yes. I wanted to know if you've thought of a name for my coffeehouse yet. I'd like to start preparing my act."

"Oh good grief!" Sally said. "What now?"

"You haven't heard, miss?" Johnny said. Sally shook her head. "Mel was telling me about a kind of coffeehouse that the intellectuals are quite keen on in the States, where poets read their material and folk singers sing their songs. He thought I'd get a bit of a run for my money if I sat and reminisced about the titans of literature whom I've had the good fortune to meet in their travels through these storied isles."

"We've rented a little shop from Jack Koo, the tailor," Mel said, taking up the explanation. "Jack's going to Taiwan for six months, and his shop is just right for a literary enterprise of this kind: it's small and dirty and dark. I'm getting Harvey to send out photographs of Stevenson, Nordhoff & Hall, Jack London, Conrad, Melville, Maugham, Rupert Brooke, James Michener — the whole bunch — and we'll tack 'em up on the walls to create the right tone."

"You won't forget to inscribe the pictures, lad?" Johnny asked.

"You think I'd forget *that*?" Mel said, hurt. "I've got most of 'em written already in my notebook. 'To Johnny. Ever in your grateful debt for putting us on the trail of the "Bounty." With deep admiration, Charley Nordhoff and Jim Hall.' Is that about right?"

"It's a lovely sentiment, Mel," Johnny said, dabbing at his eyes.

"We'll scatter some books around and build a little platform at one end where you can sit — a rocking chair would be best — and smoke a pipe and tell your stories. I see you in a slightly frayed alpaca jacket and . . . is it too hot to wear one of those scarf cravats?"

"It's murder, lad, much as I'd like to oblige."

"Well then, a beard."

"Done and done. I had my last shave this morning."

"Good. You'll do two shows — one at nine and one at midnight — and in between a folk singer will come and do some freedom songs."

"Is Harvey bringing the folk singer, too?" Sally asked.

"No, I've found the folk singer," Mel said. "A boy named Tom Falonga with a beautiful voice. Now all I've got to do is write the freedom songs. I'm working on one called 'There's a Great Day A-Comin' When Cession Day Is Gone.' "

"And what about the name of the coffeehouse, lad?" Johnny asked.

"No trouble," Mel said. " 'The White Whale' . . . 'The Bloody Mary' . . . 'The Lord Jim' . . . or how about 'The Narrow Corner': you know, from Maugham's novel?"

"Of course I know," Johnny said. "I remember when Willie finished it he told me he was stuck for a title and I . . ."

"Or 'Club Tusitala,' " Mel went on.

"Why that?" Sally asked.

"It was the Samoans' name for Robert Louis Stevenson. It means 'teller of tales.'"

"I like that, Sally said.

"So do I," Mel agreed, "but it won't turn a buck."

"Speaking of that, lad," Johnny said, "what about the little art gallery next to my coffeehouse?"

"Some progress," Mel said. "I've already found two good artists — a girl named Valoma and a man named Peter Fa'olo. The trouble is they're *too* good — their paintings are quite sophisticated."

"What's wrong with that?" Sally asked.

"Oh, you know how hipped Americans are on finding a primitive. They don't want to come out here and find Gauguin — that's been done. So I tried to get Valoma and Peter to locate the paintings that they did when they were just beginning. Unfortunately, Valoma threw hers away — she was ashamed of them when she got better. Peter was ashamed of his, too, but his mother kept them in a little hut. Twelve altogether."

"What are they like?"

"They're crude and bright and childlike, and they have a certain charm. We'll hang them in the gallery and they'll be discovered within a half-hour by the lady from 'Vogue' — Perdita Fox-Martin, the What-to-Wear-Where Editor — and she'll buy all twelve and tell everybody how 'amusing' they are. Then the rest of the journalists will come charging down and buy a lot of other paintings and wood carvings, and that'll put them in a cultural mood to go next door and hear Johnny's literary memoirs."

"Are you sure the folk singer won't be excessive?" Johnny ventured.

"Not a bit," Mel said. "Folk singing is very 'in,' and we'll need a guitar to go with it. Americans are on a guitar kick, too — you'd think it was a goddam *Stein*way, or something. And of course we've got to have dance: that's also been certified as 'culture.' I've promised to book some authentic

South Sea dancers into 'Jerry's Authentic South Sea Emporium.' "

"Where are you going to get them?" Sally asked. "Fly them in from Grossinger's?"

"You're going to get them," Mel said. "I want the most authentic village dancers in Tonji."

"What do you mean 'most authentic'? If I find 'em in Tonji they're *all* going to be authentic. You drive me crazy."

"*You* know what I mean, for God's sake. A tourist can go into any dive from Frisco to Noumea and see Polynesian girls doing the hula and shaking their tails. They may be authentic but they don't look it. For Jerry's I want a troupe that's *ob*viously authentic — like maybe they could be dramatizing one of their myths or legends. The old migration bit in the double canoes. You know?"

"I know," Sally said. "I'll find an act that's so authentic you won't be able to tell it from the real thing."

Mel looked puzzled. "How?" he asked.

"I'll *get* you the real thing, for God's sake," she said, her voice rising with exasperation. "Oh dear, now you've got me swearing — which I never do. But honestly, Mel, you're so profane."

"Jack London — *there* was a chap who could burn your ears," Johnny remarked. "Why, he'd as soon say . . ."

"Forget it," Mel cut in. "And don't put any of that stuff in your act, either. Americans have been told they're on a culture boom and they're very proud of it, so the whole point of your routine — and the folk singer and the guitarist and the painters and the authentic dance troupe — is to create that atmosphere for the journalists. Then they'll all write stories about how they stumbled into a remote art colony of unsuspected richness and depth, which is the thing that gave Bali such a shot-in-the-arm in the 'thirties, touristwise. So don't hesitate to lay it on thick about literary influences and Rupert Brooke's flawed vision and all that jazz."

"Leave it to me, lad," Johnny said. "I'll trace Michener to Robert Dean Frisbie . . . and Maugham to Louis Becke. Or vice versa."

"Perfect," Mel said. "None of 'em will have heard of Frisbie or Becke. It'll give class to your monologue."

"Can't have too much of that, my boy," Johnny said. "I think I'll nip off now and run up a few notes. Thanks for the whiskey." He trotted down the steps.

"And I'm going to type up *my* notes," Sally said. "I want to get them onto paper while they're still fresh. I'll make a copy for you — you're bound to find plenty of authentic ideas in them. Then next week I'll go out and line up your dance act. I saw some good dancers in a village called Tongali and the chief was very friendly, so if you tell me the working conditions I can probably make a deal."

"Great," Mel said. "I'm going to edit this tape of yours and get it off to Buddy Eleganto at Titan on Thursday's plane. But I'll want you here when the furniture and appliances arrive so we can fix up the bungalow out on Moona-Moona. I need your feminine touch to make it cozy for the new owners."

"When's the stuff coming?"

"It was shipped on the 'Koala Bear,' bound for Sydney and due here any day now. It damn well *better* get here any day now. Time is short and I've got a million things to do, not even counting the 'Queen of Tonji' festival."

"Queen of . . . ?"

"This is Tuesday the twenty-sixth already — if it comes on Friday that only leaves two weeks."

"It'll come," Sally said. She gave him a reassuring pat on the shoulder and started to go inside when she saw Denis walking along the sidewalk with a white-haired old man. He saw her and waved.

"Come on down a minute," Denis called. "I'd like you to meet a friend of mine. You too, Mel." They both came down to the peeling white fence and shook the bony hand that the old man extended.

Denis said: "I'd like you to meet Mr. Quaritch. This is Miss Merrill and Mr. Parker."

"How d'you do?" Quaritch said. "One's been wanting to meet you, and as Denis and I were just passing by . . ."

"Pleasure's ours," Mel said, genially.

"Mr. Quaritch," Denis explained, "is the owner and editor — and I should say founder, fifty years ago — of the 'Tonji Times,' your good companion at breakfast every morning."

"Which is more than Millie's breakfast is," Mel said. He burped involuntarily. "It's a mighty good little paper, sir."

"One tries to fight the good fight," Quaritch said. "Be the conscience of the colony and all that."

"I must say one of your writers fights a *very* good fight," Mel said. "I mean the columnist who signs himself 'Old Settler.' That piece this morning about Section 37A of the Land Act gave me a real scare — made it sound as if the Government acted illegally in leasing Kula-ha'i to us. Of course there's nothing to that . . . is there?"

"I shouldn't wonder," Quaritch said.

"If there isn't?" Mel asked.

"If there is."

"Good God!" Mel said. "But I don't suppose they ever see Old Settler's column in London. I mean, it would take the Colonial Office six months to learn of any irregularity through normal channels."

"Normally I daresay it would," Quaritch replied. "But Old Settler sends all his columns by airmail every fortnight to the Deputy Under Secretary for Colonial Affairs, Lord Hargreave. One doesn't always trust the Government to tell the complete story of its activities in an out-of-the-way spot like this."

"Do you think Lord Hargreave will . . . I mean, Old Settler's columns are cutting deeper every day. He could do a lot of damage by the middle of August."

"One doesn't know how it will turn out, actually," Quaritch said, "because one isn't going to be able to stick around to see. Dr. Davis feels that one's prostate is acting up a bit and he's making one sail to Sydney on Friday to have it treated. On the 'Koala Bear.'"

"The 'Koala Bear' is coming Friday?" Mel asked.

"She's due Thursday and going out the next day."

"And you're going with her?"

Quaritch nodded. He looked old and wan.

"I'm awfully sorry," Sally said.

"One will be sailing away from Tonji for the first time since 1914," Quaritch said. "So you can imagine one isn't keen to leave. When one's an old settler, one gets attached. Luckily, my son Peter in Sydney and my daughter Heather in Auckland will . . ."

"Of course!" Mel broke in. "*You're* 'Old Settler'!" Quaritch nodded. "Well, I must express my admiration, sir. The high quality of your column, day after day . . ."

He stopped in mid-sentence.

"So the column will be suspended on Friday, until you get back?" Mel asked.

"The column has never been suspended since one started it in 1917," Quaritch said.

"What a record!" Mel exclaimed. "Forty-nine years! Just one more and you would have made it fifty."

"The column has never been suspended, Mr. Parker," Quaritch said. "Goodbye, old boy. Goodbye, Miss Merrill — we'll meet again, one has a feeling. Cheerio."

He took Denis's arm and the two men continued their walk, ambling very slowly along the waterfront. They chatted like old friends, their voices gradually ebbing away. Once, the white-haired man lifted his cane to point at something in the harbor. They didn't look back.

13

IF there were an instrument subtle enough to measure the rhythm of an island, as the electrocardiograph can catch with one thin line any fluctuation of the heart, it would have begun to act strangely in Tonji on Thursday afternoon when the "Koala Bear" arrived. Not only would the graph have risen in a steady curve, registering a higher intensity at the end of every day. The line itself would have contained dozens of jagged little peaks and odd little gulleys, never seen before and telling no coherent story. A reader of the chart would only know that erratic forces were at work throughout the colony. But where those forces were leading he couldn't possibly predict.

There was nothing special about the "Koala Bear" herself. It was just that the cargo which she disgorged onto the wharf had a quickening effect on the metabolism of the islands. Part of this was purely psychological. The ship had sailed from Liverpool and had made only two stops: one at Panama and another at San Diego. She was carrying three hundred-odd men, women and children — mostly families who had chosen to leave the constricted British Isles for the wide open spaces of Australia. Pale homesteaders, pent up in the narrow corridors and dark saloons of the "Koala Bear," they could hardly contain themselves from jumping overboard as the ship nosed in toward the dock. The magnetic pull of the islands was upon them as strongly as it had been on their ancestors who sailed with Captain Cook, and when the gangway was attached they spilled down it pell-mell, streaming through the town and out into the villages to drench themselves in the tropics, fertile beyond the imagination of Anglo-Saxon man. At night they straggled back to the ship carrying bunches of bananas and mangoes and other fruits — happy, wonder-struck, gorged with a concentrated glimpse of paradise. It was the only glimpse that most of them would ever have — in the morning the "Koala Bear" would sail away again, across a bare Pacific to an even barer Australia. But it was a memory that would remain with them forever.

It would also remain with the people in Tonji who saw them come and go — especially with Mel and Sally and Cy, and with Denis, and with the Governor, who came through town to watch a cricket match. Each was touched by the valor of the emigrating families, as well as by their vulner-ability, cast up briefly on an unimportant speck of land that happened to lie between the homes that they had left and the homes that they were going to make. And all five watchers, conditioned now to think of Tonji in terms of tourism, sub-consciously saw the English families as an advance guard, a symbol of the future, and either beamed or blanched at the vision, as did Millie Hawkes and Literary Johnny, Jerry and Doc Bligh and Dirty Eddie, the Rev. Bloodgood and the Rev. Boggs and other dealers in material or spiritual wares. This was the first electrical current that the "Koala Bear" sent through the islands.

Deeper shocks followed on Friday morning when the crates that had been loaded at San Diego were unloaded and uncrated. Millie Hawkes, notified by phone that a huge wooden box had arrived for her, ran all the way from her boardinghouse to the tin-roofed cargo shed, her dress flying behind, a hammer and crowbar in her hand. "It's here! It's here!" she cried as she pattered along the harbor, and half the town fell into a ragged column at her heels. Into the shed they swarmed at full speed, past two drowsy policemen who were stationed there to stop "unauthorized personnel," past three startled customs officials in prim British khaki. Once inside, they fanned out like ants among the crates and burlap

bales and sacks that smelled of coffee, looking this way and
that, until finally a small boy found a label that said:

U-PICK-'EM MUSIC PRODUCTS
"Jukeboxes Our Specialty"
MEMPHIS, TENNESSEE

His whoop of discovery brought the human swarm to a
wooden case tightly bound with metal strips and stenciled
with signs at the bottom that said THIS SIDE UP.

"Miserable bastards, can't they even *read?*" Millie shouted,
motioning to her followers to turn the crate over. They
pushed it upright while Millie stood back and yelled "Be
*care*ful, goddamit!" and "Don't break that sweet little son-of-
a-bitch *now!*"

Attacking the crate with ferocious zeal, Millie quickly
snapped the metal bands, pried one side open, and pulled
vast amounts of excelsior from the interior, revealing a flash
of chrome here, a glint of crimson plastic there, until at last
the monster from Memphis stood naked in its wooden shell.
Forty-four titles were neatly printed on the white slips, from
"Downtown" (A 1) to "I Wanna Hold Your Hand" (V 2);
forty-four buttons pleaded to be pushed, and yards of orange
tubing awaited the electrical impulse that would send green
bubbles coursing through them in perpetual splendor.

"Oh, isn't it beautiful!" Millie said again and again, clasp-
ing her hands in joy. "Son-of-a-bitch if that isn't one mighty
nice little piece of machine! Come on — let's get her home
and plug her in. The beers are on Millie." A dozen of the
faithful lifted the jukebox onto their shoulders and staggered
toward the door.

"Have you anything to declare, Mrs. Hawkes?" a customs
man asked, stopping the procession.

"I declare I have, Inspector Gooch," Millie said. "One
jukebox, forty-four records and a lot of bubbles, and if you
don't mind we'd like . . ."

"I have to calculate the import duty," Inspector Gooch
said.

"Why don't you drop around tonight, Inspector honey, and you and me'll do a little calculating together? I believe Teacher's Scotch is your brand?"

In another part of the shed Inspector Fitz-Ross surveyed with despair the several dozen crates that had come for Mel Parker. They formed an enormous circle, Stonehenge-like, with smaller boxes piled on top of larger ones, and in the center Mel himself paced nervously, looking at the different labels and checking them against a list. Simeon Lafonga followed him around like an obedient dog. Sally sat on one of the crates, sluggish in the morning heat which was already trapped under the tin roof, her slender arms batting away the flies. Cy was also there, preparing to take a picture of one of his native girls. He lifted her by the waist and sat her on a high crate and crossed her legs in the manner of a movie star posing on top of a steamer trunk. Cy felt a twinge of regret that so few movie stars now traveled by steamer. Mel looked up just as Cy was completing his arrangement of the legs.

"Christ, Cy, it's just a bunch of lousy crates," he snapped. "Let's at least get 'em open first."

"It's cheesecake, baby — don't knock it," Cy said, amiably. He stood back and took several pictures. "Okay, Melura doll — you can get down now."

"But Cy," she called, "I can't *get* down."

"Old Cy'll help you," he said. He reached up and swung her through the air, using a grip that elicited a squeal compounded in equal parts of pleasure and surprise. "Good girl," he said, giving her a congratulatory pat as she regained her balance and her integrity on the cement floor.

"Come *on*," Mel said. "You're turning into a dirty old man."

"It's the hobby that I've chosen for my declining years."

"What was it before?" Sally asked.

"I was a dirty young man," Cy replied. "You want me to take up bird-watching or power tools, just because I've turned forty?"

"No, no," Sally said with compassion. "That's not your style."

Cy walked over to Mel. "So what can I do to help?" he asked.

Mel handed Cy his notebook. "Read me the names of these companies while I see if everything's here."

"Roger!" Cy said. He peered at Mel's scribbled list. "First there's . . . Number One on Your Plug Parade . . . Slumberama!"

"They're over here," Mel said. "Seven crates. Let's see. This would be one bed. And this would be a mattress and spring. And this would be another bed. And another mattress and spring. And this long one would be headboards. And this box would have two reclining TV chairs. And this one would have the other two TV chairs — in case they have guests."

"Even if they don't have TV," Sally said.

"Maybe someday they will," Mel said. "Who knows? Next?"

"In second place," Cy intoned. "Number Two on your . . ."

"Can it!" Mel snapped.

"Cook-Eez Kitchen Products," Cy said.

"Right. This big crate has got to be the stove. This bulky one is the sink. And these would be the counters and cabinets."

"I hope it isn't an electric stove," Sally said. "That island's not exactly wired for appliances."

"Christ, they wouldn't . . . no, I specified gas. Or did I? And where's the refrigerator?"

"Over here, Boss Mel," said Simeon. He repeated the words on the shipping tag: "Ever-Kool Corp., 'Snowball' Brand, Tarzana, Calif. Is that him?"

"That's him," Mel said. "Cy?"

"Snug-Fit is next," Cy said. "That's the one I thought was a bra."

"It's contour sheets," Mel replied. "And pillow cases and bath towels. I saw the box earlier — it was on the Slumberama crate."

"How about I take a picture of Melura up there?" Cy asked. "She'd be reclining, like, on top of the Snug-Fit box. I see her legs kind of curled around . . ."

"Okay, but make it fast," Mel said. Cy began to lift Melura.

"Ooooooh!" she squealed.

"Palmer!" boomed a familiar voice. "Can't you find anything better for your assistant to do than fondle our Tonjian women? Ehh? Hmm?"

Mel turned at the sound of his name, or its near facsimile, to see Sir Reginald scowling at the accumulated crates and at Cy's efforts to use them as a set. He had come to say goodbye to Quaritch, who, along with Denis, stood near by. Denis put down Quaritch's suitcases, which he had been carrying, and watched the scene with amusement. His eyes met Sally's, but she was less amused.

"Well, sir," Mel explained, "Mr. Rumble had a conception for a photographic essay . . ."

"Too much conception begins in the islands that way, if you ask me," the Governor said. "Hahahaha. Ehh, Foote? What?"

"Yes, sir," Denis said, laughing weakly.

"There's a joke to put in your column, Quaritch," the Governor said, jabbing the thin old man in the chest with his forefinger. "Pity you're going away. Pffff."

The "Koala Bear" gave two loud blasts.

"I think Mr. Quaritch and I will just go on ahead, sir," Denis said, picking up the suitcases.

"Ahead? Where?" the Governor asked. "Oh I see. Quite. The beggars wouldn't give damn-all about leaving without you. I'll be right along."

Denis and Quaritch walked toward the gangway. The old man gave a last look of repugnance at the crates that had come for Mel, which the Governor now saw, as if for the first time, in all their size and profusion.

"What the devil are these boxes, Palmer? Hmmm?" he asked.

"They're the furnishings for the bungalow, sir. Beds, stoves, patio chairs . . ."

"Potty chairs? Whatever for? I'll be damned if I see why grown people . . ."

"No, sir. Pat-ee-o chairs. For sitting on the pat-ee-o."

"I don't catch your drift, Palmer," the Governor said. "Some new fiddle-faddle you chaps have run up in the States, I suppose. One doesn't always get the latest word out here in the Commonwealth."

"And a stove and a refrigerator," Mel went on, deflecting the talk back to the crates. "And a kitchen sink and cabinets and curtains — that sort of thing."

"Your kit. That what it is, Palmer?"

"You might call it that, sir, yes. My kit."

"Lot of contraptions — is that what you're trying to say?" He yanked at his moustache.

"The latest appliances, sir. I'm eager for this enterprise to be of first quality."

"Most important," the Governor agreed. "Pffff. Not having any trouble getting your gear through customs, are you?"

"No, sir. Not yet."

"Well, if the blighters make any fuss, you know who to call. Hahaha."

"Yes, sir. Thank you, sir."

"Easy enough to throw 'em in the boob."

"Yes, sir. Easy enough."

"What's that? What did you say?"

"I said 'Yes, sir. Easy enough.' About the boob, sir."

"Quite right. Foof. Well, I've got to say goodbye to old Quaritch. Chap's had a bit of a kick-up in the male department, from what I understand."

"Yes, sir. A bit of a kick-up."

"Poor show," the Governor said. He turned and strode toward the gangway, preceded by two guards from Government House who cleared a path through the sweating dock workers. His malacca walking stick made a stern click-clack on the cement floor and eventually died away, smothered in the noise of derricks and winches.

On Monday morning, August 1, Mel sent Sally into "the field" again. She was to spend a week visiting the four biggest islands in the Tonji group, going from village to village and "wrapping up" various details, as Mel put it.

"Only two weeks left, Sal," he said. "The shoes are getting tight."

He gave her a number of different assignments. First she was to be his talent scout. He not only wanted an authentic dance troupe for Jerry's Authentic South Sea Emporium. He also wanted anyone who could sing or play the guitar or the drums or do any other act. She was to keep her eye out for girls who could do "a hula-type solo — you know, one of those nymphets who can really shake it." And she was not to be too high in her critical standards, because there were sixteen dives along Victoria Street and "all of them had to have something going." He would be the final judge; she only had to send all likely prospects into town to see him. She was also to send in painters with their paintings, sculptors with their carvings, and any other artists who might work in "some screwball medium, like maybe they make pictures out of shells, or pillows that say 'Mother' in tapa cloth." In short, as he summed up this part of the assignment, "the whole culture bit is in your hands."

Secondly, she was to take ample notes on picturesque aspects of Tonjian life, which she would write up for the press kit. When Sally said she didn't know what a press kit was, he explained that it was "a vast sheaf of mimeographed releases which every journalist on a junket expects to receive." Its purpose, he said, is to inundate the scribes in impressive facts and figures which they will weave into their stories. Mel said that he himself would write all the material dealing with the movie, emphasizing its lavish cost and production values; with the win-an-island contest, mentioning all the tie-in companies and products, and with the week's events related to the premiere, stressing the fabulous nature of a promotion unrivaled in motion-picture annals. She, Sally, was to cover "the travel and anthropology angle," gathering colorful lore and folk tidbits and putting them into short, breezy paragraphs for journalists too lazy, too dumb or too drunk to gather colorful lore and folk tidbits for themselves.

Finally, she was to "gumshoe around and see if anything is brewing." Sally had told Mel about the men chanting at night by the lagoon, and it still bothered him. She had also mentioned Denis's strange hints of a battle soon to be joined, and he knew from his own gumshoeing that the five Protestant ministers and one Catholic priest were discussing some kind of counter-move, throwing their ancient differences at least briefly into the shiny new bucket of ecumenism. And then there were Old Settler's recent columns punching legal holes in the entire fabric of his work. Well, at least Old Settler was gone. But it was no time to be complacent.

Sally listened gravely to Mel's instructions and set out. Whatever fears she had about doing a good job were offset by the pleasures of touching base once more with life as it was lived and not as it was managed. She felt the relief of Dorothy leaving the vaporous land of Oz and sighting again the comfortable realities of Kansas.

The first two parts of her assignment turned out to be satisfying. No end of talented men and women were discovered and sent back to Mel, and no end of wonderful facts were teased out of the village elders at night and recorded in her notebook. But as for any clear idea of what was brewing, if anything, she proved to be a poor detective. She saw — or imagined that she saw — clues at every point in her journey. Like Dr. Watson, however, she had no gift for putting one clue next to another. On the contrary, instead of making the jigsaw puzzle come into focus, every new piece made it fuzzier.

Many of the real or imagined clues were connected with Denis. Wherever she went, it turned out that Denis had been there a day or two earlier. He, too, was obviously making a systematic tour of the islands. Once she saw his jeep, parked at the village where she had heard the men chanting "Kula-ha'i-i-i-i!" at night. And once she saw Denis himself as she bicycled past the royal village of Mui, sitting at a table with a Tonjian man of tremendous size and dignity. Denis, glancing up as she went by, called to her to come and meet Chief Malalonga.

The Chief greeted her with solemn warmth and they chatted for several minutes, but neither he nor Denis asked her to stay, and she bicycled off again. As she left she noticed quite a few large sheets of paper on the table where Denis and the Chief had been sitting. They looked like maps of the different Tonji islands, on which the two men had scrawled various arrows and circles, rather like the plans of elaborate football plays that she used to see chalked on the blackboard of the Pembleton gym.

The other clues were less specific in detail, though no less conspiratorial. In certain villages, as she approached, all talk would suddenly stop. In other villages she saw small knots of men whispering and gesturing. Or were these just figments of a mind fevered by listening to Mel? Work with him a month and your nerves get all shot, Sally thought. She'd be glad when it was over, the whole damn thing. Whole darn thing, she corrected herself.

Only once did she meet someone who she felt was following his private trail through the islands, allied with no faction, driven by no force except his own endocrine glands. It was Dr. Kalbfleisch, who scared her half to death by bursting out of a mango grove, a copy of Henry Miller's "Sexus" under his arm, while a Tonjian girl beat a hailstorm upon his retreating back with her fists.

"Good afternoon, Mademoiselle," he said, tipping his Panama hat with European formality as the blows continued to rain around his spine. "I was zimply trying to purzue my rezearch. Zis particular lead I can now azzume to be false. Ze girl is like a tiger, *nicht?* Zuch ztrong fizts! *O mein Gott!* How we zcientists muzt zuffer when our work is not underztood!"

In town the even tenor of life became more and more uneven. Millie Hawkes's jukebox turned out to have a loudness unsuspected by the most ardent admirers of American technology, and the very trees along Victoria Street trembled to its blast. The Beatles and Rolling Stones now wailed from the machine where Bing Crosby and Dinah Shore had so long been sovereign. The Mersey sound, the Tijuana sound, the Nashville sound and the Good Guys' sound echoed along the waterfront while the ghosts of Glenn Miller, Harry James

and Guy Lombardo, disenfranchised at last, tiptoed out of
Millie's back door.

An electric guitar, never heard in Tonji before, whined out
of Dirty Eddie's, adding a shrill new timbre to the old
Polynesian instrument. Eddie explained to curious bystanders
that Mel Parker had done the modernizing job himself "with
just an extension cord and a funny little box."

From Jerry's Authentic South Sea Emporium came the
authentic sounds of a dance troupe in rehearsal: the rhythmic
stomping of feet and the abrupt starting and stopping of
music. Periodically the voice of Mel Parker filled one of the
silences: "All right, kids, let's take it from the top."

Literary Johnny's beard grew longer and he was often seen
to comb it.

Doc Bligh announced that a happening would be held at
his Bounty Hotel on August 18. He didn't know exactly what
a happening was, but he had been assured by Mel Parker
that it was "the real avant-garde stuff." Hence his hotel was
the perfect place to hold it, as he told a local reporter who
came around to ask, kicking away a land crab that dragged
itself across the mottled rug in his lobby, "because I've always
been ahead of my time out here."

Mrs. Beezley, wife of the Presbyterian minister, whose
Wednesday Club met in the front room of a malted milk
parlor that she had started as an antidote to "all the wicked
saloons," announced that she had agreed to Mel Parker's
suggestion that she hold poetry readings during the week of
August 15, "just like they do at Aspen."

The Danish explorers began to make trial runs in their
balsa raft. Karl Ullstrad announced that Mel Parker had
graciously offered to act as public relations consultant to the
official departure of the raft for Peru on August 18 "as a token
of international amity and in the larger cause of scientific
exchange."

On the island of Moona-Moona, née Kula-ha'i, the eerie cry
of the bad-luck bird was blotted out by the more insistent
sounds of hammering, grunting and swearing as Simeon and
his men tried to install the appliances that they brought out

daily in their small boat. Mel and Cy also made regular trips
to the island in a speedboat to supervise the work and to help
decipher the "instructions for assembly" that came with every
product — sentences that were positively Etruscan in their
refusal to be cracked.

One morning, when Mel went out early to adjust the
defroster and try a new spray paint on the grass, he noticed
footprints in the sand left by two men who had visited the
island during the night. One of the men had been big and
barefooted; the other had been thin and wore sneakers. Who
wore sneakers?

Had he gone several mornings later Mel would have
noticed two other sets of footprints, one belonging to a man,
the other to a girl, which led to a rumpled section of beach
where the two visitors appeared to have had a fierce struggle.
Simeon came back in late afternoon and reported this to Mel,
who mentioned it to Cy, who was just waking up from an all-
day sleep.

Cy said it wasn't "any goddam mystery" to him. The two
combatants were himself and Maud Weems. She had stopped
him on the dock, pushed him into the Governor's launch and
told the native pilot to go to Kula-ha'i, which she was "fright-
fully keen to see." She took Cy to the galley, which she had
provisioned with gin and vermouth, and commanded him to
mix a batch of "those lovely drinks you gave me up at
Government House," adding that "if you're going to be
naughty and refuse, I'll tell Daddy and he'll throw a spanner
in your whole scheme."

"Jesus, Mel, I was in a spot," Cy said, dredging back the
events of the night before. "I didn't even know what a
spanner *was*. Turns out it's a monkey wrench. Well, I didn't
want to screw things up *now*: I mean, get Big Daddy mad at
us. But I didn't want to be stuck out in the middle of the
ocean with Big Daughter, either. So I figured, 'What the hell,
I'll make us both a weak one and play it by ear — maybe
bribe the guy at the wheel to take us back in.' But she kept
knocking 'em back — four or five at least. How was I to know
that gin would affect her like *that*? Or that I remind her of

Paul Newman? When she got me on that beach she had the strength of ten. Ten horsepower."

"Did you . . . ?" Mel began, appalled at this turn in the story. Of all the possible ways in which his project could be shattered, all the threats that he had anticipated and arranged to parry, one that he had not foreseen was the deflowering of Sir Reginald's womenfolk. He shuddered. He didn't want to hear Cy's answer. But he also wanted to hear Cy's answer.

"No . . . I didn't," Cy said, his voice a concentrate of gravel. "Of course I had no way of knowing if Maud would be madder if I *didn't*, or if I did — you know, next day when she cooled off? If there was gonna *be* a next day . . . which I doubted. I thought I was gonna die right there from the strain of fighting her off. Anyway, some instinct told me to abstain."

"An instinct you've never had before," Mel said.

"Never," Cy said.

"You did well, old friend. You saved the Alamo."

Mel was confident now, buoyant with the momentum of things going as he wanted them to go. Only one event jolted his equanimity, and that was the continued appearance of "Old Settler's" column after Old Settler sailed away. At first it was merely a surprise and not a shock to see the familiar heading, OLD SETTLER SAYS, framed in its box of typographical garlands and encrusted with the ink of a thousand yesterdays, because the column dealt only with general island matters. Mel realized with relief that Quaritch had somehow mustered the energy to write a number of columns in advance.

After three days, however, which "Old Settler" devoted to chiding Sir Reginald's Government for having bungled the vanilla quota, the Indian problem and "the ground nuts scheme" (whatever that was), his column turned once again on Mel Parker and his activities, striking with more scorn every morning. No plan which could be construed as despoiling the islands seemed to escape the columnist's X-ray eye. It was all there — the electric guitar, the hula acts, the appliances, the happening — and in lethal detail. He wondered if Quaritch had only feigned going to Australia. Yes, that was it. The old man had boarded the "Koala Bear" and then had himself lowered through a porthole on the other side. Tonjian men had paddled him in an outrigger to a secret cove where they brought him news every day and took his column for the printer. Certainly there was no mistaking the style, that distinctive blend of righteous outrage and sardonic tone:

One cannot blink the fact that the Beatles, whose strident keening from Mrs. Hawkes's "jukebox" have shattered the calm of Victoria Street, are recipients of the royal favour of Her Majesty herself (although one can still express dismay at the prudence of Buckingham Palace in this particular instance). The Beatles are chargeable to our conscience as Englishmen, just as Mrs. Hawkes's infernal machine is chargeable to our collective conscience in Tonji. If this were all, it would be too much.

But the sounds being spewed forth from one "jukebox," raucous and vulgar though they may be, are but the merest foretaste of what lies in store for our hapless islands. Sleazy forces, manipulated from the cheap factories of Hollywood, will soon multiply tenfold — nay, fiftyfold — the assaults of the kind exemplified by Mrs. Hawkes's instant frozen music. One need only mention the "belly dancers" now being recruited for Jerry's no-longer-authentic South Sea Emporium. Nor could one miss the replacement yesterday of the sign at Alfie's alehouse ("Alfie's, That's All"), long one of the most popular corporate names in the islands, by an enormous orange sign, THE BEATNIK BEACHCOMBER. Further evidence of the rapid degeneration which . . .

Maybe I can put a watch on the office of the "Tonji Times," Mel thought. See where the stuff is coming from. Track him down, wherever he is. The old bastard'll get me yet.

By Monday morning, August 8, with Sally due back and the bungalow almost finished, the only big factor still unknown to Mel was the outcome of the win-an-island contest. He had been impatient for a cable. The contest deadline was August 1, and only a few days should have been necessary to

choose a suitably folksy couple and see if they were willing to
fly out.

That afternoon a Tonjian boy walked down from the
mountains with a scribbled message from M. LeClercq, the
French planter with the shortwave radio. It said that "un
homme qui s'appelle M. Pierre Bleu" in Los Angeles had
tried to reach him and would try again tonight "at seven
hours." Who the hell, Mel thought. Some wise guy putting
me on. Pierre Bleu. He didn't know anybody named Bleu.
Blau, yes — plenty of them in Hollywood. Irwin and Leonard
and what's-his-name over at Paramount . . . Theodore. But
Pierre Blau. It didn't figure. Like Raoul Levy. Except there
was a Raoul Levy. He studied the name like an anagram, but
not until he began thinking in French did its defenses yield.
Pierre, stone. Bleu, blue. Stone, blue. Stone-blue. Bluestone.
BLUESTONE! Harvey Bluestone! Sure! It was old Harv,
wanting to tell him about the contest.

That night at seven hours, Mel huddled over M. LeClercq
as the Frenchman huddled over his shortwave equipment,
alternately calling and listening as he tried to conjure Los
Angeles out of the air. If he gets his goddam doctor in Kyoto
I'm cooked, Mel thought. But M. LeClercq was intent on his
mission, and within ten minutes his face brightened and he
handed his earphones and microphones to Mel. "*Le voilà*," he
said.

"Mel, baby, are you there?" called a thin voice from far
away.

"Harv? Yeah, it's me. How the hell are you?" Mel shouted.

"Great. I'm over at Shel Sheldrake's. Shel sends his best.
Sandra too. Listen, Mel . . . you still there? . . . Good. I
just want to give you a quick wrap-up. The contest went over
colossal and we've got our winning couple. There were two
top entries just about even, so I went to see 'em both.
That's what held me up. The first was a Mr. and Mrs.
Fothergill in Dallas. I rang the doorbell at eleven in the
morning and old Fothergill was stoned already, so he didn't
strike me as a good risk. The other couple is from a little
town in Iowa, farm people about sixty years old, real nice, as

American as hot dogs. Mr. and Mrs. Hal C. Mudge. Can you hear me? . . . Yes, Mudge. They're thrilled at winning a South Sea island and they're eager to come out and start living there. How's the bungalow? . . . Good. I told 'em it was. I sent a story out to the wire services on Saturday and we made all the Sunday papers. A real heartwarmer. With pictures, too. Mr. and Mrs. Mudge looking at photographs of Moona-Moona. The ones that Cy took. Which reminds me: Perdita Fox-Martin wants to bring along 'Vogue's' winter line of ski clothes and photograph them out on Moona-Moona. That ought to grab you. The point is, can she hire Cy as her photographer? Regular space rates? . . . Swell. Oh, and about that neon sign for Dirty Eddie's à Go-Go. I couldn't get red, so I'm bringing yellow and green. Okay? . . . Look, you're fading out on me, old buddy, so I'm gonna wrap it up. Everything's falling into place. We all got our shots this week and we leave Saturday at four. We'll see you Monday. Don't forget to meet the plane."

14

NEWLY rechristened the "Moona Marone," newly
decorated in the manner of a World War II bomber
with a huge painting of that chesty starlet, the seaplane of
Trans-Sky Airways droned southward from Honolulu. The
blue Pacific glittered far below in the morning sun. It was
Monday, August 15.

In the rear of the plane, shielded from the vulgar gaze of
sixteen journalists and two agents, Moona Marone nibbled at
her breakfast, stared at her recently awakened face in a
mirror, and pondered the grim fate of a Hollywood "person-
ality" forcibly separated from her coiffeur and cosmetician.

"God!" she moaned to Harvey Bluestone, who had assigned
himself the adjoining seat in order to protect his prize
heifer — as far as that was within human possibility — from
her own solecisms, witticisms and other such assaults against
man and nature.

"I can't *stand* it," Moona Marone said in a voice sprinkled
with sand. "You got a cigarette, darling?"

Harvey lit a cigarette for her and she disappeared into a
nimbus of smoke, coughing heavily. The plane had left
Honolulu the previous evening and had come down at Fanning Island to refuel between two and three A.M., an interval
which the journalists, already drugged with alcohol, put to
the same use as the plane, refueling themselves from their
flasks as they stood on the tarmac beneath the Southern
Cross. Consequently the noises that filled the cabin when the

plane resumed its flight — the snoring, the incoherent mumbling, the singing of Irish chanteys by Farley Grogan of the Hearst newspaper chain — almost obliterated the roar of the engines. It was not a merciful night for an actress who needs her beauty sleep, and now, at nine A.M., the piper was demanding to be paid.

Harvey felt as terrible as everybody else — the tinkle of aspirin bottles sang a story of pain around him — and he wished that he had been able to give the position of Moona Marone's scatmate to his assistant, Sammy Kelp. Sammy was coming along fast, Harvey reflected, and some day he'd be one of the best press agents in the business. But he was just a kid and this was his first junket. He'd never seen a Hollywood actress in dawn's grisly light, and he might panic. Whereas he himself had shepherded hundreds of stars on that treacherous voyage beyond the studio gate to meet the public and the press, far from that snug harbor where makeup men know an actress's smallest wrinkle and photographers know her "good angle," where audio engineers dub out any trace of Tulsa or Tallahassee and publicity men repaint in golden strokes the paltry girlhoods that were spent there.

Now Harvey looked at the defenseless face of Moona Marone with the clinical eye of a doctor who has seen it all. What he saw was a twenty-eight-year-old girl named Gertrude Fossenkemper, who won a screen test at nineteen and ceased at that moment to be herself — or so Titan Pictures had completely persuaded the outside world and almost completely persuaded her. Gertrude Fossenkemper was dead that Moona Marone might live. It was Moona Marone who had reality. But Harvey knew that the girl sitting beside him now, the glamour goddess he was delivering to Mel Parker, was really Gertrude Fossenkemper, an aging teen-ager from Tulsa, insecure and not very bright, her empty head an echo chamber for a thousand fears that she would try to hide behind the famous smile and walk and voice that had been grafted onto her by the studio's charm coach, posture coach and diction coach in lessons so relentless that they had largely robbed her of her twenties. Harvey felt sorry for her.

"Tell me again what I'm supposed to do," she said to Harvey, applying a black pencil to her red-rimmed eyes, the first of many artifices with which she would try to banish Gertrude Fossenkemper for another day.

"Don't worry about a thing, baby doll," Harvey said. "Mel will keep telling you what to do, and if he's not there old Harvey will be right beside you."

"And there's Norbert," she purred. "He's so sweet."

"Yeah," Harvey muttered. Up ahead in the plane he could just see one of his least favorite sights in creation: the curly red locks of Norbert de Paul, Moona Marone's "personal representative," bobbing in conversation with Olivia O'Connell, venerable doyenne of Hollywood gossip columnists. Miss O'Connell, though eighty, still ruled her dominion with an iron glove; she wrought so much vengeance on actresses who failed to give her the first inkling of their pregnancy that many of them now telephoned her before they even took a rabbit test. If the test subsequently turned out negative, that was no problem. On the contrary, it brought them another "mention" in the column and kept their credit good with Miss O'Connell, who had the satisfaction of printing two items — one a rumor and one a fact — that might otherwise have fallen to the pen of her archrival, Una Urquhart.

"Are you still mad at me about Norbert?" Moona Marone said to Harvey, stroking his unshaven face in an affectionate manner which she thought, erroneously, he would regard as sincere.

"Of *course* I'm still mad," he flashed back. "What kind of bush-league stunt was that — throwing a temper fit in the ladies' room at the airport and saying that you couldn't *dream* of going on such an exh*aus*ting trip unless your personal repre*sen*tative came along?" He mimicked her studio-taught accent. "It meant I had to bounce the guy from 'Seventeen' to make room for Norbert. Mel will be mad as a bull. He'll probably throw Norbert in the lagoon."

"Well, Norbert's important to *me*, and after all I'm the star. Don't you want to keep your star happy, lover?"

"Listen, sweetheart, take a bit of advice from old Harvey.

We're going way out in the boondocks, you understand? We're not just schlepping around Wilshire Boulevard where Sammy Kelp and I can keep knocking out press releases about what a stellar actress and a lovely person you are. These reporters are going to write about the Moona Marone that they actually *meet*, and what they want to see is a plucky little American girl who goes through the whole routine like a good sport. So whatever Mel tells you to do, do it and complain later."

"But my contract . . ."

"Screw your contract," Harvey snapped. "Is that what you brought Norbert along for — to renegotiate Clause 13B if Mel tells you to pose with a coconut on your head? So pose."

"Do you really think Mel will throw him into the lagoon?"

"Very likely. And if Mel doesn't, maybe I will. So you'd better stand back."

"Why me?"

"Because when he falls in the water he'll try to take ten per cent of you along."

"Believe me, she's a real human being," Norbert de Paul said in his watery voice to Olivia O'Connell, who had the window seat and was looking down at the Pacific.

"What did you say, dear?" Miss O'Connell asked. "I'm afraid I wasn't listening."

"I said she's a real human being."

"Moona? Yes . . . so genuine. By the way, she's not pregnant, is she?"

"*Heav*ens, no!" Norbert piped. "She's not married."

"Oh, I guess you're right," Miss O'Connell said.

"Of *course* I'm right. I'm her personal representative, aren't I?"

"I thought she married that Hungarian arranger who did the background music for 'Budapest Beach Boy.' Laszlo something."

"Oh that dreadful man. Quite frankly, I don't know what Moona ever saw in him. I *plead*ed with her to break it off. I told her, 'Moona, he's not good enough for you — you're a real human being.' "

"And what finally happened, darling? My memory gets a little fuzzy now. Last week I thought I saw Norma Talmadge on Sunset Boulevard."

"He eloped to the Springs with Nicky de Zoxas — just a week before her old man put a picture into production over at Emblem called 'Transylvanian Rhapsody' that he wanted to do the score for. She's pregnant, if that's any help to you."

"Oh you dear boy," Miss O'Connell said, scribbling in a stenographer's notebook.

"Of course I breathed the *big*gest sigh of relief when I heard about the wedding," Norbert went on. "Quite frankly, it would have *ru*ined Moona's career to marry that creep. When you've been personal representative to as many luminaries as I have, you learn to spot the phonies, believe me. But there's not one drop of phony blood in Moona Marone. She's a real human being."

"Surely you jest," said Duncan Dunnington, film critic of "Esquire," to his seat companion, Farley Grogan. "Do you think I'd actually *see* a picture called 'Desert Island for Two,' even if it *is* the world premiere?"

"I know what you mean, pal," Grogan said, emitting a loud belch that shook his frayed nerves. "I've been on about twenty of these movie junkets and I can honestly say I've never seen one of their movies yet. I'll bet you can't top that record, Dunc boy."

"Well, to be quite literal about it, no — I can't top it," Dunnington said, "because naturally I go to Cannes and Venice and the other film festivals."

"No kidding?" Grogan said. "You see all that foreign crap?"

"It's the only cinema of our time that has artistic validity. Unless you count Jonas Mekas."

"Jonas who?"

"Oh, never mind."

"So what're you gonna write your column about this month — I mean, if you don't see the movie?"

"Oh, that's never any problem," Dunnington said. "In fact, I've got it half written already."

"Yeah? What's the angle?"

"I begin by complaining that America has simply lost the knack of making a good film. I deplore the virtual extinction of directors like Capra and Lubitsch and Preston Sturges — you know as well as I do, Grogan, there hasn't been a really *strik*ingly original film made in our country since 'Citizen Kane.' I point out that America's good young directors — the ones who showed such promise a decade ago — have been corrupted by television and have absolutely *ab*dicated the medium to Kurosawa, Antonioni, Resnais, Godard and Truffaut. And the Czechs, of course. And don't overlook Poland, either: I saw a gem of a picture last month about an amputated Polish war veteran who's married to a blind Israeli girl. It's shot through a piece of cheesecloth."

"Oh balls!" Grogan said, belching again.

"Then I rip the mentality that made 'The Sound of Music,' take a few swipes at Walt Disney, and that leads me right into . . ."

"Haven't you made that point in your column before?" Grogan asked.

"Well, *cer*tainly," Dunnington said. "You don't expect me to think up a new point twelve times a year, do you?"

"You thought you were being put on," Mickey Dolan tapped with his two forefingers on the typewriter in his lap. "You'd heard Pat Hallahan, who used to fix up the bodies at Finn's Funeral Home in Canarsie, say that he'd shipped to the South Seas on a tramp steamer when he was just a punk kid and that it was so beautiful it made you want to cry. But that was long ago and you thought maybe Pat's memories were kind of on the rosy side. You knew how it was when old men sit on park benches and realize they're getting near the end of the big road. And yet here you were in the South Seas yourself, and out of the window of your flying boat you could see . . ." He craned his neck to look out the window.

"You start work mighty early, Mr. Dolan," said his seatmate, J. P. Foy of the "Wall Street Journal," a prim gray-haired man in a gray suit.

"When you've got a daily deadline it's like you've got a monkey on your back," Dolan said. "You want to knock off and take it easy — especially on a day like this when maybe you've had a little too much grog the night before — but then you think of your readers. You think of Leo Corcoran at Bleeck's and Kathleen the hatcheck girl at Mooney's Steak House and your kid sister Mary Agnes out in Ozone Park with the six kids . . . little Tom and Moira and . . ."

"Yes, I quite see," Foy broke in. What he quite saw, rapidly forming in the next seat like a summer thunderstorm, was a census of Brooklyn, Manhattan and Queens. At least the Bronx and Staten Island were still exempt.

"Or you think of Black Mike, the cop who walks the beat up on Fordham Road . . ."

"It must be very tiring — thinking of all those people," Foy said. "Fortunately, in my own modest orbit . . ."

"Say, I meant to ask you about that, J.P.," Dolan said. "What's a mugg from the 'Wall Street Journal' doing on a caper like this?"

"I've asked myself that, too. I haven't ever been on one of these junkets before, and I must say — from what I've seen so far — it's a very different view of the working press. *Very* different."

"It's a long way from the Stock Exchange."

"And wheat futures."

"Yeah, and wheat futures."

"But in a curious way it makes sense," Foy went on. "The promoter of this thing in Tonji — a man named Parker — convinced my boss that it's one of the biggest business stories of the year. It's more than just a movie promotion and a nationwide contest . . ."

"Hey, what the hell are wheat futures?"

"It's also a tie-in campaign with twenty firms. And it's *also* what Mr. Parker calls 'the first attempt to launch an instant tourist industry and develop an untapped market for venture capital overnight.' Sounds like a smart fellow, Parker — not everybody would think of inviting the 'Wall Street Journal.' Where else do you reach a million businessmen looking for new ways to invest their funds?"

"Can't say I see your sheet very often," Dolan replied. "Maybe that's because I don't have that extra dough-re-mi you're talking about." He fell into a brief financial reverie. "You ask yourself where it went, and then you remember you burned it all up on broads and booze. Ahh well, you can't take it with you. You've always known that. You've known it since Round One. From the time you were a kid in knee-pants hanging around Feinberg's Candy Store you've at least known that much." He glanced philosophically at the ceiling of the plane. "How about a drink, J.P.?"

"Now? It's only nine-thirty."

"That's starting time on junkets."

"Really?"

"Come *on*. You wanna live forever?"

"Guys like you can't help going a little stale," Adrian Struthers, Jr., said to Don Phelps of the Associated Press, who was stretching himself awake in the next seat. "Knocking out copy, day after day, you're bound to lose the fresh eye, the . . . I'm tempted to say the sensibility to a new environment."

"Go ahead and say it if you're tempted," Phelps remarked, lighting a cigarette.

"Well, it stands to reason," Struthers continued. "But a young novelist like me, with two critical successes under his belt — as you know, my novel about the human condition in suburbia, 'A Pique in Darien,' won the Hockaday Prize for first fiction — as I say, a writer like myself brings to an assignment of this kind a highly tuned set of . . . you might call them esthetic reflexes."

"Why would I call them that?"

"Perhaps you wouldn't. Perhaps that's not precisely the phrase. But it may explain why 'Holiday' chose me rather than your run-of-the-mill free-lance writer. They know that if anyone can catch the *tex*ture of Polynesian life — the sights, the sounds . . ."

"The smells."

"Yes, the smells. I happen to have a particular bent for capturing the fragrance of a wisteria blossom, or the hint of salt in the air beside a glaucous sea."

"You can actually describe a smell, Struthers? Is that what sets you novelists above us newspapermen?"

"Well, not the smell itself, but the *effect* of the smell . . . what it evokes in that incredibly receptive vessel called the human heart. I sometimes think of it as the olfactory mystique."

"I never do," Phelps said.

"That's because you fellows get stale. You can't help it, knocking out the same copy, day after day."

"This is where I came in," Phelps said, "and this is where I go out." He walked up the aisle of the plane to the lavatory. At the door he turned and caught Struthers's attention. "Don't miss that sea," he called, pointing out the window. "It's getting a little glaucous."

"You say you brought *ski* clothes?" Sammy Kelp asked Perdita Fox-Martin, who was idly sketching on a pad printed with the words MEMO FROM PERDITA FOX-MARTIN.

"The complete winter line," she said. "Stretch pants and hoods and those adorable knitted caps that come down over your face like a mask. And of course *après ski*."

"And you're gonna *wear* those things? It's hot out here."

"Not *me*, silly. I'm going to find some Polynesian girls and dress *them* in ski clothes and take them to that island of yours and shoot pictures *there*. Won't it make a fabulous spread?"

"It's kind of, uh, far out."

"But that's the whole *point*. In fashion journalism the race isn't to the swift — it's to the zany. You've got to *force* people to notice the new styles by shooting them in an exotic location. The trouble is, we're running out of locations."

"Like where've you been lately?"

"Well, last winter I went to Baalbek to shoot the new

bathing suits. I had my models pose against those marvelous columns of the temple of Jupiter, and the contrast was simply stunning — I mean those *new* bikinis next to those *old* columns. The gals at our shop liked it so much that I went over in April to Leptis Magna — you know, those heavenly Roman ruins in Libya? — to do the fall collection of miniskirts. And next I'm going to do the spring underwear in the medina at Fez. That's a kicky idea because Fez is one of the *holi*est cities in Islam and the women are veiled so heavily they can't even *see*."

"Is that true about running out of locations?" Sammy asked.

"Oh, maybe you can find a *few* colorful places where the fashion magazines haven't done a spread, but I can't think of any offhand. In my own case — just for openers — I've done the Greek monastery bit, up in the mountains of Thessaly, and a layout on sandals at a Shinto shrine in Osaka — you know, because the Japa*nese* wear sandals — and I've done girls in formal gowns arriving at Jerash by camel caravan, and . . . let's see . . . there was Ayutthaya and Udaipur and Dar es Salaam and Ibiza and . . . I can't even remember them all."

"I think I saw the Dar es Salaam job," Sammy said. "A lot of girls in sailing clothes on an Arab dhow — right?"

"Right. It comes back to me because I wrote a text that began 'Don't get in bad with Sinbad.' Meaning, of course, that whoever your Sinbad happens to be — Greek shipowner or just a Joe who hacks around in a sloop — you've got to look your best."

"That's cute," said Sammy, who didn't think it was.

"Well, I always like to do an article to go with the layout. It's a fun thing because these trips take me to places that nobody's ever heard of. But after I write my story they get *scads* of tourists."

"So you'll be doing a piece on Tonji — besides the spread on ski clothes?" Sammy Kelp asked, his voice betraying the hope that bubbles eternal in a press agent's soul.

"You wouldn't mind, would you, Mr. Kelp," said Miss Fox-

Martin, "if I proclaimed the charms of Moona-Moona to all our rich and restless subscribers?"

"Just as long as they don't expect to find skiing when they get there."

"This your first trip to the Pacific, Mr. Eposcu?" Vern Walters said to Emerich Eposcu, the 'Life' photographer.

Eposcu was stunned at the question. He ran his hand over his matted black hair in an elaborate gesture of disbelief at the areas of ignorance remaining in the world.

"You asked me," he said, "if this is my first trip to the Pacific — me, Emerich Eposcu. Correct?"

"That's correct," Walters said, startled by the immediate return of his own question.

"How do you like that?" Eposcu said, addressing himself.

"Like what?" Walters asked.

"Do you mean to say," Eposcu went on, "do you honestly mean to say you've never heard of my book, 'Magical Melanesia'? One hundred and seventy-two color plates, voted by the Quill Club as one of the ten best gift books of 1959? You haven't seen my sixteen-page photo essays in 'Life' on 'Stone-Age Papua,' or 'Guadalcanal Revisited,' or 'Last Voyage of the "Bounty," ' or 'Melville's Marquesas,' or 'Firewalkers of Fiji'? My God — I go to the Pacific the way other people go to Scarsdale." He fell back into his seat weary and aggrieved.

"Well now, I'm real sorry, Mr. Eposcu," Walters said. "I'm so everlastingly bad at remembering people's names . . ."

"I suppose you never heard about the exhibition of carved canoes that I brought back from the Sepik River in New Guinea for the Beverly de Rothstein Gallery on Fifty-seventh Street? Or the collection of figures in the lost wax process of the Ashanti tribe in Nigeria that I gave to Yale University, where I happen to be a member of the faculty."

"You're on the faculty of Yale?" Walters asked. "That's mighty impressive."

"Well, actually I'm a visiting lecturer, but I have faculty status. It's the same thing. So don't ask me if I've ever been to Africa, either. Or Japan or India or Egypt, because I've done

color essays on them all, though I don't suppose you noticed
that they were 'Photographed for "Life" by Emerich Eposcu.'
I don't suppose you noticed *that*." He took an expensive cigar
out of a silver tube and lit it. "*Where* in Ohio did you say you
were from?"

"Iowa," Walters said. "Des Moines. I'm a reporter with the
'Des Moines Register.' "

"What's a guy from a hick town doing on a big-time junket
like this?"

"Well now, I might just disagree with you that a city of
two hundred thousand is so goldarn insignificant."

"Small potatoes," Eposcu said.

"As a matter of fact, I'm not even too partial to that word
'hick.' Though I'd a darn sight rather be a hick than a city
feller who's gotten too big for his britches."

Eposcu blew a large cloud of cigar smoke toward the seat
ahead of him, where it briefly enveloped Mickey Dolan and
J. P. Foy.

"The reason I'm on this trip," Walters went on, "is that the
couple who won the island are from Iowa, and Mr. Parker
felt that someone from the Iowa press ought to be there to
write it up for the folks back home. Mighty nice of him to
think of it, if you ask me."

"Well at least you'll be able to tell the folks back home you
were on a trip with Emerich Eposcu."

Tom Carpenter of United Press International felt a sharp
light pressing against his still closed eyelids. On opening
them — a process which reminded him, for sheer gumminess,
of prying apart clamshells — he found that it was the morning sunlight reflected off the pincurls of Bobbie Baxter,
proprietor of the "Bobbie Sez" column in 142 newspapers. So
profusely were the pins embedded in Miss Baxter's auburn
hair that the effect was like one of the mirrored balls that
revolve from the ceiling of a skating rink. Carpenter turned
away.

"Yoo hoo! Good *mor*-ning!" Miss Baxter warbled. "Rise and

shine!" She whistled a few bars of reveille. "How's the great
Tom Carpenter today? Bright-eyed and bushy-tailed?"

How the hell did *that* expression come into the vocabulary
of every cornmonger in America, Carpenter wondered. Who
wanted to be bushy-tailed anyway — why was that such hot
stuff? He closed his eyes again and feigned falling back to
sleep.

"Oh-no-you-don't," his seatmate said. "I *saw* you. Naughty-
naughty!"

Jesus, this is worse than Vietnam, Carpenter thought. He
forced his two clamshells open again and blinked at Bobbie
Baxter. "Christ, Bobbie, you're too bright for me with those
things in your hair," he said.

"Then why don't you look in my big blue eyes?" she said,
giving him a wink, the first in a series — they came at the
rate of one every four sentences, Carpenter had estimated —
which would terminate, at least for him, only with the plane's
arrival in Tonji.

"When are we getting there?" he asked, peering out the
window as strenuously as if to pull the islands into view with
his optical muscles.

"Coupla hours," she said. "You getting impatient, lover
boy? Why don't you grab your typewriter and bat out some
manly prose?"

"Is that what you're doing?" he asked. Her handwriting
was scribbled all over the customs declaration form.

"You rat," she said, giggling to indicate that this was a
comical term. "I'm writing *femi*nine prose. Wanna hear
some? It's my first 'Bobbie Sez' column from the islands —
ready to give to the cable office."

"Maybe a little later," Carpenter mumbled.

"It starts like this: 'Moona, moona, moona, it's a long way
from Altoona, so away we go. Wanna comb a beach? I'm a
beachcomber now, so come along with Aunt Bobbie to the
fabled South Seas. The Maugham the merrier, I say, or Bali
Ha'i-there, everybody! Here comes Lady Bounty-ful. Gonna
sing-along with Mich-ener. Bloody Mary, anyone? I got the

moon and sixpence and that's all you need for a Captain Cook-out. So . . ."

"Excuse me, Bobbie," Carpenter said, his voice reduced to a low moaning sound. "There's a personal call I've got to make." He stepped over her black slacks into the aisle.

"Don't tell me — I know," she called after him. "You're gonna see a dog about a man."

As he walked slowly toward the men's room, Carpenter noticed with envy that Blake Hewitt, the NBC television reporter, and his cameraman, Tony Fiorello, were still asleep. Lucky bastards, he thought. How did *they* get to sit together? He had a blind impulse to grab them both by the collar and toss them to new partners — Hewitt to Bobbie Baxter, Fiorello to . . . who? The voices of Emerich Eposcu, Duncan Dunnington and Adrian Struthers, Jr., eddied around the cabin in gusts of equal flatulence. Tony didn't deserve any of them.

The only other person being spared the hardships of professional talk was Bill Stanton of the Scripps-Howard papers, whose seat companion, columnist Arnold Arkin, had donned black eyeshades when the plane left Fanning Island and was locked in perfect slumber behind them. The use of these eyeshades in several hundred junkets now enabled Arkin to sleep better in a plane than in his bed on West Fifty-eighth Street, and when he did awaken it was not in painful stages, like his journalistic brothers, but all at once. Off would come the black patches, and there — his brown eyes dancing amiably, his every nerve-end aquiver for the reception of anecdotes — would be the functioning Arnold Arkin, tireless custodian for forty years of "Arnie's Alley." Even as Tom Carpenter paused beside Arkin's seat, in fact, this metamorphosis took place, the columnist sliding from a gentle snore into full conversation with no evident change in his vital processes.

"You know how the limbo was invented?" he said to Bill Stanton, tugging his eyeshades off.

"The what? Oh hi, Arnie — good morning," Stanton said, astonished to find him awake.

"The limbo. You know how it was invented? Harvey Bluestone told me last night."

"No. How was it invented?"

"When they put bathrooms in at the El Tropiques Hotel."

"I don't get it, Arnie," Stanton said, scratching his sandy hair.

"Ask Harvey — he'll explain."

Stanton turned in his seat and called back to Harvey. "Hey, Harvey, how was the limbo invented?"

"When they put pay toilets in at the El Tropiques Hotel," Harvey called back.

Stanton laughed. "That's a good joke," he said, settling back down in his seat.

"Didn't I tell you?" Arkin said. "I'm going to lead my column with it today."

15

Less has been written about the art of running a successful press junket than about the art of running a successful boarding school or summer camp. Yet the two skills are surprisingly alike. As proved by every headmaster who has lasted in his job, or every camp director who has weathered July and August, the trick is to keep the inmates occupied from morning to night, coaxing or chivying them into a series of activities that they would never voluntarily undertake until, depleted by fatigue or numbed by mindless pastimes, they collapse into sleep — the only realm where they can do no harm to themselves or, more important, to the reputation of the compound. It is by putting one such day after another, year after year, that the titans of secondary education have been formed and camp owners have survived into that golden sunset where they can visit upon sons and grandsons the same sins that they visited upon their fathers.

A good press junket moves to the same relentless drummer. Time cannot be allowed to hang heavy on the captive journalists. Into their every hour some amusement must be shoved, no matter how artificial its nature or transparent its purpose: publicity abhors a vacuum. Endurance, however, is not as big a factor as in the world of school and camp. Where the headmaster makes his mark by outwitting the forces of adolescence for thirty or forty years, the average junket lasts only three or four days, or at the most a week. Yet after any such junket Mel Parker felt equal in weariness and wisdom

with Endicott Peabody retiring after half a century at
Groton.

This was because the Peabodys had an unfair advantage.
They operated within a rigid set of rules, weaving a tight
web of Puritanism around their students, secure in the approval of society. Pleasures of the flesh they simply snuffed
out by banning whiskey and cigarettes and by hinting darkly
of saltpeter in the food. But on a press junket the rulebook
was loose and the web of morality porous. In fact, the
providing of pleasure was not only permitted; it was counted
on. Every junketing newsman expected to be plied with
exotic dinners, drenched with liquor and exposed to the most
beautiful local girls, at least visually. Thus a junket-master's
task was to win the favor of the scribes with continual treats,
yet keep them from being rendered so insensible as to get
lost, get sick, get hurt, get mugged, or get too drunk to write
a story. Such a delicate balance might have taxed even
Boyden of Deerfield or Arnold of Rugby.

This kinship with formal education whirled through Mel's
head as he waited at the end of a wharf on Monday afternoon for the press plane to arrive. He paced up and down, an
athlete tensed up for the biggest game of his career. He had
the week's schedule blocked out in his head as precisely as
any headmaster, and he was impatient for the opening
whistle. His eyes swept the pale Pacific sky. Nothing. He lit a
cigar and took a long tug on his can of beer.

At his left, Sally sat dangling her legs over the edge of the
wharf. Cy Rumble, sitting on a wooden crate, his two arms
around his two Tonjian girls, sang "There is nothing like a
d-a-a-a-me." Simeon Lafonga, sprawled across a copra sack,
slept the sleep of those who have labored long and well. Denis
sat near by on a keg, sipping a rum punch that he had brought
down from the Kon-Tiki Bar, in aimless conversation with
Millie Hawkes, who had brought a bottle of Haig & Haig,
and with Literary Johnny, who was trimming his new Van-
dyke beard with scissors and a little mirror. On a wooden
platform, just completed by native carpenters, the band of
Palmerston Boys' College, hired by Mel, practiced without

conviction a medley of welcoming songs, and beyond them
two dozen Tonjian girls put the last flowers in frangipani *leis*
that they would hang around the necks of the dignitaries
from America, first giving them what Mel had called, in a
speech delivered with the rhetorical gusto of a judge's charge
to the jury, "a good sincere kiss" on both cheeks.

It was a moment of lull, an oasis of time that Sally hugged
tight, as though to make it last forever. Mel had driven her at
full speed all week. The two of them had worked feverishly
together, tying up a thousand untied ends, getting little sleep.
She had dug in the Hollywood substratum to its deepest
sedimentary layers, in beds of social anthropology un-
dreamed of by Pembleton College or U.C.L.A. or Dr. Feldspar. No Ph.D. would crown her efforts, yet she had learned
more than in any cram course that she had ever taken in the
Gothic halls of pedagogy. Were the preparations really over,
the final scenes really about to be played? She could hardly
believe it.

In the "Tonji Times" that morning, Old Settler's column
had been moved from its accustomed spot in the interior to
the top of Page 1. WEEK OF DECISION, it was titled. "Early
this afternoon," it began, "there will appear in the unde-
fended skies over Tonji a speck no bigger than a handful of
dust." It went on to say that gunpowder and dynamite were
also forms of dust, and that when this particular speck floated
down onto the lagoon, in the form of an airplane from
California, it would bear similar powers of destruction. The
column then described the "swollen tides of hoopla" that
were building up around the welcome of "a sex symbol"
named Moona Marone, "the care and liquid feeding" of the
journalists, the arrival of the cruise ship "Tonalela," the
unlawful occupation of Kula-ha'i island by its new tenants
from Iowa, and the world premiere there of "a tinseled
Hollywood charade." In proof of the litter being carried on
these tides, it said, "one need only note that Victoria Street
has changed its aspect almost overnight from one of the
prettiest thoroughfares in Oceania to a sleazy imitation of Las
Vegas or Soho." Truly, the column concluded, "today begins

a week of decision for our beloved islands, one which will profoundly alter the lives of many actors who may not even realize that they are on the stage."

Sally, who found the daily appearance of Old Settler's column more than a little spooky — the articles jolted her and Mel at breakfast every morning, especially one which implied that Lord Hargreave might fly out from London for "a firsthand view of the hanky-panky" — was nevertheless moved by today's piece. There was something about it that touched her and seemed to speak directly to her doubts. It *was* a week of decision, for her as well as for the islands. When it was over she would have to pick up the remnants, like a hostess after an all-night party, and sort out her jumbled emotions. There wouldn't be much time — the minutes would start running out quickly now. Mel would want her to go back to America; Amos Pembleton would want her to stay. She gazed at the gay and rickety buildings around the harbor and at the quiet blue lagoon, savoring a view that had already become part of herself, stamped into her more deeply than she would have thought possible in so short a period. She glanced at Mel and Cy on her right, and at Denis at her left, and felt a surge of affection for all three. If only the plane would never arrive.

The band swung listlessly into "Yankee Doodle," or its near approximation. The girls braiding their *leis* chattered and laughed. Simeon snored. Derricks whined and dock workers chanted in rhythm, one playing a conch shell to set the tempo, as they unloaded an inter-island schooner at the next wharf. Millie Hawkes crooned, "I wanna hold your ha-a-a-nd." Literary Johnny, rehearsing, declaimed a turgid passage by Joseph Conrad about the malign power of the sea. Seagulls screamed over fishermen's boats returning with their day's catch. And far to the north, no louder than a mosquito that has just squeezed through a window screen, the engines of an airplane pricked the afternoon air.

Mel watched through binoculars as the launch that met all planes, a relic of some nautical era which had otherwise vanished without a trace, nosed up to the "Moona Marone" at its mooring in the middle of the bay. The plane's engines, their precious cargo safely delivered, sputtered out and were still. The door remained shut. It's Pandora's boxville when that door opens, Mel thought.

After a while the door retracted and a large slovenly man loomed into the empty space. He leaned out and gave a jovial, uncoordinated wave to the crowd on the wharf. Then he emitted a loud bellow, lurched heavily, and fell into the water between the launch and the plane. A geyser of foam, displaced by his considerable weight, shot upward and engulfed a tiny woman starting to step out behind him. After an interval which struck Mel as long enough to swim the Yale pool, the man surfaced where he had gone down – a sight gratifying to Mel, who had expected the sunken journalist to come up under the launch like a rogue whale and bash it in. Two Tonjian boys groped for him with a boat hook.

"Christ!" Mel said.

The Tonjian girls on the wharf squealed with joy, their giggles alternating with the laughter from the band of Palmerston Boys' College, an antiphonal chorus that grew louder in succeeding billows until every tin shed reechoed the music.

"Shut up, goddam it!" Mel yelled.

Millie Hawkes choked on her Scotch and had to be brought back to respiration by Denis, pounding on her back. "Thanks, Denis," she coughed, wiping her tears on her calico skirt. "Whoo-ee! Did you see that old bastard *go!*"

"Who the hell was that?" Cy asked.

"That would be Farley Grogan," Mel said.

"And the little dame who got wet?"

"Olivia O'Connell. Blue hair and all."

"How terrible," Sally said, offering sympathy. "The poor man must have just lost his balance."

"Drunk as a billy goat," Mel said, in a voice that rejected the sympathy being invoked for Grogan. "We're lucky he didn't drown."

"He's still got tomorrow," Cy said. "Or maybe Wednesday he'll get around to it."

The laughter slowly subsided.

"Okay, you guys — play!" Mel called to the band. The musicians, wheezing into their brass instruments, blew out a fitful rendition of "Happy Talk."

Out at the launch, Farley Grogan was pulled unceremoniously aboard and the nineteen other passengers stepped down from the plane without mishap. Mel tried to identify them through his binoculars, but as a group they had a pervading neutrality of color, their suits gray, their faces pale. Only a lime-green beach hat with an enormous brim, which Mel assumed to belong to Perdita Fox-Martin, and a conical tower of silver cotton candy, which he knew to be Moona Marone's hair, stood out as landmarks recognizable from afar.

As the boat came closer he saw Emerich Eposcu rise, in a stance reminiscent of Washington crossing the Delaware, and shoot some pictures of the wharf and its expectant crowd. He saw Harvey Bluestone smiling the smile of a man who is off the hook. He saw the hair-curlers of Bobbie Baxter twinkling in the afternoon sun. He saw Mickey Dolan taking a swig from a flask. He saw Arnold Arkin writing in his little black notebook. He saw the sodden Grogan and the damp Olivia O'Connell. But the others still had that faceless look as common to the fourth estate when it goes grazing in a distant pasture as to a flock of sheep. Oh well, Mel thought, soon enough they'll look just as terrible at the opposite extreme — the men in garish hula shirts and shorts and shoes and funny little brown socks, the women in flowered halters and cerise slacks and high-heeled sandals. And speaking of looking terrible, Mel thought, who's that faggot with red hair sitting next to Moona Marone? The creep is even holding her hand. In his lap yet.

"God-*damn!*" Mel said when he made his identification of the unwelcome bird.

"Whatsa matter?" Cy asked.

"You know that fink, Norbert de Paul? Moona's agent?"

"Know him! I'd like to kick his ass from here to Bora-Bora,"
Cy said.

"Well, start today. Boot him into the lagoon, like acci-
dental."

"Can I, Mel? No crap? You mean it?"

"Your salary goes up ten dollars when I hear the splash."

Cy got down from his crate and began to stretch. "Don't go
away now, girls — hear?" he said to his two playmates.

Mel signaled to the band and they struck up a facsimile of
"Put on a Happy Face." He motioned to the two dozen
Tonjian girls; they clustered at the edge of the wharf, giggling and throwing kisses to the people in the launch, almost
beneath them now. The journalists waved back. So did
Moona Marone, first extracting her hand, well moistened,
from that of Norbert de Paul. "Hiya, sweetheart," Farley
Grogan shouted to one of the Tonjian girls from within the
wet bundle that constituted his person and his apparel.

The launch reached the dock and its passengers climbed up
a shaky ladder. Mel greeted each one warmly at the top.

"Hello, Miss O'Connell. Great to have you here. We're
most honored, ma'am . . . Hello, Arnie. Howza boy? Swell.
Got some good anecdotes for you . . . Hello, I'm Mel
Parker. Mr. Foy? A pleasure to meet you, sir. Wonderful that
you could come . . . Mickey Dolan, isn't it? Hi, Mickey:
Mel Parker. Been reading your stuff for a long time. Quite a
job you're doing. . . . Miss Fox-Martin? How d'you do? I'm
Melville Parker. My pleasure. Cy's all set to work with you on
that layout. Whenever you want. Good . . . Adrian
Struthers? Oh, Mr. *Dunnington*. Sorry. I'm Mel Parker. Welcome to Tonji. It's not Cannes or Venice, but it has its
points . . . *You're* Mr. Struthers? I think we've met before,
haven't we? No? Well, we're meeting now, that's the main
thing. Nice reviews on that novel, by the way . . . Hello, I'm
Mel Parker. Mr. Walters? Hello there! Delighted to have a
son of Iowa out here to cover the big event. How's the corn
this summer? Was it 'knee-high by the Fourth of July'? . . .
Hi, Emerich. Good to see you back in the Pacific. That was a

beautiful layout last spring on 'Enigma of Easter Island.' Sensitive but gutty: you know? . . . Hi, Bobbie. How was the all-girl safari? As if I didn't know. I wouldn't miss that column of yours . . . Hey, Don Phelps! How've you been. Haven't seen you since that 'Lydia Bailey' junket to Haiti. You still got dysentery? . . . Hello, I'm Mel Parker. You're Blake Hewitt of NBC. I used to see you on that late news wrap-up. 'World Focus,' right? This your photographer? Hi, Tony — let me give you a hand with that camera. It looks kind of heavy . . . Hello, Grogan. Couldn't resist taking a little swim, I see. I don't blame you. We'll get that suit over to Fong's laundry right away . . . Hiya, Tom. How's things at the old UP? I see they had you down at Cape Kennedy. Don't let 'em shoot you up in one of those things by mistake . . . You must be Bill Stanton. Hello, I'm Mel Parker. Welcome aboard. What? Yeah, seventeen saloons on that street right over there. Take your pick. No, we'll have you through customs in five minutes . . . MOONA! Doll! How are ya, baby? Got a kiss for old Mel? Mmmmmmm-mm! You're looking fabbo, honey. Just like a movie star. That's a joke. Give the folks a big wave. Say 'Hello everybody.' Good. Once more. Swell. See you later, doll . . . Norbert! Who let you in? Moona insisted? How nice. Well, you'd better not screw anything up, old buddy, or you'll find your ass out there with the sharks . . . Hiya, Sammy boy. Feeling strong? I'm gonna need plenty of help keeping this bunch of schlemiels from killing themselves . . . HARVEY! Am I glad to see you! Well, you got 'em here. Good work. Grogan looks a little wet, but otherwise they seem fine. Come on up and see fabled Tonji. I think you'll appreciate some of the changes we've made."

The new arrivals stood in a haphazard circle while the Tonjian girls swarmed over them with *leis* and kisses. Vern Walters and J. P. Foy flushed at the intensity of passion being bestowed by complete strangers, in excess of anything that they had encountered in years of marriage. But Emerich Eposcu, Bill Stanton and Farley Grogan took the kisses at their intended value, as a token of Polynesian friendship, and replied by locking their girls in embraces that lasted up to three minutes.

Mel Parker stood on a crate and quieted the crowd. "Thanks, girls," he said. "That was very nice."

"Once again, a big welcome to you all," he went on, as the voices died down and the girls gradually stopped giggling. "We're happy to have you here and we hope you'll enjoy your stay." Mickey Dolan belched. "First I'd like you to meet my assistants. Harvey Bluestone and Sammy Kelp, of course, you already know. They'll be working with me very closely. And this is Sally Merrill, my girl Friday and every-other-day."

He pulled Sally up onto the crate, where she stood in acute self-consciousness and jumped back down.

"Yay Sally!" Grogan roared.

"Sally is a student of Polynesian life," Mel continued, "so if there's anything you want from that angle I know she'll be more than glad to help. And this is Cy Rumble, whom many of you have probably met in the course of . . ."

"Hey Cy, where's the tail?" came a voice from the journalistic deeps.

"So just ask Cy," Mel went on, "if there's anything — and I see there is. We're gonna get you through customs fast and out to the El Tropiques Hotel for a swim. That's where you'll be staying. You'll find a press kit in your room that we think will be helpful. The cable office is at 172 Victoria Street, which is right over there next to the French consul, and we'll have it open from eight A.M. to midnight. The time difference, incidentally, is four hours to the Coast and seven to New York. The next airmail plane goes out Friday. Press headquarters is at Millie Hawkes's Boarding House — it's that big house with a red roof that you can just see. I should add that Mrs. Hawkes's bar is unusually well stocked. And while we're on the subject, we want you to sign for any drinks that you may possibly wish to consume. Just show the bartender the little identification card that you'll find in your press kit and leave the paying to us. Any questions?"

Seven voices simultaneously asked, "Is there a drugstore?"

"Sure is," Mel said. "Mrs. Walker's Strictly Reliable Pharmacy and Notions. It's on Disraeli Street, just off Victoria Street."

There was a restless stir among the journalists at the thought of Mrs. Walker, the druggist, so near at hand with relief for travel's hundred and one physical indignities.

"Any more questions?"

A thin hand went up.

"Yes?" Mel asked.

"I'd just like to say on behalf of my client, Moona Marone," came the parabolic voice of Norbert de Paul, "that she is exceedingly fatigued by her long journey, and though I'm sure we all agree that Moona is a real human be-eeeeeee-eeeee . . ."

A tremendous splash concluded his statement.

"I guess that's all," Mel said, genially. "Shall we go through customs?"

As a press agent Mel never tried to save money at the expense of comfort. He automatically spent the extra dollar — or thousand dollars — to do things right, however small the detail. One of his principles was not to put more than two people in a car. Therefore the caravan that took his press party to the El Tropiques, including the twenty new arrivals plus Sally and Cy and himself, consisted of twelve cars, nearly the entire local population of automobiles. They were mostly taxis, but he had also found two open touring cars. One of these, a 1932 Renault that belonged to the French consul, he put at the beginning, with himself and Olivia O'Connell as passengers. The other brought up the rear, with Moona Marone and Harvey. Norbert de Paul rode alone.

Mel instructed his driver to go at twenty miles an hour and to keep blowing his horn in a festive manner. The motorcade left the customs wharf and crept down the full length of Victoria Street, doubling back to pass various tourist attractions that Mel wanted the visitors to see. Consequently the trip to the El Tropiques Hotel, hardly a mile outside town, took ten minutes instead of the usual two. Nobody minded, however, except for Adrian Struthers, Jr., whose medicinal needs were so pressing that he jumped out when his car passed Mrs. Walker's Pharmacy. For the street was overhung with huge banners, the buildings were festooned with bunting, and the sidewalks were lined with women and children waving so eagerly that anyone might have thought that they were responding from pure joy, rather than from the money and lollipops that Mel had given them earlier. Several of the banners said WELCOME AMERICAN JOURNALISTS! and other such endearments. The rest reveled in the glorious events that were to occur within the next four or five days, such as the launching of the Danish raft, the arrival of Mr. and Mrs. Hal C. Mudge, the premiere of the movie, and the Queen of Tonji festival.

Music also serenaded the passing parade. Millie Hawkes had moved her jukebox onto the verandah, where the Beatles, wailing like sirens from their platter of wax, drew every eye to a blinking electric display that said MILLIE'S ORIGINAL DISCOTHÈQUE & CELEBRITY BAR. On the steps of Dirty Eddie's à Go-Go, two Tonjian girls danced the hula to an electric guitar, their breasts outdistancing their narrow halters by such a generous margin that Tom Carpenter thought his optician had mistakenly put trick lenses in his new glasses, and leaped out to see. Still not trusting his vision, he confirmed the wonderful news with his hand, by which time the motorcade had passed him by. Running after it, he dove headlong into Moona Marone's open car and reemerged to accept the plaudits of the crowd, along with Moona herself, who was waving to her subjects in a regal style that her charm coach at Titan Pictures had taught her only last week. Huge blownup photographs of Moona Marone waved back at her and smiled their vacuous smile. At Jerry's Authentic "Original Topless" South Sea Emporium, his new authentic dance troupe went through a sinuous ballet on the porch, and from "The Beatnik Beachcomber, Formerly Alfie's That's All" came the recorded voice of Barbra Streisand.

As the caravan wheeled into Disraeli Street the attractions took a cultural turn. Literary Johnny, in an alpaca coat, sat in a rocking chair outside the New Joseph Conrad Coffee House, smoking his pipe. Beside him a large theatrical poster announced:

Recital Tonight
"LITERARY JOHNNY"
Special Guest Appearance
TOM FALONGA
and his freedom songs

Just beyond him, at the Trade Winds Art Boutique & Gallery Shop, a sign plastered on the window said: CURRENT EXHIBI-TION: PRIMITIVES. VERNISSAGE TONIGHT AT 5. REFRESHMENTS.

Farther on, at the ex-"Presbyterian Milk Parlor," where Mrs. Beezley and her Wednesday Club had for so many years gathered to read Wordsworth and Edgar Guest, a new sign was now up, gold letters incised into wood:

the broken/cadence
poetry
readings
roethke/lowell
ginsberg/
dickey
et
al

Beyond, Herb's Psychedelic Pizza Parlor, newly opened by Mel to create a four-way tie-in — he had persuaded Herb to buy out Ralph's Frozen Custard — called to the gawking scribes not only with its aroma, but with a sign suggesting that they buy a pizza to eat while listening to the poetry, or to Literary Johnny's recital, or "après art."

Not all the signs, however, extended a hospitable hand. Mel was startled to see that quite a few had gone up since he last checked Victoria Street at noon. There was, for instance, the huge banner hanging from the belfry of Rev. Boggs's Methodist church. YANKEE HEATHEN, GO HOME!!! it said in dripping red capitals. HOLLYWOOD, REPENT! screamed a gigantic sign across the front of Rev. Bloodgood's Baptist church, and on the lawn of the First Presbyterian Church a poster had been nailed up, saying: GOD IS ALIVE IN TONJI — LET'S KEEP HIM THAT WAY!

From the second-floor office of the London Missionary Society, over Cheung Ho's Grill, a long streamer fluttered with the warning: VERILY, THE TITANS SHALL FALL AND THE DESERT ISLANDS FOR TWO BE LAID WASTE. AS IT WAS IN THE BEGINNING. Mel, shaken by the Biblical wrath of the message, still had to admire the brilliant allusion to Titan Pictures. Who was *their* press agent, he wondered?

Finally, most unsettling of all, Mel saw — too late to deflect the motorcade — a notice hanging from a window of the "Tonji Times" at the edge of town. JOURNALISTS! it cried in big black letters painted on a sheet, DO YOU KNOW THAT THE APPROPRIATION OF 'MOONA-MOONA' ISLAND CONSTITUTES AN ILLEGAL INTERNATIONAL ACT BY THE BRITISH CROWN AGAINST THE JUST CLAIMS AND DECENT ASPIRA-TIONS OF THE TONJIAN PEOPLE? INQUIRE WITHIN FOR PARTICULARS.

"What's that all about, Mel dear?" asked Olivia O'Connell, straining her rheumy eyes to puzzle out the tangled question.

"Oh, you know how many hotheads there are in these emerging nations," Mel scoffed. "It's just some kind of nut."

"Still, it sounded like a nice little item for my column. I think I'll go around tomorrow and see if they can explain what they're so upset about."

Mel swore under his breath. Old Settler strikes again, he mumbled to himself. Tune in Tuesday for another installment of "The Phantom Columnist."

Arnie Arkin lolled in his batik bathing trunks on a foam-rubber cushion in the middle of the El Tropiques's new swimming pool, writing with the waterproof ballpoint pen that Harvey had brought. The pool had arrived from Hous-

ton on Wednesday and had been sunk by Simeon and a gang
of laborers into a flat area formerly used as a tennis court.
Only a metal sign attached to the diving board, bearing the
promised plug, betrayed its expedient origin:

FRIENDS:
SWIM IN GOOD HEALTH
Irving Polowitz
President
BIG-AS-ALL-OUTDOORS
Houston 17, Texas

It was late afternoon. Arnie Arkin was at peace. He was
committing to paper, in his own words, six anecdotes that he
had found typed up, "exclusive" for him, on a table in his
hotel room. Mel had constructed them in such a way that, no
matter how Arnie might reshape them or obfuscate their
meaning, it would be impossible to omit the words "Moona-
Moona," "Moona Marone," "Tonji" and "Desert Island for
Two."

At a poolside table, where he was draining a rum and
tonic, Duncan Dunnington pricked up his ear at a hint that
had just been dropped disingenuously into it by Sammy Kelp.

"Did you say, old boy," he asked, "that both Flaherty *and*
Murnau were here?"

"That's what Mel told me," Sammy said. "Of course I
haven't been in Tonji any longer than *you* have. But Mel said
that when Flaherty was filming 'Moana of the South Seas'
and Murnau was working on 'Tabu,' they both came to scout
locations at a little village on one of these islands. Valonga."

"Good heavens, do you suppose I could *go* there?" Dunnington asked. "It's the least one can do, when one considers
the debt that the entire aesthetic of documentary cinema
owes to those two men. By any standard they earned the
right to be called '*maître.*' "

"Mel thought you'd be interested," Sammy said, "so he
arranged some kind of excursion over there tomorrow."

"Good," Dunnington said. "It'll make a nice piece for one of the little magazines: a pilgrim to one of the loneliest shrines in the collective intellect of film. Too recondite for the masses, of course, but that's the difference between a critic and a reviewer."

"Nobody would call you a reviewer, Mr. Dunnington," Sammy said.

"I should hope not," Dunnington shot back.

"Yoo-hoo, everybody," came the voice of Bobbie Baxter. "Look what I just bought — the cutest li'l dress you ever did see. It's called a 'moona' — isn't that *camp?* It's like a Lilly, only it's made of tapa-cloth, which is some kind of crazy bark-printing they've got out here, and it's slit up the side in case you want to show your legs."

Don Phelps looked up from the thick press kit, which he seemed to be trying to memorize, and reflected that the last view he wanted to be shown in Polynesia was Bobbie Baxter's legs. He was grateful in this respect, though not in any other respect, for the black slacks that Miss Baxter continued to wear, just as he dreaded the moment when the curlers would come out of her hair and release it into the atmosphere.

"Where did you get it?" Norbert de Paul asked about the dress. "It's adorable."

"At Madame Ye's. She's got an entire line in different sizes. I'm gonna take them back for all my friends at Christmas."

"Me too," Norbert said.

"I don't think that's quite what Mel has in mind, Norbert," Sammy Kelp said.

"Thank you, darlings," said Perdita Fox-Martin to four Tonjian boys who had followed her to the pool. Put them down against those patio chairs, will you?" The boys laid down the twelve paintings that they had carried from the Trade Winds Art Boutique, and Miss Fox-Martin gave them each a quarter. "Anybody want to see the most absolutely *stun*ning primitives?" she called to the idling journalists. They clustered in desultory fashion around the gay canvases, and Arnie Arkin paddled over on his foam cushion from the middle of the pool. "I bought all twelve," she announced, as proudly as if she had just reconstructed the palace at Knossos. "It's the most en*chant*ing little gallery — really, everything in the shop was quite divine — but these paintings were the best." She looked at her acquisitions with a maternal glow.

"Say, what did you get?" asked an enthusiastic new voice. It was Mel Parker, back with Mickey Dolan, whom he had taken to see maidens dancing at sunset.

Miss Fox-Martin showed him her collection. "I'll bet you never saw anything like *them* before," she said.

"Certainly didn't," Mel said. "You've got a great eye, Miss Fox-Martin."

Dolan sidled over to Adrian Struthers, Jr., who, inspired by frequent glances across the Pacific, was making a list of adjectives.

"Halcyon," "roseate," "umber," "rufous," "iridescent" and "tessellated" were already written in his small, tight script.

"Sorry you missed the maidens dancing next to the lagoon, Struthers," Mickey Dolan said. "It was just your kind of novelist's setting."

"Where? When?" Struthers asked.

"Just now — at a village about eight miles down the coast. Some kind of hymn to the setting sun that the virgins of Tonji dance out. Once a month."

"Once a *month?*"

"That's all, old buddy. Maybe if you come back on September fifteenth you'll catch it."

"What was it like?" Struthers asked.

"Suddenly it was there," Dolan said. "And you could hardly believe it. You were just an ordinary Joe from Flatbush and you were too old to believe in miracles. You'd seen the posters and the brochures and the travelogues and you knew it wasn't that way. Not really. You weren't going to be suckered by some two-bit dream."

"Yes, but what was it *like?*" Struthers asked.

"Suddenly it was there. You thought maybe you were on pot and yet you wanted it to be for keeps. You knew . . ."

"Oh hell, I'll fake it," Struthers said. "Nobody'll know the difference."

The sun was now almost down, an immense red globe on the horizon. Mel climbed up on a chair and called his sheep around him.

"First of all," he said, "are you all comfortably settled? Got your suitcases? Plenty to drink? Any complaints?"

A satisfied murmur rose from the ranks.

"Good," Mel went on. "Now it's getting around to the hour when you'll probably want to change and have drinks and dinner and see some local night life. I don't want you to feel that you're being 'organized' — if you'd like to go off by yourself that's fine. But I was going to propose that we make a relaxed tour of the town, and that'll give you an idea of where everything is."

"That sounds mighty nice to me," said Vern Walters.

"First I thought we might go have a drink at the Kon-Tiki Bar & Surfers' Club," Mel continued. "The bartender over there is a guy named Fat Lou who can tell you how the whole surfing bit got its start here in Tonji."

"It did?" asked J. P. Foy.

"That's what Fat Lou claims, and I must say he's got enough pictures on the wall." Mel felt a reflex of pain in his thumb from the two hours that he had spent thumbtacking pictures from surfing magazines on Fat Lou's wall, while also teaching him the argot of the sport.

"Then I thought we might stop at Dirty Eddie's à Go-Go," he went on, "for a real Polynesian dinner. I've reserved some tables, and you guys who've been asking me about a genuine South Sea hula dance can take the tables nearest the stage. Just don't get your heads knocked off when the girls begin to shake. After that we'll have coffee at Literary Johnny's, which I think you'll enjoy because you're writers and Johnny knew all the authors who came through the islands — Conrad and Maugham and Nordhoff & Hall and the whole bunch.

"Then we'll stop at Millie Hawkes's Discothèque. I've asked some Tonjian girls to meet us there around ten to help you overcome your natural shyness. Then we can go over to

Jerry's, which has a dance troupe that reenacts the old Polynesian legends, and after that . . . well, there are plenty of other spots — this Tonji is a swinging little place. But that'll probably be enough for one night, because tomorrow we've got an all-day trip lined up to a beautiful island called Valonga. Does that sound O.K.?"

"How about that Club Gauguin we passed driving through town?" asked Bill Stanton. "I saw a pair of knockers coming out of there today that . . ."

"We'll try to fit it in," Mel said.

"What about the Beatnik Beachcomber?" asked Farley Grogan. "It looked like a place that would turn you on."

"Let's save it for tomorrow night. So . . . let's see . . . it's half-past six . . . how about we all meet in the lobby at seven? . . . Great."

The journalists dispersed to their rooms, Arnie Arkin dragging his foam-rubber cushion behind him, Perdita Fox-Martin commanding four hotel boys to carry her pictures, Bobbie Baxter taking the curlers out of her hair. Mel and Sally and Sammy Kelp watched them go with relief, their human burden briefly unburdened. Harvey Bluestone was still off on a diplomatic errand, having taken Moona Marone to meet Sir Reginald, and Cy had gone along to photograph the royal audience.

Sammy Kelp told Mel about his conversation with Dunnington. "Did Flaherty and Murnau really go to that island we're visiting tomorrow?" he asked.

"Are you kidding?" Mel said.

16

Tuesday began badly. In purely physical terms there was not a journalistic head that didn't throb from the night's mixture of potent drinks, foods, sights and spectacles — even the teetotaling Vern Walters had a hangover — and there was hardly a pelvis that didn't ache from the dance lessons given by various Tonjian girls at Millie Hawkes's Discothèque. Mel had stuck to his announced itinerary, steering his charges from one dive to another with a precision that appeared entirely casual, until at two A.M. he pushed them off to bed, giddy with the spell of the islands and the pleasures of total release. Now they were at breakfast on the outdoor terrace of the El Tropiques, silent and staid, each trying in his own fashion, with coffee and with pills, to set his metabolic house in order.

In psychological terms, too, there was an ill wind blowing across the terrace. It came from the "Tonji Times," and Mel was helpless to fan it away. He had known all along that this puny gazette, this "two-minute silence," would be the worm in his daily apple — a worm that he would give anything not to have the journalists eat every morning with their papaya and breadfruit. But he also knew that a newspaperman without a morning newspaper, however meager it might be, is a man bereaved, a soul lost from mortal reach. Not to deliver the "Times" to each member of the press party at breakfast would be to generate the blackest of moods.

Still, on this of all mornings, this first morning when he

wanted his guests to relish the clean beauty of a new Pacific day, the worm was unusually tart. The lead story dealt at extraordinary length with the arrival of the journalists. Though it was strictly reportorial, the writer had selected his facts with surgical care. A whole paragraph was devoted to Farley Grogan's drunken plunge, another to Tom Carpenter's dash from the motorcade to feel the hula dancers, and a third to Moona Marone's wave, "the first sample that Tonji has seen of American automation." Bobbie Baxter's hair-curlers and Norbert de Paul's hair were also mentioned.

Mel saw immediately that the writer of the article was the same person as the current writer of Old Settler's column, for in an adjacent spot on Page 1, under the all-too-familiar ensign of OLD SETTLER SAYS, he went over the same terrain, this time dipping his pen in the special ink of personal opinion that is every columnist's lifeblood:

CLASH OF SYMBOLS
By Old Settler

The British people are no strangers to symbolism. On the contrary, in the elaborate rituals and rubrics that hedge our Kings and Queens, our Peerage and our Parliament, we have long since learned to apprehend certain truths about the English character and heritage which speak more eloquently than words.

Hence it required no special gift yesterday for British residents of Tonji, or for Tonjians reared in the historical warp and woof of Albion, to read the symbols of decay written in the debarking from Hollywood of 16 journalists, one peroxided star, and three studio lackeys. From the initial moment of their invasion, when the door of the aircraft "Moona Marone" opened and a flagrantly inebriated reporter fell out of it into the lagoon, it was patent that the iconography of our islands is in imminent peril of . . .

Don Phelps looked up from the column to greet Mel, who had just come to see how everybody was getting along.

"That old guy can really write," Phelps said, pointing at the newspaper.

"What makes you think he's old?" Mel asked.

"I went to see him yesterday. He's got some good stuff on Section 37A of the Land Act."

"You went to *see* him? At his office?"

Phelps nodded.

"Who *is* he?" Mel asked. "What's he look like?"

"Just a nice old guy. Thin, with white hair. He was very helpful — gave me everything I need."

"What was his name?"

"It began with a 'Q' . . . Quaritch. That was it."

"Quaritch!" Mel repeated.

"Hey, is anything wrong?" Phelps asked.

"No, no," Mel said, composing himself. "I guess I'm just a little shaky from last night."

"That was a gasser all right," Phelps agreed. "You really showed us a time."

"Give the credit to Tonji," Mel said. "This little place has got a lot of zap."

At ten o'clock the journalists were herded into cars and driven to the harbor, where four speedboats were waiting to take them to Valonga. Just as into every junket some liquor must fall, so one day must be set aside for sightseeing. Its ostensible purpose is to show the journalists as many "points of interest" as possible, thus humoring the need of Mr. and Mrs. America to see and take pictures of every certified "tourist attraction," wherever their ship comes in or their plane comes down.

But its more important purpose is to change the rhythm of the junket. It gets the scribes out of town, reminds them that lavish planning has gone into their entertainment, gives them a sense of adventure, and binds them in the convivial fellowship of mild discomforts shared and overcome.

"And it's *also* the day," Mel explained to Sally before the journalists arrived, "when starlet falls from horse."

"What on earth does that mean?" she had asked.

"Oh, that's just my name for it," Mel said. "But what it means is that something newsworthy has got to happen. Which it almost never does. So one of the press agents usually ends up pushing the starlet off her horse, and that's worth a headline in every newspaper that says 'Starlet Falls from Horse.' It's not as extreme as 'Starlet Breaks Leg' and it gets the same results."

"Poor starlet," Sally said.

Now, on the wharf, Mel methodically assigned his flock to the four speedboats, putting a member of his staff in each. He himself took Arnie Arkin, Bobbie Baxter, Mickey Dolan and Farley Grogan, journalists whose needs he felt peculiarly suited to fill, sharing as he did their bent for overstatement and their impatience with fact. He also took Norbert de Paul to keep him subdued. Harvey Bluestone was given Moona Marone and he also got Olivia O'Connell, Mel thinking it politic to keep that dowager queen of gossip close to its principal fount. Into Sally's boat he loaded the writers who were proud of their sensitivity to exotic detail, like Adrian Struthers, Jr., and Perdita Fox-Martin, confident that she would ply them with lore both picturesque and accurate, and Sammy Kelp got the remainder, including Duncan Dunnington, for whom he would continue to recall the visit to these very waters, so many years ago, of the sainted Flaherty and Murnau.

It took an hour for the boats to reach Valonga, threading their way outside the reefs of several smaller islands and then making a twenty-minute run across the open ocean. Sally, a scholar at last turned teacher, pointed out villages along the shore, described their daily life and tribal structure, identified tropical birds and flying fish, made the boat stop when it crossed a reef so that her pupils could look down at the brilliant coral through a glass face mask that she had brought along for the purpose, and generally reveled in talking about a culture which she had long admired in print and which now, alive, she loved. Her enthusiasm bubbled over and her passengers were caught up in it.

"We're mighty lucky to get you in our boat, Miss Merrill," Vern Walters said. "You've added a great deal to my appreciation of these islands."

"You're right, Vern," J. P. Foy agreed. "It makes all the difference."

Adrian Struthers asked why Valonga had been chosen for the day's excursion. He had just looked up from adding "opaline" and "prismatic" to his list of adjectives applicable to the sea.

"Well, Mr. Parker felt," Sally said, referring to him with the formality of a teacher defining the goals of her principal, "that this island combined the most appealing features of Tonji as a whole. In the first place, it's very beautiful — if you look now you can just begin to see its twin volcanoes, which, incidentally, are held sacred by the Tonjian people. We'll be landing at a pretty little village that's built around a lagoon, so you'll be able to see what Polynesian life is like in its purest form, away from the influence of a town. The chief is going to meet us and have a welcoming ceremony — we'll probably sit in a circle and drink kava, which is made by grinding the root of a plant that belongs to the pepper family."

"There's a description of that in the press kit," Vern Walters said. "I'll bet you wrote that material, Miss Merrill. Am I right?"

"Right," Sally said, blushing slightly. "Is it helpful at all?"

"Intriguing," Perdita Fox-Martin said. "I know I can use it in my captions."

"Most informative," said Adrian Struthers, adding "peregrine" to his list.

"After that," Sally continued, "we'll walk to a nearby village where they make tapa cloth, so you can see how *that's* done. I guess you know they make it from white strips of bark. The women soak the bark in water and then they pound it for hours until it's as thin as paper. Then they paint it in their own designs with dyes that they get from different plants."

"Can we buy any?" asked Perdita Fox-Martin, her question a surrogate for the vast body of American tourists who don't feel that travel is travel until it has been ratified by purchase and by postcard.

"I suppose so," said Sally, who hoped not.

"If I give them enough money they're bound to sell me some," Miss Fox-Martin said.

"You thinking of having a dress made?" J. P. Foy asked.

"Oh, something more kicky than that. Like maybe a slip-cover for the ottomans in my conversation pit at West-hampton."

"Then," Sally went on, "we're going to go up the side of that volcano — Nui-Nui — to the old capital of Tonji. It's on a plateau that was cleared away, maybe a thousand years ago, by a race that might have been ancestors of the present Tonjians, or might have been a different race altogether. Anyhow, we know that this was their capital — it's in the most commanding location and it has monuments that could only have been built by a king who had tremendous power."

"What kind of monuments, Miss?" Foy asked.

"The most famous is the hexalithon, or six stones. It's four immense vertical slabs of coral rock, twenty-five feet high, with two horizontal lintels mortised into them. And next to it you can see a group of burial mounds that have a border of huge coral rocks that must have taken a thousand men to drag up there. It's very impressive. Incidentally, there's a time gap between this ancient burial ground and the tombs of the present Tonjian chiefs, over on Saloma, which only go back five hundred years. Where the kings of the intermediate period are buried we still have no idea."

"Any clues?" Struthers asked.

"Not yet."

"How are we going to get *up* to that monument?" Miss Fox-Martin asked, shading her eyes to look at the volcano, which now loomed over them as their boat neared the shore.

"Don't laugh," Sally said, "but we're going up on burros."

"*Bu*rros!" her passengers said in unison.

"Well, at least you didn't laugh," Sally said.

"Arnie Arkin on a burro — this I gotta see," Struthers said. He started to laugh.

"Burros aren't indigenous to the islands," Sally said, "but there was a phosphate mine over here many years ago and the British imported burros to work it. They're tame little things — ideal for taking tourists up to Nui-Nui."

"If I'd only known we were going to visit that old monument," Perdita Fox-Martin said, "I would have brought my ski clothes. Can't you just *see* a girl in stretch pants leaning against those coral slabs?"

When the entire press party had landed and been welcomed by Chief Fa'a Nui and his attending maidens; when the ceremonial kava had been drunk and everyone agreed it tasted like toothpaste; when Duncan Dunnington had been taken for a walk down the beach by Sammy Kelp to put his sandals into the ghostly footprints of Flaherty and Murnau; when the village ladies had demonstrated Polynesian cooking and the journalists had eaten a sticky lunch of *poi* with their fingers; and when the women in the adjoining village had blocked sample bolts of tapa cloth for the visitors and Miss Fox-Martin had bought twenty yards of "the most heavenly pattern," all was in readiness for the climb. The scribes were led to a field where several dozen burros were idly munching on voluptuous shrubs, tended by three hags who had a variety of straw and sisal hats on sale.

"Hey gentleman! Keep off Mister Sun," they shouted, approaching each journalist in turn, and each journalist in turn bought a hat and put it on. It only remained for them to mount the burros, an act so foreign to their urban origins that they kept sliding off.

"You think I'm gonna get up on that *horse?*" Moona Marone hissed at Harvey Bluestone.

"It's not a horse, sweetheart," he hissed back. "It's a little ol' burro, so get your little ol' bottom up there pronto."

"Burro shmurro, I'm not getting up on any *an*imal."

"I'll count to five, sugar," Harvey said. "One . . . two . . ."

"Nor-*bert!*"

"Three . . ."

"My contract says . . ."

"Four . . ."

". . . I'm not required to . . ."

"Five!"

The thwack of a flat hand resounded on the eminent behind of Moona Marone, one of her few domains not insured by Lloyd's of London, and almost before the others could turn to see what might have caused a noise so sharp yet spongy, Miss Marone was astride her burro and starting up the trail.

"Moona wants to go first," Harvey called back to the journalists, poised on their burros in a ragged file. "O.K., fellas?"

Cries of "Sure!" and "Lead on, Moona!" came from the scribes, still somewhat surprised at finding themselves aloft.

"She's a plucky kid," Harvey said, turning his burro to follow his leader.

"Real guts!" said Sammy Kelp, taking up the cry and passing it back.

"A trouper!" Mel said, bringing up the rear.

"I *told* you!" said Norbert de Paul, his voice jiggling as his burro joined the cavalcade. "She's a real human being."

Sally had announced that it would take the burros an hour and a quarter to climb to Nui-Nui. They picked their way nimbly up the trail, which curved through stands of bamboo and giant ferns and other garish plants. Its steep angle tilted the riders backward, but they hung onto the reins and soon convinced themselves that they were having a ball. Miss Fox-Martin said she hadn't done such a fun thing since she rode to Petra on a dromedary, Bobbie Baxter said she hadn't had such a fun trip since she rode to Amber on an elephant, and Emerich Eposcu said he hadn't been on such a fun kick since he rode through the Sudd on a water buffalo to photograph his four-color essay on the Dinka tribe, "Strange Legacy of the Stork People." Had anybody seen it? Nobody seemed to have seen it. "*I* saw it," Mel's voice came racing into the vacuum. "Deeply moving, Emerich." Arnie Arkin said that this was turning out to be the best junket since the opening of the Istanbul Hilton. Farley Grogan said it wasn't as good as the opening of the Comrade Hilton in Moscow, which led to a swift exchange of Hilton jokes.

"They're in a great mood," Sally said to Mel. She was riding with him at the end of the column. "I don't know how you do it."

"Partly by sending Moona first," he explained. "A lot of these guys would complain like hell if you even showed 'em a *pic*ture of a burro. But they think, 'If that little girl can ride up a volcano, by God so can I.'"

"Did you ever think of being a psychologist?" Sally asked, looking at him with genuine admiration. Of all the miracles that he had passed so far, this was the most miraculous. In front of them, twenty straw-hatted heads bobbed along (only the aging Olivia O'Connell had remained below), following each other in a forty-five-degree ascent through the matted greenery, and they were loving it, though if you had asked any of them during the year to play so much as a game of quoits they would have recoiled.

"I don't think psychology would be as enjoyable," Mel answered, smiling, pleased to have won a compliment at last from his severest critic — the critic whose approval, he suddenly realized, he wanted more than anybody else's. "Are you having a good time?" he said to Sally with a tenderness that took her by surprise.

"It's a day I'll never forget," she said. She gave him a warm and appreciative smile. "You know, I didn't think Moona would agree to go off on that burro."

"She didn't," Mel said.

After they had been climbing for three-quarters of an hour, Mel felt a sharp plink on his straw hat. Rain. He looked up anxiously at the sky, which had turned gray, and another drop fell into his eye.

"You feel anything, Sal?" he asked.

"I thought I felt rain," she said. "It's probably just a brief shower. It'll cool us off."

But the shower gave no hint of brevity, or of remaining a shower. The sky turned from gray to black, the clouds descended to hover on the riders' heads, and the raindrops ceased to be individual raindrops. In the ranks, however, there was no sign of anarchy; if anything, the troops were more resolute than ever. Cries of "We're almost there," "Let's go on," and "We can't get any wetter" echoed through the column. The journalists pulled their straw hats down and rode on.

Whoever had said "We can't get any wetter" undoubtedly thought he was speaking the truth. When someone is caught in the rain, soaked from head to toe, he is as easily persuaded as if he were in a bathtub that he is wet all over. Still, there are degrees of being wet all over that are beyond the imagining of anyone who has not lived in the tropics, as the journalists discovered. What had begun as a sprinkle grew into a drizzle and then into a rain, then into a downpour, then into a cloudburst, then into a deluge, and finally into a raging cataract. The effect was as close as any of them would come to sitting at the base of Niagara Falls. Water of incredible volume beat down upon the cowering heads.

And still the caravan moved onward and upward, its psychological spark still dry, the riders hanging tenaciously to the slippery burros, the burros hanging tenaciously to the slippery trail, until Moona Marone, and then Harvey Bluestone, and then their twenty followers straggled into a clearing and saw, dimly, through sheets of rain, six coral slabs that constituted the ruins of Nui-Nui. Bringing their burros to a halt, they jumped off and ran for shelter under the two lintels of the hexalithon, trying to borrow at least the memory of dryness, huddling in tight knots to keep warm. Desperate for a smoke, they remained desperate — every cigarette had decomposed into its original element of loose tobacco, every match was a sodden strip of cardboard. Shivers ran through them and shook them to the marrow.

"Anyone got a drink?" came a weak voice.

Farley Grogan had a drink. Producing a flask from his pocket, he unscrewed the top, took a long swallow, and passed it from person to person, rationing the golden elixir, ministering to the stricken, even prevailing on Vern Walters to forget his Baptist code. No dog arriving with a serum was ever welcomed more gratefully than Grogan, who only yesterday had disgraced their arrival. Monday's sinner was Tuesday's saint, and all was forgiven.

The flask empty, the lofty destination reached, there was nothing left to do but look at the ancient monuments. In the oppressive grayness, however, there was little to look at and no zest to learn. The sightseeing flame, seemingly unextinguishable in the American breast, was washed out, and through the entire party ran a single impulse to get back down the mountain. Sally made one effort to engage their interest and to fix the site, so dearly won, in their minds. Standing apart from the wretched forms huddled under the lintel, she called their attention to certain engineering feats, pointed out the burial mounds and their huge encircling stones, and explained that on a good day — which, she regretted, this had ceased to be — it was possible to see for twenty miles in all directions; hence the capital was in an ideal spot. She looked beautiful, as Mel told her later, her blue eyes shining with pleasure out of a face shining with rain, her black hair hanging wet down her back. But her students were beyond the call of beauty. Their thoughts were turned inward onto their own misery, and only Vern Walters and J. P. Foy could muster a polite question to acknowledge her effort.

"Do you think it'll clear off, Sally, if we stay up here awhile?" Tom Carpenter asked in an attempt to be helpful.

"I doubt it," Sally said, glancing up — not very far — at the clouds. "I think Valonga is getting its entire rainfall for the year this afternoon."

"Let's go, then," came a voice, and with one motion the journalists sprang out from under the lintel, ran to their burros, clambered on, and started pell-mell down the trail.

If the downward trip went faster than the climb up, it was because the burros soon dropped the formality of using their feet. The trail had turned into a running stream — white water cascaded down it in rapids. At first the burros tried to keep their footing, but they slipped and stumbled, fell to their knees and got back up, tried again and tripped, until at last they sat on their rumps and used the trail as a slide. Down, down, down the slippery chute they were borne, around corners, caroming off rocks, occasionally standing up to make a fresh start and again losing their balance.

To their riders, instinct gave special powers of stamina and grit. "Hang on," the instinct told them, "however outlandish the burro's position, and you will get home to a hot bath and a warming drink." They hung on, their bodies tilted so far back that they were almost parallel with the hurtling stream and sometimes in it. Across their faces was written the vacant stare seen on infantrymen in newsreels about Guadalcanal, a withdrawal from the world into some private prison of the soul. "Hang on," the instinct repeated. "Nothing else matters." Nothing else did. They hung on, and on, and on.

And then, mercifully, they were at the bottom. How they got there they hardly knew. But they did know that the boats were near, and they abandoned their burros and half-ran through the village where, earlier, they had drunk kava and eaten such a tranquil lunch beside a blue lagoon. Could the lagoon really have been blue? Had the village really been circled by foliage of brilliant green? Such colors were almost washed off the palette of their minds, leaving nothing but gray. And had the village really been full of laughing women and dancing children in gaudy fabrics? Now everyone was inside, and only an occasional dark face peeping out from a thatched hut was proof that the village hadn't been deserted and left to the rain god.

Mel quickly shoved all the journalists into three of the four boats. He pushed the three boats out into the water and told the Tonjian pilots to get home as fast as possible. So hastily did he manage the departure that none of the journalists noticed who was there and who wasn't. They crouched low in their boats, pressing against each other for warmth, and didn't look back.

Sally and Cy and Sammy Kelp watched them go.

Mel looked at his watch. "Exactly four-thirty," he said.

"They'll be home by five-thirty and dried out and drinking by six. Perfect. But Jesus what a rain!"

He took a last look at the saturated island. "O.K.," he said, motioning to his three friends to get into the fourth boat. "Let's get this show on the road."

At six o'clock Mel strode rapidly into the bar of the El Tropiques Hotel. He had had a hot shower and a quick bourbon at Millie's. His eye made a rapid tour of the room and saw that most of his sheep were there, dry at last, seeking balm in the whiskey of their choice. Arnie Arkin's face, however, was contorted in pain, and when he caught sight of Mel he came running to meet him.

"Look at this, willya?" he shouted. "Just *look* at it!" He waved a soggy and shapeless object in front of Mel's face.

"What *is* it, Arnie?" Mel asked.

"My *note*book, for Chrissake. Every note I've taken since the junket began. Hollywood, Honolulu, Tonji — the whole bit."

Mel examined the limp pages. Here and there he could make out the faint remains of a word, as on a fragment of pottery just unearthed at Ur of the Chaldees, but the letters were pale beyond recognition. All was lost. Not one immortal word of Arnie's had been spared by the devouring rain.

"Don't worry, Arnie," Mel said. "I've got plenty of good stuff. I'll see that you don't run short."

"Run short! How's not to run short? I began making notes in the taxi going to the airport at L.A. I had a swell anecdote about What's-His-Name . . . not Steve McQueen . . . not . . . you know, the guy who was in that picture about the drummer who's got a hangup on mind drugs . . . it'll come to me in . . ."

"Excuse me, Arnie," Mel broke in, "but this is kind of important. Have you seen Moona?"

Arkin's nose quivered slightly. "Moona?" he said. "Moona Marone?"

Mel nodded. His expression was serious.

"No, why?" Arkin asked.

"Was she in your boat? I mean, coming back from the island?"

"No. Wasn't she in yours?"

"I thought she was in *yours,*" Mel said. "Hey, Emerich! Was Moona in your boat?"

"No such luck. What's the matter?"

"I can't find her," Mel said. The room was suddenly quiet. "Was anybody here in the *fourth* boat? Duncan?"

"Not me, old boy," Dunnington said. "I was with Emerich."

"Miss O'Connell?" Mel asked, his voice rising with apprehension.

"No, darling. I was with Arnie. You don't mean the poor girl was left on that horrible volcano?"

"Aouuuuuuuuu!" came a high wailing sound from a corner of the room, followed by Norbert de Paul, stumbling crazily towards Mel. "*I* was in the fourth boat," he screamed. "I thought she was with you! You *monster!*" He beat his fists against Mel's chest. "What have you done with my client?"

"Easy," said Mel, catching the whirlwind of fists. "We'll find her in the morning — she'll be perfectly all right."

"*Mo*rning!" cried Norbert. "We'll find her *now!* As her personal representative I demand that we go back to the island *this minute.*"

"I'm afraid that's impossible, Norbert," Mel said with solicitude. "Sunset's in another fifteen minutes and that passage can't be navigated after dark. Very tricky reefs — you saw that for yourself today."

"Nevertheless I de*mand* . . ." Norbert began, but his sentence was swallowed in a babble of journalistic voices.

"It's four hours' time difference to the Coast?" asked Don Phelps of the Associated Press.

". . . catch the late edition," said Tom Carpenter of UPI.

". . . all papers west of Denver," said Bill Stanton of the Scripps-Howard chain.

". . . make over Page One," said Farley Grogan of Hearst.

". . . my readers!" said Mickey Dolan. "Leo Corcoran at Bleeck's, and Mary Agnes out in Ozone Park, and little Tom . . ."

All five men ran out of the bar to get their typewriters, trailed by Bobbie Baxter, Arnie Arkin and Vern Walters. J. P. Foy asked Mel if the cable office was still open.

"Yes," Mel said, "but I'd better call and get some extra operators." He walked to the main desk and feigned making a phone call. He had already told Mr. O'Hara to have five extra men on duty at 6 P.M. J. P. Foy watched him for a moment and then hurried down the hall to his room. In the bar, Olivia O'Connell scribbled furiously on her stenographer's pad. Only six journalists went back to their drinking and allowed the reportorial storm to blow over their heads: photographer Emerich Eposcu, the two men from NBC television, and three writers representing monthly magazines — Perdita Fox-Martin, Adrian Struthers and Duncan Dunnington.

Mel told Sammy Kelp to make sure that there were enough taxis at the front door to take the scribes to the cable office. Then he sat down at a table where Sally was having tea.

"Starlet falls from horse?" she asked.

"Starlet gets left on mountain," Mel replied.

"Where *is* starlet?" she asked.

"Starlet's on mountain."

"No kidding? All alone?" She looked at Mel with amazement.

"Not quite. Harvey's with her, and they'll be put up tonight in that village where we had lunch, perfectly safe and comfortable, though *Moona* probably won't think it's so comfortable."

"And then what?"

"I'll go over and get starlet tomorrow morning in the Royal Coast Guard's one helicopter and bring her back for a triumphal press conference. Plucky film queen found alive. Recalls night of terror."

"But are these guys going to believe a story like that?" Sally nodded her head toward the vanished journalists. "Won't they even check it?"

"They don't have time to check it," Mel said. "I think you'll agree that the planning is rather good in that respect. If they're gonna make the late edition their story has to be written and cabled by seven o'clock — a little less than an hour from now — and none of them can afford to be beaten by the others. They've got scoop fever: you could smell it in the air."

"So the story will be in the morning papers?"

"West of Chicago," Mel said. "And it'll make the afternoon papers in New York and the East. And of course it'll get picked up by all the TV and radio news programs. Then tomorrow I'll bring Moona back and the poor schlumps will have to write another story saying she's been found."

"Brother!" Sally said, dazed at the sight of so many jagged pieces falling into place.

"Two front-page stories in two days," Mel murmured. "Not bad, eh?"

"You're a genius," Sally said.

"Thanks, doll," Mel said.

"So why don't you look happier?" Sally asked.

"Because there are six journalists left in this bar and I'm supposed to be deeply worried. Want to see my worried face?" He contracted his features in an elaborate display of anguish.

Sally laughed and then caught herself. "Oh dear," she said. "I almost gave you away. But what a look — really, if you could see it."

"I don't want to," Mel said. "Let's get out of here and go someplace where I can smile. My work's done for the day, anyhow. We'll have a quiet dinner and then drop around to the cable office and see what the boys have written."

He took Sally's arm and steered her out the front door. "Look after the store, willya, Sambo?" he said to Sammy Kelp as he left. "We'll be at the Club Gauguin if you need me."

The lights were low at the cable office. Mr. O'Hara was asleep with his head on the teletype machine. The extra operators had gone home, and the floor was ankle-deep in crumpled balls of paper on which the journalists had made a false start or failed to think of a phrase florid enough to do justice to the epic story which destiny had put at their fingertips.

Mel signaled to Sally not to wake up Mr. O'Hara, resting from the busiest hour of his professional life and due for another in the morning. They took his "out" basket to a table in the corner and scanned the urgent dispatches which, even now, half an ocean away, converted into type, transferred to stereotype plates and strapped onto rotary presses, were bearing to the American public the kind of story that it likes best:

BY DON PHELPS

FALOLO, TONJI, AUG. 16 (AP). — BOSOMY FILM QUEEN MOONA MARONE BELIEVED LOST LATE TONIGHT HIGH SLOPES VOLCANO ASSERTEDLY HELD SACRED MEMORY ANCIENT KINGS CHIEFS PRIMITIVE TONJI ISLANDS STOP LAST SEEN NEAR GIGANTIC BURIAL MOUNDS THOUGHT BY SUPERSTITIOUS TONJIANS POSSESS EVIL SPIRITS, SHAPELY BLONDE HOLLYWOOD SEX SYMBOL VANISHED AFTER PLUCKY RIDE BURROWISE RE UPCOMING WORLDPREEM LATEST STARRER QUOTE DESERT ISLAND FOR TWO UNQUOTE STOP WORRIED NATIVES EXPRESSED FEAR WILD BOAR OTHER BEASTS MIGHT . . .

BY TOM CARPENTER

FALOLO, TONJI, AUG. 16 (UPI). — STUNNED DISBELIEF SWEPT REMOTE FABLED TONJI ISLANDS TONIGHT AT ALLEGED DISAPPEARANCE BUXOM STARLET MOONA MARONE FROM WEIRD MONUMENT GIANT CORAL SLABS HELD BUILT BY LEGENDARY RACE POLYNESIAN KINGS WHOSE HISTORY LOST MISTS TIME STOP AWED VILLAGERS REPORTEDLY REFUSED SEARCH VOLCANO REPUTEDLY STILL INHABITED WRATHFUL GODS SPIRITS STOP BRITISH OFFICIALS HOWEVER EXPRESSED QUOTE GLIMMER HOPE UNQUOTE PLUCKY ACTRESS MIGHT . . .

One after another the cables passed in review beneath the yellow light bulb. Sally studied them in wonder, Mel in pure contentment. For him it was the perfect end of a perfect day, as sweet as reading a good novel in bed on a cold winter night, and no report gave more sensuous pleasure than the one which concluded the long parade:

BY MICKEY DOLAN

FALOLO, TONJI, AUG. 16. — YOU LAST SAW HER HUDDLED AGAINST MAMMOTH CORAL PYRAMID ATOP TYPHOON-WHIPPED VOLCANO IN MIDDLE NOWHERE STOP YOU'D SEEN FACE ON THOUSAND MOVIE SCREENS BILLBOARDS YET NOW COULD HAVE BEEN YOUR YOUNGER SISTER JUST PRETTY BLUE-EYED KID FROM TULSA WITH NICE PAIR PINUPS WHO WENT SCREENLAND HAP-PENED GRAB BRASS RING STOP YOU WERE JUST MIDDLE-CLASS MICK FROM FLATBUSH BUT YOU KNEW CLASS WHEN YOU SAW IT STOP IT HIT YOU DASH POW DASH WHEN YOU WATCHED PLAIN KID TULSA CALLS HERSELF MOONA MARONE THROW FAMOUS GAMS OVER WILD BURRO TODAY UPGALLOP TONJIAN MOUNTAIN BLANKETED VIRTUALLY THICKEST JUNGLE GROWTH YOU'D SEEN YEARS SLOGGING NEWSMAN'S WORLDBEAT STOP YOU WERE RE-MINDED JIMMY BRADDOCK WHEN CLIMBED INTO RING AT END CAREER KNEW UNHAD IT ANYMORE STOP GUTS AND CLASS STOP REAL CLASS STOP YOU'D SEEN ENOUGH BIGTIMERS COME DOWN MAIN PIKE TO KNOW . . .

"What a beautiful writer," Mel said. He put the wire basket back on Mr. O'Hara's desk. "Good night, old scout — and well done," he whispered to the sleeping man.

He tiptoed out the door with Sally and closed it softly. The town was empty tonight, the journalists exhausted and in bed. Tomorrow it would jump back to life. The cruise ship "Tonalela" would arrive with two hundred passengers, and so would the biweekly plane with Mr. and Mrs. Hal C. Mudge of Iowa, and so would Moona Marone. But for now the neon signs were out, the electric guitars unplugged, the muses of Literary Johnny silent.

Mel put his arm around Sally's waist and they walked slowly down Victoria Street to Millie Hawkes's Boarding House.

17

O N Wednesday morning Mel got up and flew over to Valonga. The English pilot brought his helicopter down on the beach where the press party had sailed away so hurriedly in the rain. Now the sun was out, the lagoon was blue, and gaily dressed villagers came running to wave at the strange bird that had dropped from the sky. In their midst Mel saw Harvey Bluestone and jumped out to meet him.

"How'd it go?" Harvey asked, impatient for news.

"Great!" Mel said. "Ten stories cabled out by seven o'clock. Starlet left on mountain. Feared lost to wrathful volcano god."

"Sensational! The masterpiece of your career. Congratulations!"

"Thanks, old buddy. How'd it go with you?"

"Moona was mad as hell. I kept her up on the mountain for half an hour, just to make sure."

"And then you came down to the village?"

"Yeah — Moona swearing at me all the way. The women gave us a warm welcome and dry clothes and a hot meal, and later the rain stopped and the moon came up and everyone sat around the lagoon and sang. It was lovely."

"Did Moona think it was lovely?" Mel asked.

"Moona didn't think it was lovely."

"Where is she now?"

"Down at the women's bathing pool, washing off the makeup that she put on when I said you were coming."

"*Make*up! Doesn't the dumb broad know that starlet left on mountain isn't found wearing cosmetics?"

"Dumb broad doesn't," Harvey said. "I told her to wash off every ounce of that cruddy pancake and to mess her hair up, too. Like, for instance, it was caught in the rain."

"Has she got her story straight for the press?"

"I rehearsed it with her. Which is not to say she's got it straight."

A slight commotion ran through the crowd of villagers. "*There* you are, you rotten fink!" came the shrill voice of Moona Marone, pushing the children aside to reach Mel. "I'll get you for this if it's the last thing I do, you two-bit Mike Todd. Bastards like you I need like a hangover."

"Good morning, Moona," Mel said, genially. "Sleep well?"

"Rat!" she shouted. "Crumby son-of-a-bitch!" Her face, scrubbed of every artifice, was inalienably her own: hollow-eyed, drawn, old before its time. Her hair, rinsed of stiffening lacquers and deprived of metal props during the night, flew Medusa-like in all directions.

"Ready to go?" Mel asked. She nodded. "Wave goodbye to your friends." She waved weakly to the villagers. Mel went over to the chief, hugged him in a grateful farewell and presented him with a wristwatch. Then he hopped into the helicopter after Moona and Harvey and pulled the door shut. The strange bird rose as gently as it had come down.

Fifteen minutes later the helicopter circled over the terrace of the El Tropiques Hotel where the journalists were having breakfast. Mel could see them look up from their copies of the "Tonji Times" which, though he didn't yet know it, had a stinging account of their abject return from Valonga. He told the pilot to bring his plane low over the swimming pool, and while it was hovering there he pushed Moona Marone to a window and had her wave to the scribes.

The effect, seen from above, was dramatic. No other hair in all of Tonji was quite the same color or shape. There could be no mistake: starlet had been found. From every table the journalists jumped up and waved back to the lost goddess, whereupon Mel asked the pilot to bring his plane down on the lawn. The blades whirred to a stop, the door opened and Moona was lifted out onto the grass by Mickey Dolan and Norbert de Paul, who said "Moona, darling, you're a *sight!*"

Cries of "What happened?" and "Are you all right?" and "Tell us about it" pierced the morning air. Moona feigned a spell of exhaustion and asked Harvey Bluestone to stand beside her for support. He dug her imperceptibly in the ribs as a signal to start talking.

"Shaddap!" called several members of the press. "Let's hear Moona!" They got out their notebooks.

"My friends," Moona began in a frail voice, "I'm deeply thankful to be alive today, and I know I owe it to the prayers of each and every one of you."

"Oh, shucks," said J. P. Foy. Pencils flew to record the star's first sentence in all its fullness.

"I only know," Moona went on, and then turned to Harvey. "What do I only know?" she whispered.

"I was sustained," Harvey whispered back.

"I was sustained on the mountain last night by the thought that your — thoughts were — thinking of me. Which was very thoughtful of you."

Emerich Eposcu was taking photographs of the bedraggled star. Tony Fiorello was catching her speech on his TV camera.

"How did it happen, Moona?" asked Don Phelps.

"When we got up to that old monument," she replied, speaking very slowly, as if trying to dredge back a memory too ghastly to recall, whereas in fact she was trying to dredge back the memory of what Harvey had taught her, "I was intrigued by the thought of those mighty kings who lived so many cen-, centu- . . . you know, hundreds of years ago. I started looking at those big burying piles and went from one to another until . . ."

She half-choked, half-sobbed, re-creating an emotional seizure that Harvey had remembered from her role as Nurse Stella Bates in "Angel of the Marijuana Ward."

"Give her time!" called Tom Carpenter.

"Can you go on, Baby?" Harvey asked.

"I must have lost my footing," Moona persevered, "because the next thing I knew I had slipped down a kind of . . . what we used to call a gulch back home where I was born 'n' raised." She took out a handkerchief and cleared her seven nasal sinuses of excess sentiment. "It was too wet to climb back up, and when I tried to shout for help I couldn't make my voice heard through the rain and fog."

"Poor thing," said Olivia O'Connell.

"She's a real human being," said Norbert de Paul.

"Could be your kid sister," said Mickey Dolan.

Moona Marone started again and faltered. "Do I have to go on?" she asked Harvey Bluestone.

"There's not much more, honey. Try."

"I can't seem to remember the rest very well," Moona explained to the waiting journalists. Which was true: Harvey's prefabricated tale was fast ebbing out of her brain cells. She finished by stitching together a loose patchwork of scenes that she might or might not have enacted after her fall into the gulch. The general thread was that she had made her way — "how, I'll never know" — back to the trail, bleeding from thorns and brambles. (Mel had scratched her legs during the helicopter ride and tied a bandage around her calf.) On the trail she had finally met Harvey Bluestone, who had gone back up the mountain calling her name. By then it must have been three o'clock in the morning and she was faint from exposure and shock. "We groped and stumbled down to the village," she concluded, "where kind people gave us . . ." She looked at Harvey.

"Food and shelter," he said.

"Food and shelter," she went on. "And here I am."

A cheer welled up from the journalists. Several ran and gave her a hug.

"Yay Moona!" roared Farley Grogan.

A seconding "ya-a-a-y!" echoed around the circle, and the press conference was over.

A quarter of an hour later Mr. O'Hara looked up from his desk at the cable office and saw three, then four, then seven, then ten journalists come tumbling through the door. "Hello, boys," he said. "Got something to go?"

He took the first page of Don Phelps's dispatch, already written at the hotel, and clipped it up next to his machine. Then his fingers began to tap out the glad tidings.

In midmorning Perdita Fox-Martin took the winter line of ski clothes and went with Cy to Moona-Moona island to photograph a fashion layout, bringing along two Tonjian girls whom she had hired as models. Adrian Struthers, Jr., engaged a taxi and tried to find the village where Mickey Dolan had seen the maidens dancing at sunset. With his novelist's imagination, he told himself, he would not only be able to reconstruct the scene; he would make it better. Duncan Dunnington sat down beside the swimming pool to knead into rough shape his appreciation of Flaherty and Murnau for one of the little magazines, perhaps "Ambiance" or "Charisma." Later there would be time to bevel it with adverbs and decorate it with allusions to other pioneers of documentary film. The main thing now was to set down his impressions while they were still pristine.

In midmorning, too, a ship's whistle announced that the "Tonalela" had docked. The periodic arrival of these cruise ships was a big event in Tonji, for the passengers were unfailingly frantic to buy souvenirs, and they streamed through the town dispensing American capital to every shopkeeper and sidewalk vendor in sight. So feverishly did they buy, in fact, that they could barely stagger back to their ship under the weight of carved mahogany heads and fluted teak lamp-bases. Later, when the fever had passed and they surveyed the objects heaped in their staterooms so thickly that they could hardly reach their beds, they wondered how they had even remotely imagined their powder room in Montclair being improved by a huge ebony figure of the Tonjian vanilla god.

But those were afterthoughts. It was the during-thoughts that mattered to the local economy — and to Mel. The two hundred passengers represented that golden will-o'-the-wisp so hungrily sought by publicists and so seldom captured: "word of mouth." Here were two hundred affluent Americans who would carry back to their communities the story of a tourist paradise, rich in every delight, yet still "undiscovered." To make sure that this concept would not escape them, Mel had prepared a special press kit which was handed to the passengers as they spilled down the gangway, fiddling with their cameras and checking their wallets to see if they had brought enough money.

The press kit, attractively printed to look like a brochure instead of a press kit, began by listing — with a street map — the many diversions which the travelers might want to sample that evening, such as Millie Hawkes's Discothèque, Literary Johnny's coffeehouse and Mrs. Beezley's poetry center. The brochure then called the tourists' attention to their good luck in being able to witness the arrival, that very afternoon, of Mr. and Mrs. Hal C. Mudge to claim the island of Moona-Moona, which they had won in a nationwide contest connected with the world premiere of a $3,000,000 romantic comedy in Technicolor called "Desert Island for Two," and to see the historic departure for Peru in the morning of Karl Ullstrad's "Modern Viking Expedition" in an 18-foot balsa raft.

Now, standing on the pier, Mel watched the debarking tourists as they took the brochures from his beautiful Tonjian girls and fanned out into the town — two hundred sub–press agents, and all his for twenty-four hours. He beamed with professional pride.

At 2:30 an enormous crowd gathered on the customs wharf to meet Mr. and Mrs. Mudge. The journalists were there, and so were most of the "Tonalela's" passengers, and so were a large number of townspeople, eager to see what kind of couple had opted to live on an island where nobody had ever lived before. An immense banner shouted WELCOME MR. AND MRS. MUDGE! to the launch arriving with the plane's passengers, and a brass band struck up what even Richard

Rodgers might have had trouble recognizing as a medley from "State Fair."

Recognizing the Mudges, however, was no trouble. Amid the tourists, businessmen, beachcombers and British colonial families grouped loosely in the launch, the couple from Iowa stood out like two stalks of corn in a field of tomatoes: tall and straight and plain. Seeing the hospitable banner, hearing the music meant just for them, seeing the merry crowd, they smiled and waved and called "Hello, everybody!" On their faces it was Christmas morning and Thanksgiving dinner and Fourth of July night. The unaffected warmth of the Midwest went forward from them and brushed the people on the pier.

Harvey Bluestone, the only person whom the Mudges had met before, was waiting at the ladder. He pulled them up onto the wharf and introduced them to Mel, who enveloped them in the sincerest greeting he had given in a career of sincere greetings and turned them over to Sally, who fussed over them and took Mrs. Mudge's handbags and asked if they had had a good trip.

And then the journalists were on them in a pack. Emerich Eposcu barked at them to smile for his camera, to wave, to look pleased, to look stunned, to hold hands, and to accept a barrage of kisses from four Tonjian girls. Tony Fiorello's TV camera whirred and into its microphone Blake Hewitt spoke with the heightened jollity of his craft: "It's a great day for this little island, folks, ho-ho-ho, and especially for these two wonderful people from Iowa, Mr. and Mrs. Hal C. Mudge, who still look a little dazed at this rully incredible turnout, and who can blame them? It's the dream of a lifetime, rully kind of like a fairy tale come true. For don't you and I and everybody sometimes lie awake and think that if we had our druthers what we'd rully like to do is fly away to a South Sea island and . . ."

The reporters plied the winning couple with characteristic questions.

"What did you think, Mr. Mudge, when you heard that you'd won a desert island? I mean, just what was your general reaction, sir?"

"We were mighty excited," Mr. Mudge said.

"And you, Mrs. Mudge?"

"We were real pleased," Mrs. Mudge replied in a cheerful voice. "Yessir, I'd say we were real pleased."

"Did you have any thoughts about leaving Iowa?" asked Tom Carpenter.

"Yes, I'd say we had a few," Mr. Mudge answered. "Wouldn't you say so, Mother?"

"Oh, indeed we did," Mrs. Mudge replied brightly. "Quite a few. I should say so!"

"Just what were those thoughts, sir?" Carpenter went on, amplifying his question to what should have been its original form. "Could you tell us in your own words?"

"Those are the only words I've got, son," Mr. Mudge said diffidently. He wondered who else's words the reporter expected him to use.

"That's what I mean," Carpenter said. "Just tell us in your own words."

"What was the question again?"

"Could you tell us just what your thoughts were, sir, about leaving Iowa?"

"Well now, both Mrs. Mudge and I were born and brought up in Iowa, and we've brought up a family of our own there, too — three fine boys and a girl — and they've grown up now and have youngsters of their own, and they live on farms not too far from ours, so you can see our roots go down real deep. Isn't that so, Mother?"

"It's like the song says: 'All I owe I owe Ioway,'" Mrs. Mudge agreed.

"So it must have been a wrench," Bill Stanton prompted, "to pull up and . . . you know."

"Well, naturally it was," Mr. Mudge said, answering what he assumed, from its abrupt halt, to be a question. "There was the corn coming along, and some of our neighbors probably wondered what would possess a retired couple to go sashaying out to the South Sea islands. But we've worked hard all our lives and never had a vacation. Come to think of it, I don't reckon we've ever been farther than Davenport."

"You went over to Council Bluffs once," Mrs. Mudge said.
"Remember? When your brother Earl was sick?"

"But I mean to*gether*, dear," Mr. Mudge explained.

"Oh that's true. I believe you're right, Hal."

"Would you tell us in your own words," said Farley
Grogan, "what went through your mind when the telephone
rang and you heard . . . ?"

The press conference ran its redundant course. For half an
hour the Mudges told in their own words what went through
their mind and what their thoughts were and what their
general reaction was, until at last Mel took pity.

"I'm going to get Mr. and Mrs. Mudge through customs
now," he announced, "and drive them over to the El
Tropiques Hotel, where they'll want to catch their breath. But
I've promised to take them out to see their island this
afternoon, and then tomorrow they're going to move out
there to live. So if any of you would care to go along, the
boat will leave from here . . ." He looked at his watch. "At
four o'clock. That'll get us back here in time for drinks and
dinner."

He pushed the Mudges through the applauding crowd,
helped by Harvey Bluestone and Sally. At the customs desk
Harvey took Mel aside.

"Did you notice that V.I.P. type who came off the plane?"
he asked.

"No, I was too busy with the Mudges," Mel said. "Say,
aren't they a couple of dolls? You picked well."

"Thanks. This V.I.P. was very British — real Colonel Blimp
— red face, big moustache, the whole image. Everyone
treated him like royalty, so I asked who it was."

"And who was it?"

"Lord Hargreave. They said he was Deputy . . ."

". . . Under Secretary for Colonial Affairs," Mel finished
the sentence. "Damn! That meddling 'Old Settler'! . . .
Sally!"

Sally excused herself from Mrs. Mudge. "Yes, Mel? What is
it? Are you all right?"

"Sally, honey," he said, "I've got to take the Mudges and the press out to Moona-Moona and . . ."

"I'll take 'em, Mel," Harvey volunteered.

"No, we've both got to be there. So what I'd like you to do, Sal, is go over to the 'Tonji Times' and do a little detective work. Like maybe you could pretend you're looking something up in the clips. See who comes and goes, and find out if Quaritch really is there. O.K.?"

"I'll try my best."

"Thanks, doll."

At four o'clock Sally went to the office of the "Times." Just as she was arriving, the door opened and out strode Chief Malalonga, followed by half a dozen Tonjian men of almost equal majesty. The chief looked solemn, but, noticing Sally, he gave a courtly bow and said "Good day, Miss Merrill." Then he hurried on.

Inside, Mrs. Pedley looked up from typing her social notes and asked, "Can I help you, miss?"

"I . . . I'd like to look through your back issues," Sally said.

"They're over on that table, dearie, under the pot of glue. Help yourself and don't mind the mess."

"Thank you so much," Sally said. "And I wondered . . ."

"*Bitch* of a linotype!" came Mr. Glubb's voice from the back room.

"I wondered whether . . . that is . . . would . . . Mr. Quaritch be in today?"

"He's in," Mrs. Pedley replied. Sally gave a slight shudder. With her own eyes she had seen Mr. Quaritch climb up the gangway of the "Koala Bear" and not come back down. "But he's busy with three visitors right now. Did you want to see him?"

"Yes. I mean . . . if I could."

"I don't know why not. I'll call you when he's through. Who shall I say wants him?"

"Miss Merrill," Sally said. She went to the disorderly table, moved the glue and began thumbing through recent issues of the paper. They were as familiar as her college roommates, each edition giving her a twinge of recollected emotion, especially the columns by "Old Settler" with their disquieting titles and Churchillian prose. After a while an office door opened and three men came out. Sally recognized them as the Rev. Bloodgood, the Rev. Boggs and the Rev. Beezley. Their features, though lacking in fire, were amply daubed in brimstone.

"Then it's agreed?" Rev. Boggs asked, turning to someone in the office that they had just left. "We'll hold the service tonight in the mission church at Mui and assure them that it's God's will for the Tonjian people. Good. Let's get started," he said to the other two ministers and they trotted out into the street.

A white-haired man with metal-rimmed glasses appeared in the office door. "Come in, Miss Merrill," he said, extending his hand. "How nice to see you again. Won't you have a seat?" He pointed to a cracked leather armchair, closed the door, and sat down at the editor's rolltop desk. Sally peered at him, momentarily flustered.

"You're not Mr. Quaritch," she said at last. "You're . . ." She looked again at the humorous eyes and at the hair so silky white as to be made of silk. "You're . . . DENIS!" She ran over and gave him an impulsive hug. "Oh darling, you look wonderful! You're going to make a very handsome old man."

"I've aged a lot in two weeks, putting out this paper," Denis said. "Quaritch left it to me in sacred trust until he gets back."

"He'll be proud of you," Sally said. "Your columns have been just beautiful."

"Did you like them?"

"I didn't like them, but they've been just beautiful. There was one I felt was written specially for me."

" 'Week of Decision' — was that it?" Sally nodded. "I've *missed* you, Sally. Lord, how I've missed you. You've been so busy, and heaven knows so have I. When can we have an evening together? Tonight?"

"*Too-night, too-night,*" she sang and then burst out laughing. "Oh, Denis, it's like a 'thirties musical — you in that crazy disguise."

"Dear sweet Carlotta," he declaimed, seizing both her hands. "Fly away with me this evening. Sir Reginald must not find us here together — it would be rew-in."

"I'm afraid tonight's out," Sally said. "The boss has got me on the run. I can't even think beyond that crumby movie tomorrow."

"And then what?"

"I really don't know. Too many things have happened. But I've missed you, too, Denis — I've missed you a lot. Is that enough of an answer?"

"It's a lovely answer."

"And now that we're finally together I can't even *see* you behind those silly glasses and that stupid wig. Where ever did you get it?"

"Mrs. Tunwell of the dramatics society. She altered it from a wig that her husband wore in a play about . . ."

"Who, for heaven's sake?"

"George Washington, I think."

"Oh Denis," Sally said, "did you fool *any*body with it?"

"*Everybody*. Most of all, those journalists of yours who came around to ask about Section 37A of the Land Act. My elderly mien lent authority to my account of the illegal international act by the British Crown against the just claims and decent aspirations of the Tonjian people. I trust you saw my little sign?"

"I did," Sally said. Then, putting two and two together, she added, "and all your other signs. On the churches, right?"

"Right."

"You're getting pretty good at the managed event yourself."

"I'm only trying to unmanage an event that's been managed — and superbly managed," Denis said. "As an objective observer I must say that Mel's feat has been brilliant. But I'm not an objective observer. I'm partial to Tonji and — have you seen the town today, with all those trippers going from one neon-signed dive to another? Fat women doing the twist?

Paunchy old men in shorts throwing dollar bills to Tonjian boys playing the electric guitar? It's a glimpse of the future."

"I've hardly had time to look," Sally said.

"They'll go back home and send all their sisters and their cousins and their aunts out here on the next plane and . . ."

"BALDERDASH!" thundered a voice in the outer office. "YOU CAN'T STOP ME! NOBODY STOPS ME!"

"Hark!" Denis cried, a Shubert tenor again.

"DON'T YOU KNOW WHO I AM? WHAT?" the voice beyond the door bellowed.

"Quick! There is no time to lose," Denis said, not moving.

The door crashed open under the impact of Sir Reginald Weems. His small eyes darted from side to side and finally lit on Denis.

"Who the devil are you?" he roared. "You're not Quaritch. Pfff. The beggar's flat out on a hospital bed in Sydney — chap who came on the plane said he saw him two days ago. Weak as water, from what I hear. Took bloody-all out of him in the male department. Ehh? What's that?"

"Yes, sir," Denis said. "Bloody-all."

"So if you're not Quaritch . . ." He glanced over and saw Sally. "I remember *you* well enough, Miss Marple — wore a bathing suit to my dinner, if I'm not mistaken."

"Oh no, sir, I beg to contra . . ."

"Contra *what*, Miss Marple? Contra*dict?* Nobody contradicts Sir Reginald Weems, you may be sure of that. Very sure. Very sure indeed. I know chalk from cheese."

"Yes, sir," Sally said.

"What?"

"Chalk, sir. . . . From cheese."

"Quite right. And *you*, sir," the Governor went on, turning back to Denis, "have had the temerity to contradict my policies in print. You have dared to question the wisdom of my blwgrrm-frooff-vmmm." The words were swallowed up in rage and saliva.

"Freedom of the press, sir, if I may point out . . ."

"I'll press the freedom out of you, you impostor! Ruffian!" The Governor grabbed Denis by the shoulders and shook him so violently that his wig slid half off. Sir Reginald grabbed the wig and hurled it across the room. Then he pulled the metal glasses off Denis and threw them after the wig. Then he seemed on the verge of pulling Denis's own hair out. But he stood still, his stomach heaving, his fists clenching and unclenching, his mouth working rapidly — not rapidly enough, however, to catch and transmit the word clusters that were forming in his brain.

Sally retreated toward the door. Sir Reginald raised his arm and pointed his index finger at Denis.

"I should have known it was you!" he shouted. "Foote, you may consider your services for Her Majesty's Government terminated, as of now. I shall direct Judge Grimshaw to bring you to the dock for the treason of subverting the Crown's tourist scheme whilst receiving the Crown's wages as tourist director. Furthermore, I shall direct Mulgrew of the Land Board to appropriate your house and grounds, and I *personally* shall take steps to revoke your permit of residence. In other words, Foote, *you are no longer wanted in Tonji.* Her Majesty's Government, in their wisdom, regard you as an undesirable."

He paused for breath. Denis's face was white. Sally stood at the door, aghast.

"I propose," the Governor went on, his voice soaring, "to make an example of you, Foote. I intend to make it clear — *quite* clear — that there is no place in the English-speaking democracies for troublemakers of your stripe. No place at all. None whatever. Fmmmmm. Where Sir Reginald Weems is Governor, no quarter will be given to you young Communists! You will be stamped out! Exterminated! Driven into the sea! Aourrgghhhh!" A high wail completed his speech.

"I say, Reggie," came a quiet voice at the door. "Isn't that rather intemperate language for a man in your position? I mean the Communist part?"

Sir Reginald wheeled around. "Lord Hargreave!" he stammered. "What brings you here?"

"A little inspection tour," said the Deputy Under Secretary for Colonial Affairs. "And not a second too soon, I should judge. What the devil have you been up to? The ruddy town looks like Blackpool."

"Easy enough to explain, sir," the Governor said, putting his dental problem into service as a smile. "There's the man you're looking for." He jerked his thumb toward Denis. "It's that radical, Foote. These young agitators move to the colonies and they get all cock-a-hoop."

"I shall receive your explanation at Government House in precisely forty-five minutes," Lord Hargreave said. "See that you are punctual. In the meantime I should like a word in private with Mr. Foote. One learns a lot, I've found, by talking with young Communists. You may go."

Sir Reginald stood frozen for a moment. Then he withdrew his gums into an ingratiating smile and hurried away. Sally threw a last look of encouragement to Denis and followed the Governor out.

Sally's thoughts were in such a swirl as she hurried along Victoria Street that she hardly noticed the rising tempo of activity. Only when she had been jostled several times by passengers from the "Tonalela" did she realize how many neon signs and electrical displays were lighting up, how many places of entertainment were exerting their strident call. Did I help to manage all *this*, she asked herself, amazed that the project had swelled to such proportions.

In her room at Millie Hawkes's Boarding House she found a little pile of mail that had come on the plane. There was a letter from her mother, and one from her father, and one from her classmate Betty Begley in the Kurdish village of Wadi Ma'zoom, and one from Ted and Helen (Parkinson) Ross in Jogjakarta, and a copy of the Pembleton Alumni Magazine. This she opened first, turning immediately to the Class of '65 notes. Sam Washburn was in Luang Prabang, Ray and Priscilla (Thorne) MacDonald were in Dacca, Gail Underwood was in Botswana, and a square blur of ink turned into a picture of a baby boy, "Skipper," just born to the Ron Redfields at their little mission clinic in the mountains of Paraguay — "really a fun birth," as Liz put it in her letter to the class secretary, adding that she and Ron and "Skipper" would love to see any Pembletonians passing through the mountains of Paraguay. Sally went through the column with interest and pleasure: all was well.

Her mother's letter, a wholly different creature, was written with chatty affection:

You've missed some lovely parties this summer, Sally dear. "Pootie" Douglas had a darling coming-out dance at the Piping Rock Club — pink tent, and lots of beaux from Yale, and Ben Hubris's band playing all the songs from "Mame." And the following Saturday we went to Westbury for a cunning "dansant discothèque" that the Finches gave for "Muffin" after the horse show. We tried to get your brother Harry to come with us, because you know how we feel about "Muffin," but he just refused. You remember how queer Harry gets about those things. Now he's talking about going into the Peace Corps after he graduates. Your father thinks that *some*body in the family should stay home and learn how to make a living. He spoke to his partners at Maltby, DeKooning and they were very nice about wanting Harry to start there.

By the way, last week when I was driving to Oyster Bay for the Vassar benefit house-and-garden tour (Peg Bigelow is running it this year and not me, thank heavens), I happened to turn on the car radio and hear a tune which the announcer said comes from Tonji. Isn't that a coincidence? He said it was a song that the natives sing to attract turtles and that it's sweeping America as a dance called "Doing the Moona-Moona." I also saw a terribly cute dress called a "moona" at the Cockles 'n' Muscles Beach Shop in Glen Cove that's run by Barbara Skipworth '37 (you remember, who used to be Barbara Poole?). Barbara says it comes from Tonji, too, and is all the rage. Funny, how I never even heard of Tonji until you went there and now I hear about it all the time.

Not so funny, Sally thought. Everybody's on a proper course except me. The Redfields and the MacDonalds and Betty Begley and the others are giving something to the country that they're in, and I'm taking something away. I've taken away the innocence of Tonji and I've even taken away its turtle song and let it be huckstered to the disk-jockeys. I'd have done less damage at "Pootie" Douglas's coming-out party or "Muffin" Finch's dance or the Vassar house-and-garden tour (Peg Bigelow '35, who used to be Peggy Lord). All those people are at least true to their codes. My mistake was that I thought this would be just a simple promotion. A few phony events and then back to California. But I didn't know Mel. Nothing's just a simple promotion — publicity's his life, and nothing else matters. No guilt, no second thoughts: the end justifies the means. And the real trouble is that he's so good at it. Just my luck to sign up with a mere promoter and find out he's some kind of crazy genius.

She took the rest of the letters, lay down on her iron bed, and fell into a tormented sleep.

It was dark when she woke up. What woke her was Mel knocking on the door and calling her name, and it took her a minute to disengage his real voice from his P. T. Barnum voice in the dream that she was having, wherein he was ornately dressed as a carnival barker and was extolling the wonders to be found inside a mammoth tent.

"Oh hi, Mel," she said drowsily.

"You O.K., Sal?"

"Yes. I'm afraid I fell asleep. How did it go with the Mudges?"

"Great," Mel said. "They loved the bungalow, which I must say looked damn nice, and the journalists flipped over it, so we got good coverage."

"That's fine," Sally said, not caring now whether the Mudges liked it or not. "What's next?"

"The journalists are out on the town tonight — the whole joint is jumping, and I wondered if I could take you to dinner."

"I'm not very hungry, Mel. Do you really need me?"

"I don't really need you, but I really want you."

"Where do you want to go?"

"First to Literary Johnny's for a drink. Tom Falonga is gonna sing the freedom song that I wrote. It's folk rock."

"A preem?" she asked.

"A preem — my debut as a tunesmith."

"Well, I didn't think anything would get me out into Times Square again tonight, but *that* I've got to hear."

They could hardly reach the New Joseph Conrad Coffee House because of the crowds surging along the sidewalks, and, once there, they could hardly get in. Several hundred people were bunched on folding chairs in the dark and disheveled room. There was only enough light to see the autographed photographs of Maugham, Stevenson and the other authors pinned to the wall. On a platform Literary Johnny, in an alpaca jacket, was finishing his act:

"So I said to Jimmy Hall, the *real* story is what happened to Bligh and those chaps when they got into that little boat. All alone on the trackless ocean and not a whaler or clipper ship for thousands of miles: that's *literature*, lads! Well, my friends, I remember as clearly as I'm looking at you tonight that Hall turned to his partner and their eyes met. For half a minute neither of 'em uttered a word. Then Hall spoke up. 'By God, Nordhoff,' he said. 'Johnny's right. The yarn was right there under our noses and we never even saw it.' "

The crowd burst into applause and Johnny took a series of bows. He held up his hand and told his listeners that the late show would feature Conrad, Stevenson and Rupert Brooke. But next, he said, Tom Falonga would sing his new freedom song, "There's a Great Day A-Comin' When Cession Day Is Gone." He explained briefly what Cession Day was and then beckoned Tom Falonga, who came trotting onto the stage in a hula shirt and tapering black pants and black motorcycle boots. He strummed a few chords on his electric guitar, and Mel looked at Sally with satisfaction.

"It's been another perfect day for you, hasn't it?" she whispered.

He nodded. "I want to hit every spot in town tonight — see my creation in full swing. Will you come along?"

"I guess so," she whispered back. Then the room was quiet

and in a voice that was strikingly Beatle-like the singer began
to sing:

There's a great day a-comin'
When Cession Day is gone,
Ev'ry trade wind's a-hummin'
That it's freedom's day to dawn.

Back to Britain, all you Limeys,
Take your cricket when you go,
Take your "smashings" and your "blimeys,"
"Jolly good" and "half a mo'."

Shout the news:
Comin' soon,
Throw your blues
In the lagoon,
Nothin' to lose
When you croon
Mister Freedom's hap-hap-happy
Happy-go-lucky tune.
Still got the sun,
Still got the moon,
Yeah, yeah, yeah, yeah, yeah!

Oh, there's a great day a-comin'
When Cession Day is gone,
There'll be guitars a-strummin'
On the bowls and croquet lawn . . .

18

Mr. and Mrs. Hal C. Mudge
Request the Pleasure of Your Company
At Cocktails and Buffet Dinner
On Thursday, the Eighteenth of August
At Half After Five O'Clock

At Their Home, "Moona-Moona"

Prior to the World Première
Of the Motion Picture
"Desert Island for Two"

THE engraved invitation glittered on the breakfast table of every journalist at the El Tropiques on Thursday morning. It had also gone by mail to Sir Reginald and Lady Weems, to the Misses Maud and Winifred Weems, to Justice and Mrs. Grimshaw, and to fifty other ranking couples in the colonial government, as well as to Tonji's leading citizens and their wives — two hundred people altogether, the maximum that could fit in the outdoor theater that Mel had improvised in the bamboo clearing on Kula-ha'i. Everyone on the list had accepted: Tonji's entire ruling class would be gathered in one place that night.

Mr. and Mrs. Mudge were surprised to learn that they were giving a party for two hundred on their first day in residence, but Mel assured them that it would be "fully catered." Titan Pictures was providing the food, Walter of

Waikiki had donated the liquor in return for certain "mentions," and a platoon of Tonjian bartenders, waiters and cooks would do all the work. The Mudges need only meander among the guests, and perhaps Mrs. Mudge would also like to point out the major appliances to the wives, most of whom had never seen an automatic dishwasher or an electric can-opener. After dinner everybody would walk to "Moona Marone Theater," in the interior of the island, and then they would go home and leave Moona-Moona for the new owners to enjoy in peace. Did that sound all right? Mrs. Mudge said it sounded real nice. She would have baked some pies if she had only known about it earlier.

The journalists, starting their fourth day on Tonji, began to show their age. Again they had spent a long night drinking, eating, dancing and straining their eyes at Tonjian hula girls garbed in two narrow strips of grass. They had gone from dive to dive, saloon to saloon, and not come home until dawn. Some, in fact, had won or otherwise obtained the friendship of Polynesian girls and not come home at all. Except for the detonations now going off in their heads, it had been the best bash of their lives, the quintessential dream of the islands made real, and they were grateful to Mel Parker, grateful to Titan Pictures, grateful to Tonji for making it possible. Tonight the junket would reach its climax; tomorrow it would slacken off with the "Queen of Tonji" festival, and on Saturday they would fly back to the binding clothes and customs of Western civilization. But today they had their memories, and between frequent applications of aspirin and coffee they would convert these memories into rich, golden, delicious, adjective-filled prose and carry it to Mr. O'Hara at the cable office, who would feed it to the outside world. And thus the spell of the South Seas, never reported with any objectivity since the white man first set foot there, would be wafted once again around the globe and magnified still another time.

Mel was almost sorry that he had to deflect the journalists from this literary orgy to watch the Danish raftmen set sail for Peru. Still, he knew that this was the sight that they would probably remember longest. Of all the events unfolded for their pleasure, it was the only one that had an organic life of its own. Mel had not managed it; it was in process when he arrived, and all that he had done was to accent it, as a theatrical lighting expert breathes glamour into a merely well-written play.

At 10:30 the three Danes were ready to sail. Years of dreaming and months of planning had gone into this moment, and they stood on the dock encircled by the reporters, photographers, TV cameramen and tourists whom Mel had conjured there to see them off. The explorers, however, were oblivious of the milling crowds. Their thoughts were already at sea, far ahead in the lonely Southern latitudes, beyond the help of press and press agents. Withdrawn, reticent, uneasy with the turmoil and with the English language, they answered the reporters' questions with the few words that they knew and listened in discomfort as Sir Reginald Weems made a valedictory speech. The speech was not long, but it had the trappings of length. Sir Reginald stood at a lectern on a platform that had been draped with bunting. He was dressed in his white ceremonial uniform and plumed hat, and the words that he declaimed, though incomprehensible to the Danes, had a rotund quality which told them exactly what he was saying: that Her Majesty's Government were most singularly honoured to have been vouchsafed the esteemed privilege of being chosen by the gallant Karl Ullstrad and his two dauntless compatriots, etc.

When he was finished the photographers called for a picture, and Ullstrad climbed onto the platform, clad only in a blue sweater and faded denim slacks, and shook hands with the resplendent Governor while blinking into the Leica of Cy Rumble, the Rolleiflex of Emerich Eposcu, the box Brownie of the "Tonji Times," and the TV camera of Tony Fiorello.

"It's rully incredible," Blake Hewitt of NBC said into his microphone, "to think of these three men — each one, if you will, a modern Leif Ericson — sailing out of this safe harbor onto virtually unknown seas where nature and not man calls the shots. It's rully something to see."

Bobbie Baxter, overhearing his commentary, scribbled a note to herself: "turned over a new Leif." Then she added: "Toodle-oo, see you in Peru!" and "What three Danes are gonna run out of Danish pastry?"

Mickey Dolan took out his pad and wrote: "Your mind boggled. You were just a city punk who'd never seen a body of water bigger than the Gowanus Canal."

When the ceremony seemed to be over, Sir Reginald stepped reluctantly down and Karl Ullstrad was about to follow when Mel pushed Moona Marone up onto the platform. The blonde goddess threw her arms around the wiry old Dane and gave him a wet kiss on behalf of America. Cameras duly recorded the sacrament and then Miss Marone took Ullstrad by the wrist and pulled him to the lectern.

"The thoughts and prayers of my countrymen and I," she said into the microphone, "will be thinking of you and praying for you. Believe me."

Then Mel waved them both down and they walked to the end of the wharf, where the raft was tied. The three Danes jumped nimbly onto it and raised a canvas sail. Moona Marone, less nimble because of her high-heeled sandals, lowered herself on a rope ladder. Her lemon-yellow slacks shimmered in the morning sun. She reached up to take a bottle of champagne from Harvey Bluestone and then bent over the bow of the raft.

"I christen thee . . . *Moona-Tiki!*" she said, swinging the bottle against the balsa logs. Glass tinkled, champagne fizzed, and Karl Ullstrad pushed his raft with relief out into the harbor. There it was joined by ten Tonjian canoes, each occupied by a chief in tribal regalia and his parents and wife and children. As Mel had explained in his press kit, lest the obvious symbolism not be obvious, the original Tonjians had come in canoes of this type, and now that a voyage was setting out to trace that ancient migration, it was only natural for their descendants to escort the raft beyond the reef and see it dispatched toward the horizon. Mel had impressed this symbolism on the ten chiefs and their families with wristwatches and candy, and now they formed a convoy around the Danes and led them out through the harbor, singing old Polynesian songs as they went. Propelled by wind and by oars, the little fleet threaded its way past freighters and tankers, motorboats and trawlers, copra schooners and tuna clippers — all the noisy vessels that served Tonji today. The singers' voices floated back to the people on the wharf, who were still standing there, rooted by an emotion as old as seafaring. Their eyes followed the raft until it bobbed through the passage in the reef and turned into a speck, indistinguishable from the ocean itself. Then they slowly dispersed and re-entered their ordinary lives.

Sally's day was clouded, as her night had been, by worry over Denis. She tried to find him at the "Times," but Mrs. Pedley said he had gone to the royal village of Mui, where he had "a great many things to do," and wouldn't be back till midafternoon. So Sally left a note to express a "concern," and at 2:30, restless and fretful, she went to the Kon-Tiki Bar & Surfers' Club to wait. Inside, the atmosphere of Fat Lou's bar was cheaper for its conversion into a temple of surfing lore, but the verandah was still intact — one of the few places that she and Mel had not defiled. It was their fault that Denis had had to tilt against the Crown almost single-handed, risking everything that he valued and, as of yesterday, losing it. She felt guilty and depressed, and for a long time she sat staring vacantly at the harbor.

Suddenly she felt a comforting squeeze on her shoulder and a voice said "Cheer up, Sal, the game's not over."

"Denis!" she said, jumping up to greet him. Her heart pounded — whether from feminine sympathy or girlish joy she didn't quite know.

Denis sat down and whistled for Fat Lou, who came shambling out the screen door. "Bring me a beer, Lou," Denis said, "and none of that bloody surfing talk either, or I'll hang five across your stomach."

"Right away, Denny boy," Lou said. "Say, where've you been?"

"Busy."

"Me too! I've never done so much business. It's been like real wipe-out."

"That can't be right," Denis said.

"Oh hell, I don't know what the stuff means. Mel gave me a list of surfing terms and I just throw them in any old place. Nobody seems to care."

"Well, get me a beer. I care about beer."

Fat Lou ambled off. Sally put her hand on Denis's arm. "Denis?" she said.

"What is it, Sal?"

"Did Lord Hargreave — I mean, did he give you any hope that he might . . . you know, reverse what Sir Reggie said?"

"No," Denis said. "Oh, I had a good talk with him, but as far as reversing the Governor goes, it's like being in the army. The officers protect each other. In the long run it's 'Them' against 'Us' and no guff from the troops."

"But he was furious at Sir Reggie."

"Sure," Denis agreed, "and he should have been — the town *does* look like Blackpool. But if you're wondering what happened at Government House, he probably just ordered Sir Reggie to take all the neon signs down and then they played snooker and drank Scotch and talked about Harrow till two A.M."

"Gosh," Sally said. "I sort of hoped . . ."

"There's still hope. Are you going to the movie tonight?"

"Yes. Not that I expect it to be 'Brief Encounter.' Even Mel says it sounds like Dog City."

"Dog City?"

"A turkey. A bomb."

"Even with Moona Marone? She seems a person of rare sensibility."

"She's a real human being."

"Is that what they say?"

"That's what they say."

"How nice. Where *exact*ly are you going to be tonight?"

"First I'm going to the Mudges' for cocktails. A little party for two hundred. And they've also invited me to stay for dinner."

"So generous," Denis said. "I love the Mudges, don't you?"

"They're real human beings," Sally said. "Will you be there? I do want you to see their Formica countertops."

"Maybe. It depends."

"Then after dinner," Sally went on, "I'm going to the world premiere of the three-million-dollar romantic comedy in Technicolor, 'Desert Island for Two.'"

"And where will you be sitting?" Denis asked.

"Gosh, I don't know. Is it important?"

"Yes."

"It is?" She looked at him inquisitively. "Well then, I'll sit . . ."

"Hi, kids! Can an aging press agent pull up a chair?" Mel Parker sat down wearily. "Looks like we've come full circle. The three of us sat here at the beginning and we're back here at the end — the calm before the final storm."

"How *are* you, Mel?" Denis asked affably. There was none of the first day's acrimony in his voice. He seemed to have made peace with himself about Mel as a person, if not about Mel as an instrument.

"Tired," Mel said. "Four days with these nutniks is like a thousand with anybody else. Oh well, the pressure'll be off after tonight."

"Where'd you go this afternoon?" Sally asked. "I forget the schedule."

"Over to the Bounty Hotel — it was Doc Bligh's happening."

"What happened?" Denis asked.

"I'll tell you what happened. First a bat flew down from the ceiling and bounced off Olivia O'Connell's chest. Then a land crab came tearing out from under one of those moth-eaten sofas — we were all sitting in that grimy lounge — and bit Bobbie Baxter on the ankle. Then a sick dog hobbled out of Bligh's office and threw up on the rug. Then the downstairs toilet . . ."

"You're kidding," Sally said, consumed with giggles. "All that happened?"

"That and more. Some happening, eh, baby?"

"It's authentic," Denis said. "You couldn't get closer to the true conditions if you had written the script and trained the animals."

"You're right about that," Sally said. "I spent a night there."

"Anyway it was a fiasco," Mel said. "Imagine taking the venerable Olivia O'Connell all the way to the South Seas so she can get hit by a bat."

"Make a nice item for her column," Denis said.

"So I guess that's why I'm tired," Mel went on. "Boy, have I had my fill of the culture boom!"

"How are the poetry readings?" Sally asked.

"Didn't I tell you? Mrs. Beezley came across a word beginning with 'f' seventeen times in one poem by Allen Ginsberg last night. She had hysterics on the podium. Dr. Thurlow had to come and give her a sedative, and today she won't read anything but James Whitcomb Riley."

"There goes your culture boom," Denis said.

"Just about. Well, I'm lucky only these two things have gone wrong. Keep your fingers crossed . . . Hey, Sal! It's almost four-thirty. We've got to be dressed and down at the dock by five. That's when the boats leave for Moona-Moona and you're my social hostess. Are you ready?"

"You're the boss," Sally said, stretching to her feet. "How about a day off tomorrow? I'm getting kind of tired myself."

"Anything you want," Mel said. "If we get through tonight we're home free."

The island of Moona-Moona, formerly Kula-ha'i, almost looked good. Guests began arriving at 5:30 in launches which Mel had engaged and festooned with bright flags and pictures of Moona Marone. They stepped out onto a beach newly sprinkled with white sand. Its lone palm tree gave the appearance of health, Cy's two coats of paint having lost their sheen and worked into the texture of the bark. Beneath it, the little bungalow looked like the adman's creation that it was. From thatched roof to patio chairs it represented every couple's vision, nurtured in a thousand color advertisements, of two weeks in Bermuda or Barbados or Bora-Bora.

At the door Mel Parker, neat, refreshed, jovial, stood with Mr. and Mrs. Hal C. Mudge and welcomed the guests. Inside, his aides — Sally, Cy, Harvey Bluestone and Sammy Kelp — circulated with strenuous charm. Simeon Lafonga, chief steward for the housewarming of the house that he had built, stood behind the bar in a white linen coat and directed his scurrying waiters. Moona Marone took a regal position in one of Slumberama's TV chairs and received the ardent stares of the crowd, while Norbert de Paul sat on an arm of the chair and patted her wrist. Harvey Bluestone noticed that because Moona's chair was quite low, and because she had chosen to wear a low-cut dress to validate her image as a sex goddess, the men hovering over her got a better view of her most famous feature than had ever been granted her fans on the screen. Thinking it undignified, Harvey considered telling her to stand up. But he quickly realized that there was no surer way of fostering a jolly atmosphere, and when he heard Mr. Satterthwaite take Brigadier Chitty aside and say "By Jove, Chitty, it reminds one of the ruddy Himalayas," he decided to leave well enough alone.

Every once in a while Mrs. Mudge pushed through the crowd to show various wives her Ever-Kool refrigerator and freezer, her Cook-Eez kitchen cabinets and counters, her Snug-Fit sheets and towels in coordinated decorator colors, and the many appliances that had been wheedled out of American industry in an abundance that she found embarrassing. The electric carving set, for instance, as she pointed out to her guests, would probably not be practical; here on Moona-Moona there was only enough current from a generator to operate the lights, and the major appliances ran on gas. But she hastened to add that she was "real pleased" with the house, and she was — Mel had made it as trim and modern as a new home in Brentwood or Bronxville. Her sole objection was the bar, which Walter of Waikiki had stocked with such a catholic assortment of liquors that it looked like a bottle museum. Mrs. Mudge averted her eyes when she passed it and pretended that it was not there.

The journalists, however, subscribed to no such fiction.

Having toured the house on the previous day, they were absolved of reportorial duties and they clustered at the bar making deep inroads into Walter of Waikiki's forest of whiskeys and rums. To Mel it was already clear that many of them would not reach the theater and many others would be too glazed to see the screen. But he didn't care. Though the announced purpose of every junket is to fly journalists thousands of miles to see the premiere of a movie, very few of them — when the moment finally arrives — have the desire or the ability to see it. Nor do the hosts mind. As long as the newsmen mention the picture in their stories, it doesn't matter what they think of it. Often, in fact, it is a blessing that they don't say what they think. For if junkets have an unannounced purpose, it is to salvage with "word of mouth" a high-budget film that has gone wrong, thereby offsetting at the box office much of the scorn that critics will heap upon it in print.

Consequently Mel felt, as he surveyed his boisterous scribes, that the premiere was off to a good normal start. Everything was going according to form — like a Japanese ritual or any stylized drama, it merely had to be played out. His only displeasure came when the bungalow quieted and Sir Reginald and Lady Weems entered. It was not their entry itself that displeased him, though as he remembered from his evening at Government House there were few more displeasing sights in Polynesia. It was Farley Grogan, who roared into the silence: "Hiya, Guv! Come on over and have a snort! You too, lady." Grogan thereupon draped his arms around Tonji's first couple and dragged them toward the bar. As Sir Reginald and Lady Weems struggled to get loose, alcohol gave Grogan new strength, and for a moment the three figures seemed tangled beyond salvation, like Laocoön and his sons. It took the full force of Mel and Cy, rushing into the breach, to wrest them apart.

Freed at last, Lady Weems straightened her dress, trying to restore a line that was never there; Sir Reginald tweaked his moustache to make sure that it had not been torn loose, and the two resumed their processional, smiling within their limited capacity at the radiant crowd. Never in Tonji was there such a glamorous event, never such a distinguished company, never so much fun.

And so the preliminaries of the evening were accomplished. Dinner was handsomely served, songs were sung by Tonjian girls, coffee was poured at the beach beneath the sheltering palm, and over the glassy Pacific a full moon rose. Mel watched it without resentment — though it was another event that he hadn't managed, he had to admit that it was a nice touch. He was as happy as he had ever been.

"All right, everybody!" he called when coffee was over. "Let's go see the movie. Follow me!"

He took a torch and plunged into the path that he and Simeon had cleared so crudely a month before. Now it was wide and smooth underfoot and merrily lit by Japanese lanterns overhead. The guests fell into line behind him, laughing and chattering like children at a party.

19

EVERYONE was soon seated on folding chairs in the bamboo clearing. As it obviously had on some occasion long ago, the clearing made a perfect theater, binding the spectators in a mystical communion. On the raised ground in front, where priests might once have conducted some kind of liturgy, a giant movie screen stood ready to conduct the arcane rites of Hollywood.

Mel Parker stepped to a microphone and an expectant hush fell over the crowd. He made a brief speech thanking "all you good people" for making such a memorable occasion possible. Then he introduced Moona Marone "in person," and in person she said that she wanted to thank not only "you folks who have so kindly taken me to your hearts, but the little people wherever they may be, from the humblest studio grip to the youngest girl in the Moona Marone Fan Clubs in like Timbuctoo." Applause resounded through the clearing, Moona waved and trotted off, and Mel said: "And now . . . *on with the show!*"

Lush music welled up from the soundtrack, and on the screen the huge words TITAN PICTURES PRESENTS were superimposed over a long shot of the blue Pacific, which, Mel saw, had been filmed in Titan's miniature tank on Sound Stage 6. (It had served as the South China Sea in "Opium-Runners of Macao" and as the Indian Ocean in "Peace Corps Gal.") The simulated Pacific dissolved into a close-up of

sand, in which a girl's finger wrote "Desert Island for Two."
Seeing the title, everyone clapped again and Mel sagged with
relief. The movie had begun: the acoustics were good, the
picture was in focus, and it was even on the screen.

Suddenly a ripping noise intruded on the soundtrack and a
large hole was poked in the lower right-hand corner of the
screen. An object was coming through it from the other side.
The projectionist stopped the film, freezing there the sullen
face of Moona Marone's co-star, Tab Torn, and the soundtrack went silent. The object continued its progress through
the jagged screen — it appeared to be a long stone shaft,
borne on the shoulders of half a dozen men. Reaching the
microphone, the first man stopped and blinked into the light
and into the horrified eyes of Mel Parker, who had rushed
back onto the stage.

"Ach, zo!" he said. "It iz you. I was *won*dering what made
zo much light."

"Kalbfleisch, you blundering ass!" Mel yelled. "Take that
damn thing out of here!"

"Ze phallus!" Dr. Kalbfleisch said. "I have found ze
eighteen-foot phallus of ze lost civilization of Tonji!"

"You dirty old man!"

"Zcholars will thank me!"

"You creep! Beat it!"

"My finezt hour!"

"Pervert!"

"Immenze burial mounds — right over there!"

"Sex maniac!"

". . . Priapic Press!"

"OUT!"

The microphone, still on, carried the exchange of words
across the audience in shrill metallic tones. Mel shoved Dr.
Kalbfleisch to one side and the long stone shaft slowly turned,
like some enormous serpent of mythology, and stumbled off
into the night.

Mel mopped his brow and stepped back to the microphone. "Ladies and gentlemen," he said, "I regret this most

unfortunate occurrence. Dr. Kalbfleisch, the German anthropologist, has evidently been engaged on a clandestine project and has found an . . . uh, an icon which he believes was left by an earlier Tonjian race. While the scientific community may thank him, I'm certain that you will join me in wishing he had not chosen this particular moment . . ."

"What's *that?*" a woman's voice said.

"*Listen!*" said another.

"Drums!" a man shouted.

"Eeeeeeeeeeeeee!" screamed several ladies.

Brigadier Chitty bounded up and seized the microphone from Mel.

"QUIET!" he commanded. "Keep calm! Let's hear what the beggars are up to!" He raised both hands for silence.

The noise encircling them was so loud and eerie that at first the listeners could not identify it. But as it continued they were able to separate it into various components. Some heard a steady and insistent drumming. Some heard a steady and insistent chanting. Others heard a high, singsong wail. Sally heard the sinister war cry that she had heard in the village: "Kula-ha'i-i-i-i-i!" Over and over again, faster and faster, it cut through the night, weaving in and around and through the other sounds.

"They're not on the island," Brigadier Chitty boomed, "so we're quite safe. Quite. The beggars are a*round* the island, if I'm not mistaken."

"A*round* the island!"

"Help!"

"We're trapped!"

". . . . . . *trapped!*"

". . . . . TRAPPED!"

"Cannibals!"

". . . human flesh!"

". . . . . . die like flies!"

"Revolution!"

". . . blood feud!"

". . . . . . civil war!"

"To the boats!"

". . . . . . boats!"

". . . . . boats!"

The cries, touching each other off like firecrackers, started panic and pandemonium. The guests left their chairs and ran headlong for the path leading back to the beach. Screaming and moaning, knocking each other down, trampling over bodies in the dark, getting up and starting forward again, all two hundred spectators left the theater once more to the spirits who had dwelled there long ago, and only the truculent face of Tab Torn, staring down from the giant screen across rows and rows of empty chairs, remained as trustee for the new gods who had so abruptly come and gone.

But at the beach the hysterical hordes found that their boats had been taken away. Worse, they could see the enemy. Out in the water, hundreds of Tonjian war canoes formed a cordon around the island. In the orange light of their torches it was possible to see eight or nine men in every canoe. Spears glinted in the darkness, and the chants and drumbeats, the war cries and wails pounded in upon the shore.

Once again Brigadier Chitty tried to hold the thin red line. Climbing up on the Mudges' thatched roof, he invoked his Gurkha voice from some bygone campaign. "In God's name, act like Englishmen!" he bellowed, and the voices died out as if shot. "Form two lines!" he commanded. "Now sit and be quiet and await further orders."

He jumped down from the roof and strode through his terror-stricken ranks to the water's edge, where he was met by Lord Hargreave and Sir Reginald Weems.

"Well, Weems," Lord Hargreave said, "you've made a proper balls-up this time." Sir Reginald's face twitched. "How do you propose to get us out of it? You're the Governor."

Brigadier Chitty said, "I'd put a load of grape across their bow, sir. Cheeky Wogs!"

"That's all you military chaps can ever think of," Lord Hargreave said. "Has it occurred to you, Chitty, that our ordnance posture here is not good? Where *is* this grape that you're nattering on about?"

"I only know that when the Eighty-eighth Bugles was at the Khyber . . ."

"You're not there now," Lord Hargreave snapped. "You're with the Two Hundred Civilians on a mile of scrub in the middle of the Pacific, surrounded by British subjects who appear to be dissatisfied with Sir Reginald's administration. Well, Reggie?"

"Most unusual, sir," the Governor replied. "Can't see what got into the beggars. Can't see it at all. Not one bit. Fmmmmm." He yanked at his moustache.

"But what are you going to *do* about it?"

"*Do* about it, sir?"

"Yes, do about it. What are you going to *do* about it?"

"Do about it," the Governor repeated. "Fffff. Exactly."

"Exactly what?"

"I thought we might wait the beggars out. They're bound to miss us in town tomorrow — rather a lot of people to be missing, you know — and then the Navy might send out one of its gunboats and give the blighters a bit of a shoot-up."

"How many gunboats do you have?"

"One, I believe, sir. Yes, I remember now: one."

"I thought so," Lord Hargreave said. "And what about these people?" He pointed to the men and women huddled on the beach. "How do you plan to protect them?"

"I . . . I . . . I . . ." The Governor's mouth worked a long and complicated pattern, but no further words emerged. The muscles in his cheek twitched rapidly and a vein in his temple throbbed. Seldom, Lord Hargreave thought, had he seen the central nervous system labor so hard to produce so little.

"Speak up!" he said. "Good God, man, don't you *know* these Tonjians? Aren't you their Governor?"

"Mmmm-brmmmm-ff," Sir Reginald said.

"Can't you go out to them in a canoe? See what they want?"

"Go *out* to them, sir?"

"Yes, out to them."

"In a canoe?"

"You can *swim* out to them, Weems, for all I care. But someone has to make contact."

"I . . . I . . ." Sir Reginald's face decomposed into a flutter of little movements and Lord Hargreave saw that he was not going to go out to them. The canoes were nearer, the sounds definitely louder.

Lord Hargreave was at a loss. Twenty minutes more and he would have an international incident on his hands. He could see the headlines: BRITISH COLONY ANNIHILATED; SAVAGES REBEL AGAINST ENGLISH RULE; WOMEN RAPED, TAKEN CAPTIVE. Such headlines were the stuff of his worst dreams every day as he studied the incoming cables at the Colonial Office, and now they were coming true and he was in the middle, powerless. To see the Crown humiliated was his idea of perdition. What could he do? Nothing came to mind. He felt clammy and alone.

"I'll go out to them, sir," a voice said.

"What? Who's that?" Lord Hargreave said to the figure approaching through the dark.

"Foote, sir. Denis Foote. You remember we met yesterday at the newspaper?"

"Oh yes, Foote. Jolly good. You say you'll go out?"

"If you wish, sir. The Tonjian people are my friends. Perhaps I could arrange some kind of talk."

"It's our only hope, my boy. The prayers of a grateful nation will go with you."

"Yes, sir."

"How will you go, Foote?"

"There's a new canoe up at the bungalow. If Mr. and Mrs. Mudge don't mind I thought . . ."

A dozen men sprinted to their feet and dragged the Mudges' canoe down to the beach. Denis took a Japanese lantern and jumped in. The crowd cheered as he paddled out into the night.

Half an hour later he came back, accompanied by a long

Polynesian canoe full of men and ornately carved on the sides. Denis shouted from offshore: "Lord Har-greave?"

"Right here, lad. Are you all right?"

"Quite all right, sir. I have the honor of presenting Chief Malalonga III, hereditary sovereign of the Tonjian people. Do you wish to hear his terms?"

"I do."

"Do you pledge safe conduct to him and his men?"

"On my word as an Englishman, I do."

Denis and Chief Malalonga brought their canoes in to the beach and got out. The Chief, ceremonially dressed, towering over everyone else, shook hands with Lord Hargreave.

"Good of you to come," Lord Hargreave said.

"We have you surrounded," the Chief said. "We are armed — there is no escape."

"I understand."

"This island is sacred to the Tonjian people," the Chief went on. "Our ancestors are buried in the large mounds beyond that little cottage."

"They are? How extraordinary! D'you mean that the graves of the intermediate period have been found?"

"They have. Our holy island has been violated by the British Crown. Now the spirits of our fathers demand that it be purged."

"Just what is it that you demand?" Lord Hargreave asked nervously. "Could you be specific?"

"Our demands are in writing," the Chief said, taking out a piece of paper. "Shall I read them?"

"If you please."

"First: Title to the island of Kula-ha'i shall be deeded in perpetuity to the Tonjian people, effective immediately. Mr. and Mrs. Hal C. Mudge, however, are granted permission to occupy their home for a period of one month, if they so desire.

"Second: Mr. Melville Parker, his staff, and all American journalists shall leave the colony of Tonji before the setting of the next sun." A hum of anger went up from the newsmen scattered in the crowd. "Miss Sally Merrill, however, shall be permitted to remain, if she so desires.

"Third: Sir Reginald Weems is no longer acceptable to the Tonjian people as supreme British authority. He shall be dismissed prior to the signing of this agreement." A gasp rose from the English contingent.

"Fourth: The British Government shall take steps to admit the Tonjian people as partners in the Legislature, commencing January 1, with a view towards granting them self-government no later than 1970. The celebration of Cession Day will cease."

The Chief paused. "Those are our terms."

"No! No!" cried the crowd.

Brigadier Chitty jabbed his finger at Chief Malalonga and said, "See here, old boy — if you think we're going to swallow all that flapdoodle about Brown Brother, you're bloody well wrong."

Sir Reginald Weems seconded the Brigadier's remarks. "Unthinkable!" he piped. "Utterly out of the question! We will fight on the beaches, we will fight on the . . ."

"That will do, Weems," Lord Hargreave said.

Chief Malalonga listened to the outburst with patience.

"We will need time to consider our answer," Lord Hargreave said. "Certain of the conditions may not be within my power to grant."

"My people will not wait indefinitely," Chief Malalonga said. He handed Lord Hargreave a tubelike object. "Send up this flare when you have reached a decision." He climbed into his canoe and pushed out.

Immediately the crowd pressed around Lord Hargreave, Sir Reginald and Brigadier Chitty and urged them to hold out. Defend at all costs. British honor. God save the Queen. Show the Wogs who's boss. No flapdoodle about Brown Brother. Fight on the beaches. Blood, sweat and tears. Eighty-eighth Bugles. Remember Khartoum. Ladysmith. Sun never sets.

Lord Hargreave called for silence again. "I take it, then, that you do not wish to accede to these terms?"

"NEVER!"

"Very well. We shall dig in here for the night and try to draw up a plan. Foote, I shall want your advice. Foote?"

"Yes, sir — here I am."

"Good."

"I just want to have a look around the island," Denis said. "Can you give me a few minutes?"

"Mmpph. Don't be long."

What Denis wanted to find was Sally. He peered frantically at the dark faces clustered on the beach and around the bungalow. At last it was she who broke through the crowd to find him.

"Oh Denis! Did you do all this?" she said, pointing to the flotilla of canoes.

"One managed event deserves another," he said. "Are you all right?"

"Yes. I was frightened at first, but then I guessed that you . . ."

"Good," he broke in. "It can still go either way. Will you do something for me?"

"If I can."

"I've got to get back to Lord Hargreave. I'd like you to find the Associated Press man — Phelps, I think his name is — and the fellow from United Press . . ."

"Carpenter. Tom Carpenter."

"That's the one," Denis said, "and lead them to a boat that I've got waiting on the other side to take them back to the cable office. There's a native pilot who knows what to do. Tell Phelps and Carpenter they're the only two reporters who'll get off this island tonight."

"But if the story gets out," Sally said, "Mel will be ruined."

"And Tonji won't," Denis said. "It's the only way to kill the tourist fever."

"Why?"

"Look: if Lord Hargreave agrees to the Chief's terms, the problem will be solved locally. Mel will go, and Sir Reggie will go, and I'll stay, and there'll be some changes in the government. But the outside world won't even hear about it.

They'll still think of Tonji as the swinging little tourist paradise that Mel's journalists have been writing about. The damage will live after him."

"That's true," Sally admitted. "There'll be a picture spread in 'Life' and a fashion layout in 'Vogue' and . . ."

"Right," Denis interrupted. "But if the AP and the UP send out a story tonight about bloodthirsty natives holding the English population in siege with war canoes on a desert island, it'll be on every front page, and people won't come near Tonji for twenty years."

"But I owe it to Mel . . ."

"I warned you that a moment might come when you'd have to choose sides. The moment is here."

"Poor Mel," Sally said. "All his dreams."

"The hell with dreams!" Denis shouted. "And images! This is life — remember? Or can't you tell them apart any more?"

"Gosh, have I got so muddled that I . . ."

"Life!" he repeated, shaking her by the shoulders. "That's all that matters: life, and truth, and love, and compassion. Everything else is cynical, and I hate cynics."

"So do I," Sally said, quietly. "Tell me what to do. I'll go find Carpenter and Phelps."

One night on Kula-ha'i was enough to thin the blood of the thin red line. The air turned damp, the island's mosquitoes fully compensated for their previous lack of human blood, the land crabs scuttled up from their holes in battalion strength, and the bad-luck bird sang an obbligato of doom.

The English men and women, as many as could fit, swarmed into the Mudges' bungalow and threw themselves in untidy heaps on the floor, seeking sleep. But new arrivals kept stepping on and over them. Some slept on the Cook-Eez counters, some on the color-coordinated pillows, one on the Ever-Kool refrigerator, six in the Perma-Tile shower, and several on Moona Marone, who slept in the Slumberama reclining TV chair. The frozen foods were unfrozen and eaten; the seemingly inexhaustible whiskeys of Walter of Waikiki were exhausted. Stale cigarette smoke hung in the room, and butts were ground into the ethnic designs of the Acrilan acrylic rugs woven by Folklore Fabrics in Brooklyn. Memories of Khartoum went dim and the 88th Bugles went sour. Sweat and tears were thicker than blood, and of water there was none at all: like the morale of the two hundred, it was consumed during the endless night.

And just as there was no water, there was no plan for vanquishing Chief Malalonga. The combined military experience of Brigadier Chitty and the colonial wisdom of Lord Hargreave failed to overcome the shortage of weapons, ammunition and boats — a shortage abated only by Brigadier Chitty's sword and the Mudges' canoe. Dawn over Kula-ha'i therefore witnessed a sight to make proud Albion weep. As a brilliant sun announced that Friday had irreversibly arrived, a single flare announced to Brown Brother that the flapdoodle would, after all, be swallowed.

On the beach, shortly thereafter, a solemn ceremony began. The ragged English company formed a circle, their ranks punctuated by the American journalists, whose appearance and temper the night had worn raw. The Moona Marone of nine P.M. was the Gertrude Fossenkemper of daybreak; Bobbie Baxter's hair, as untamed without pins as the vines of Angkor, seemed on the verge of strangling her head. In the middle of the circle Lord Hargreave, Sir Reginald Weems and Brigadier Chitty stood with Chief Malalonga and six lesser chiefs.

"By virtue of the power vested in me as Deputy Under Secretary for Colonial Affairs," Lord Hargreave declared, "and in the presence of these witnesses, I hereby declare you, Sir Reginald Weems, relieved of your duties as Governor of the British Crown Colony of Tonji, and of all rights and favors pertaining thereto."

A horrified moan, as at a hanging, rose from the listeners. Sir Reginald's mouth worked arabesques of shock and disbelief. Lord Hargreave led him off to a more inconspicuous spot. "Sorry about that, old fellow," he said. "We'll chase up something else for you when I go back to London. Ever fancy Mauritius or the Seychelles? Or Saint Helena? That's coming open soon, I'm told." The arabesques turned into rhomboids, rigid and geometrical, and Sir Reginald Weems spoke no more.

Lord Hargreave stepped back to Chief Malalonga and asked for the paper on which the terms were written. Then he took a pen and with an elaborate motion scrawled: AGREED — HARGREAVE. He gave the paper back to the Chief and they shook hands.

"Your boats will be returned immediately," the Chief said.

"Very good," Lord Hargreave said. He turned to the crowd. "Mr. Parker?" he called. "Is Mr. Parker here?"

"Yes, sir," came a voice hoarse from drink and cigars and lack of sleep, followed by its owner, Mel Parker, his face ashen and dead.

"You will see that your chaps are out of the colony by sundown?"

"Yes, sir," Mel said.

"And yourself, too, of course?"

"Yes, sir, I understand. We'll leave as soon as possible."

"Splendid! Now is there anything else?"

Chief Malalonga leaned over and mumbled something.

"Oh yes," Lord Hargreave said. "Chief Malalonga reminds me — quite correctly, hahaha — that no successor to Sir Reginald Weems has been appointed, and as I shall be returning to London myself on the afternoon plane it seems imperative that I . . . I . . ." He scratched his head. "Good heavens, I simply haven't given the matter any thought." He stood in the middle of the circle, befuddled. His eyes scanned the crowd, lighting briefly on Sir Reginald's many under secretaries and ministers, men from whose faces all mark of authority was now erased.

Brigadier Chitty stepped forward. "Perhaps, sir," he boomed, "as an interim measure . . ."

"Not you, Chitty!" Lord Hargreave roared. "Good God, you'd blow the whole place up by Monday."

A nervous laugh ran through the English men and women, recovering their humor with the prospect of recovering their tea and plumbing.

"Silence!" Lord Hargreave bellowed. He thought a moment more and then whispered something to Chief Malalonga. The Chief nodded.

"There is only one obvious choice," he announced, "at least — in Brigadier Chitty's phrase — as an interim measure." The crowd murmured restlessly.

"By virtue of the power vested in me as Deputy Under Secretary for Colonial Affairs," he proclaimed, "and in the presence of these witnesses, I hereby appoint as Acting Governor of the Crown Colony of Tonji, with all rights and favors pertaining thereto . . . the Honorable . . . Denis Foote."

20

"You sure you won't come along?" Mel said to Sally. "There's still time."

"No," she said. "I want to stay — if that's really all right with you."

"You're the boss," he said. "You've got your plane ticket home — it's good any time."

"I think I should give it back to you."

"I wouldn't take it. You did your job faithfully and well, to the very end."

"Almost to the very end," Sally said.

"Why 'almost'?"

"I helped get Don Phelps and Tom Carpenter off the island last night so they could report the great revolution."

"'Foote's Native Uprising' — it was the best promotion I ever saw."

"I'm sorry I had to do it," Sally said.

"You told me at the beginning that it could happen. And you were right to do it."

"I hope so. Mel, are you terribly disappointed?"

"No," he said. "You can't win 'em all. I had a good time, it was one hell of a junket, and the best man won."

"And what will you do now?" Sally asked.

"There's always another promotion," he said. "And another and another."

They were walking down Victoria Street to the customs wharf. It was noon, and Trans-Sky's plane was to fly the journalists out at one. Mel was dressed in a business suit and was carrying an attaché case. Simeon Lafonga followed behind with his suitcase. Overhead, Tonjian men were taking down the banners that had welcomed the American newsmen, hailed Moona Marone and announced the "Queen of Tonji" festival, now canceled.

Eddie Terhune, seeing Mel and Sally go by, stopped dismantling the neon sign that said "Dirty Eddie's à Go-Go" and came down his ladder. "We'll miss you, boy," he said. "You gave us a real pickup."

At Jerry's Authentic "Original Topless" South Sea Emporium, Jerry waved from an upstairs window. An electric guitar lay broken on the front steps. "So long, baby," he called. "Come back soon."

Beyond that, Alf McGowan looked up from a can of paint. He had taken down his sign, "The Beatnik Beachcomber, Formerly Alfie's That's All," and on its back he was painting "Alfie's That's All, Formerly the Beatnik Beachcomber." Up and down the street Mel heard the sounds of banging and demolition. "Godspeed, Mr. Mel," Alfie said. "We'll remember you."

At the Kon-Tiki Bar they saw that the words "& Surfers' Club" had been sawed off the wooden sign. "Come on, Sal, we've got time for a final beer," Mel said. They walked through the bar, where Fat Lou was prying off the last surfing photographs, and walked out onto the verandah. Literary Johnny was at one of the tables.

"Ah, lad, I *knew* you'd be by," he said. "I remember when Robert Louis Stevenson left these islands he said, 'Johnny, my bairn, I'm going off to Samoa to live and die — I'll not be seeing you again. But there's always time to sip a last wee drop on this verandah for auld lang syne.' "

"And there's time now," Mel said. "I wouldn't want to leave without it."

"Here are your pictures back," Johnny said. He handed over the photographs of Conrad, Melville, Nordhoff & Hall and the others, all admiringly signed. Mel looked over the inscriptions in his counterfeit handwriting: "To my dear friend Johnny — remember that rain in Pago-Pago? Ever gratefully, W. Somerset Maugham." The pictures seemed to Mel like some product of his distant past, almost forgotten. Tonji was already behind him; the compass of his mind was swinging its needle back toward the true north of Los Angeles.

Fat Lou brought three beers. "Thanks, you hodad," Mel said. Then he raised his glass. "To you, Johnny. If you ever get to L.A., look me up. You've got talent — and I like you."

Johnny drank his beer quickly. "Gonna run along now, lad," he said. "Never did care for goodbyes."

"Here, take your pictures," Mel said. "I don't want them." Johnny took the photographs and hurried off.

"Well, I guess I'd better be going, too," Mel said. He paid Fat Lou, who embraced him warmly, and he and Sally strolled on. Almost immediately they bumped into Doc Bligh.

"Moving out of Millie Hawkes's, I see," Bligh cackled. "I knew you would. The rats get to 'em all sooner or later. I expect you're on your way to my place."

"I'm headin' for the Beverly Hilton, Doc," Mel said, "so stand back."

"You'll be sorry," he said. "Flies as big as footballs there, they tell me." He scuttled to one side. "You'll miss the islands," he called after Mel. "Mark my words!"

"I guess I will," Mel said to Sally when they had left Bligh in their wake. "Most of all I'll miss you. When do you think you'll come back?"

"I just don't know," she said. "A year, maybe." They had reached the customs shed.

"I don't suppose," Mel began, "that you'd consider . . ." He stopped and fumbled for the remainder of the sentence. "I don't suppose," he began again, "that you could ever conceive of . . . conceive of marrying someone who may not seem to be doing anything very . . . very substantial, but who loves you and would take good care of you?"

Sally stopped and took his hand and looked in his eyes. The eyes were smiling again, as they had from the first day — optimist's eyes. He had lost, but he was not defeated.

"Thank you, Mel," she said. "Thank you very much. Nobody has ever asked me that before."

"I know you think I've got a crazy set of values, but maybe if I picked up some of yours . . ."

"No!" Sally said. "Don't you *dare* change. Stick with your own dream. It's yours and nobody else's, and it's not as insubstantial as you think. I *know!*"

"How come?"

"Because you've taught me how to live a little. You've loosened me up and given me a sense of gaiety, and that's *anoth*er thing nobody's ever done for me before. I'll never be quite so serious again."

"I love both Sallys — the old and the new."

"I'll never forget you, Mel dear. Thank you for believing in me — from the very beginning. But if I loved you, I don't think I would have let Denis talk me into finding Don Phelps and Tom Carpenter last night. I think it must mean that I love him."

"It could be that you just thought it was the right thing to do."

"Yes, it could. I'm not sure. But I think the right thing to do now is stay and find out. If I'm wrong . . ."

"The offer will still be good — if it *is* any good. Anyway, it'll still be open."

"The offer *is* good," Sally said. "Thank you, Mel," Sally said. "I'll keep in touch."

"Promise?"

"I promise."

She reached up and put her arms around his neck and gave him a kiss.

"Goodbye, Sal," he said and hurried into the customs shed.

Sally sat on a burlap bag at the edge of the wharf and waited for the departure. Millie Hawkes sat at her left, and on her right Mr. and Mrs. Hal C. Mudge stood uncertainly, bemused to find their guardian angels about to vanish into thin air.

"We wanted to say goodbye to dear Mr. Parker," Mrs.

Mudge explained to Sally, "and to that nice Mr. Bluestone. Have they come through the gate yet?"

"No, they should be coming soon."

"I hate to see that fellow of yours go," Millie Hawkes said to Sally. "I'll be damned if he isn't the most amiable old bastard to come along since Mr. Hawkes got swallowed by the grouper."

"What was that, ma'am?" Mr. Mudge asked.

"The story of my late husband," Millie replied. "Maybe you'd care to hear it. Will you be staying long?"

"About a month," Mr. Mudge said. "Wouldn't you think, Mother?"

"I think a month will be just fine."

"Then why don't you come for tea this afternoon?" Millie said. "I'm sure you don't want to go back to that island just yet."

"No, we thought we'd stay in town a few days."

"I tell you what," Millie said. "Come for dinner — it's bloaters and fish-eyes tonight — and I'll fix you up with a nice room, too. No charge: I want to do it for Mel."

"That's very kind," Mrs. Mudge said. "Who's Mel?"

"*That's* Mel," Millie said, pointing, as several people straggled out of the customs shed. She waved and Mel came over to the fence separating the passengers from the non-passengers.

"Goodbye, Millie," he said, reaching over to give her a big hug. "Thanks for everything. Goodbye, Mr. Mudge! Mrs. Mudge! You all enjoy your stay now, hear? And give me a call when you get back — I'll take you around the studios." Then he gave Sally a last smile and went down the ladder.

Harvey Bluestone saw the Mudges next and came over and said goodbye. "Sorry about last night," he added. "You're wonderful sports — it's been a privilege to know you. Goodbye now. G'bye."

Then Cy Rumble emerged from the shed. "Cy! Cy!" Sally called, waving and jumping up and down. He saw her and came to give her a final hug. "So long, doll," he said. "We had a time. I'll miss you."

"Me too," Sally said. She realized how sorry she was to see him go. "When I come home I'll call you and we'll have a blintz on Mosholu Parkway."

"It's a deal," he said. "Don't be long."

One by one the journalists climbed down into the launch. No band brightened their going-away with music, no speech saluted their stay and told them they would be missed. Only a few Tonjian girls were there to giggle and throw *leis* after the departing boat, and even these the newsmen were too numb to acknowledge. Their faces were drained by fatigue, by indulgence, by more new sensations than Mel himself had imagined possible. It had indeed been one hell of a junket.

In the rear of the launch Mel stood up and waved with obvious affection to someone on the dock. Sally followed the wave and saw that it was Denis, standing at the very edge.

"So long, old buddy," Mel called. "Look after the store while I'm away."

"Will you come back and see us?" Denis shouted.

"Yes!" Mel shouted as the distance between them widened. "Social visit. No business. Take care of . . ." The last word didn't reach the dock. Mel sat down in the boat. Denis continued to wave.

Sally went over and stood next to him. He was dressed as usual, in sneakers and denim pants. "You don't look any different," she said. "Shouldn't you be in your white-plumed hat?"

"New regime," he said. "In me you see the twilight of the British empire."

"It looks more like a sunrise," she said. "Government by cooperation instead of by clothes."

"I hope so," Denis said. He nodded toward the receding launch. "You'll miss him, I think."

"I think I will. It already seems too quiet around here."

"But nice," he said.

"But nice," she agreed. They both looked at the launch again. The passengers were merging into a blur. Only the lime-green beach hat of Perdita Fox-Martin, the soaring silver hair of Moona Marone and the myriad pincurlers of Bobbie Baxter, reflecting the Pacific sun, still gave the group a corporate identity.

"That must be the most beautiful sight of your life," Sally said to Denis. "Watching them go."

"No," he said. "The most beautiful sight of my life is watching you stay." They sat down at the end of the wharf, their legs dangling over the harbor.

"I've got to stay," she said. "It was written into an international treaty. Who could refuse such a compliment?"

"That was my favorite phrase in the whole agreement," Denis said.

"You wrote those terms yourself, of course?" Sally said.

"No. Chief Malalonga and I drafted them together. *He* thought of allowing you to stay — which saved me having to bring it up. And it was *his* idea to let Mr. and Mrs. Mudge use the island."

"He sounds like an unusual man."

"He's a good man," Denis said. "He'll make a good first president of Tonji."

"Speaking of the Mudges' island, what about those burial mounds? Did you *really* find any? Come clean."

"I think we really did," Denis said. "At least we found some honest-to-God mounds. The Chief and I went out to the island one night to look things over, and we found several dozen mounds in a spot terribly overgrown with vines. We also found a slab that had a powerful symbol carved in it: two triangles locked inside a double circle."

"I've never heard of that design," Sally said.

"Anyway, it'll take three or four months to clear the site and make a proper archeological study, but my hunch is that they really are the lost graves of the intermediate period. If you'd like to head the dig and write it up for a scholarly journal, the Mudges' bungalow would make a nice office. You could cook lunch there every day on the Formica counters and have a siesta on the color-coordinated sheets."

"Oh Denis, do you think I *could* — I mean head the dig?"

"There's nobody better qualified," he said. "And it's important — you could make a real contribution."

"Gosh, if I really could!"

"But my problem last night," Denis went on, "was to have some documentary proof on the island, in case anyone thought we were bluffing. Luckily, I remembered Dr. Kalbfleisch and his eighteen-foot phallus."

"And *that* was on the island?"

"Unfortunately it wasn't. I found it in an old quarry over on Tuva — just a long piece of stone. I had a team of twenty men working for a week with pickaxes to split it off at eighteen feet and also to give it, uh . . . more verisimilitude. Then we almost broke our backs taking it over to Kula-ha'i on a raft, and then I had to find Kalbfleisch and bring him out there to 'discover' it. But I didn't *dream* my work would be rewarded by having him come right through the movie screen."

"You didn't?" Sally said. "I thought that was your masterpiece."

"It was the hand of God, outdoing the manager of the managed event. Wasn't it lovely?"

"Lovely."

"It was the perfect trigger for the panic that followed," Denis said, "because it made the whole business of the avenging war canoes seem authentic."

"And what timing! Right at the opening title of the world premiere of 'Desert Island for Two.' "

"He works in mysterious ways."

"Do you think we'll *ever* see that movie?"

"I hear it's Dog City," Denis said.

"Is that what they say?"

"That's what they say."

"You might get a print," Sally suggested, "and have a showing at Government House."

"I'm not going near that place," Denis said. "I didn't want to be Governor — that was the other surprise of last night. So if I've got to be Acting Governor, Acting Government House is going to be *my* house. It'll do for about three weeks, by which time Lord Hargreave will send someone else out who likes to dress for dinner and play the cork game, and then I'll get back to what I want to do."

"Which is . . . ?"

"Look for shells. Study the flight patterns of birds. Trace the route of the early Polynesians. Write. Paint. Listen to music. Help Quaritch put out a good newspaper. Visit my friends in the villages and have them visit me. Teach: there's a lot of teaching to be done, now that self-government is in sight. And try to persuade you to stay here and do all these things with me. Do you think you might?"

"I think I might," Sally said.

Millie Hawkes ambled up and sat beside them. "There they go," she said, pointing out to the launch, which had just reached the "Moona Marone." The door of the plane opened and one little, two little, three little, sixteen little journalists, three little press agents, one little photographer, one little personal representative and one little sex goddess climbed laboriously up, like working ants, and disappeared inside. The last ant, larger than the others, had a hard time negotiating the ladder, and when he seemed to be at the very top Denis and Sally lost sight of him for a moment. Then they saw a mountainous splash.

"Farley Grogan," Sally said.

"The old *bas*tard!" Millie roared. "Hoo-eeeee!"

Several Tonjian men with boat hooks dredged Farley Grogan out and pushed him up the ladder again. Two other people pulled from above and Grogan was duly taken aboard. The door of the plane closed, its engines rattled across the quiet lagoon, and the "Moona Marone" turned and taxied out toward the opening in the reef.